GREAT HOUSE

GREAT HOUSE

Nicole Krauss

WINDSOR
PARAGON

First published 2011
by Viking
This Large Print edition published 2011
by AudioGO Ltd
by arrangement with
Penguin Books Ltd

Hardcover ISBN: 978 1 445 85864 7
Softcover ISBN: 978 1 445 85865 4

I am deeply grateful to the Dorothy and Lewis B. Cullman Center for Scholars and Writers at the New York Public Library, the Rona Jaffe Foundation, and the American Academy in Berlin for their warmth and support, and for giving me a quiet room to work in when I needed it most. Rafi's story of looking across no-man's land in Jerusalem is from Sophie Calle's *Eruv* project. My account of Yochanan ben Zakkai is indebted to Rich Cohen's *Israel is Real*.

British Library Cataloguing in Publication Data available

Printed and bound in Great Britain by
MPG Books Group Limited

For Sasha and Cy

I

II

I

ALL RISE

Talk to him.

Your Honor, in the winter of 1972 R and I broke up, or I should say he broke up with me. His reasons were vague, but the gist was that he had a secret self, a cowardly, despicable self he could never show me, and that he needed to go away like a sick animal until he could improve this self and bring it up to a standard he judged deserving of company. I argued with him—I'd been his girlfriend for almost two years, his secrets were my secrets, if there was something cruel or cowardly in him I of all people would know—but it was useless. Three weeks after he'd moved out I got a postcard from him (without a return address) saying that he felt our decision, as he called it, hard as it was, had been the right one, and I had to admit to myself that our relationship was over for good.

Things got worse then for a while before they got better. I won't go into it except to say that I didn't go out, not even to see my grandmother, and I didn't let anyone come to see me, either. The only thing that helped, oddly, was the fact that the weather was stormy, and so I had to keep running around the apartment with the strange little brass wrench made especially for tightening the bolts on either side of the antique window frames—when they got loose in windy weather the windows would shriek. There were six windows, and just as I finished tightening the bolts on one, another would start to howl, so I would run with the wrench, and then maybe I would have a half hour of silence on the only chair left in the apartment. For a while, at least, it seemed that all there was of the world was that long rain and the need to keep the bolts fastened. When the weather finally cleared, I went out for a walk. Everything was flooded, and there was a feeling of calm from all that still, reflecting water. I walked for a long time, six or seven hours at least, through neighborhoods I had never been to before and have never been back to since. By the time I got home I was exhausted but I felt that I had purged myself of something.

* * *

She washed the blood from my hands and gave me a fresh T-shirt, maybe even her own. She thought I was your girlfriend or even your wife. No one has come for you yet. I won't leave your side. *Talk to him.*

* * *

Not long after that R's grand piano was lowered through the huge living room window, the same way it had come in. It was the last of his possessions to go, and as long as the piano had been there, it was as if he hadn't really left. In the weeks that I lived alone with the piano, before they came to take it away, I would sometimes pat it as I passed in just the same way that I had patted R.

A few days later an old friend of mine named Paul Alpers called to tell me about a dream he'd had. In it he and the great poet César Vallejo were at a house in the country that had belonged to

Vallejo's family since he was a child. It was empty, and all the walls were painted a bluish white. The whole effect was very peaceful, Paul said, and in the dream he thought Vallejo lucky to be able to go to such a place to work. This looks like the holding place before the afterlife, Paul told him. Vallejo didn't hear him, and he had to repeat himself twice. Finally the poet, who in real life died at forty-six, penniless, in a rainstorm, just as he had predicted, understood and nodded. Before they entered the house Vallejo had told Paul a story about how his uncle used to dip his fingers in the mud to make a mark on his forehead—something to do with Ash Wednesday. And then, Vallejo said (said Paul), he would do something I never understood. To illustrate, Vallejo dipped his two fingers in the mud and drew a mustache across Paul's upper lip. They both laughed. Throughout the dream, Paul said, most striking was the complicity between them, as if they had known each other many years.

Naturally Paul had thought of me when he'd woken up, because when we were sophomores in college we'd met in a seminar on avant-garde poets. We'd become friends because we always agreed with each other in class, while everyone else disagreed with us, more and more vehemently as the semester progressed, and with time an alliance had formed between Paul and me that after all these years—five—could still be unfolded and inflated instantly. He asked how I was, alluding to the breakup, which someone must have told him about. I said I was ok except that I thought maybe my hair was falling out. I also told him that along with the piano, the sofa, chairs, bed, and even the silverware had gone with R, since when I met him I'd been living more or less out of a suitcase, whereas he had been like a sitting Buddha surrounded by all of the furniture he'd inherited from his mother. Paul said he thought he might know someone, a poet, a friend of a friend, who was going back to Chile and might need a foster home for his furniture. A phone call was made and it was confirmed that the poet, Daniel Varsky, did indeed have some items he didn't know what to do with, not wanting to sell them in case he changed his mind and decided to return to New York. Paul gave me his number and said Daniel was expecting me to get in touch. I put off making the call for a few days, mostly because there was something awkward about asking a stranger for his furniture even if the way had already been paved, and also because in the month since R and all of his many belongings had gone I'd become accustomed to having nothing. Problems only arose when someone else came over and I would see, reflected in the look on my guest's face, that from the outside the conditions, my conditions, Your Honor, appeared pathetic.

When I finally called Daniel Varsky he picked up after one ring. There was a cautiousness in that initial greeting, before he knew who it was on the other end, that I later came to associate with Daniel Varsky, and with Chileans, few as I've met, in general. It took a minute for him to sort out who I was, a minute for the light to go on revealing me as a friend of a friend and not some loopy woman calling—about his furniture? she'd heard he wanted to get rid of it? or just give it out on loan?—a minute in which I considered apologizing, hanging up, and carrying on as I had been, with just a mattress, plastic utensils, and the one chair. But once the light had gone on (Aha! Of course! Sorry! It's all waiting right here for you) his voice softened and became louder at the same time, giving way to an expansiveness I also came to associate with Daniel Varsky and, by extension, everyone who hails from that dagger pointing at the heart of Antarctica, as Henry Kissinger once called it.

He lived all the way uptown, on the corner of 101st Street and Central Park West. On the way, I stopped to visit my grandmother, who lived in a nursing home on West End Avenue. She no longer recognized me, but once I'd gotten over this I found myself able to enjoy being with her. We normally sat and discussed the weather in eight or nine different ways, before moving on to my grandfather, who a decade after his death continued to be a subject of fascination to her, as if with each year of his absence his life, or their life together, became more of an enigma to her. She liked to sit on the sofa marveling at the lobby—All of this belongs to me? she'd periodically ask, waving in a gesture that took in the whole place—and wearing all of her jewelry at once. Whenever I came, I brought her a chocolate babkah from Zabar's. She always ate a little out of politeness, and the cake would flake onto her lap and stick to her lips, and after I left she gave the rest away to the nurses.

When I got to 101st Street, Daniel Varsky buzzed me in. As I waited for the elevator in the dingy lobby it occurred to me that I might not like his furniture, that it might be dark or otherwise oppressive, and that it would be too late to back out gracefully. But on the contrary, when he opened the door my first impression was of light, so much so that I had to squint, and for a moment I couldn't see his face because it was in silhouette. There was also the smell of something cooking which later turned out to be an eggplant dish he'd learned to make in Israel. Once my eyes adjusted I was surprised to find that Daniel Varsky was young. I'd expected someone older since Paul had said his friend was a poet, and though we both wrote poetry, or tried to write it, we made a point of never referring to ourselves as poets, a term we reserved for those whose work had been judged worthy of publication, not just in an obscure journal or two, but in an actual book that could be purchased in a bookstore. In retrospect this turns out to have been an embarrassingly conventional definition of a poet, and though Paul and I and others we knew prided ourselves on our literary sophistication, in those days we were still walking around with our ambition intact and in certain ways it blinded us.

Daniel was twenty-three, a year younger than I was, and though he hadn't yet published a book of poems he seemed to have spent his time better, or more imaginatively, or maybe what could be said is that he felt a pressure to go places, meet people, and experience things that, whenever I have encountered it in someone, has always made me envious. He had traveled for the last four years, living in different cities, on the floors of the apartments of people he met along the way, and sometimes apartments of his own when he could convince his mother or maybe it was his grandmother to wire him money, but now at last he was going home to take his place alongside the friends he had grown up with who were fighting for liberation, revolution, or at least socialism in Chile.

The eggplant was ready and while Daniel set the table he told me to look around at the furniture. The apartment was small, but there was a large southern-facing window through which all the light entered. The most striking thing about the place was the mess—papers all over the floor, coffee-stained Styrofoam cups, notebooks, plastic bags, cheap rubber shoes, divorced records and sleeves. Anyone else would have felt compelled to say, Excuse the mess, or joked about a herd of wild animals passing through, but Daniel didn't mention it. The only more or less empty surface was the walls, bare aside from a few maps he'd tacked up of the cities he had lived in—Jerusalem, Berlin, London, Barcelona—and on certain avenues, corners, and squares he had scribbled notes that I didn't immediately understand because they were in Spanish, and it would have seemed rude to have gone up and tried to decipher them while my host and benefactor set down the silverware. So I turned my attention to the furniture, or what I could see of it under the mess—a sofa, a large wooden desk with lots of drawers, some big and some small, a pair of bookshelves crammed with volumes in Spanish, French, and English, and the nicest piece, a kind of chest or trunk with iron braces that looked as if it had been rescued from a sunken ship and put to use as a coffee table. He must have acquired everything secondhand, none of it looked new, but all the pieces shared a kind of sympathy, and the fact that they were suffocating under papers and books made them more attractive rather than less. Suddenly I felt awash in gratitude to their owner, as if he were handing down to me not just some wood and upholstery but the chance at a new life, leaving it up to me to rise to the occasion. I'm embarrassed to say that my eyes actually filled with tears, Your Honor, though as is so often the case, the tears sprang from older, more obscure regrets I had delayed thinking about, which the gift, or loan, of a stranger's furniture had somehow unsettled.

We must have talked for seven or eight hours at least. Maybe more. It turned out that we both loved Rilke. We also both liked Auden, though I liked him more, and neither of us cared much for Yeats, but both felt secretly guilty about this, in case it suggested some sort of personal failure at the level where poetry lives and matters. The only moment of disharmony came when I raised the subject of Neruda, the one Chilean poet I knew, to which Daniel responded with a flash of anger: Why is it, he asked, that wherever a Chilean goes in the world, Neruda and his fucking seashells has already been there and set up a monopoly? He held my gaze waiting for me to counter him, and as he did I got the feeling that where he came from it was commonplace to talk as we were talking, and even to argue about poetry to the point of violence, and for a moment I felt brushed by loneliness. Just a moment, though, and then I jumped to apologize, and swore up and down to read the abbreviated list of great Chilean poets he scribbled on the back of a paper bag (at the top of which, in capital letters overshadowing the rest, was Nicanor Parra) and also to never again utter the name of Neruda, either in his presence or anyone else's.

We talked then of Polish poetry, of Russian poetry, of Turkish and Greek and Argentine poetry, of Sappho and the lost notebooks of Pasternak, of the death of Ungaretti, the suicide of Weldon Kees, and the disappearance of Arthur Cravan, who Daniel claimed was still alive, cared for by the whores of Mexico City. But sometimes, in the dip or hollow between one rambling sentence and the next, a dark cloud would cross his face, hesitate for a moment as if it might stay, and then slide past, dissolving toward the edges of the room, and at those moments I almost felt I should turn away, since though we talked a lot about poetry we had not yet said much of anything about ourselves.

At a certain point Daniel jumped up and went rifling through the desk with all the drawers, opening some and closing others, in search of a cycle of poems he'd written. It was called *Forget Everything I Ever Said*, or something like that, and he had translated it himself. He cleared his throat and began to read aloud in a voice that coming from anyone else might have seemed affected or even comic, touched as it was with a faint tremolo, but coming from Daniel seemed completely natural. He didn't apologize or hide behind the pages. Just the opposite. He straightened up like a pole, as if he were borrowing energy from the poem, and looked up frequently, so frequently that I began to suspect he had memorized what he'd written. It was at one of these moments, as we met eye-to-eye across a word, that I realized he was actually quite good-looking. He had a big nose, a big Chilean-Jewish nose, and big hands with skinny fingers, and big feet, but there was also something delicate about him, something to do with his long eyelashes or his bones. The poem was good, not great but very good, or maybe it was even better than very good, it was hard to tell without being able to read it myself. It seemed to be about a girl who had broken his heart, though it could just as easily have been about a dog; halfway through I got lost, and started to think about how R always used to wash his narrow feet before he got into bed because the floor of our apartment was dirty, and though he never told me to wash mine it was implicit, since if I hadn't then the sheets would have gotten dirty, making his own washing pointless. I didn't like sitting on the edge of the tub or standing at the sink with one knee to my ear, watching the black dirt swirl in the white porcelain, but it was one of those countless things one does in life to avoid an argument, and now the thought of it made me want to laugh or possibly choke.

By then Daniel Varsky's apartment had gotten dim and aquatic, the sun having gone down behind a building, and the shadows that had been hiding behind everything began to flood out. I remember there were some very large books on his shelf, fine books with tall cloth spines. I don't remember any of their titles, perhaps they were a set, but they seemed somehow to be in collusion with the darkening hour. It was as if the walls of his apartment were suddenly carpeted like the walls of a movie theater to keep the sound from getting out, or other sounds from getting in, and inside that tank, Your Honor, in what light there was, we were both the audience and the picture. Or as if we alone had been cut loose from the island and were now drifting in uncharted waters, black waters of unknowable depth. I was considered attractive in those days, some people even called me beautiful, though my skin was never good and it was this that I noticed when I looked in the mirror, this and a faintly perturbed look, a slight wrinkling of the forehead that I hadn't known I was doing. But before I was with R, and while I was with him, too, there were plenty of men who made it clear they would have liked to go home with me, either for a night or longer, and as Daniel and I got up and moved to the living room I wondered what he thought of me.

It was then that he told me the desk had been used, briefly, by Lorca. I didn't know if he was joking or not, it seemed highly improbable that this traveler from Chile, younger than I, could have gotten hold of such a valuable item, but I decided to assume that he was serious so as not to risk offending someone who had shown me only kindness. When I asked how he had gotten it, he shrugged and said he had bought it, but didn't elaborate. I thought he was going to say, And now I am giving it to you, but he didn't, he just gave one of the legs a little kick, not a violent one but a gentle one, full of respect, and kept walking.

Either then or later we kissed.

*　　*　　*

She injected another dose of morphine into your drip, and fixed a loose electrode on your chest. Out the window, dawn was spreading over Jerusalem. For a moment she and I watched the green glow of your EKG rise and fall. Then she drew the curtain and left us alone.

*   *   *

Our kiss was anticlimactic. It wasn't that the kiss was bad, but it was just a note of punctuation in our long conversation, a parenthetical remark made in order to assure each other of a deeply felt agreement, a mutual offer of companionship, which is so much more rare than sexual passion or even love. Daniel's lips were bigger than I expected, not big on his face but big when I closed my eyes and they touched mine, and for a split second I felt as if they were smothering me. More than likely it was just that I was so used to R's lips, thin non-Semitic lips that often turned blue in the cold. With one hand Daniel Varsky squeezed my thigh, and I touched his hair, which smelled like a dirty river. I think by then we'd arrived, or were about to arrive, at the cesspool of politics, and at first angrily, then almost on the edge of tears, Daniel Varsky railed against Nixon and Kissinger and their sanctions and ruthless machinations that were, he said, trying to strangle all that was new and young and beautiful in Chile, the hope that had carried the doctor Allende all the way to Moneda Palace. Workers' wages up by 50 percent he said, and all these pigs care about is their copper and their multinationals! Just the thought of a democratically elected Marxist president makes them shit in their pants! Why don't they just leave us alone and let us get on with our lives, he said, and for a minute his look was almost pleading or imploring, as if I somehow held sway with the shady characters at the helm of the dark ship of my country. He had a very prominent Adam's apple, and every time he swallowed it bobbed around in his throat, and now it seemed to be bobbing continuously, like an apple tossed out to sea. I didn't know much about what was happening in Chile, at least not then, not yet. A year and a half later, after Paul Alpers told me that Daniel Varsky had been taken in the middle of the night by Manuel Contreras' secret police, I knew. But in the winter of 1972, sitting in his apartment on 101st Street in the last of the evening light, while General Augusto Pinochet Ugarte was still the demure, groveling army chief of staff who tried to get his friends' children to call him Tata, I didn't know much.

What's strange is that I don't remember how the night (by then it was already an enormous New York City night) ended. Obviously we must have said goodbye after which I left his apartment, or maybe we left together and he walked me to the subway or hailed me a cab, since in those days the neighborhood, or the city in general, wasn't safe. I just don't have any recollection of it. A couple of weeks later a moving truck arrived at my apartment and the men unloaded the furniture. By that time Daniel Varsky had already gone home to Chile.

Two years passed. In the beginning I used to get postcards. At first they were warm and even jovial: Everything is fine. I'm thinking of joining the Chilean Speleological Society but don't worry, it won't interfere with my poetry, if anything the two pursuits are complementary. I may have a chance to attend a mathematics lecture by Parra. The political situation is going to hell, if I don't join the Speleological Society I'm going to join the MIR. Take good care of Lorca's desk, one day I'll be back for it. Besos, D.V. After the coup they became somber, and then they became cryptic, and then, about six months before I heard he'd disappeared, they stopped coming altogether. I kept them all in one of the drawers of his desk. I didn't write back because there was no address to write back to. In those years I was still writing poetry, and I wrote a few poems addressed, or dedicated, to Daniel Varsky. My grandmother died and was buried too far out in the suburbs for anyone to visit, I went out with a number of men, moved apartments twice, and wrote my first novel at Daniel Varsky's desk. Sometimes I forgot about him for months at a time. I don't know if I knew about Villa Grimaldi yet, almost certainly I hadn't heard of 38 Calle Londres, Cuatro Alamos, or the Discoteca also known as Venda Sexy because of the sexual atrocities performed there and the loud music the torturers favored, but whatever the case I knew enough that at other times, having fallen asleep on Daniel's sofa as I often did, I had nightmares about what they did to him. Sometimes I would look around at his furniture, the sofa, desk, coffee table, bookshelves, and chairs, and be filled with a crushing despair, and sometimes just an oblique sadness, and sometimes I would look at it all and become convinced that it amounted to a riddle, a riddle he had left me that I was supposed to crack.

From time to time, I've met people, mostly Chileans, who knew or had heard of Daniel Varsky. For a short time after his death his reputation grew, and he was counted among the martyred poets silenced by Pinochet. But of course the ones who tortured and killed Daniel had never read his poetry; it's possible they didn't even know that he wrote poetry at all. Some years after he disappeared, with the help of Paul Alpers, I wrote letters to Daniel's friends asking if they had any poems of his that they could send to me. I had the idea that I could get them published somewhere as a kind of memorial to him. But I only received one letter back, a short reply from an old school friend saying he didn't have anything. I must have written something about the desk in my letter, otherwise the postscript would have been too strange: By the way, it said, I doubt Lorca ever owned that desk. That was all. I put the letter in the drawer with Daniel's postcards. For a while I even thought of writing to his mother, but in the end I never did.

Many years have passed since then. I was married for a while, but now I live alone again, though not unhappily. There are moments when a kind of clarity comes over you, and suddenly you can see through walls to another dimension that you'd forgotten or chosen to ignore in order to continue living with the various illusions that make life, particularly life with other people, possible. And that's where I'd arrived, Your Honor. If it weren't for the events I'm about to describe, I might have gone on not thinking about Daniel Varsky, or very rarely, though I was still in possession of his bookshelves, his desk, and the trunk of a Spanish galleon or the salvage of an accident on the high seas, quaintly used as a coffee table. The sofa began to rot, I don't remember exactly when but I had to throw it away. At times I thought of getting rid of the rest, too. It reminded me, when I was in a certain mood, of things I would rather forget. For example sometimes I am asked by the occasional journalist who wishes to interview me why I stopped writing poetry. Either I say that the poetry I wrote wasn't any good, perhaps it was even terrible, or I say that a poem has the potential for perfection and this possibility finally silenced me, or sometimes I say that I felt trapped in the poems I tried to write, which is like saying one feels trapped in the universe, or trapped by the inevitability of death, but the truth of why I stopped writing poetry is not any of these, not nearly, not exactly, the truth is that if I could explain why I stopped writing poetry then I might write it again. What I am saying is that Daniel Varsky's desk, which became my desk of more than twenty-five years, reminded me of these things. I'd always considered myself only a temporary guardian and had assumed a day would come, after which, albeit with mixed feelings, I would be relieved of my responsibility of living with and watching over the furniture of my friend, the dead poet Daniel Varsky, and that from then on I would be free to move as I wished, possibly even to another country. It isn't exactly that the furniture had kept me in New York, but if pressed I have to admit this was the excuse I'd used for not leaving all those years, long after it became clear the city had nothing left for me. And yet when that day came it sent my life, at last solitary and serene, reeling.

It was 1999, the end of March. I was at my desk working when the phone rang. I didn't recognize the voice that asked for me on the other end. Coolly, I inquired who was calling. Over the years

I've learned to guard my privacy, not because so many people have tried to invade it (some have), but because writing demands that one be protective and adamant about so much that a certain a priori unwillingness to oblige spills over even to situations where it isn't necessary. The young woman said that we'd never met. I asked her the reason for her call. I think you knew my father, she said, Daniel Varsky.

At the sound of his name I felt a chill through me, not only from the shock of learning that Daniel had a daughter, or the sudden expansion of the tragedy I'd perched on the edge of for so long, or even the certain knowledge that my long stewardship had come to an end, but also because some part of me had waited for such a phone call for years, and now, despite the late hour, it had come.

I asked how she'd found me. I decided to look, she said. But how did you know to look for *me*? I only met your father once, and it was a very long time ago. My mother, she said. I had no idea who she was referring to. She said, You once wrote her a letter asking if she had any of my father's poems. Anyway, it's a long story. I could tell it to you when I see you. (Of course we would be seeing each other, she knew perfectly well that what she was about to ask for couldn't be denied, but all the same her assurance threw me.) In the letter you wrote that you had his desk, she said. Do you still have it?

I looked across the room at the wooden desk at which I had written seven novels, and on whose surface, in the cone of light cast by a lamp, lay the piles of pages and notes that were to constitute an eighth. One drawer was slightly ajar, one of the nineteen drawers, some small and some large, whose odd number and strange array, I realized now, on the cusp of their being suddenly taken from me, had come to signify a kind of guiding if mysterious order in my life, an order that, when my work was going well, took on an almost mystical quality. Nineteen drawers of varying size, some below the desktop and some above, whose mundane occupations (stamps here, paper clips there) hid a far more complex design, the blueprint of the mind formed over tens of thousands of days of thinking while staring at them, as if they held the conclusion to a stubborn sentence, the culminating phrase, the radical break from everything I had ever written that would at last lead to the book I had always wanted, and always failed, to write. Those drawers represented a singular logic deeply embedded, a pattern of consciousness that could be articulated in no other way but their precise number and arrangement. Or am I making too much of it?

My chair was turned slightly away, waiting for me to return and swivel it back to attention. On such an evening I might have stayed up half the night working, writing and staring out at the blackness of the Hudson, as long as the energy and clarity lasted. There was no one to call me to bed, no one to demand that the rhythms of my life operate in a duet, no one toward whom I had to bend. Had the caller been almost anyone else, after hanging up I would have returned to the desk that over the course of two and a half decades I'd physically grown around, my posture formed by years of leaning over it and fitting myself to it.

For a moment I considered saying that I had given it away or thrown it out. Or simply telling the caller that she was mistaken: I'd never been in possession of her father's desk. Her hope was tentative, she had offered me a way out—*Do you still have it?* She would have been disappointed, but I would have been taking nothing away from her, at least nothing that she had ever had. And I could have continued writing at the desk for another twenty-five or thirty years, or however long my mind stayed agile and the pressing need didn't subside.

But instead, without pausing to consider the repercussions, I told her that, yes, I had it. I've looked back and wondered why I so quickly uttered those words that almost immediately derailed my life. And though the obvious answer is that it was the kind and even the right thing to do, Your Honor, I knew that wasn't the reason I'd said it. I've wronged people I've loved far more gravely in the name of my work, and the person asking something of me now was a complete stranger. No, I agreed to it for the same reason I would have written it in a story: because saying yes felt inevitable.

I'd like to have it, she said. Of course, I answered, and, without pausing to give myself a moment to change my mind, asked her when she wanted to come for it. I'm only in New York for another week, she said. How about Saturday? That, I calculated, would leave me five more days with the desk. Fine, I said, though there couldn't have been a greater discrepancy between the casual tone of my voice and the distraught feeling taking hold of me as I spoke. I have a few other pieces of furniture that belonged to your father, too. You can have them all.

Before she hung up, I asked her name. Leah, she said. Leah Varsky? No, she said, Weisz. And then, matter-of-factly she explained that her mother, who was Israeli, had lived in Santiago in the early seventies. She'd had a brief affair with Daniel around the time of the military coup, and soon afterwards had left the country. When her mother had found out that she was pregnant, she'd written to Daniel. She'd never heard back from him; he had already been arrested.

When, in the silence that followed, it became clear that we had run out of all the small manageable bits of the conversation, leaving only the pieces too unwieldy for such a phone call, I said, that, yes, I'd been holding on to the desk for a long time. I always thought someone would come for it one day, I told her, though of course I'd have tried to return it sooner had I known.

After she hung up I went to the kitchen for a glass of water. When I came back into the room—a living room I used as a study, because I had no need for a living room—I walked over and sat down at the desk as if nothing had changed. But of course something had, and when I looked at the computer screen to the sentence I'd abandoned when the telephone rang I knew it would be impossible to go any further that night.

I got up and moved to my reading chair. I picked up the book from the side table, but found, somewhat uncharacteristically, that my mind was wandering. I stared across the room at the desk, as I had stared at it on countless nights when I'd reached an impasse but wasn't ready to capitulate.

No, I don't harbor any mystical ideas about writing, Your Honor, it's work like any other kind of craft; the power of literature, I've always thought, lies in how willful the act of making it is. As such, I've never bought into the idea that the writer requires any special ritual in order to write. If need be, I could write almost anywhere, as easily in an ashram as in a crowded café, or so I've always insisted when asked whether I write with a pen or a computer, at morning or night, alone or surrounded, in a saddle like Goethe, standing like Hemingway, lying down like Twain, and so on, as if there were a secret to it all that might spring the lock of the safe housing the novel, fully formed and ready for publication, apparently suspended in each of us. No, what I was distraught to be losing was the familiar conditions of my work; it was sentimentality speaking and nothing else.

It was a setback. Something melancholy clung to the whole business, a melancholy that had begun with the story of Daniel Varsky, but now belonged to me. But it was not an irreparable problem. Tomorrow morning, I decided, I would go out to buy a new desk.

It was past midnight by the time I fell asleep, and, as always when I go to bed entangled in some difficulty, my sleep was uneven and my dreams vivid. But by morning, despite the receding sense that I had been dragged through something epic, I only remembered a fragment—a man standing outside my building, freezing to death in the glacial wind that blows down the Hudson corridor from Canada, from the Arctic Circle itself, who, as I passed, asked me to pull a red thread that was hanging from his mouth. I obliged, bullied by the pressure of charity, but as I pulled the thread continued to pile up at my feet. When my arms tired the man barked at me to keep pulling, until over a passage of time, compressed as it only can be in dreams, he and I became joined in the conviction that something crucial lay at the end of that string; or maybe it was only I who had the luxury to believe or not, while for him it was a matter of life and death.

The next day I did not go out to look for a new desk, or the day after that. When I sat down to work, not only was I unable to muster the necessary concentration, but when I looked over the pages I'd already written I found them to be superfluous words lacking life and authenticity, with no compelling reason behind them. What I hoped had been the sophisticated artifice that the best fiction employs, I now saw was only a garden-variety artifice, artifice used to draw attention away from what is ultimately shallow rather than reveal the shattering depths below the surface of everything. What I thought was a simpler, purer prose, more searing for being stripped of all distracting ornament, was actually a dull and lumbering mass, void of tension or energy, standing in opposition to nothing, toppling nothing, shouting nothing. Though I had been struggling with the mechanism behind the book for some time, unable to work out how the pieces fit together, I'd believed all along that there was something there, a design that if I could only dislodge and separate it from the rest would prove to have all the delicacy and irreducibility of an idea that demands a novel, written in only one way, to express it. But now I saw that I had been wrong.

I left the apartment and went for a long walk through Riverside Park and down Broadway to clear my mood. I stopped at Zabar's to pick up some things for dinner, waving to the same man in the cheese department who'd been there since the days when I visited my grandmother, weaving past the old, heavily powdered hunchbacks pushing a jar of pickles around in a cart, standing in line behind a woman with an eternal and involuntary nod—yes, yes, yes, yes—the exuberant yes of the girl she once was, even where she meant no, no, enough already, no.

But when I got back home it was exactly the same. The next day was worse. My judgment of all I'd written over the last year or more took on a sickening solidity. In the days that followed, all I accomplished at the desk was to box up the manuscript and notes, and empty the drawers of their contents. There were old letters, scraps of paper on which I'd written things now incomprehensible, scattered odds and ends, remaindered parts of objects long ago thrown away, assorted electrical transformers, stationery printed with the address where I'd lived with my ex-husband, S—a collection of mostly useless things, and, underneath some old notebooks, Daniel's postcards. Lodged at the back of one drawer I found a yellowed paperback Daniel must have forgotten so many years ago, a collection of stories by a writer named Lotte Berg, inscribed to him from the author in 1970. I filled a large bag with things to be thrown out; everything else I put away in a box except for the postcards and paperback. Those I placed, without reading them, into a manila envelope. I emptied all the many drawers, some very small, as I said, and some of average size, except for the one with a small brass lock. If you were sitting at the desk the lock would be located just above your right knee. The drawer had been locked for as long as I could remember, and though I'd looked many times I'd never found the key. Once, in a fit of curiosity, or maybe boredom, I tried to break the lock open with a screwdriver, but only managed to scrape my knuckles. Often I'd wished that it were a different drawer that was locked, since the one on the top right was the most practical, and whenever I went to look for something in one of the many drawers, I always instinctively reached for it first, awakening a fleeting unhappiness, a kind of orphaned feeling that I knew had nothing to do with the drawer but that had somehow come to live there. For some reason I always assumed that the drawer contained letters from the girl in the poem Daniel Varsky once read to me, or if not her then someone like her.

The following Saturday at noon Leah Weisz rang my bell. When I opened the door and saw the figure standing there I caught my breath: it was Daniel Varsky, despite the intervening twenty-seven years, exactly as I'd remembered he'd stood that winter afternoon when I rang his bell and he opened the door for me, only now everything was reversed as in a mirror, or reversed as if time had suddenly come to a halt then begun to hurtle backwards, undoing everything it had done. The same thinness, the same nose, and, despite it, the underlying delicateness. This echo of Daniel Varsky now extended her hand. It was cold when I shook it, despite the warmth outside. She wore a blue velvet blazer scuffed at the elbows and a red linen scarf around her neck, the ends slung over her shoulders in the rakish way of a college student bent under the burden of her first encounter with Kierkegaard or Sartre, battling the wind to cross a quadrangle. She looked as young as that, eighteen or nineteen, but when I did the math I realized Leah must have been twenty-four or twenty-five, almost exactly the age Daniel and I had been when we'd met each other. And, unlike a fresh-faced student, there was something foreboding about the way her hair fell in her eyes, and the eyes themselves, which were dark, almost black.

But inside I saw that she was not her father. Among other things, she was smaller, more compact, almost puckish. Her hair was auburn, not black as Daniel's had been. Under the overhead lights of my hallway, Daniel's features fell away enough that had I passed Leah in the street I might not have noticed anything familiar about her.

She saw the desk immediately and walked slowly toward it. Stopping in front of the hulking mass, more present to her, I imagine, than her father could ever have been, she put her hand to her forehead and sat down in the chair. For a moment I thought she might cry. Instead she laid her hands on the surface, ran them back and forth, and began to fiddle with the drawers. I stifled my annoyance at this intrusion, as well as those that followed, as she wasn't content to open only one drawer and look inside, but proceeded to look in three or four before she seemed satisfied that they were all empty. For a moment I thought I might cry.

To be polite, and in order to put a halt to any further inquisition of the furniture, I offered her tea. She rose from the desk and turned to look around the room. You live alone? she asked. Her tone, or the expression on her face as she glanced at the leaning stack of books next to my stained armchair and the dirty mugs collecting on the windowsill, reminded me of the pitying way friends had sometimes looked at me when they came to see me in the months before I met her father, when I lived alone in the apartment emptied of R's things. Yes, I said. How do you take your tea? You never married? she asked, and perhaps because I was taken aback by the bluntness of the question, before I could think I answered, No. I don't plan to either, she said. No? I asked. Why not? Look at you, she said. You're free to go wherever you want, to live as you please. She tucked her hair behind her ears and took in another sweeping glance across the room, as if it were the whole apartment or maybe even the life itself that was about to be transferred to her name, not just a desk.

It would have been impossible, at least for the moment, to ask all that I wanted to about the circumstances of Daniel's arrest, where he was detained, and whether anything was known about how and where he had died. Instead, over the course of the next half hour, I learned that Leah had lived in New York for two years, studying piano at Juilliard, before she decided, one day, that she no longer wished to play the giant instrument she had been chained to since she was five, and a few weeks later she went home to Jerusalem. She had been living there for the past year, trying to figure out what it was she wanted to do now. She had only come back to New York to pick up some of the things she had left behind with friends, and she planned on shipping it all, along with the desk, back to Jerusalem.

Perhaps there were other details that I missed, because as she spoke I found myself struggling to accept the idea that I was about to hand over the single meaningful object in my life as a writer, the lone physical representation of all that was otherwise weightless and intangible, to this waif who might sit at it from time to time as if at a paternal altar. And yet, Your Honor, what could I do? Arrangements were made for her to return the following day with a moving truck that would bring the furniture directly to a shipping container in Newark. Because I couldn't bear to watch the desk being carted away, I told her that I would be out, but that I would make sure that Vlad, the gruff Romanian superintendent, was there to let her in.

Early the next morning I left the manila envelope with Daniel's postcards on the empty desk, and drove up to Norfolk, Connecticut, where S and I had rented a house for nine or ten summers, and to which I hadn't returned since we'd separated. It was only once I'd parked next to the library, stepping out of the car to stretch my legs in view of the town green, that I realized any reason I had for being there shouldn't be indulged, and, moreover, I desperately wanted to avoid running into anyone I knew. I got back into the car and for the next four or five hours drove aimlessly along the country roads, through New Marlborough to Great Barrington, beyond to Lenox, tracing routes S and I had taken a hundred times before we looked up and noticed that our marriage had starved to death.

As I drove, I found myself thinking of how, four

or five years after we'd gotten married, S and I were invited to a dinner party at the home of a German dancer then living in New York. At the time S worked at a theater, now closed, where the dancer was performing a solo piece. The apartment was small and filled with the dancer's unusual possessions, things he had found on the street, or during his tireless travels, or that he had been given, all arranged with the sense of space, proportion, timing, and grace that made him such a joy to watch onstage. In fact, it was strange and almost frustrating to see the dancer in street clothes and brown house slippers, moving so practically through the apartment, with little or no sign of the tremendous physical talent that lay dormant in him, and I found myself craving for some break in this pragmatic façade, a leap or turn, some explosion of his true energy. All the same, once I got used to this and became absorbed in looking at his many little collections, I had the elated, otherworldly feeling I sometimes get entering the sphere of another's life, when for a moment changing my banal habits and living like *that* seems entirely possible, a feeling that always dissolves by the next morning, when I wake up to the familiar, unmovable shapes of my own life. At some point I got up from the dinner table to use the bathroom, and in the hall I passed the open door of the dancer's bedroom. It was spare, with only a bed and wooden chair and a little altar with candles set up in one corner. There was a large window facing south through which lower Manhattan hung suspended in the dark. The other walls were blank except for one painting tacked up with pins, a vibrant picture from whose many bright, high-spirited strokes faces sometimes emerged, as if from a bog, now and then topped with a hat. The faces on the top half of the paper were upside down, as if the painter had turned the page around or circled it on his or her knees while painting, in order to reach more easily. It was a strange piece of work, unlike the style of the other things the dancer had collected, and I studied it for a minute or two before continuing on to the bathroom.

The fire in the living room burned down, the night progressed. At the end, as we were putting on our coats, I surprised myself by asking the dancer who had made the painting. He told me that his best friend from childhood had done it when he was nine. My friend and his older sister, he said, though I think she did most of it. Afterwards they gave it to me. The dancer helped me on with my coat. You know, that painting has a sad story, he added a moment later, almost as an afterthought.

One afternoon, the mother gave the children sleeping pills in their tea. The boy was nine and his sister was eleven. Once they were asleep, she carried them to the car and drove out to the forest. By this time it was getting dark. She poured gasoline all over the car and lit a match. All three burned to death. It's strange, the dancer said, but I was always jealous of how things were in my friend's house. That year they kept the Christmas tree until April. It turned brown and the needles were dropping off, but many times I nagged my mother about why we couldn't keep our Christmas tree up as long as they did at Jörn's.

In the silence that followed this story, told in the

most straightforward manner, the dancer smiled. It's possible that it was because I had my coat on, and the apartment was warm, but suddenly I began to feel hot and light-headed. There were many other things I would have liked to ask about the children and his friendship with them, but I was afraid I might faint, and so after another guest had made a joke about the morbid end to the night, we thanked the dancer for the meal and said goodbye. As we rode down in the elevator I fought to steady myself, but S, who was humming quietly, seemed not to notice.

At that time, S and I were thinking of having a child. From the beginning both of us had imagined that we would. But there were always things we felt we had to work out first in our own lives, together and separately, and time simply passed without bringing any resolution, or a clearer sense of how we might go about being something more than what we were already struggling to be. And though when I was younger I believed I wanted to have a child, I was not surprised to find myself at thirty-five, and then forty, without one. Maybe it seems like ambivalence, Your Honor, and I suppose in part it was, but it was something else, too, a feeling I've always had, despite mounting evidence to the contrary, that there is—that there will always be—more time left for me. The years went by, my face changed in the mirror, my body was no longer what it had been, but I found it difficult to believe that the possibility of having my own child could expire without my explicit agreement.

In the taxi home that night I continued to think about that mother and her children. The wheels of the car softly rolling over the pine needles on the forest floor, the engine cut in a clearing, the pale faces of those young painters asleep in the backseat, dirt under their fingernails. How could she have done it? I said aloud to S. It was not really the question I wanted to ask, but it was as close as I could get just then. She lost her mind, he said simply, as if that were the end of it.

Not long afterwards I wrote a story about the dancer's childhood friend who had died asleep in his mother's car in the German forest. I didn't change any of the details; I only imagined more of them. The house the children lived in, the buoyant smell of spring evenings seeping through the windows, the trees in the garden that they had planted themselves, all rose up easily before me. How the children would sing together songs that their mother had taught them, how she read the Bible to them, how they kept their collection of birds' eggs on the sill, and how the boy would climb into the sister's bed on stormy nights. The story was accepted by a prominent magazine. I didn't call the dancer before it was published, nor did I send him a copy of the story. He lived through it, and I made use of it, embellishing it as I saw fit. Seen in a certain light, that is the kind of work I do, Your Honor. When I received a copy of the magazine I did wonder for a moment if the dancer would see it and how it would make him feel. But I did not spend very long on the thought, basking instead in the pride of seeing my work printed in the illustrious font of the magazine. I didn't run into the dancer for some time afterwards, nor did I think about what I would say if I did. Furthermore, after the story was published, I stopped thinking about the mother and her children who had burned to death in a car, as if by writing about them I had made them disappear.

I continued to write. I wrote another novel at the desk of Daniel Varsky, and another after that, largely based on my father who had died the year before. It was a novel I could not have written while he was alive. Had he been able to read it, I have little doubt that he would have felt betrayed. Toward the end of his life he lost control of his body and was abandoned by his dignity, something he remained painfully aware of until his final days. In the novel I chronicled these humiliations in vivid detail, even the time he defecated in his pants and I had to clean him, an incident he found so shameful that for many days afterwards he was unable to look me in the eye, and which, it goes without saying, he would have pleaded with me, if he could have brought himself to mention it, never to repeat to anyone. But I did not stop at these torturous, intimate scenes, scenes which, could my father momentarily suspend his sense of shame, he might have acknowledged as reflecting less on him than the universal plight of growing old and facing one's death—I did not stop there, but instead took his illness and suffering, with all of its pungent detail, and finally even his death, as an opportunity to write about his life, and more specifically about his failings, as both a person and a father, failings whose precise and abundant detail could be ascribed to him alone. I paraded his faults and my misgivings, the high drama of my young life with him, thinly disguised (mostly by exaggeration) across the pages of the book. I gave unforgiving descriptions of his crimes as I saw them, and then I forgave him. And yet even if in the end it was all for the sake of hard-won compassion, even if the final notes of the book were of triumphant love and grief at the loss of him, in the weeks and months leading up to its publication a sickening feeling sometimes took hold of me and dumped its blackness before moving on. In the publicity interviews I gave, I emphasized that the book was fiction and professed my frustration with journalists and readers alike who insisted on reading novels as the autobiographies of their authors, as if there were no such thing as the writer's imagination, as if the writer's work lay only in dutiful chronicling and not fierce invention. I championed the writer's freedom—to create, to alter and amend, to collapse and expand, to ascribe meaning, to design, to perform, to affect, to choose a life, to experiment, and on and on—and quoted Henry James on the "immense increase" of that freedom, a "revelation," as he calls it, that anyone who has made a serious artistic attempt cannot help but become conscious of. Yes, with the novel based on my father if not flying then at least migrating off the shelves in bookstores across the country, I celebrated the writer's unparalleled freedom, freedom from responsibility to anything and anyone but her own instincts and vision. Perhaps I did not exactly say but certainly implied that the writer served a higher calling, what one calls only in art and religion a vocation, and cannot worry too much about the feelings of those whose lives she borrows from.

Yes, I believed—perhaps even still believe—that the writer should not be cramped by the possible consequences of her work. She has no duty to earthly accuracy or verisimilitude. She is not an accountant; nor is she required to be something as ridiculous and misguided as a moral compass. In her work the writer is free of laws. But in her life, Your Honor, she is not free.

*   *   *

Some months after the novel about my father was published, I was out walking and passed a bookstore near Washington Square Park. Out of habit, I slowed as I reached the window to see whether my book was on display. At that moment I saw the dancer inside at the register, he saw me, we locked eyes. For a second, I considered hurrying on my way without remembering exactly what it was that made me so uneasy. But this quickly became impossible; the dancer raised his hand in greeting and all I could do was wait for him to get his change and come out to say hello.

He wore a beautiful wool coat and a silk scarf knotted around his throat. In the sunlight I saw that he was older. Not by much, but enough that he could no longer be called young. I asked how he was, and he told me about a friend of his who like so many in those years had died of AIDS. He spoke of a recent breakup with a long-term boyfriend, someone he had not yet met the last time I saw him, and then about an upcoming performance of a piece he had choreographed. Though five or six years had passed, S and I were still married and lived in the same West Side apartment. From the outside, not very much had changed, and so when it was my turn to offer news I simply said that everything was fine and that I was still writing. The dancer nodded. It's possible he even smiled, in a genuine way, a way that always makes me, with my unrelenting self-consciousness, feel slightly nervous and embarrassed when I encounter it, knowing I could never be so easy, open, or fluent. I know, he said. I read everything you write. Do you? I said, surprised and suddenly agitated. But he smiled again, and it seemed to me that the danger had passed, the story would go unmentioned.

We walked a few blocks together toward Union Square, as far as was possible before we each had to turn off in separate directions. As we said goodbye, the dancer bent down and removed a piece of fluff from the collar of my coat. The moment was tender and almost intimate. I took it down off my wall, you know, he said softly. What? I said. After I read your story, I took the painting down off my wall. I found I couldn't bear to look at it anymore. You did? I said, caught off guard. Why? At first I wondered myself, he said. It had followed me from apartment to apartment, from city to city, for almost twenty years. But after a while I understood what your story had made so clear to me. What was that? I wanted to ask, but couldn't. Then the dancer, who though older was still languid and full of grace, reached out and tapped me with two fingers on the cheek, turned, and walked away.

As I made my way home, the dancer's gesture first baffled and then annoyed me. On the surface, it had been easy to mistake for tenderness, but the more I thought about it, the more there seemed something condescending in it, even meant to humiliate. In my mind the dancer's smile became less and less genuine, and it began to seem to me that he had been choreographing the gesture for years, turning it over, waiting to run into me. And was it deserved? Hadn't he gamely told the story, not only to me but all of the dinner guests that night? If I had discovered it through surreptitious means—reading his journals or letters, which I couldn't possibly have done, knowing him as little as I did—it would have been different. Or if he had told me the story in confidence, filled with still-painful emotion. But he had not. He had offered it with the same smile and festivity with which he had offered us a glass of grappa after dinner.

As I walked, I happened to pass a playground. It was already late in the afternoon but the small fenced-in area was full of the children's high-pitched activity. Among the many apartments I've lived in over the years, one had been across the street from a playground and I'd always noticed that in the last half an hour before dusk the children's voices seemed to get noisier. I could never tell whether it was because in the failing light the city had grown a decibel more quiet, or because the children had really grown louder, knowing their time there was almost through. Certain phrases or peals of laughter would break away from the rest, rising up, and hearing one of these I would sometimes get up from my desk to watch the children below. But I didn't stop to watch them now. Consumed by my run-in with the dancer, I barely noticed them until a cry rang out, pained and terrified, an agonizing child's cry that tore into me, as if it were an appeal to me alone. I stopped short and jerked around, sure I was going to find a mangled child fallen from a great height. But there was nothing, only the children running in and out of their circles and games, and no sign of where the cry had come from. My heart was racing, adrenaline coursing through me, my whole being poised to rush to save whoever had let loose that terrible scream. But the children continued to play, unalarmed. I scanned the buildings above, thinking that perhaps the cry had come from an open window, though it was November and cold enough to need the heat. I stood gripping the fence for some time.

When I got home, S was still out. I put on Beethoven's String Quartet in A Minor, a piece I'd always loved since a college boyfriend first played it for me in his dorm room. I still remember the knobs of his spine as he bent over the record player and slowly let the needle down. The third movement is one of the most moving passages ever written, and I've never listened to it without feeling as if I alone have been lifted up on the shoulders of some giant creature touring the charred landscape of all human feeling. Like most music that affects me deeply, I would never listen to it while others were around, just as I would not pass on a book that I especially loved to another. I am embarrassed to admit this, knowing that it reveals some essential lack or selfishness in my nature, and aware that it runs contrary to the instincts of most, whose passion for something leads them to want to share it, to ignite a similar passion in others, and that without the benefit of such enthusiasm I would still be ignorant of many of the books and much of the music I love most, not least of all the third movement of Opus 132 that bore me up one spring night in 1967. But rather than an expansion, I've always felt a diminishment of my own pleasure when I've invited someone else to take part in it, a rupture in the intimacy I felt with the work, an invasion of privacy. It is worst when someone else picks up the copy of a book I've just been enthralled by and begins casually to thumb through the first pages. Simply reading at all in the presence of another did not come naturally to me, and I suppose I never really got used to it, even after years of being married. But by that point S had been hired as a booking manager of Lincoln Center and his work required longer hours than it had in the past, and sometimes even took him away on trips to Berlin or London or Tokyo for days at a time. Alone, I could slip into a kind of stillness, into a place like that bog those children once drew, where faces rise up out of the elements, and all is quiet, like the moment just before the arrival of an idea, a stillness and peace I've only ever felt when alone. When at last S came through the door I always found it jarring. But in time he came to understand and accept this, and took to entering by whichever room I wasn't in—the kitchen if I was in the living room, the living room if I was in the bedroom—and occupying himself there by emptying his pockets for some minutes, or organizing his foreign change in little black film canisters, before gradually merging into wherever I was, and this small gesture always melted my resentment into gratitude.

When the movement came to an end I turned off the stereo without listening to the rest, and went to the kitchen to start a soup. I was cutting the vegetables when the knife slipped and sliced deeply into my thumb, and at the instant I shouted out I heard a double of my cry, one belonging to a child. It seemed to come from the other side of the wall, in the next apartment over. I was overcome by a feeling of regret, so sharp that I felt it as a kind of physical pain in my gut, and I had to sit. I admit that I even cried, sobbing until the blood from my finger began to drip onto my shirt. After I'd gotten control of myself and wrapped the cut in a paper towel, I went to knock on my neighbor's door, an old woman named Mrs. Becker who lived alone. I heard her slow footsteps shuffling to the door, and then, after I announced myself, the patient unlocking of various bolts. She peered up at me through enormous black glasses, glasses that somehow made her look like a small, burrowing animal. Yes, dear, come in, so nice to see you. The smell of ancient food was overwhelming, years and years of cooking odors clinging to the rugs and upholstery, thousands of pots of soup that allowed her to scrape by. I thought that I heard a cry coming from here just a moment ago. A cry? Mrs. Becker asked. It sounded like a child, I said, peering past her into the dark recesses of her apartment, cluttered with claw-footed furniture that would only be moved, with great difficulty, when she died. Sometimes I watch the television, but no, I don't think it was on, I was just sitting here looking at a book. Maybe it came from downstairs. I'm fine, dear, thank you for your concern.

I didn't tell anyone what I'd heard, not even Dr. Lichtman, my therapist of many years. And for some time I didn't hear the child again. But the cries stayed with me. Sometimes I would suddenly hear them within me when I wrote, causing me to lose my train of thought or become flustered. I began to sense in them something mocking, an undertone I had not heard at first. Other times I would hear a cry just as I woke, as I crossed over into wakefulness or departed from sleep, and on those mornings I rose with the feeling of something wound around my neck. A hidden weight seemed to attach itself to simple objects, a teacup, a doorknob, a glass, hardly noticeable at first, beyond the sense that every move required a slightly greater exertion of energy, and by the time I negotiated among these things and arrived at my desk, some reserve in me was already worn down or washed away. The pauses between words became longer, when for an instant the momentum of pressing thought into language faltered and a dark spot of indifference bloomed. I suppose it's what I've battled most often in my life as a writer, a sort of entropy of care or languishing of will, so consistently, in fact, that I barely paid it any attention—a pull to give in to an undertow of speechlessness. But now I often became suspended in these moments, they grew longer and wider, and sometimes it became impossible to see the other shore. And when I finally got there, when a word at last came along like a lifeboat, and then another and another, I greeted them with a faint distrust, a suspiciousness that took root and did not confine itself to my work. It is impossible to distrust one's writing without awakening a deeper distrust in oneself.

Around that time a houseplant I'd had for many years, a large ficus that had grown happily in our apartment's sunniest corner, suddenly became diseased and began to drop its leaves. I gathered them into a bag and brought it to a plant store to ask how to treat it, but no one could tell me what it had. I became obsessed with saving it, and explained again and again to S the various methods I'd used to try to cure it. But nothing eradicated the disease and in the end the ficus died. I had to throw it out on the street, and for a day, until the garbage truck picked it up, I could see it from my window, bare and ruined. Even after the garbagemen took it away, I continued to page through books on care for houseplants, to study the pictures of mealybugs, of twig blight and canker, until one night S came up behind me, closed the book, put his two hands on my shoulders and held them strongly there while staring fixedly into my eyes, as if he had just applied glue to the bottom of my feet and needed to hold me in place, applying steady pressure until it dried.

That was the end of the ficus, but it was not the end of my agitation. No, I suppose you could say it was just the beginning. One afternoon I was alone in the house. S was at work, and I had just come back from an exhibition of paintings by R. B. Kitaj. I made myself lunch, and as I sat down to eat I heard the shrill laughter of a child. The sound of it, its closeness and something else, something somber and unsettling behind that little ascension of notes, made me drop my sandwich and stand so suddenly that my chair fell back. I hurried into the living room and then the bedroom. I don't know what I expected to find; both were empty. But the window next to our bed was open, and leaning out I saw a boy, no more than six or seven, disappearing alone down the block, pulling a small green wagon behind him.

I remember now that it was that spring that Daniel Varsky's couch began to rot. One afternoon I forgot to close the window before I went out, and a storm blew up and soaked the sofa. A few days later it started to give off a terrible stench, the smell of mold, but something else too, a sour, festering smell as if the rain had unloosed something foul hidden in its depths. The super removed it, grimacing at the smell, the sofa on which Daniel Varsky and I had once kissed all those years ago, and it too sat dejectedly on the street until the garbagemen came for it.

Some nights later I woke suddenly out of a cavernous dream that took place in an old dance hall. For a moment I was unsure of where I was, and then I turned and saw S sleeping beside me. I was comforted for a moment until I looked closer and saw that instead of human skin he seemed to be covered in a tough gray hide like that of a rhinoceros. I saw it so clearly that even now I can remember the exact look of that scaly gray skin. Not quite awake and not quite asleep, I became frightened. I wanted to touch him myself to be certain of what I saw, but I was afraid to wake the beast lying next to me. So I closed my eyes and eventually fell asleep again, and the fear of S's skin became a dream about finding my father's body washed up on the shore like a dead whale's, only instead of being a whale it was a decomposing rhinoceros, and in order to move it I had to stab it deeply enough that my spear would lodge there, allowing me to drag the body along behind me. But no matter how hard I drove the spear into the rhino's flank I couldn't get it in deeply enough. In the end, the decomposing corpse found its way to the sidewalk outside the apartment where the diseased ficus and the rotting couch had also been discarded, but by this time it had morphed again and when I looked down at it from our fifth-floor window, I realized that what I took to be a rhinoceros was the body of the lost, decomposing poet Daniel Varsky. The next day, passing the super in the lobby, I thought I heard him say, You make good use of death. I stopped and spun around. What did you say? I demanded. He looked me over calmly, and I thought I saw the hint of a smirk at the corners of his mouth. They're fixing the roof on the tenth, he said. Lots of noise, he added, and clanged the gate of the service elevator shut.

My work continued to go badly. I wrote more slowly than I ever had before, and continued to second-guess what I'd written, unable to escape the feeling that all I'd written in the past had been wrong, misguided, a kind of enormous mistake. I began to suspect that instead of exposing the hidden depths of things, as all along I'd supposed I was doing, perhaps the opposite was true, that I'd been hiding behind the things I wrote, using them to obscure a secret lack, a deficiency I'd hidden from others all my life, and, by writing, had kept, even, from myself. A deficiency that became larger as the years passed, and harder to conceal, making my work more and more difficult. What sort of deficiency? I suppose you could call it a deficiency of spirit. Of strength, of vitality, of compassion, and because of this, welded to it, a deficiency of effect. So long as I wrote, there was the illusion of these things. The fact that I didn't witness the effect didn't mean it didn't exist. I made a point of answering the question I received with some frequency from journalists, Do you think books can change people's lives? (which really meant, Do you actually think anything you write could mean anything to anyone?), with a little airtight thought experiment in which I asked the interviewer to imagine the sort of person he might be if all of the literature he'd read in his life were somehow excised from his mind, his mind and soul, and as the journalist contemplated that nuclear winter I sat back with a self-satisfied smile, saved again from facing the truth.

Yes, a deficiency of effect, born of a deficiency of spirit. That is the best way I can describe it, Your Honor. And though I had been able to hide it for years, countering the appearance of a certain anemia in life with the excuse of another, more profound level of existence in my work, suddenly I found I couldn't any longer.

I didn't talk about it with S. In fact, I didn't even bring it up with Dr. Lichtman, whom I saw regularly during my marriage. I thought I would, but each time I arrived at her office a silence overtook me, and the deficiency hidden under hundreds of thousands of words and a million small gestures remained safe for another week. Because to have acknowledged the problem, to have said it aloud, would have kicked loose the rock on which everything else rested, ringing in an emergency, and afterwards interminable months, years perhaps, of what Dr. Lichtman called "our work" but which was really just an excruciating excavation of myself with an array of blunt instruments while she sat by in a worn leather chair, feet on the ottoman, occasionally noting something on the legal pad she kept balanced on her knees for moments when I clawed up out of the hole, face blackened and hands scratched, clutching a little nugget of self-knowledge.

So instead I went on as before, only not as before, because now I felt a creeping shame and disgust with myself. In the presence of others—especially S, to whom I was of course closest—the feeling was most acute, while alone I could forget it a little bit, or at least ignore it. In bed at night I recoiled to the farthest edge, and sometimes when S and I passed each other in the hall I couldn't bring myself to meet his eyes, and when he called my name from another room I had to exert a certain force, a strong pressure, to goad myself to answer. When he confronted me I shrugged and told him it was my work, and when he did not press me on the subject, laying off as he always did, as I had taught him to do, giving me a wider and wider berth, I secretly grew angry at him, frustrated that he did not notice how dire the circumstances were, how awful I was feeling, angry at him and perhaps even disgusted. Yes, disgusted, Your Honor, I didn't save it only for myself, for not noticing that for all these years he had been living with someone who had made a life's work of duplicity. Everything about him began to annoy me. The way he whistled in the bathroom, and moved his lips as he read the paper, the way he had to ruin every nice moment by pointing its niceness out. When I was not aggravated with him I was angry at myself, angry and full of guilt for causing so much grief to this man for whom happiness, or at the very least gladness, came easily, who had a talent for putting strangers at ease and drawing them over to his side so that people naturally went out of their way to do him favors, but whose Achilles' heel was his poor judgment, proof being that he had willfully roped himself to me, a person who was always falling through the ice, who had the opposite effect on others, immediately making them raise their hackles, as if they sensed that their shins might be kicked.

And then one evening he came home late. It was raining out and he was soaking wet, his hair plastered down. He came into the kitchen still wearing the dripping coat and shoes muddy from the park. I was reading the paper as I always do in the evening, and he stood above me showering droplets on the pages. He had a terrible look on his face, and at first I thought he had been through something awful, a near-fatal accident, or seen a death on the subway tracks. He said, Do you remember that plant? I couldn't imagine what he was trying to get at, soaking wet like that, with shining eyes. The ficus? I said. Yes, he said, the ficus. You took more interest in that plant's health than you have taken in me for years, he said. I was taken aback. He sniffed and wiped the water from his face. I can't remember the last time you asked me how I felt about something, about anything that might matter. Instinctively I went to reach for him, but he pulled away. You're lost in your own world, Nadia, in the things that happen there, and you've locked all the doors. Sometimes I look at you sleeping. I wake up and look at you and I feel closer to you when you're like that, unguarded, than when you're awake. When you're awake you're like someone with her eyes closed, watching a movie on the inside of your eyelids. I can't reach you anymore. Once upon a time I could, but not now, and not for a long time. And I don't think you give a damn about reaching me. I feel more alone with you than I feel with anyone else, even just walking by myself down the street. Can you imagine how that feels?

He went on for some time while I sat listening in silence because I knew he was right, and like two people who have loved each other however imperfectly, who have tried to make a life together, however imperfectly, who have lived side by side and watched the wrinkles slowly form at the corner of the other's eyes, and watched a little drop of gray, as if poured from a jug, drop into the other's skin and spread itself evenly, listening to the other's coughs and sneezes and little collected mumblings, like two people who'd had one idea together and slowly allowed that idea to be replaced with two separate, less hopeful, less ambitious ideas, we spoke deep into the night, and the next day, and the next night. For forty days and forty nights, I want to say, but the fact of the matter is it only took three. One of us had loved the other more perfectly, had watched the other more closely, and one of us listened and the other hadn't, and one of us held on to the ambition of the one idea far longer than was reasonable, whereas the other, passing a garbage can one night, had casually thrown it away.

And as we spoke a picture of myself emerged and developed, reacting to S's hurt like a Polaroid reacting to heat, a picture of myself to hang on the wall next to the one I'd already been living with for months—the one of someone who made use of the pain of others for her own ends, who, while others suffered, starved, and were tormented, hid herself safely away and prided herself on her special perceptiveness and sensitivity to the symmetry buried below things, someone who needed little help to convince herself that her self-important project was serving the greater good, but who in fact was utterly beside the point, totally irrelevant, and worse, a fraud who hid a poverty of spirit behind a mountain of words. Yes, next to that pretty picture I now hung another: a picture of someone so selfish and self-absorbed that she had been unconcerned enough about her husband's feelings to give him not even a fraction of the care and attention she gave to imagining the emotional lives of the people she sketched out on paper, to furnishing their inner lives, taking pains to adjust the light on their faces, brushing a stray hair from their eyes. Busy with all of this, not wishing to be disturbed, I'd hardly stopped to think of how S might have felt, for example, when he walked through the door of our home and found his wife silent, with back turned and shoulders hunched so as to defend her little kingdom, how he felt as he removed his shoes, checked the mail, dropped the foreign coins into their little canisters, wondering just how cold my mood would be when at last he tried to approach me across the rickety bridge. I had barely paused to consider him fully at all.

After three nights of talking as we had not in many years, we arrived at the inevitable end. Slowly, like a great hot-air balloon drifting down and landing with a bump in the grass, our marriage of a decade expired. But it took us time to split apart. The apartment had to be sold, the books divided up, but really, Your Honor, there is no need to go on about this, it would take too long, and I feel I haven't got a lot of time with you, so I won't go into the pain of two people prying apart their lives inch by inch, the sudden vulnerability of the human situation, the sorrow, regret, anger, guilt, and disgust with oneself, the fear and suffocating loneliness, but also the relief, so incomparable, and I will only say that when it was all finished I found myself alone again in a new apartment, surrounded by my belongings and what was left of Daniel Varsky's furniture, which followed me like a pack of mangy dogs.

I suppose you can imagine the rest, Your Honor. In your line of work you must see it all the time, the way people continue to repeat the same story of themselves over and over, complete with the old mistakes. One would think that someone like me, with enough psychological acumen to supposedly uncover the little delicate skeleton that organizes the behavior of others, would be able to learn from the painful lessons of self-scrutiny, and correct a little, to find the way out of the maddening circular game where we are forever eating our own tails. Not so, Your Honor. The months passed, and before long I'd turned those pictures of myself to face the wall, and lost myself in writing another book.

* * *

By the time I got back from Norfolk it was dark. I parked the car, then walked up and down Broadway, inventing various errands in order to delay returning to confront the absence of the desk for as long as possible. When at last I went home, there was a note on the hall table. Thank you for this, it said, in surprisingly small handwriting. I hope to meet you again one day. And then, below her signature, Leah had put her address on Ha'Oren Street in Jerusalem.

I was only in the apartment for fifteen or twenty minutes—enough time to glance at the yawning emptiness where the desk had stood, fix myself a sandwich, and, full of decisive purpose, go to fetch the box containing the various worked-up sections of the new book—when I experienced the first attack. It came over me quickly, with almost no warning. I began fighting for air. Everything seemed to close around me, as if I'd been dropped into a narrow hole in the ground. My heartbeat became so rapid I wondered whether I was going into cardiac arrest. The anxiety was overwhelming—something like the feeling of having been left behind on a dark shore while everyone and everything I'd ever known in my life had departed on a great, illuminated ship. Clutching my heart and talking aloud to try to calm myself, I paced the former living room that was now also a former study, and only when I turned on the television and saw the face of the anchorman did the feeling at last begin to subside, though my hands continued to shake for ten minutes more.

In the week that followed I experienced similar attacks daily, sometimes even twice a day. To the original symptoms were added terrible stomach pain, extreme nausea, and more varieties of terror hidden in the smallest things than I ever imagined possible. Although at first the attacks were set off by glancing at or being reminded of my work, very quickly they spread out in all directions, and threatened to infect everything. Just the idea of going out of the apartment and trying to accomplish some tiny, inane task that in my infinite wellness I would have thought nothing of filled me with dread. I stood trembling at the door, trying to think myself through it and out the other side. Twenty minutes later I would still be standing there, and all that had changed was that I was now drenched in sweat.

None of it made sense. I'd been steadily writing and publishing books at the rate of about one every four years for half of my life. The emotional difficulties of the profession were legion, and I had stumbled and fallen again and again. The crises that had begun with the dancer and the child's cry had been the worst, but there had been others in the past. Sometimes a depression, the result of the war writing wages on one's confidence and sense of purpose, all but incapacitated me. It had happened often between books, when, used to having my work to reflect myself back to me, I had to make do with staring out onto an opaque nothingness. But no matter how bad it had gotten, my ability to write, however haltingly and poorly, had never abandoned me. I'd always felt the surge of the fighter in me, and had been able to drum up the opposition; to turn the nothingness into something to push, and push, and push against, until I'd broken through to the other side, still swinging. But this—this was something entirely different. This had bypassed all of my defenses, had slipped unnoticed past the halls of reason, like a supervirus that has become resistant to everything, and only once it had taken root in the very core of me had it reared its terrifying head.

Five days after the attacks began I phoned Dr. Lichtman. After my marriage had ended I'd stopped seeing her, having slowly given up on the idea of undertaking vast renovations on the foundation of my self in order to make myself more suitable for social life. I'd accepted the consequences of my natural tendencies, letting my habits slide, not without relief, back to their ungirdled state. Since then I had seen her only from time to time, when I couldn't find the exit to a long-standing mood; more often, because she lived in the neighborhood, I ran into her on the street, and like two people who had once been but were no longer close, we waved, paused as if to stop, but continued on our ways.

It took a gargantuan effort for me to get myself from my apartment to her office nine blocks away. At regular intervals I had to stop and grip some pole or railing, to borrow from it a sense of permanence. By the time I was sitting in Dr. Lichtman's waiting room filled with evocative, musty books, the armpits of my shirt were soaked in sweat, and when the door opened and she appeared, light streaming through her finely spun, goldish hair that for two decades she'd worn puffed at the top in a fashion I've never seen on anyone else, as if she had needed quickly to hide something and had put it there, I nearly threw myself on her. Folded into the familiar gray wool couch, surrounded once again by the objects I'd stared at so often in the past that they now seemed to me landmarks on the map of my psyche, I described the past two weeks. Over the course of the hour and a half (she'd managed to clear a double session for me), a feeling of calm began slowly, tentatively, to return for the first time in days. And, even as I was speaking about being incapacitated by panic, narrating my experience of being in the grips of a monster that seemed to have sprung from nowhere and made me a stranger to myself, on another level of mind, freed from thinking about what was now being attended to by Dr. Lichtman, I began to take hold of an idea that was wholly preposterous, Your Honor, beyond that it offered me an escape. The life I had chosen, a life largely absent of others, certainly emptied of the ties that keep most people tangled up in each other, only made sense when I was actually writing the sort of work I had sequestered myself in order to produce. It would be wrong to say that the conditions of such a life had been a hardship. Something in me naturally migrated away from the fray, preferring the deliberate meaningfulness of fiction to unaccounted-for reality, preferring a shapeless freedom to the robust work of yoking my thoughts to the logic and flow of another's. When I had tried it in any sort of sustained way, first in relationships, and then in my marriage to S, it had failed. Looking back, perhaps the only reason I had been happy, for a while, with R is that he had been as absent as I had been, or even more so. We were two people locked in our antigravity suits who happened to be orbiting around the same pieces of his mother's old furniture. And then he had drifted off, through some loophole in our apartment, to an unreachable part of the cosmos. After that there was a series of doomed relationships, then my marriage, and once S and I parted ways I'd promised myself that it was the last time I would try. In the five or six years since then I'd had only brief affairs, and when these men tried to turn it into something more I refused, and soon afterwards brought things to an end and returned alone to my life.

And what of it, Your Honor? What of my life? You see, I thought—One has to make a sacrifice. I chose the freedom of long unscheduled afternoons in which nothing happens but the slightest shift in mood as captured in a semicolon. Yes, work was that for me, an irresponsible exercise in pure freedom. And if I neglected or even ignored the rest, it was because I believed the rest conspired to chip away at that freedom, to interfere and force upon it a compromise. The first words out of my mouth in the morning spoken to S, and already the constraints began, the false politeness. Habits are formed. Kindness above all, responsiveness, a patient show of interest. But you also have to try to be entertaining and amusing. It's exhausting work, in the way that trying to keep three or four lies going at once is exhausting. Only to be repeated tomorrow and tomorrow after that. You hear a sound and it's truth turning in its grave. Imagination dies a slower death, by suffocation. You try to put up walls, to cordon off the little plot where you labor as something apart, with a separate climate and different rules. But the habits seep in anyway like poisoned groundwater, and all you were trying to raise there chokes and withers. What I'm trying to say is that it seems to me you can't have it both ways. So I made a sacrifice, and let go.

The idea I began to entertain during that first session with Dr. Lichtman took hold, so that after seeing her ten or eleven times in almost as many days, and, aided by Xanax, having managed to scale the panic down from a nightmare to a threatening menace, I announced to her that I had decided, in a week's time, to take a trip. She was surprised, of course, and asked where I was going. A number of possible answers crossed my mind. Places I had, over the years, received invitations from that perhaps could be extended again. Rome. Berlin. Istanbul. But in the end I said what I knew I was going to say all along. Jerusalem. She raised her eyebrows. I'm not going in order to claim back the desk, if that's what you're thinking, I said. Then why? she asked, the light through her windows spinning her hair, the rising wave of hair drawn up high above the scalp, into something almost transparent—almost but not quite, so that it seemed like the secret to wellness, however unlikely, could still be hidden there. But my time was up, and I was excused from the need to answer. At the door we shook hands, a gesture that always struck me as strangely out of place, as if, with all one's organs spread on the table and the allotted time in the operating room almost up, the surgeon were to wrap them each neatly in plastic wrap before putting them back and hurriedly sewing you up again. The following Friday, having given Vlad instructions to look after my apartment while I was away, taken one Xanax to get through security, and another hurtling down the runway, I was aloft on a night flight bound for Ben Gurion airport.

TRUE KINDNESS

I don't support the plan, I told you. Why? you demanded, with angry little eyes. What will you write? I asked. You told me a convoluted story about four, six, maybe eight people all lying in rooms joined by a system of electrodes and wires to a great white shark. All night the shark floats suspended in an illuminated tank, dreaming the dreams of these people. No, not the dreams, the nightmares, the things too difficult to bear. So they sleep, and through the wires the terrifying things leave them and flood into the awesome fish with scarred skin that can bear all the accumulated misery. After you finished I let a sufficient amount of silence pass before I spoke. Who are these people? I asked. People, you said. I ate a handful of nuts, watching your face. I don't know where to begin on the problems with this little story, I told you. Problems? you said, your voice rising and cracking. In the wells of your eyes your mother saw the suffering of a child raised by a tyrant, but in the end the fact that you never became a writer had nothing to do with me.

* * *

So what? Where to begin? After everything, after the millions of words, the endless conversations, the relentless goings on about, the phone calls, the explaining, the badgering, the emphasizing, the obfuscating and the clarifying, and then the silence of all these years—where?

It's almost dawn. From where I sit at the kitchen table I can see the front gate, and any minute now you'll return from your nocturnal rambling. I'll see you appear in your old blue windbreaker, the one you dug out of your closet, and you'll bend over to unhook the rusted latch and let yourself in. You'll open the door, take off your wet sneakers, ridges of mud on the edges and blades of grass stuck to the soles, and then you'll come into the kitchen and find me waiting for you.

* * *

When you and Uri were very young your mother lived in fear of dying and leaving you alone. Alone with me, I pointed out. She would look three, four times before crossing the street. Every time she came home safely she had won a small victory against death. She gathered you and your brother up in her arms, but it was always you who clung to her the longest, burying your little runny nose in her neck as if you sensed what had been at risk. Once she woke me up in the middle of the night. It was soon after the Suez War, in which I fought just as I fought in '48, just as anyone fought who could hold a gun or throw a grenade. I want us to leave, she said. What are you saying? I asked. I won't send them into a war, she said. Eve, I said, it's late. No, she said sitting up, I won't let it happen. Why are you worrying, they're babies, I said. By the time they're old enough there will be no more fighting. Go to sleep. Three weeks earlier a guy in my battalion was walking outside our tent when a shell hit and vaporized him. He was blown to bits. The next day a dog that everyone fed their scraps to brought his hand back and sat chewing on it in the noonday sun. It fell to me to wrestle the severed hand from the hungry animal. I wrapped it in a rag and kept it under my bed until someone could send it back to his family. Later I was informed that such minimal parts were not returned. I didn't ask what would become of it. I gave the hand over and they disposed of it as they saw fit. Did I have nightmares afterwards? Did I scream out in the night? Pass over it. What's the use of going into these things? Don't think about it now, I said to your mother, and turned to sleep. I've already thought about it, she said. We'll move to London. And how will we live? I asked, flipping back over and grabbing her wrists. For a moment she was silent, sucking in her breath. You'll find a way, she said quietly.

But we did not move, I did not find a way. I came to Israel when I was five, almost everything in my life happened here. I would not leave. My sons would grow up in Israeli sunshine, eating Israeli fruit, playing under Israeli trees, with the dirt of their forefathers under their nails, fighting if necessary. Your mother knew all of this from the beginning. In the light of day, in light of my obstinacy, she went out in the street with a scarf tied around her hair, went out to battle death, and came home victorious.

When she died I called Uri first. Make of that what you will. All of these years it was Uri who came when the garage door was stuck, Uri when the stupid DVD player was on the fritz, Uri when the piece-of-shit GPS system that nobody needs in a country the size of a postage stamp kept barking over and over, At the next light, turn left! Left, left,

left! Fuck you, bitch, I'm going right. Yes, Uri who came over and knew the right button to silence her, so that I would be free to drive again in peace. When your mother got sick, it was Uri who drove her to the chemotherapy twice a week. And you, my son? Where were you during all of that? So tell me, why the hell would I call you first?

Go by the house, I told him, and get your mother's red suit. Dad, he said, his voice unraveling like a ribbon dropped from a roof. The red one, Uri, with the black buttons. Not the white buttons, that's important. It has to be the black ones. Why did it have to be? Because there is great comfort in specifics. After a silence: But Dad, she won't be buried in clothes. Uri and I stayed with her body the whole night. While you were waiting for a plane in Heathrow we sat with the corpse of the woman who brought you into this world, who was afraid to die and leave you alone with me.

*   *   *

Explain it to me again, I said to you. Because I want to understand. You write and you erase. And you call this a profession? And you, in your infinite wisdom, you said, No, a living. I laughed in your face. In your face, my boy! A living! and then the laughter dropped from my lips. Who do you think you are? I asked. The hero of your own existence? You shrank into yourself. You pulled your head in like a little turtle. Tell me, I said, I'd really like to know. What is it like to be you?

*   *   *

Two nights before your mother died I sat down to write her a letter. Me, who hates writing letters, who would rather pick up the phone to say my piece. A letter lacks volume, and I am a man who relies on volume to make myself understood. But, OK, there was no line that would reach your mother, or maybe there was still a line but no telephone on the other end. Or just an endless ringing and no one picking up, Jesus Christ, my boy, enough with the fucking metaphors. So I sat down in the hospital cafeteria to write her a letter, because there were things I still wanted to tell her. I'm not a man who has romantic ideas about the extension of the spirit, when the body fails it's over, finished, curtains, kaput. But I made up my mind all the same to bury the letter with her. I borrowed a pen from the overweight nurse and sat under the posters of Machu Picchu, the Great Wall of China, and the ruins of Ephesus as if I were there to send your mother to a faraway place rather than no place. A gurney rattled by carrying the almost-dead, bald and shrunken, a little bag of bones that opened an eye in which all the sentience had been concentrated, and fixed me in its gaze as it rolled past. I turned back to the paper in front of me. *Dear Eve.* But after that, nothing. Suddenly it became impossible to write another word. I don't know which was worse, the plea of that pathetic little eye or the rebuke of the blank page. To think that you once wanted to make a life of words! Thank God I saved you from that. You might be a big macher now, but it's me you have to thank.

Dear Eve, then nothing. The words dried up like leaves and blew away. All that time I'd sat by her side as she lay unconscious it had been so clear in my head, the many things I still needed to tell her. I'd held forth, I'd carried on, all in my head. But now every word I dredged up seemed lifeless and false. Just when I was ready to give up and crumple the page into a ball I remembered what Segal once told me. You remember Avner Segal, my old friend, translated into many obscure languages but never English so he always stayed poor? A few years ago we met for lunch in Rehavia. It had surprised me how old he'd gotten in the few years since I'd seen him. No doubt he thought the same of me. Once we worked side by side among the chickens, full of ideals of solidarity. The kibbutz elders had decided the best way to make use of our youthful talent was to send us to inoculate a flock of birds, then to clear up their shit in the hay. Now we sat together, the retired prosecutor and the aging writer, hair growing out of our ears. His body was bent. He confided that despite the fact that his last book had won a prize (I never heard of it), he was having a terrible time. He couldn't get a paragraph out without condemning it to the trash. So what do you do? I asked. You want to know? he said. I'm asking, I told him. All right, he said, between you and me, I'll tell you. He leaned across the table and whispered two words: Mrs. Kleindorf. What? I said. Just what I said, Mrs. Kleindorf. I'm not following you, I told him. I pretend I'm writing to Mrs. Kleindorf, he said. My seventh grade teacher. No one else is going to see it, I tell myself, only her. It doesn't matter that she's been dead already twenty-five years. I think of her kind eyes and the little red smiley faces she used to draw on my papers, and I begin to relax. And then, he said, I can write a little.

I turned back to the paper in front of me. *Dear—* I wrote, but stopped again there, because I couldn't remember the name of my seventh grade teacher. Not the sixth, fifth, or fourth either. The smell of the floor polish mingling with unwashed skin I remembered, and the dry feel of chalk dust in the air, and the stench of glue and urine. But the names of the teachers were lost to me.

Dear Mrs. Kleindorf, I wrote, *My wife is dying upstairs. For fifty-one years we shared a bed. For a month she's been lying in a hospital bed, and every night I go home and sleep in our bed alone. I haven't washed the sheets since she left. I'm afraid that if I do I won't be able to sleep. The other day I went into the bathroom and the maid was cleaning the hair out of Eve's brush. What are you doing? I asked. I'm cleaning the brush, she said. Don't touch that brush again, I said. Do you understand what I'm trying to say, Mrs. Kleindorf? And while we're on the subject of you, let me ask a question. Why is it that there was always a unit on history, math, science, and God knows what other useless, totally forgettable information you taught those seventh graders year after year, but never any unit on death? No exercises, no workbooks, no final exams on the only subject that matters?*

* * *

Do you like that, my boy? I thought you would. Suffering: just the sort of thing that's up your alley.

Anyway, I got no further than that. I tucked the unfinished letter in my pocket and went back to the room where your mother lay among the wires and tubes and beeps and drips. There was a watercolor of a landscape on the wall, a bucolic valley, some distant hills. I knew every inch of it. It was a flat and crude painting, terrible actually, like something out of one of those paint-by-numbers kits, like one of those landscapes-out-of-a-can they sell in the souvenir booths, but right then I decided that when I left that room for the last time I would take it off the wall and carry it away with me, cheap frame and all. I had stared at it for so many hours and days that in a way I can't explain that shitty painting had come to stand for something. I had begged it, reasoned with it, argued with it, cursed it, I had gone into it, I had bored my way into that incompetent valley and by and by it had come to mean something to me. So I decided, while your mother was still clinging to the last inhumane shred of life given to her, that when it was all over I would take it down off the wall, stick it under my jacket, and make off with it. I closed my eyes and drifted off. When I woke, the nurses were gathered in a little clot around the bed. A flare of activity, and then they parted and your mother was still. Gone from this world, as they say, Dova'leh, as if there is any other. The painting was nailed to the wall. Such is life, my boy: if you think you're original in anything, think again.

* * *

I rode with her body to the mortuary. It was I who looked on her last. I pulled the sheet over her face. How is this possible? I kept thinking. How am I doing this, look at my hand, it's reaching out, now it's taking hold of the cloth, how? The very last time I will ever look on the face that I spent a lifetime studying. Pass over it. I went to reach in my pocket for a tissue. Instead I pulled out the crumpled letter to Avner Segal's seventh grade teacher. Without stopping to think I smoothed it out, folded it up, and slipped it in with her. I tucked it next to her elbow. I trust that she would have understood. They lowered her into the ground. Something gave way in my knees. Who had dug the grave? Suddenly I needed to know. He would have had to spend the night digging. As I approached the abysmal hole the absurd thought crossed my mind that I had to find him to tip him.

At some point in all of this, you arrived. I don't know when. I turned around and there you were in a dark raincoat. You've gotten old. But still slim, because you always had your mother's genes. There you stood in the cemetery, sole surviving carrier of those genes because Uri, as I don't need to tell you, Uri always took after me. There you stood, the big-shot judge from London, holding out your hand, waiting for your turn with the shovel. And do you know what I wanted to do, my boy? I wanted to slap you. Right then and there, I wanted to slap you across the face and tell you to go find your own shovel. But for the sake of your mother who never liked a scene, I handed it over. It took everything I had to restrain myself, but I handed it over to you and watched as you bent down, drove the spade into the pile of loose dirt, and, with the slightest tremor in your hands, approached the hole.

Afterwards everyone gathered at Uri's house. I thought that was the most I could bear—not my house, not seven days—and even that was too much. The children were closed up in the den watching television. I looked at the guests around me and suddenly I couldn't stand to be among them a moment longer. Couldn't stand either the shallowness of their mourning or the depth of it—which of them had any true idea of what had been lost? Couldn't stand the righteousness of their consolations, the idiotic justifications of the pious, nor the empathy of Eve's old friends or the daughters of those friends, the carefully placed hand on my shoulder, the pursed lips and furrowed brow their faces so naturally assumed after years of raising children, sending them to the army, and shepherding their husbands through the dark valley of middle age. Without another word, I put down the untouched plate someone had filled, a heaping plate that could not have held a morsel more and whose slightness, in the ratio of food to grief, disgusted me, and went to the bathroom. I locked the door and sat down on the toilet.

Soon I heard my name called. In time others joined in the search. I saw you walk across the garden, distorted through the glass, calling. You! Calling me! It almost made me laugh. Suddenly I saw you as you were at the age of ten on the trail in Ramon Crater, pacing wildly, out of breath, your little mouth agape, sweat trickling down your face, the ridiculous sun hat drooping around your head like a wilted flower. Calling and calling to me because you thought you were lost. Guess what, my boy. I was there the whole time! Crouched behind a rock, a few meters up the cliff. That's right, while you called, while you screamed out for me, believing yourself to be abandoned in the desert, I hid behind a rock patiently watching, like the ram that saved Isaac. I was Abraham *and* the ram. How many minutes passed while I let you shit in your pants, a ten-year-old boy facing his smallness and helplessness, the nightmare of his utter aloneness, I don't know. Only when at last I decided that you'd learned your lesson, that it had been made clear to you just how much you needed me, did I pop out from behind the rock and saunter down to the path. Relax, I said, what are you shrieking for, I was just taking a piss.

Yes, that's what I suddenly remembered while I watched you through the bathroom window thirty-seven years later. There is a fallacy that the powerful emotion of youth mellows with time. Not true. One learns to control and suppress it. But it doesn't lessen. It simply hides and concentrates itself in more discreet places. When one accidentally stumbles into one of these abysses, the pain is spectacular. I find these little abysses everywhere now.

You went on calling me for twenty minutes. The children were drawn into it, too, lured away from the television by a real-life mystery, perhaps if they were lucky even an emergency. I saw the smallest one through the window, trailing my sweater across the grass. Leaving my scent for the dogs, perhaps. They are all so educated, the grandnephews and grandnieces. Pooled together, their knowledge could run a small, terrifying country. They speak with confidence; they hold the keys to the castle. I was the afikomen they searched for. A few minutes into the game I heard the pack of them scratching at the door. We know you're in there, they called. Open up, one said in a little hoarse voice, and then the rest joined in, their little fists raining down. I tapped a giant bruise on my knee that I couldn't remember getting. I've reached the age where bruises are formed from failures within rather than accidents without. Uri arrived, calling off the beasts. Dad? he said through the door. What are you doing in there? Are you all right? Many ways to answer the question, but none sufficient. You have no toilet paper? one of the kids piped up. A pause, footsteps receding, then returning again. The sound of a struggle with the knob, and before I had time to prepare the door shuddered and sprang open. The crowd peered at me. Among the children, giggles and scattered applause. The smallest one, my little Cordelia, approached and touched my bruised knee. The others, rightly, backed away. In Uri's face I saw a look of fear I hadn't seen before. Relax, my son, I was just taking a piss.

* * *

No, I am not a man who harbors romantic ideas about the extension of the spirit. It's something I'd like to think I taught my sons, to partake of the physical world while it is yours to take, because that is one meaning of life with which no one can argue. To taste, to touch, to breathe in, to eat and stuff yourself—all the rest, all that takes place in the heart and mind lives in the shadow of uncertainty. But the lesson didn't come easily to you, and you never accepted it in the end. You shot yourself in the foot, and then you spent years trying to account for the pain. It was Uri who embraced my lessons about physical appetite. You can knock on Uri's door at almost any hour of the day or night and he'll answer with food in his mouth.

* * *

That night after the guests had gone, leaving behind the tubs of humus crusting over, the egg salad, the stinking whitefish, the pita growing stale before our eyes, I saw you and Uri huddled together in the kitchen. You'd left him alone to shoulder the burden of your aging parents—of chauffeuring us here and there, passing the time with us in waiting rooms, schlepping to our house to look into this problem, investigate that complaint, to find the pair of glasses no one could find, sort out this or that confusion with the life insurance forms, organize a roofer to come fix a leak, or, without a word to anyone, install a chairlift after he found out that I'd been sleeping on the downstairs sofa for a month because I could no longer climb the stairs. Imagine, Dovik, a *chairlift*, so that whenever I want I can fly up and down the stairs like an alpine skier. And if all that wasn't enough, calling us every morning to find out how the night was, and every night to find out how the day was? All that he did without complaint, without resentment, even though he had every right to be furious with you. I looked into the kitchen and there were the two of you, head to head, two grown men speaking in hushed tones just as you did as kids, intensely discussing whatever it was you two used to discuss, girls, probably, their shiny long hair and their asses and breasts. Only this time I knew you were talking about me. Trying to figure out what to do with me now, your old man, without having a clue, just as once you had no clue what to do with a pair of tits. If it had been Uri who had been doing the figuring, that would have been fine with me, I was used to it already, he had a way of doing it that didn't cost me my dignity. God forbid I ever lose the ability to hold my own dick while I piss, Uri will find a way to do it for me that will let me keep my dignity, with just the right joke and a funny story about something that happened to him the other day at the supermarket. That's Uri. But the fact that now suddenly you were involved, you who for so long lived over there in silence while your mother and I fumbled and grew old, who suddenly now decided to sweep in to bestow your magnanimity, to pretend that you were part of it all, with that disgusting look of concern on your face—that was more than I could bear. What the fuck is going on here? I said. And you turned to me, and in your eyes, behind all of that false magnanimity, I thought I saw a flare of the old anger, the one you kept boiling, that you stirred and stirred for me when you were seventeen, nineteen, twenty. And I was happy, my boy. I was happy to see it again, the way one is happy to see a long-lost relative.

Nothing, you said. You were always a bad liar. We're talking about what to do with all this food. I ignored you. I'm ready to go home, Uri, I said. Dad, he said, you sure you don't want to stay here? Ronit can make up the guest bed, the mattress is brand-new, very comfortable, I've been forced to try it a few times myself, and then he cracked one of his grins, because he is a man who can make jokes at his own expense. It costs him nothing. Just the opposite: the more he jokes about himself, the more he encourages people to laugh at him, the happier he is. Does that baffle you, Dov? That a man can accept, can even *invite*, the mocking laughter of others? You were always too afraid of being made a fool. If anyone dared to laugh at you, you turned sour and privately registered a strike against him in your little accounting book. That was you. And look at you now: a Circuit judge. One day, if all goes well, they will ask you to sit on the High Court of England. To sit in judgment on the serious crimes, most serious of all. But you started training long ago. To sit above the rest, to judge, to condemn—all of this came naturally to you.

Thanks all the same, I said, but I want to go home, and Uri shrugged, called to Ronit to pack up some food, and went to find the car keys. Gilad, who for the first time in ages I was seeing without an enormous pair of earphones stuck to his head, came into the room with a determined look on his face and made a beeline in my direction. I looked over my shoulder, thinking he was focused on something behind me, and when I turned back we collided. The boy, hardly a boy anymore, a fifteen-year-old man-child, was applying something to me, a kind of pumping or pressure that turned out to be a hug. An embrace, Dovik, my grandson who for years had not answered a single one of my questions with anything more than a monosyllable was now clinging to me, his eyes squeezed shut, his teeth bared. Apparently trying to hold back tears. I thumped him on the back, There, there, I said to him, Grandma loved you very much. Which was all it took for the boy to sputter, spraying me with spit, and break down into a blubbering mess. Because no one taught him anything, not even here in this country where death overlaps life, and now he is getting his first taste of it. And he isn't crying for her, not for his grandma, he's crying for himself: that he, too, is going to die one day. And before that his friends will die, and the friends of his friends, and, as time passes, the children of his friends, and, if his fate is truly bitter, his own children. So there he is crying. And while I am trying wordlessly to comfort him (I have a sense that even in this weakened, alert state, the man-child is deaf to all words except those that come to him through the enormous, furry portals of the earphones), Uri returns jingling the keys. And then out of nowhere you put your hand out to stop him. You, who, as far as I was concerned, knew nothing about anything. I'll take him, you said. Him? I almost shouted. *Him?* As if I were a child waiting to be taken to dance lessons. Uri glanced at me to gauge my reaction. Uri who keeps the clicker to my garage clipped to the sun visor of his car, right next to the clicker of his own garage, that's how often he uses it. And yet what could I say? There was Gilad still clinging to me. You put me in a position. How could I tell you what I really thought of your offer with that overgrown child gripping onto me for support and comfort as he absorbed the shock that all of this, all of us, everything he has ever known, is temporary?

And so five minutes later, against my wishes, I found myself in the rental car with you, Ronit's bag filled with little plastic tubs of food on my lap. The interior was black leather. What is this thing? I demanded. A BMW, you said. A German car? I said. You're driving me home in a German car?

You're such a big shot that you can't accept a Hyundai like everyone else? It's not good enough for you? You have to specially pay extra for a car made by the sons of Nazis? Of death camp guards? Haven't we had enough of black leather? Let me out of this thing, I said, I'd rather walk. Dad, you pleaded, and I heard something in your voice I didn't recognize. Something hiding there, in the upper registers. Please, you said. Don't make me beg. It's been a long day. And you weren't wrong, so I turned away from you to glare out the window.

* * *

When you were a boy, I used to take you with me to the shuk on Friday mornings. You remember, Dova'leh? I knew all the merchants and they knew me. They always had something for me to taste. Get some dates, I would tell you while I locked horns with Zegury, the fruit man, over politics. Five minutes later I would look over and you were plucking them between two fingers, one by one, studying each with exotic remove. I would grab the bag containing the little pathetic collection. Like that we'll starve, I'd say. I'd pick up two, three heaping handfuls and drop them in. I never saw you eat a single one. You claimed they looked like cockroaches. There was an old Arab at the shuk who used to cut people's profiles out of black paper. The person would take his place on a crate and the Arab would look at him and snip away. You used to wince as you watched, afraid the Arab would cut himself, which he never did. He would snip maniacally, then hand over the paper essence of his subject's face. To you he was a genius on the level of Picasso. You were mute in his presence. When no one came to sit, the Arab sharpened the scissors on a stone and hummed a long, convoluted passage. One day I had you and Uri with me and when we reached the Arab, feeling proud or magnanimous, I said, Who wants a portrait, boys? Uri leaped up onto the crate. He summoned all his youthful gravitas and struck a pose. The Arab regarded him through lowered lids, snipped, and out came the proud outline of my Uri. All the glory of a potent life could be read in the aquiline nose. He hopped off the seat and took his likeness, utterly delighted. What did he know of disappointment and death? Nothing, as the Arab's portrait made clear. Nervously, you took your place on the crate where so many had been sized up and reduced to a single unbroken line by the tremendous artist. The Arab began to snip. You sat very still. Then I saw your eyes flutter and drop to the floor where the accumulated clippings had fallen, the scraps of black paper. You looked up again into the Arab's eyes, opened your mouth, and screamed. You screamed and sobbed and wouldn't stop for anything. You're acting crazy, I told you, shaking you by the shoulders, but you carried on. You cried all the way home, lagging three feet behind us. Uri clutched his profile, worriedly glancing back at you. Later your mother put it into a frame for him. I don't know what became of yours. Maybe the Arab threw it away. Or kept it in case I came back to claim it, since I'd already paid. But I never went back. After that, you stopped coming with me to the shuk. You see, my boy? You see what I was up against?

*   *   *

You drove me back to our house, your mother's and mine, only now it was no longer hers. She was spending her first night underground. Even now I can't think it. Mrs. Kleindorf, it makes me gag, to think of my wife's lifeless body packed under two meters of earth. But I don't shy away from it. I don't comfort myself by imagining that she is sprinkled around me in the atmosphere, or has come back in the form of the crow who arrived in the garden days after her death and stays on, strangely, without its mate. I don't cheapen her death with little fabrications. The gravel crunched under the wheels of your German car, we glided to a stop, and you cut the motor. The sky above the hills was deep indigo with the last glow of the day, but the house was already closed up in darkness. And listening to the little, dying pings of the engine in the fresh silence, I suddenly remembered the day we moved here from the house in Beit Hakerem. Do you remember? All morning you had been locked up in your room, transferring the fish from your aquarium into plastic bags filled with water—worrying over them, opening and closing the bags. While the rest of us hurried around taping up boxes and moving furniture, you measured out your fish and readied your beloved turtle for the journey. The care you lavished on that reptile! You used to let him stretch his legs in the garden; every day you gave him his moment in the sun. You stared into his little beady eyes for the secret of his soul. When your mother bought the wrong kind of cabbage you got so angry that you cried—*screamed and cried* because she had been so insensitive as to buy red instead of green. And I screamed back that you were an ungrateful wretch. In my fury, I grabbed your little friend and dangled him above the whirring blade of the blender. Desperately, it tried to wrestle the leg back into the safety of its shell, but I pinched it between my fingers and revved the motor. You screamed a bloodcurdling scream. What a scream! As if it were you yourself I was prepared to sacrifice to the blade. A pleasant tingling spread through the ends of my nerves. Afterwards, once you had fled to your room cradling the pathetic creature in your arms, your mother's face turned to stone. We fought, as we always did when it came to you, and I told her she was crazy if she thought I was going to indulge such behavior. And she, who since you were a toddler had inhaled every last book of child psychology, had eaten whole every theory, tried to convince me that to you that turtle was a symbol of yourself, and for us to act cavalier about its needs and desires was, to you, the same as disregarding your own. A symbol of yourself, for God's sake! Following the orders of those ridiculous books, she found a way to contort herself to fit into your little skull, so that she could not only understand but *empathize* with you in your belief that the purchase of red cabbage over green constituted an emotional assault. I let her finish. I let her wear herself out, tangling herself up in theories. Then I told her she had lost her mind. That if you saw yourself as a smelly, disgusting, brainless reptile then it was time to start treating you like one. She stormed out of the house. But half an hour later she was back again, clutching a sad little head of green cabbage, and pleading with you, whispering and begging through the crack of your door, to be let in. A few months after that we bought the house in Beit Zayit and you were up all night scheming about how best to transport the turtle. All morning you spent divvying up the fish in bags and counseling the turtle psychologically. You held the tank on your lap as we drove to the new house, and with every turn I took the turtle skid and bumped into the corners. Your eyes welled up with tears, believing I was being cruel, but you overestimated me: even I wasn't capable of such deliberate torment. In the end, it wasn't at my hands that your precious pet met its tragic end. One day you left it out in the sun, and when you came back it was lying on its back, its shell cracked open, dying from an assault by a real beast.

* * *

It was soon after we moved that you started your nighttime ramblings. You thought no one knew, but I knew. You trusted me with nothing, but I kept your little secret. In those days it often happened that I woke up ravenous in the middle of the night. I would go down to the kitchen and stand in front of the fridge and tear meat from the roasted chicken, too hungry to take a plate or sit or even turn on the light. One night, I was standing there eating in the dark and I saw a figure crossing the front garden, a kind of stick figure who had been lent some kinetic energy moving across the grass. It stopped for a minute as if it had seen or heard something that pricked its interest. There was a little moonlight, and from what I could see the stick figure looked like neither a man nor a woman, and not a child either. An animal, maybe. A wolf, or a wild dog. Only when the figure began to move again around the side of the house, and a moment later I heard the door open softly, then the quick, solid movements of one who knew exactly where he was—only then did I realize it was you.

I remained still in the kitchen until I heard you disappear upstairs to your bedroom. I went to study your muddy sneakers lying exhausted on their sides by the door in order to guess what your stealth little outing had been about, what trouble you had gotten up to, and with whom—though if it involved anyone it could only have been Shlomo. Whatever happened to him? Shlomo, whom you were attached to like a Siamese twin, with whom you communicated under the radar of others in a private, ingrown language of grimaces, eye-rolls, and tics. Yes, I was almost certain your midnight outing involved some half-baked scheme you two had wordlessly cooked up with a few twitterings of the facial muscles you'd somehow managed to send and receive in class while with pained expressions the Mrs. Kleindorfs hammered into your heads the two thousand years, always the two thousand years, and sent you to sit at opposite corners of the room. I intended to confront you about it the next morning, but when you appeared at breakfast nothing on your face gave away even the slightest hint of your adventure, and I began to wonder whether it was possible you had been sleepwalking. But four or five nights later I was up at 2 a.m. devouring the last of the schnitzel when I saw you come up the front path again. The moon was bright and I caught a glimpse of your face bathed in the most peaceful expression.

* * *

Now you walked me up the same front path and waited as I fumbled with the keys, and for once I was glad I had forgotten to leave on a light so that you couldn't see that suddenly my hands were shaking. At last I got the lock open and turned on the lights. I'm fine, I said. You can go now. And only then did I look down and see that you were holding a small suitcase in your hand. I looked at the suitcase and then I looked back at you. At your face, which I hadn't looked at, truly looked at, for a long time. You've gotten old, it's true, but there was something else there, something in your eyes or the tilt of your mouth, a kind of pain—but not just pain, more than that, a look as if you had been beaten down by the world, like you had finally been defeated. And something happened in me. A kind of ravaged feeling entered. As if now that your mother was gone, now that she was no longer there to absorb your pain, to tend to it, to feel it as her own, it had been left to me. Try to understand. All your life your pain infuriated me. Your stubbornness, your determination, your inwardness, but most of all your pain that always made her come running to your rescue. And at that moment, looking at you in the light of the hall, I saw something in your eyes. She was gone, she had finally abandoned us, left us alone with each other, and I saw something in your face and I was overwhelmed.

I looked from your suitcase to your face and back to your suitcase. And I waited for you to explain.

*　　*　　*

When you were a boy your mother told me she would kill to save you. You would kill another so that he could live, I repeated. Yes, she said. And would you let five die so that he could live, too? I asked. Yes, she said. A hundred? I asked. She didn't answer, but her eyes turned cold and hard. A thousand? She walked away.

*　　*　　*

No, it isn't my fault that you didn't become the writer you wanted to be. You wanted to write about a shark that takes the brunt of human emotions. Suffering, I said to you. What? you said, a quiver in your lips. Listen to me, Dov, you have to take control of it. You have to grab it by the horns and wrestle it down. You have to suffocate it or it will suffocate you. You looked at me as if I had never understood anything in my life. But it was you who didn't understand. You stood in your army uniform, your kit bag slung over your shoulder. In a uniform a man can go about detached from himself, can lose himself in the flank of a great beast of which he has never seen the head. But not you, my boy. In plainclothes you suffered, and in a uniform it was no different. You'd come home on leave for the first time in three months. Do you remember this? You were still in love with Dafna. It was her you'd come home for. Maybe in the beginning she had been drawn to your suffering, but even I could see it was already beginning to bore her. She came over and the two of you closed yourselves in your room, but not as you used to close yourselves in, epically, against the world; now she came out after only an hour wearing your army-issued T-shirt to explore the refrigerator or turn on the radio. Make yourself at home, I said as she picked through the bowls of chicken salad and cold pasta. I sat across from her and watched her eat. Such a small girl and such a large appetite. She was sure of her beauty; it was evident in her smallest gestures. She flung her arms and legs around with unstudied carelessness, but they always landed with grace. There was an inner logic that organized her thoroughly. Tell me something, I said. She looked at me, still chewing. A musky odor clung to her. What? she said. I sat there, hair growing out of my ears. Never mind, I said, and let the giant shark swim off away from me. She finished eating in silence and got up to clean her plate. At the door she paused. The answer to your question is no, she said. What question? I said. The one you didn't ask, she said. Oh? Which one is that? About Dov, she said. I waited for her to go on, but she didn't. There was much in that instant I failed to grasp. I heard the front door close behind her.

All throughout your service, before what happened to you, you used to send packages home addressed to yourself. Your mother passed on your instructions that these packages were not to be touched except to be placed in a drawer of your desk. You lavished no end of tape on them, so that you would know if anyone tampered with them. Well, guess what? I did. I opened them up and read the contents, and then I closed them back up exactly as you had, with more tape, and if you ever asked I would have told you it was the army censors who were to blame. But you never asked. As far as I could tell, you never again looked at what you had written. Sometimes I even convinced myself that you knew I broke open the packages and read what you wrote; that you meant for me to read it. And so, at my leisure, when your mother was out and the house was empty, I steamed open the envelopes and read about the shark, and the interconnected nightmares of many. About the janitor who cleaned the tank every night, wiping the glass and checking the tubes and the pump that sent fresh water in—who would pause in his work to check on the feverish, shivering bodies asleep in their beds, who would lean on his mop and stare into the eyes of the tormented white beast covered in electrodes, attached to tubes, who every day grew sicker and sicker from absorbing the pain of so many.

The girl, Dafna, left you of course. Not immediately, but in time. You discovered that she had been with another man. Could you blame her? Maybe this other man took her out dancing. Cheek to cheek, groin to groin, in one of those noisy discos with a tribal drumbeat, and she was intoxicated by her nearness to a man whose body was not a distant country to himself, a distant and at times enemy country. No, the story isn't difficult to imagine. Already at twelve or thirteen you began growing inward. Your chest collapsed, your shoulders rounded, your arms and legs became caught out in awkward positions, as if they had become disassociated from the whole. You closed yourself in the bathroom for hours on end. God knows what you did in there. Tried to make sense of things. When Uri used the bathroom he would burst out, the water still gurgling down the toilet, rosy cheeked and even singing. He could have done it in front of a live audience. But when you at last emerged you looked pale, sweaty, troubled. What were you doing all that time, my boy? Waiting to let the smell pass?

She left you, and you threatened to kill yourself, came home on leave, and sat in the garden like a vegetable, your shoulders draped with a blanket. No one came to see you, not even Shlomo, because a few months earlier, because of God knows what injury that you judged unforgivable, you cut him off, your best friend of ten years, as close to you, closer, than your own limbs. What is it like, I once demanded of you, to be a man of such high principles that no one else can live up to them? But you only turned your back on me, just as you turned your back on everyone who betrayed you with their shortcomings. So you sat hunched in the garden like an old man, starving yourself because the world had disappointed you again. When I tried to approach, you stiffened and became mute. Perhaps you sensed my disgust. I left you to your mother. The two of you whispered together, and fell silent whenever I entered the room.

There was another girl after that. The one you met in the army, when you were stationed together at Nachal Tzofar. You stopped coming home on the weekends; you wanted to stay close to her. Later she was sent to the north, wasn't she? But you found ways of seeing each other. When she finished her tour of duty she enrolled in Hebrew University. Your mother told me that you planned to follow. The army wanted you to become an officer, but you declined. You had better things to do. You intended to study philosophy. What is the application? I asked you. You stared at me darkly. I'm not a fool; I recognize the value of expanding the human picture. But for you, my child, I wished a life of solid things. To move in the opposite direction, toward greater and greater abstraction, seemed to me a disaster for you. There are those who have the necessary constitution, but not you. From a young age, you tirelessly searched for and collected suffering. Of course it isn't that simple. One doesn't choose between the outer and the inner life; they coexist, however poorly. The question is: Where does one place the emphasis? And here, however coarsely, I tried to guide you. Sitting in the garden wrapped in a shawl, recovering from your forays into the world, you read books on the alienation of modern man. What does modern man have on the Jews? I demanded, passing you with the garden hose. The Jews have been living in alienation for thousands of years. For modern man it's a hobby. What can you learn from those books that you weren't born knowing already? And then, watering the vegetables, I let a little spray drift in your direction, soaking your book. But it wasn't me who stood in your way. I couldn't have even if I wanted to.

* * *

We stood in the hall of the house that had once been all of our house, a house that had been filled with life, every last room of it brimming with laughter, arguments, tears, dust, the smell of food, pain, desire, anger, and silence, too, the tightly coiled silence of people pressed up against each other in what is called a family. And then Uri enlisted, and, three years later, you, and after what happened you left Israel, and then it was only your mother's and my home, and we could only occupy one, at most two rooms at a time, leaving the rest empty. And now it was mine alone. Only there you were like an awkward visitor, a weary guest, clutching your suitcase. I looked at it, and then I looked at you. You shifted it from one hand to the other. I thought—you began to say, but then stopped, following some invisible thing across the room. I waited.

I thought maybe, you began again, if you didn't mind, I would stay here a little while.

I must have looked shocked because you swallowed and looked away. And I was, Dov. I was shocked. And I wanted to say, Yes. Of course. Stay with me here. I'll make up your old bed. But I didn't say that. What I said was, For your sake or mine? A faint but unmistakable grimace seized your face before it dissolved, leaving your features flat and lifeless again. And for a moment I thought I had lost you, that you would turn away from me again, as you have always turned away. But you didn't. You continued to stand there, looking past me at the living room, as if you were seeing something there, a memory, maybe, the ghost of the child you once were.

Mine, you said simply.

I scanned your face, trying to understand.

What about work? Don't you have to get back? I asked, because that was your excuse all these years when you hardly ever came, always work that you couldn't leave, that kept you away.

You winced. The lines between your eyes deepened, and with one hand you reached up and touched your temple, just above the little blue vein that used to stand out and pulse when you were angry as a child.

I resigned, you said.

I thought I'd misheard. You for whom there was nothing but your work. So I asked you again: Surely they need you back again? But I saw that you weren't really with me, standing there in the hall. You were with whatever memory it was that you saw behind me, crossing the living room floor.

* * *

A strange boy, who grew inward from the beginning. When we asked you a question, we would sometimes have to wait half a day for an answer. God forbid you should respond without thinking, without making absolutely sure of the truth. By the time the answer came no one remembered what you were talking about. When you were four you began to have fits. You would throw yourself on the floor, pound your fists and bang your head, and hurl everything around your room. Often it was when you didn't get your way, but other times something tiny and completely unexpected would set you off, a magic marker no one could find the cap for, the halves of your sandwich cut straight across instead of on a diagonal. Your kindergarten teacher called to express her concern. You stubbornly refused to participate in class activities. You sat to the side, holding yourself away from the others as if they were lepers, and pretended not to understand what they said when they spoke to you. You never laughed, she said, and when you cried it wasn't a short jag and a little whimpering like the other kids, a crying that could be appealed to, soothed away. You were inconsolable. With you, it was something existential. That was her word. Your mother had to pick you up early, had to come rescue you and bring you home so often that soon she began to hide it from me, so that I wouldn't become angry. An appointment was scheduled with the school psychologist. He invited himself to our home. He was a balding, pigeon-toed man who used a handkerchief to mop up his profuse sweat. I had to specially schedule a time when I could leave the office. Your mother served him coffee and cookies, gave you a glass of milk, and then we left you alone in the living room. For an hour the psychologist, Mr. Shatzner, pulled things out of his bag, and got you to make up stories about the little toys and action figures. We could see you through the French doors if we tiptoed past in the hallway. Afterwards, you were excused and went off to play in the garden while he interviewed us about our "home life." Before leaving, he took a tour of the house. He seemed surprised to find the place so sunny and warm, full of plants, wooden toys, and plenty of your crayon drawings taped to the walls. Looks can be deceiving, I saw him thinking, working hard to scratch the surface to uncover the neglect and brutality beneath. His gaze rested on the woolen blanket on your bed. Your mother looked concerned, and I saw her biting her lip and kicking herself that, what? It wasn't soft enough? She should have bought one with cars and trucks on it like Yoni had next door? It took all the control I had not to take him by the ear and throw him out on the street. You were playing outside. I could see your red shirt flashing behind the quince bush, where you'd found an ant colony two days before. May I ask, Shatzner said, if there are any problems I should know about at home? In the marriage, perhaps? It was all I could take. I grabbed the wooden Pinocchio marionette down off the shelf and shouted for you. You came inside, lumbering up the steps with dirt on your knees, and stood watching while I made the Pinocchio dance and sing then trip and fall on his face. Every time I made him collapse, you howled with laughter. Enough, your mother said, putting her hand on my arm, I'm sure Mr. Shatzner realizes our little Dovi isn't always so serious. But I kept going, making you laugh so hard that you wet your pants, and then I crushed the balding psychologist's hand in mine, told him he was welcome to snoop around for as long as he liked, but that I had more important things to do. I left the house, slamming the door behind me.

Your mother couldn't drop the matter so easily. Even a whiff of the suggestion that she was somehow doing something wrong as a mother wracked her with guilt. She beat herself up over it and tried to figure out where she had gone wrong. She put herself under the psychologist's tutelage, and listened once a week while he explained to her what he'd gleaned from his sessions with you that continued at the school, and instructed her on how to assuage some of your "difficulties." He developed a strategy, and laid down a set of rules that your mother clung to about how we should and shouldn't behave with you. He even gave her his number at home, and when she was unsure of how to apply one of his rules, or what the proper reaction was to some fit of yours, she would dial him up, no matter the hour of the morning or night, and explain the problem in a low, serious tone, then listen to his response in silence, nodding grievously. Mr. Shatzner said we shouldn't do that, she would say to me as soon as you left the room, Mr. Shatzner said we should let him do this, Mr. Shatzner said we should stand on our heads, bite our tongues, turn in circles, Mr. Shatzner, Mr. Shatzner, Mr. Shatzner, until finally I blew up at her and said I never wanted to hear that name in our house again, that I knew how to raise my own child, what did he think it was, a game of Scrabble or Monopoly, there are no rules, was she so blind that she couldn't see that all that mental midget had done was turn her into a nervous wreck, full of doubt about something that had come naturally to her from the beginning, something any idiot could see, which was that she was a wonderful mother, full of love and patience? He's five years old, for God's sake, I shouted, if you treat him like a special case then that's what he'll always be. Have you seen any improvement at all since you started with this clown? No. Who is he to suddenly be offering himself as a source of wisdom on human behavior? You think that little prick knows better than us, than you and me? A silence passed between us. But he is a special case, she said quietly. He has always been.

Eventually she caved in. The sessions were stopped, and you wriggled out from under Shatzner's watch like a little animal set free who goes immediately to hide in the underbrush. But the whole experience set a certain tone. Your mother continued to hover and worry, to rigorously put every one of your moods, episodes, and tantrums through a little gauntlet of analysis, searching for a clue to your hurt and our role in it. This self-lacerating attitude drove me crazy, almost as much as your crying and carrying on. One night, in the middle of you throwing a fit about the bathwater not reaching exactly the level you liked, I grabbed you from under your arms and held you naked and dripping above the floor. When I was your age, I shouted, shaking you so hard your head wobbled sickeningly on your neck, there was nothing to eat, and no money for toys, the house was always cold, but we went outside and played and made games out of nothing and lived because we had our lives, while the others were being murdered in the pogroms we could go out and feel the sun and run around and kick a ball! And look at you! You have everything in the world, and all you do is shriek your head off and make everyone's life miserable! Enough already! Do you hear me? I've had enough! You looked at me, your eyes enormous, and reflected in your pupils, small and far away, I saw the image of myself.

Seventy years ago I was a child, too. Seventy years? *Seventy?* How? Pass over it.

* * *

Now you stood holding your suitcase. There was nothing to say. You seemed no longer to need my help. Once you had perhaps, but no longer. I have a terrible headache, you said at last. The light is hurting my eyes. If you don't mind, I think I'll go lie down. We can talk later.

And just like that you walked back into the house that you had left so long ago. I heard your footsteps slowly ascend the stairs.

Were they the lepers, Dov, those other kids? Is that why you held yourself apart? Or was it you? And the two of us, closed up together in this house—are we the saved or the condemned?

A long silence while you must have stood at the threshold of your old room. Then the creak of the door, and the sound of it closing again after twenty-five years.

SWIMMING HOLES

That evening we were reading together, as we always did. It was one of those winter nights in England when the darkness that falls at three makes nine feel like midnight, reminding one of how far north one has staked one's life. The doorbell rang. We looked up at each other. It was rare for anyone to visit us unannounced. Lotte put her book down in her lap. I went to the door. A young man was standing there holding a briefcase. It's possible that the moment before I opened the door he had extinguished his cigarette, because I thought I saw a trail of smoke slip out of the corner of his mouth. Then again, it could have been just his breath in the cold. For a minute I thought it was one of my students—they all shared a certain knowing look, as if they were trying to smuggle something in or out of an unnamed country. There was a car waiting by the curb, the motor still running, and he glanced back at it. Someone—man or woman, I couldn't say—was hunched over the steering wheel.

Is Lotte Berg home? he asked. He had a strong accent, but I couldn't place it immediately. May I ask who would like to see her? The young man thought, just for a moment really, but long enough for me to notice a slight twitch at the corners of his mouth. My name is Daniel, he said. I assumed it was one of her readers. She wasn't widely known; to say she was known at all in those days would be generous. Of course it always made her happy to receive a letter from someone who admired her work, but a letter was one thing, and a stranger at the door at that hour was another. It's a bit late—perhaps if you called or wrote first, I said, immediately regretting the lack of kindness I thought this Daniel must have heard in my words. But then he shifted something he'd been holding inside his cheek from one side to the other and swallowed. I noticed then that he had quite a large Adam's apple in his throat. It crossed my mind that he wasn't one of Lotte's readers at all. I glanced down at the darkness gathered in the folds of the leather jacket where it fell around his hips. I don't know what I thought I might see concealed. But of course there was nothing. He continued standing there as if he hadn't heard me. It's late, I said, and Ms. Berg—I don't know why I called her that, it was absolutely ridiculous, as if I were the butler, but that's what happened to come out of my mouth—Ms. Berg isn't expecting anyone. Now his face crumpled, but just for a fraction of a second, really, resuming its former appearance so quickly that someone else might have missed it altogether. But I caught it, and as it crumpled I saw through to another face, the face one wears alone, or not even alone, the face one wears asleep or unconscious on the gurney, and in it I recognized something. This is going to sound foolish, but though I lived with Lotte and, as far as I knew, this Daniel had never met her at all, in that instant I felt that he and I were aligned in some way, aligned in our position toward her, and that it was only a matter of degrees that separated us. It was absurd, of course. After all, I was the one keeping him from whatever it was he wanted from her. It was a mere projection of myself onto this young man clutching his briefcase in front of the skeleton of my hydrangeas. But how else are we to make decisions about others? On top of which it was freezing out.

I let him in. In our hallway, standing in his boots under our little collection of straw hats, all the shadows fell away and I saw him clearly. Arthur? Lotte called from the living room. Daniel and I locked eyes. I posed a question, and he answered. Nothing was said. But at that moment we agreed on something: Whatever happened, he would not disturb us. He would do nothing to threaten or dismantle what we had taken such pains to build. Yes, darling, I called back. Who's there? she asked. I studied Daniel's face once more for even a glimmer of dissent. But there was none. There was only seriousness, or an understanding of the seriousness of the agreement, and something else as well, something I took for gratitude. Just then I heard Lotte's footsteps behind me. It's for you, I said.

Our lives ran like clockwork, you see. Every morning we walked on the Heath. We took the same path in and the same path out. I accompanied Lotte to the swimming hole, as we called it, where she never missed a day. There are three ponds, one for men, one for women, and one mixed, and it was there, in the last, that she swam when I was with her so that I could sit on the bench nearby. In the winter, the men came to smash a hole in the ice. They must have worked in the dark because by the time we arrived the ice was already broken. Lotte would peel off her clothes; first her coat and then her pullover, her boots and trousers, the heavy wool ones she favored, and then her body would at last appear, pale and shot through with blue veins. I knew every inch of her body, but the sight of it in the morning against the wet, black trees almost always aroused me. She'd approach the water's edge. For a moment she would stand completely still. God knows what she thought about. Up until the last she was a mystery to me. At times the snow would fall around her. The snow or the leaves, though most often it was rain. Sometimes I wanted to cry out, to disturb the stillness that in that moment seemed to be hers alone. And then, in a flash, she'd disappear into the blackness. There would be a small splash, or the sound of splash, followed by silence. How terrible those seconds were, and how they seemed to last forever! As if she would never come up again. How deep does it go? I once asked her, but she claimed not to know. On many occasions I would even leap up off the bench, ready to dive in after her, despite my fear of the water. But just then her head would break the surface like the smooth head of a seal or an otter, and she would swim to the ladder where I would be waiting to fling the towel over her.

Every Tuesday morning I took the eight-thirty train to Oxford, and returned to London on Thursday evening at nine. When we went out with colleagues of mine, Lotte would explain again why she couldn't live in Oxford. The persistence of all those bells disturbed her work, she said. On top of that, one is always being tripped over, shoved, or bumped into by some student scurrying through the streets, or someone riding a bike while engaged in the life of the mind. At least once at every such dinner I would overhear Lotte tell the story of how she saw a woman knocked over by a bus on St.

Giles'. One second she was crossing the street, she'd say, her voice rising, and the next she's slumped against the wheels of a bus. It's a crime, Lotte would go on, how they turn those children loose in the world with their heads full of Plato and Wittgenstein, but impart to them no sense of how to safely negotiate the dangers of daily life. It was a strange argument to make for someone who spent most of her days closeted in her study inventing stories and searching for ways to make them plausible. But, out of politeness, no one ever pointed that out.

The truth was more complicated, of course. Lotte liked her life in London—liked the anonymity that was hers as soon as she got off the Underground at Covent Garden or King's Cross, and which would have been impossible in Oxford. She liked the swimming hole and our house in Highgate. And I think she liked being alone while I was off teaching the long-haired youth gathered from Winchester and the polished halls of Eton. On Thursday evenings she would be waiting for me with the car at Paddington, the windows fogged and the motor idling. In those first minutes of the drive home through the dark streets, while she still held in my eyes the clarity of someone separate unto herself, I sometimes noticed in her a renewed patience—for our life together, perhaps, or for something else.

Yes, Lotte was a mystery to me, but I took comfort in those little islands I discovered in her, islands that I could always find, no matter how poor the conditions, and use to orient myself. At the center of her was her abysmal loss. She'd been forced to leave her home in Nuremberg when she was seventeen. For a year she'd lived with her parents in a transit camp in Zbaszyn, Poland, in what I can only imagine were atrocious conditions; she never spoke about that time, just as she rarely spoke of her childhood or her parents. In the summer of 1939, with the help of a young Jewish doctor also in the camp, she received a visa to chaperone eighty-six children on a Kindertransport to England. That detail, eighty-six, always struck me, both because the story as she told it had so few details, and also because it seemed such an enormous number. How did she care for so many children, knowing that everything she had ever known, that they'd all ever known, had just been lost forever? The boat left from Gdynia on the Baltic Sea. The voyage which was supposed to take three days took five instead, because in the course of the journey Stalin signed the pact with Hitler, and the boat had to be diverted to avoid Germany. They arrived in Harwich three days before war broke out. The children were scattered to foster homes throughout the country. Lotte waited until every last one of them had departed on a train. And then they were gone, carried away from her, and Lotte disappeared into her life.

No, I couldn't possibly know what it was she carried in the depths of her. But slowly I discovered certain footholds. When she shouted out in her sleep, it was almost always her father she had been dreaming of. When she was hurt by something I'd said or done, or more often failed to do or say, she became suddenly friendly, although it was a sort of lacquered friendliness, the friendliness of two people who happen to find themselves sitting together on a bus ride, a long one for which only one of them has remembered to bring food. Some days later something little would happen—I would forget to return the tea canister to the shelf, or leave my socks on the floor—and she would explode. The force and volume of her anger were shocking, and the only possible response was to make myself very still, and stick to a course of silence until the brunt of it had passed and she'd begun to retreat inward. At that moment there was a break or opening. A moment earlier and the gesture meant to calm and make amends would only stoke her fury. A moment later, and she would already have crawled into herself and shut the door, taking up residence in that obscure chamber where she could survive for days or even weeks without so much as a word for me. It took me many years to put my finger on that moment, to learn to see it coming and seize it when it arrived, to save us both from that punishing silence.

She struggled with her sadness, but tried to conceal it, to divide it into smaller and smaller parts and scatter these in places she thought no one would find them. But often I did—with time I learned where to look—and tried to fit them together. It pained me that she felt she couldn't come to me with it, but I knew it would hurt her more to know that I'd uncovered what she hadn't intended for me to find. In some fundamental way I think she objected to being known. Or resented it even as she longed for it. It offended her sense of freedom. But it isn't possible to simply look upon a person one loves in tranquility, content to regard her in bafflement. Unless one is happy to worship, and I never was. At the heart of any scholar's work is the search for patterns. You may think it sounds cold to suggest that I took a scholarly attitude toward my wife, but then I think you would be misunderstanding what drives a true scholar. The more I've learned in my life, the more acutely I've felt my hunger and blindness, and at the same time the closer I've felt to the end of hunger, the end of blindness. At times I've felt myself to be clinging onto the rim—of what I can hardly say without the risk of sounding ridiculous—only to slip and find myself deeper in the hole than ever. And there, in the dark, I find again in myself a form of praise for all that continues to crush my certainty.

*   *   *

It's for you, I said to Lotte, but I didn't turn around. I kept my eyes fixed on Daniel, and so I missed the expression on her face when she saw him that first time. Later on I came to wonder whether it had given anything away. Daniel stepped forward toward her. For a moment he seemed at a loss for words. I saw something in his face that I hadn't seen before. Then he introduced himself as one of her readers, as I'd expected. Lotte invited him inside, or further inside. He let me take his jacket, but held tightly to the briefcase—I assumed it held a manuscript inside that he wanted to show to Lotte. The jacket smelled, sickeningly, of cologne, though as far as I could tell, relieved of the coat Daniel himself smelled of nothing. Lotte led him to the kitchen, and as he followed her he looked around at everything, the pictures on our walls, the envelopes on the table waiting to be mailed, and when his eyes met his own reflection in the mirror I thought I saw the hint of a smile. Lotte gestured at the kitchen table, and he sat, placing the briefcase delicately between his feet, as if a small, live animal were contained inside of it. From the way he watched Lotte fill the battered kettle with water and put it on the stove I could tell that he hadn't expected to get so far. Perhaps he'd hoped to come away with an autographed book at best. And now he was inside the house of the great writer! About to drink tea from her cups! I remember thinking that perhaps this was just the encouragement Lotte needed: She said little about her work while in the throes of it, but I could tell from her mood exactly how things were going, and for some weeks she'd seemed listless and depressed. I excused myself politely, saying I had work to do, and went upstairs. When I glanced back over my shoulder, I felt a pang of regret for the child we'd never had who might have been almost Daniel's age by now, who might have come in from the cold, like him, full of things to tell us.

I hadn't thought about it until just now, but the night Daniel rang our bell in the winter of 1970 was the end of November, the same time of year she died twenty-seven years later. I don't know what that's supposed to tell you; nothing, except that we take comfort in the symmetries we find in life because they suggest a design where there is none. The evening she lost consciousness for the last time seems further away to me now than the June afternoon in 1949 when I saw her for the first time. It was at a garden party to celebrate the engagement of Max Klein, a close friend from my student days. Nothing could have been more lovely and genteel than the crystal bowl of punch and vases of freshly cut irises. But almost immediately on walking in I sensed something strange about the room, something interrupting an otherwise uniform light or mood. I found the source without trouble. It was a small woman, like a sparrow, with short black hair cut straight across her face, standing by the doors to the garden. She was at odds with everything around her. To begin with, it was summer and she was wearing a purple velvet dress, almost a smock. Her hairstyle was completely unlike any other woman's there, something like a flapper's, though seemingly cut for comfort over style. She wore a very large silver ring that seemed to weigh too much for her bony fingers (much later, when she took it off and put it on my bedside table, I noticed that it left a green mark of corrosion on her skin). But it was really her face, or the expression on her face, that struck me as most unusual. It reminded me of Prufrock—*There will be time, / To prepare a face to meet the faces that you meet*—because she alone in that room seemed not to have had time, or not to have thought to take the time. It wasn't that her face was open or revealing in any way. It's just that it appeared to be at rest, completely unaware of itself as the eyes took in all that happened before them. What I first took to be an uneasiness emanating from her now seemed, as I watched from across the room, to be just the opposite: the uneasiness of others, brought to light when standing in opposition to her. I asked Max who she was, and he told me she was somehow related, a distant cousin of his fiancée. She remained rooted to the same spot the entire party, holding an empty glass.

At some point I wandered over and offered to refill it.

At that time she was living in a rented room not far from Russell Square. The other side of the street had been bombed, and from her window you could see the piles of rubble where the children sometimes came to play King of the Castle (long after it became dark, you could still hear their voices), and here and there was the shell of a house whose empty windows framed the sky. In one, only the staircase with carved banisters remained rising out of the rubble, and in another you could still make out the floral wallpaper that the sun and rain were slowly erasing. Though it was melancholy it was also exhilarating in a strange way, to see the inside turned out like that. Many times I saw Lotte staring at those ruins with their solitary chimneys. The first time I visited her room I was amazed at how little was in it. She'd been in England for almost ten years by then, but, aside from her desk, there were only a few sticks of plain furniture, and much later I came to understand that in a certain way the walls and ceiling of her own room were as nonexistent to her as those across the street.

Her desk, however, was something else entirely. In that simple, small room it overshadowed everything else like some sort of grotesque, threatening monster, clinging to most of one wall and bullying the other pathetic bits of furniture to the far corner, where they seemed to cling together, as if under some sinister magnetic force. It was made of dark wood and above the writing surface was a wall of drawers, drawers of totally impractical sizes, like the desk of a medieval sorcerer. Except that every last drawer was empty, something I discovered one evening while waiting for Lotte, who had gone down the hall to use the lavatory, and which somehow made the desk, the specter of that enormous desk, really more like a ship than a desk, a ship riding a pitch-black sea in the dead of a moonless night with no hope of land in any direction, seem even more unnerving. It was, I always thought, a very masculine desk. At times, or from time to time when I came to pick her up, I even felt a kind of strange, inexplicable jealousy overtake me when she opened the door and there, hovering behind her, threatening to swallow her up, was that tremendous body of furniture.

One day I got up the courage to ask her where she had found it. She was as poor as a church mouse; it was impossible to imagine that she had ever been able to save enough money to buy such a desk. But rather than allaying my fears, her answer plunged me into despair: It was a gift, she said. And when, trying my best to act casually but already feeling my lips begin to twitch as they do whenever my emotions get the better of me, I asked her from whom, she gave me a look, a look I will never forget as it was my first introduction to the complex laws that governed life with Lotte, though it would be years before I came to understand those laws, if I ever really understood them at all, a look equivalent to the raising of a wall. Needless to say, nothing more was said on the subject.

During the day she worked in the basement of the British Library reshelving books, and at night she wrote. Strange and often disturbing stories that she left out, I assumed, for me to read. Two children who take the life of a third child because they covet his shoes, and only after he is dead discover that the shoes don't fit, and pawn them off to another child, whom the shoes fit, and who wears them with joy. A bereaved family out for a drive in an unnamed country at war, who accidentally drive across enemy lines and discover an empty house, in which they take up residence, oblivious to the horrific crimes of its former owner.

She wrote in English, of course. In all the years we lived together I only heard her utter something in German a few times. Even once her Alzheimer's became advanced and language came unbraided in her, she did not revert to the syllables of her childhood, as many do. I sometimes thought that if we'd had a child it would have given her a way to return to her mother tongue. But we never had a child. From the beginning Lotte made it clear that it wasn't a possibility. I'd always imagined that I would have children one day, perhaps just because it seemed to me that was what happened to one as a matter of course; I don't think I ever really pictured myself as a father. On the few occasions I tried to raise the subject with Lotte she immediately erected a wall between us that took me days to dismantle. She didn't have to explain herself, or defend her position; I should have understood. (Not that she expected me to understand. More than anyone I've known, Lotte was content to live in a perennial state of misunderstanding. It's so rare, when you think about it, a trait one can imagine belonging to the psychology of a race more advanced than ours.) Eventually I came to accept the idea of a life without children, and I can't say that part of me wasn't also a bit relieved. Though later, as the years passed with so little to account for them, with almost nothing in our lives that grew and changed, I sometimes regretted that I hadn't argued harder for it—footsteps on the stairs, an unknown quantity, an envoy.

But, no: our life together was organized around protecting the ordinary; to throw a child into it would have shattered everything. Lotte was unnerved by disruptions to our habits. I tried to insulate her from the unexpected; the smallest change in plans threw her completely. The day would be lost reassembling a sense of peace. It took more than a year to convince her to leave that shabby room overlooking the rubble and come to live with me in Oxford. Of course I asked her to marry me. I even moved into larger rooms in a college-owned house, very comfortable ones with a fireplace in the living room and the bedroom, and a large window that looked out onto the garden. When the day of the move arrived at last, I went to pick her up at her room. Aside from her desk and the meager bits of furniture, everything she owned fit into a couple of battered suitcases already standing by the door. Giddy with the prospect of our lives together, full of hope that we were seeing the last of that wretched desk, I kissed her face, the face I was always so overjoyed to see. She smiled up at me. I've arranged for the desk to be moved to Oxford by van, she said.

By some miracle, some miracle or nightmare depending on the perspective, the movers managed to negotiate the narrow corridors and staircases of the house, groaning with pain and shouting obscenities that rose up on the crisp autumn breeze and were carried in through the open window of the room where I sat, waiting in horror, until at last I heard a pounding at the door, and there it was, resting on the landing, its dark, almost ebony, wood gleaming with a vengeance.

Almost as soon as I brought Lotte to Oxford I realized it had been a mistake. That first afternoon she stood with her hat in her hands, and seemed not to know how to proceed. What use did she have for a stone hearth or overstuffed chairs? I would get up in the middle of the night to find the bed empty, and discover her standing in the living room holding her coat. When I asked her where she was going, she would look down in surprise at the coat and hand it back to me. Then I would lead her back to bed and stroke her hair until she fell asleep, just as I would do forty years later when she forgot everything, and afterwards I would lie awake against the pillows, staring into the shadows of the room to where the desk waited like a Trojan horse.

* * *

One Saturday not long after, we went to London to have lunch with my aunt. Afterwards the two of us took a walk on the Heath. It was a bright autumn day; the light lent itself to everything. As we walked, I told Lotte an idea I had for a book on Coleridge. We crossed the Heath and stopped for a cup of tea in Kenwood House, where afterwards I showed Lotte the late Rembrandt self-portrait, the one I'd first visited as a boy, and which I came to associate with the expression "a ruined man," a phrase that, in my childish mind, took hold and became my own private, glorified aspiration. We emerged from the Heath, and took the first turn, which happened to be onto Fitzroy Park. As we made our way toward Highgate village, we passed a house for sale. It was in poor shape, suffering from neglect, the whole thing engulfed by brambles from all sides. On the peaked roof above the door, a strange little gargoyle crouched with a terrible grimace. Lotte stood looking up at it, kneading her hands in a way she sometimes did when she was thinking, as if the thought itself were lying inside her hands and she had only to polish it. I watched her studying the house. I thought maybe it reminded her of somewhere, perhaps even her home in Nuremberg; once I knew her better, I understood that would have been impossible—she avoided anything that reminded her. No, it was something else again. Perhaps the look of it simply appealed to her. Whatever it was, I could see immediately that she was taken by the place. We walked up the little front path, crowded by overgrown shrubs. A severe-looking woman let us in after some hesitation—it turned out she was the daughter of the old woman, a potter, who'd lived in the house for years, but had grown too frail to go on living alone. There was a stuffy, medicinal smell and the ceiling of the hall had been badly damaged by water, as if someone had accidentally diverted a river to flow right above it. In a room that led off from the hall I glimpsed the back of a white-haired woman sitting in a wheelchair.

I had a small inheritance from my mother that made it just possible to buy the house. One of the first things I did was paint the attic room that became Lotte's study. It was she who chose the room for herself, but I admit that I was relieved to think that the desk would be relegated to the attic, away from the rest of the house. She chose the same dove gray for the walls and floor, and from the day I finished painting until the day she became too ill to ascend the steep stairs alone, I avoided the attic. Not because of the desk, of course, but out of respect for her work and her privacy, without which she wouldn't have survived. She needed a place to escape, even from me. If I wanted her, I stood at the bottom of the steps and called up. When I made her a cup of tea, I left it for her at the foot of the stairs.

A year or so after we moved, Lotte sold her first collection of stories, *Broken Windows,* to a small publishing house in Manchester dedicated to experimental work (a label she objected to, but not enough to refuse the offer of publication). There wasn't a single reference in the book to Germany. All she allowed for was a mention in the brief biography on the last page of the place and date of her birth—Nuremberg, 1921. But there was a story buried near the end that touched on the horror. It was about a landscape architect in an unnamed country, an egoist so taken with his own talent that he is willing to collaborate with the officials of the country's brutal regime in order to see that a large park he has designed is built near the center of the city. He commissions appropriately fascist-looking bronze busts in each of their images, scattered among the rare and tropical plants. He names an alley of palm trees after the dictator. When the secret police begin to bury the bodies of murdered children under the park's foundations in the middle of the night, he turns a blind eye. People flock from all over the country to see the enormous blooms and admire the rare beauty of the place. The title of the story was "Children Are Terrible for Gardens"—a line the landscape architect had tossed off many years earlier to a young female journalist who obviously was in love with her subject—and for a long time after I read it I would catch myself staring at my wife, feeling a little bit afraid.

* * *

That night Daniel first appeared I didn't hear the front door open and close again until well past midnight. Another quarter of an hour passed before Lotte came upstairs. I was already lying in bed. I watched her undress in the dark. The revelation of her body twice a day was one of the great pleasures of my life. She slipped under the covers. I reached out and put my hand on her thigh. I waited for her to say something, but she didn't. Instead she slid on top of me. Everything in silence, but there was a special tenderness about the way she bent her head to touch mine. Afterwards, we went to sleep. The next morning a smell of cigarette smoke lingered in the kitchen, but otherwise nothing was out of the ordinary. I left for Oxford, and nothing more was said about Daniel.

But when I came home on Thursday night and went to hang up my coat I was hit by the powerful stench of cologne. It took me a moment to connect it to Daniel's jacket, and when I did I expected to find it hanging there, forgotten. But there was no sign of it. I might not have thought about it again if, settling into the sofa to read after dinner, I hadn't noticed a metal lighter resting near a cushion. Weighing it in my hand, I thought of how to phrase the question to Lotte. But what, exactly, was the question? Has that boy been back to see you? So what if he had? Wasn't she allowed to see whomever she pleased? She had made it clear to me from the beginning that I had no claims on her freedom, nor did I wish to have any. There was much she didn't tell me, and I didn't ask. Once, in a bitter argument over our late mother's affairs, my sister said she thought I liked being married to a mystery because it turned me on. She wasn't right—she never understood the first thing about Lotte—but perhaps she wasn't entirely wrong either. At times it seemed to me that my wife was built around a Bermuda Triangle, for God's sake! Send something in and you might never hear from it again. All the same, I wanted to know—had the boy been back, and what was it about him that made her immediately accept him in? To say she was not a sociable person would be to put it mildly. And yet, no sooner had a stranger at the door introduced himself than she was brewing his tea in the kitchen.

We search for patterns, you see, only to find where the patterns break. And it's there, in that fissure, that we pitch our tents and wait.

Lotte was reading in the chair across from me. I meant to ask, I said, where was Daniel from? She looked up from her book. Always the same rumpled expression when I disturbed her from her reading. Who? Daniel, I said. The boy who rang the bell the other night. I heard an accent, but couldn't quite place it. Lotte paused. Daniel, she repeated, as if she were testing the durability of the name for one of her stories. Yes, where was he from? I repeated. Chile, she said. All the way from Chile! I exclaimed. Isn't that remarkable! That your books have reached as far as that. For all I know, he picked one up at Foyles, Lotte said. We didn't talk about it. He's read a lot, and he wanted someone to discuss books with, that's all. You're being modest, I'm sure, I said. He seemed quite amazed to find himself in your presence. He probably could quote whole paragraphs of your work. A pained look crossed Lotte's face, but she remained silent. He is alone here, that's all, she said.

The next day the lighter was gone from where I'd left it on the coffee table. But over the next few weeks I continued to find signs of the boy—cigarettes in the rubbish bin, a long black hair on the white antimacassar, and once or twice when I called Lotte from Oxford I thought I sensed in her voice an awareness of someone else's presence. Then one Thursday night, putting something away at my desk, I found a leather diary, a small black book, warped and badly worn. On the inside cover was his name, Daniel Varsky. Each page had the days of the week, Monday, Tuesday, and Wednesday on the left, Thursday, Friday, and Saturday/Sunday on the right, and every box was filled to its edges with tiny handwriting.

It was only when I saw Daniel's handwriting that the jealousy brewing hit me with full force. I remembered him walking down the hall after Lotte, and now, along with the curt little smile he'd exchanged with himself in the mirror, I thought I remembered a certain swagger. Alone here! I thought. Alone here with a leather jacket, a silver lighter, a self-congratulatory grin, and something pressing zipped into his tight jeans. I'm embarrassed to admit to this now, but that's what came to me. He was almost thirty years younger than she. It's not that I suspected that Lotte had gone to bed with him—the thought itself was simply too far afield from the laws that governed our little universe. But if she hadn't welcomed his advances, she hadn't turned him away either—she had entertained them, or him, some intimacy had been allowed, and I saw, or thought I saw, that this young man in a leather jacket who had made himself comfortable at my desk had brazenly made a fool of me.

I knew that anything I said to Lotte at that point would be met with anger—the idea that I harbored suspicions and had been keeping tabs on her would strike her as an intolerable infringement. What right did I have? You see, my hands were tied. And yet I was certain that something was going on behind my back, even if it was only desire.

I began to form a plan, a plan that might seem counterintuitive but which at the time made perfect sense. I would go away for four days, to leave them alone together as a test. I would remove myself, the tiresome obstacle in their way, and give Lotte every opportunity to betray me with this swaggering youth with his leather and his tight jeans and his lines from Neruda, which no doubt he tossed off breathlessly with his face inches from hers. As I write this all these years later, in the long shadow of that boy's tragic fate, it sounds ridiculous, but at the time it felt real. In my desperation, with wounded pride, I wanted, or thought I wanted, to force her to do what I was convinced she longed for, to realize her desires instead of harboring them in secret, and to deliver us both to the terrible consequences that would follow. Though the truth was that all I was really searching for was proof that she wanted only me. Don't ask me with what evidence I intended to prove things either way. When I return, I told myself, everything will be clear.

I informed Lotte that I was going to attend a conference in Frankfurt. She nodded, and her face gave away nothing, though later, lying in my miserable hotel room while nothing happened and things got worse and worse, I thought I recalled seeing a little glint in her eyes. Once or twice a year I attended the English Romantic conferences held throughout Europe, brief gatherings perhaps not dissimilar in feeling for the participants than the feeling Jews have when they get off the plane in Israel: the relief of at last being surrounded on all sides by your own kind—the relief and the horror. Lotte rarely accompanied me on these trips, preferring not to have her work interrupted, and for this reason I always turned down the invitations I received to conferences held on other continents, in Sydney, Tokyo, or Johannesburg, whose native Wordsworth or Coleridge experts longed to host their friends and colleagues. Yes, I would refuse these invitations because they would have taken me away from Lotte for too long.

I don't remember why I chose Frankfurt. Perhaps a conference had recently taken place or was scheduled to take place there at some point in the near future, so that should any of my colleagues run into Lotte and the subject of a conference in Frankfurt came up, no one would think twice about it. Or perhaps, never very good at lying, I'd chosen Frankfurt because the name was so commanding, and at the same time it was a sufficiently uninteresting city that it wouldn't invite suspicion, like Paris, say, or Milan, although the idea of Lotte being suspicious was, in any case, absurd. So perhaps I chose it because I knew that Lotte would never, under any circumstances, return to Germany, and could be sure that she would not offer to accompany me.

The morning of my departure I got up very early, dressed in the suit I always wore when I flew, and drank my coffee while Lotte was still asleep. Then I took one last look around our house as if I might have been seeing it for the last time: the wide-plank floors smooth from use, Lotte's pale yellow reading chair with the tea stains on the left arm, the groaning bookshelves with their endless, unrepeating pattern of spines, the French doors leading out to the garden, the trees skeletal under the frost. I saw it all and felt it like an arrow in me, not in my heart but in my gut. Then I closed the door and got into the taxi waiting at the curb.

Almost as soon as I arrived in Frankfurt I regretted the choice. The flight was plagued by turbulence, and during the rocky descent through the storm an ominous silence overtook the few passengers huddled in their coats, or perhaps it only seemed ominous as background to the loud moans of an Indian woman in a violet sari, clutching a small, terrified child to her breast. The sky outside the baggage claim was dark and immobile. I took the train to the main station and from there I walked to the hotel where I'd made a reservation, on a small street off Theaterplatz, which turned out to be a grim and anonymous-looking place whose only effort at conviviality was the red-striped awnings above the windows of the lobby and restaurant, an effort that had obviously been made long ago in a spirit since lost or forgotten, as the awnings were dingy and stained with bird droppings. A bored, pimpled bellboy showed me to my room and handed me the key attached to a large paddle, making it impractical to carry around and thus ensuring that the residents of that miserable place would deposit their keys at the reception whenever leaving the building. After switching on the heater and opening the curtains to reveal a view of the concrete building across the street, the bellboy waited around, even going so far as to make sure the minibar was stocked with the appropriate combination of tiny bottles and cans, before I finally remembered to tip him and he bid me a good morning and left.

As soon as the door closed behind him I felt overwhelmed by loneliness, a cavernous loneliness I had not felt for many years, perhaps since my student days. To calm myself I unpacked the few items I had in my suitcase. At the bottom was Daniel's black diary. I took it out and sat down on the bed. Until then I had only paged through it without trying to decipher the dwarfed Spanish, but now with nothing else to do I tried to make sense of it. From what I could tell, it seemed to be a rather dull account of his life: what he ate, what books he read, who he met, and so on, a long list lacking in any reflection about these activities, a banal march against oblivion, as ineffectual as every other. Obviously I searched for Lotte's name. I found it six times: on the date he had first rung the bell, then five more times, always on days when I was away at Oxford. I began to sweat, a cold sweat, since the heater had yet to have any effect, and helped myself to a bottle of Johnnie Walker. Then I turned on the television, and soon enough I fell asleep. In my dreams I saw Lotte on all fours being taken from behind by the Chilean. When I woke only half an hour had passed, though it seemed like much more. I washed my face and went downstairs, relinquished my key to the receptionist who was busy counting great wads of German marks, and went out into the gray street where it had just begun to rain. A few blocks from the hotel I passed a woman leaning against the buzzers of a beige apartment block and sobbing. I thought of stopping to ask her what was wrong, maybe even taking her out for a drink. I slowed down as I approached her, close enough to notice the rip in her stockings, but in the end it was too out of character for the person I have been all my life, whether I've liked it or not, and I kept walking.

Those days in Frankfurt passed with excruciating slowness, like the descent of something lifeless through the fathoms of the ocean, darker and darker, colder and colder, more and more hopeless. I spent my time walking up and down the quays of the river Main, because as far as I could tell the whole city was gray, ugly, and full of miserable people, and there was no point in venturing beyond those banks where the Franks had first stepped ashore with their javelins, and because in that whole city only the trees by the riverside, large and beautiful, had any kind of calming effect on me. Away from them, I imagined the worst. Lying in my hotel room, too agitated to read, the enormous paddle hanging from the lock, I saw Daniel Varsky strutting shirtless around the kitchen, or going through my wardrobe to choose a clean shirt, dropping those he didn't care for on the floor, or sliding into bed, the one we had shared for almost twenty years, next to a naked Lotte. When I couldn't stand it anymore I forced myself back out onto the grim, colorless streets.

On the third day it began to pour and I ducked into a restaurant, a cafeteria really, populated by zombies, or so it seemed in that muted light. It was while sitting there, feeling sorry for myself over a plate of oily pasta I didn't have the stomach to eat, that a realization suddenly hit me. For the first time it occurred to me that I might have misunderstood Lotte. I mean utterly and grossly misunderstood her. All these years that I'd thought she'd needed regularity, routine, a life uninterrupted by anything out of the ordinary, maybe the opposite had actually been true. Maybe she had been longing the whole time for something to come along and smash all that carefully maintained order to pieces, a train through the bedroom wall or a piano falling out of the sky, and the more I did to protect her from the unexpected, the more stifled she felt, the wilder her longing, until it had become unbearable.

It seemed possible. Or at least, in that purgatorial cafeteria, not impossible, more or less as likely as the other scenario, the one I'd believed the whole time, priding myself on how well I understood my wife. Suddenly I wanted to cry. Out of frustration and exhaustion and despair of ever really coming close to the center, the always-moving center of the woman I loved. I sat at the table staring into the greasy food and waited for the tears to come, even wishing them to come, so that I might unburden myself of something, because as things stood I felt so heavy and tired that I couldn't see any way to move. But they didn't come, and so I continued to sit there hour after hour watching the unrelenting rain slosh against the glass, thinking of our life together, Lotte's and mine, how everything in it was designed to give a sense of permanence, the chair against the wall that was there when we went to sleep and there again when we awoke, the little habits that quoted from the day before and predicted the day to come, though in truth it was all just an illusion, just as solid matter is an illusion, just as our bodies are an illusion, pretending to be one thing when really they are millions upon millions of atoms coming and going, some arriving while others are leaving us forever, as if each of us were only a great train station, only not even that since at least in a train station the stones and the tracks and the glass roof stay still while everything else rushes through it, no, it was worse than that, more like a giant empty field where every day a circus erected and dismantled itself, the whole thing from top to bottom, but never the same circus, so what hope did we really have of ever making sense of ourselves, let alone one another?

At last my waitress approached. I hadn't noticed that the cafeteria had emptied, nor that the waiters had cleared the tables and were laying them with white cloths for the evening when the place apparently transformed itself into something respectable. The lunch shift ends at four, she said. We're closed until dinner starts at six. She was no longer wearing her black and white uniform, and had changed into her street clothes, a blue miniskirt and yellow sweater. I apologized, paid my bill and a large tip, and stood. Perhaps the waitress, who was not more than twenty, saw a grimace on my face as I did so, the grimace of a man lifting a tremendously heavy weight, because she asked me if I had far to go. I don't think so, I said, because I didn't know exactly where I was. I'm going to Theaterplatz. She said she was going that way, too, and to my surprise asked me to wait while she got her bag. I don't have an umbrella, she explained, and pointed at mine. While I waited for her I was forced to reassess my opinion of the cafeteria, which now had candles on each table that a waiter was setting out one by one, and which, as I couldn't help but admit when the girl returned with a smile, employed such a pretty and friendly waitress.

We huddled under my umbrella and set off into the storm. Her nearness immediately softened my mood. The walk was only ten minutes, and mostly we discussed her classes at the art school, and her mother who was in the hospital with a cyst. To anyone who passed, we might have been father and daughter. When we reached Theaterplatz I told her to keep the umbrella. She tried to refuse but I insisted. May I ask you a personal question? she said just as we were about to part ways. All right, I said. What were you thinking about at the restaurant all that time? You had the most miserable look on your face, and just when I thought it couldn't get any more miserable it did.

About train stations, I said. Train stations and circuses, and then I touched the girl on the cheek, very gently, as I thought her father might, the father she should have had if the world were just, and went back to the hotel where I packed my bag, checked out, and caught the next plane back to London.

It was late by the time the taxi pulled up in front of our house in Highgate, but what I could see of it filled me with joy—its familiar outline against the sky, the streetlights falling through the leaves, the lights burning yellow in the windows, yellow as they only ever look from the outside looking in, yellow like the windows in that painting by Magritte. Then and there I decided that I would forgive Lotte anything. So long as life could go on as it had. So long as the chair that was there when we went to sleep was there again in the morning, I didn't care what happened to it as we slept side by side, didn't care if it was the same chair or a thousand different chairs, or if, during the long night, it ceased to exist at all—so long as when I sat down on it to put on my shoes, as I did every morning, it would hold my weight. I didn't need to know everything. I only needed to know that our life would go on together as it always had. With shaking hands, I paid the driver and searched for my keys.

I called out Lotte's name. A pause, and then I heard her footsteps on the stairs. She was alone. As soon as I saw her expression, I understood that the boy had gone for good. I don't know how I knew, but I did. Something wordless was exchanged between us. We embraced. When she asked me how the conference had gone, and why I had come home a day early, I told her it had been fine, nothing interesting, and that I had missed her. We made a late dinner together, and as we ate I searched Lotte's face and voice for some sign of how things had ended with Varsky, but the way was barred: in the days that followed Lotte was subdued, lost in thought, and I let her be, as I always have.

It was months before I realized that she had given him her desk. I only found out because I noticed that a table we kept in the cellar was missing. I asked her if she'd seen it, and she told me she was using it as a desk. But you have a desk, I said, stupidly. I gave it away, she said. Gave it away? I said, unbelieving. To Daniel, she said. He admired it, and so I gave it to him.

Yes, Lotte was a mystery to me, but a mystery through which I somehow found my way. She was the only child with her parents when the SS rung their bell that October night of 1938 and rounded them up with the other Polish Jews. Her brothers and sisters were all older than she—one sister was studying law in Warsaw, one brother was the editor of a communist paper in Paris, another was a music teacher in Minsk. For a year she clung to her elderly parents and they to her inside the sealed compartment of that rapidly moving nightmare. When her chaperone visa came through, it must have felt like a miracle. Of course it would have been unimaginable not to take it and go. But it must have been equally unimaginable to leave her parents. I don't think Lotte ever forgave herself for it. I always believed it was her only real regret in life, but a regret of such vast proportions that it couldn't be dealt with straight on. It reared its head in unlikely places. For example, I thought that what really bothered Lotte about the woman who was hit by a bus on St. Giles' was how she herself had reacted in the moment. She had watched it happen—the woman stepping into the street, the screech of brakes, the terrible, inanimate thud—and as a crowd gathered around the fallen woman, she had turned and continued on her way. She hadn't mentioned it until that night, when we were reading. She told me the story, and of course I'd asked what anyone would have—whether the woman had been all right. A certain look came over Lotte's face, a look I'd seen many times before, and which I can only describe as a kind of stillness, as if everything that normally existed near the surface had retreated into the depths. A moment passed. I felt something one from time to time experiences with those one is intimate with, when the distance that all the while has been folded up like a Chinese paper toy suddenly springs open between you. And then Lotte shrugged, breaking the spell, and said she didn't know. She didn't say anything else about it, but the next day I saw her scanning the newspaper, looking, I felt sure, for some report of the accident. She walked away, you see. She walked away without waiting to find out what had happened.

All her life I thought it was about her parents. When she told the story about the bus it was about her parents, and when she woke up crying it was about her parents, and when she lost her temper at me and went cold for days, it was also, I believed, about her parents in some way. The loss was so extreme there seemed no need to go looking any further. So how was I to know that lost inside the vortex of her there was also a child?

I might never have known about him at all if a strange thing hadn't happened toward the end of Lotte's life. By then the Alzheimer's was quite advanced. In the beginning she had tried to hide it. I would remind her of something we had done together—a seaside restaurant we'd eaten in years before in Bournemouth, or the boat ride we'd taken in Corsica when her hat had blown off and floated on the backs of the waves toward the shores of Africa, or so we'd later imagined lying sun-drenched, naked, and happy in bed. I would remind her of one of these memories and she would say, Of course, of course, but I could see in her eyes that beneath those words there was nothing, just an abyss, like the black-water pond she disappeared into every morning no matter the weather. Then followed a period when she became scared, aware of how much she was losing by the day, perhaps even the hour, like a person slowly bleeding to death, hemorrhaging toward oblivion. When we went for a walk she would grip my arm as if at any minute the street might drop away, the trees and houses, England itself, sending us tumbling down, turning and tumbling, unable to ever right ourselves. And then even that period passed, and she no longer remembered enough to be afraid, no longer remembered, I suppose, that things had ever been any other way, and from then on she set off alone, utterly alone, on a long journey back to the shores of her childhood. Her conversation, if one could call it that, disintegrated, leaving behind only the rubble out of which a once-beautiful thing had been built.

It was during this time that she began to wander

off. I would come back from doing the shopping and find the front door open and the house empty. The first time it happened I got into the car and drove around for fifteen minutes, becoming more and more distraught before I found her half a mile away, on Hampstead Lane, sitting at a bus stop without a jacket though it was winter. When she saw me she didn't move to get up. Lotte, I said, bending down to her, or maybe I said, Darling. Where were you planning to go? To visit a friend, she said, crossing and uncrossing her ankles. Which friend? I asked.

It became impossible to leave her alone. She didn't always wander, but there had been enough scares that I had to hire a nurse to stay with her three afternoons a week so I could go out to do the errands. The first nurse I found turned out to be a nightmare. In the beginning she had seemed very professional, arriving with a long list of references, but soon enough she revealed herself to be careless and irresponsible, only in it for the money. One afternoon I came home and she was standing nervously by the door. Where is Lotte? I demanded. She wrung her hands. What is going on here? I said, pushing past her into the hall that Lotte and I had first entered together so many years ago when it still belonged to the potter in the wheelchair, and overhead hung the damage of a diverted river, a river, I admit, that from time to time I would wake in the middle of the night and think I could hear still flowing somewhere in the walls. But the hall was empty, as was the living room and kitchen. Where is my wife? I said, or perhaps I shouted, though I am hardly the shouting type. She's fine, this nurse, Alexandra, or

Alexa, I can't remember, assured me. A very nice woman called, a magistrate if I'm not mistaken. She's bringing Lotte home right now. I don't understand, I shouted, for surely by this point I'd lost my temper and had begun to shout, How did she wander off with you sitting right next to her? Actually, said the nurse, I wasn't sitting right next to her. She was watching television, it was a program I didn't care much for myself, and so I decided to wait in the other room until she was finished. And after that program she watched another of the same kind, so I called a friend of mine and we chatted for a while, and then when she decided to watch a *third* program, one of those really awful ones where they have snakes devouring helpless animals, snakes and alligators, I believe, though I think the third one was about piranhas, well after that I went in to see if she wanted anything, and she was gone. Luckily they called from the court a few minutes later to say that they had Ms. Berg, and she was perfectly fine.

By this point I was in such a rage that I could barely speak. The court? I shouted. THE COURT? and if a car hadn't pulled up in front of the house just then I might have lunged at her. The driver, a woman in her late fifties, got out and went around to open the door for Lotte. She led her patiently up the path long since cleared of brambles, planted on either side with purple irises and grape hyacinths, purple being Lotte's favorite color. Here we are, Ms. Berg, home at last, the woman said, leading her along on her arm as if Lotte were her own mother. Home at last, Lotte repeated, and beamed. Hello Arthur, she said, smoothing her trousers, and walked past me into the house.

Afterwards the woman, who was indeed a magistrate, told me the following story: At around three o'clock she'd gone down the hallway to speak to a colleague, and when she came back there was Lotte, sitting with her handbag on her lap, staring straight ahead as if she were riding in a car and unknown landscapes were unfolding before her, or as if she were in a movie acting as if she were riding in a car while in truth she was sitting perfectly still. Can I help you? the magistrate asked, though normally they buzzed her when she had a visitor, and as far as she knew she didn't have any meetings scheduled. Later it was a mystery to her how Lotte had got past the security guard and her secretary. Slowly Lotte turned to look at her. I've come to report a crime, she said. All right, the magistrate said, taking her seat across from Lotte, because the only other option would have been to ask her to leave, which she didn't have the heart to do. What is the crime? she asked. I gave up my child, Lotte announced. Your child? she asked, and at that moment she began to sense that Lotte, who was seventy-five by then, was perhaps disoriented or not altogether in her senses. On July 20, 1948, five weeks after he was born, she said. To whom did you give him? the magistrate asked. He was adopted by a couple from Liverpool, Lotte said. In that case no one committed a crime, Madame, said the magistrate.

At this point Lotte became silent. First silent and then confused. Confused and then frightened. She stood abruptly and asked to be taken home. Stood and didn't know which way to turn, as if she had forgotten where even the door was, as if the exit had gone the way of the rest. When the magistrate asked her address, Lotte gave her the name of a German street. From down the hallway came the sound of a gavel and Lotte jumped. At last she agreed to let the magistrate look in her handbag to find her address and telephone number. The magistrate phoned the house and spoke to the nurse, and then she told her secretary that she would be back soon. As they were leaving the building, Lotte looked up as if she were seeing the magistrate for the first time.

A coldness entered my head, a kind of severe numbness as if ice had crept up my spine and begun to flow into my brain, to protect my sensorium from the blow of the news it had just received. I managed to thank the magistrate profusely, and as soon as she drove away I went in and fired the nurse, who left cursing. I found Lotte in the kitchen, helping herself from a box of biscuits.

* * *

At first I did nothing. Slowly, my mind began to thaw. I listened to the noises of Lotte moving through the house, the breathing and the cracking of bones and swallowing and wetting dry lips and allowing a little groan to escape through the mouth. When I helped her to undress or bathe, as I had to do now, I looked at her slim body that I thought I'd known every inch of, and wondered how it was possible that I'd never realized it had borne a child. I smelled her smells, the familiar ones and the newer smells of her old age, and I thought to myself, Ours is the home of two different species. Here in this house live two different species, one on land and one in the water, one who clings to the surface and the other who lurks in the depths, and yet every night, through a loophole in the laws of physics, they share the same bed. I looked at Lotte brushing her white hair in the mirror, and I knew that every day from then until the end we would grow stranger and stranger to each other.

Who had been the father of the child? To whom had Lotte given the infant? Had she ever seen him again, or been in touch with him in any way? Where was he now? I turned these questions over and over in my mind, questions that I still found hard to believe I was asking at all, as if I were asking myself why the sky was green or why a river was running through the walls of our house. Lotte and I had never spoken to each other of the lovers we'd had before we met; I out of respect for her, and she because that is how she dealt with the past: in total silence. Of course I was aware that she'd had lovers. I knew, for example, that the desk had been a gift from one of these men. Perhaps he had been the only one, though I doubted it; she was already twenty-eight when I met her. But now it dawned on me that he must have been the child's father. What else could explain her strange attachment to the desk, her agreeing to live with that monstrous thing, and not just live with it but to work in the lap of the beast day in and day out—what else but guilt and almost certainly regret? It wasn't long before my mind arrived, inevitably, at the ghost of Daniel Varsky. If what she had told the magistrate was true, he would have been almost exactly the same age as her child. I never imagined that he actually was her child—that would have been utterly impossible. I couldn't say exactly how she would have responded had her grown son walked through the door, but I knew it would not have been in the way she had when she first laid eyes on Daniel. And yet, suddenly I understood what had drawn her to him, and all at once the whole thing became clear, or at least a glimpse of the whole, before it dissolved into more unknowns and more questions.

It must have been four years after Daniel Varsky first rang our bell that Lotte picked me up at Paddington one evening, a winter evening in 1974, and as soon as I got into the car I realized that she had been crying. Alarmed, I asked her what was wrong. For some time she didn't speak. We drove in silence over the Westway and through St. John's Wood, along the dark edge of Regent's Park where from time to time the headlights would illuminate the ghostly flash of a runner. Do you remember that Chilean boy who visited a few years ago? Daniel Varksy? I asked. Of course. At that moment I had no idea what she was about to say to me. Any number of things flashed through my mind, but none of them even approached what she told me next. About five months ago he was arrested by Pinochet's secret police, she said. His family hasn't heard anything from him since, and they have reason to believe he was killed. Tortured first and then killed, she said, and as her voice slid over those nightmarish last words it didn't catch in her throat or contract to hold back tears, but rather expanded, the way pupils do in the dark, as if it contained not one nightmare but many.

I asked Lotte how she knew, and she told me

that she had been corresponding with Daniel from time to time, until one day she stopped hearing from him. At first she hadn't been concerned since it often took time for her letters to reach him, as they were always forwarded on by a friend; Daniel himself moved around quite a bit, and so he had an agreement with a friend who lived in Santiago. She wrote again, and still heard nothing. At that point she became worried, aware of how bad the situation was in Chile. So this time she wrote directly to the friend and asked him whether Daniel was all right. Almost a month passed before she finally got a letter back from the friend who gave her the news that Daniel had disappeared.

That night I tried to console Lotte. And yet even as I tried, I was aware that I didn't know how to, that what we were performing together was a kind of empty pantomime, since I couldn't hope to know or understand what the boy had meant to her. It was not for me to know, and yet she wanted or perhaps even needed my comfort, and though I suppose a better man might have felt differently, I couldn't help feeling a grain of resentment. Just a drop, nothing more, but as I held her in the car outside our house I felt it. After all, wasn't it unfair of her to erect walls and then ask me to comfort her for what went on behind them? Unfair and even selfish? Of course I said nothing. What could I have said? Once upon a time I had promised to forgive her everything. The violent tragedy of the boy loomed over us in the darkness. I held her and comforted her.

A week or ten days after the magistrate brought Lotte home, while she was napping on the sofa, I went up to her study. It had been a year and a half since she had been there, and on her desk were her papers exactly as she had left them on the last day she had tried to battle her failing mind and lost for good. The sight of her handwriting on those curling pages pained me deeply. I sat down at her desk, the simple wooden table she had been using since she gave the other away to Daniel Varsky twenty-five years before, and spread my hands on the surface. Most of the writing on the top page was crossed out, leaving only lines or phrases here or there. What I could make out was largely senseless, and yet in the manic cross-outs and shaky letters Lotte's frustration was clear, the frustration of someone trying to transcribe a fading echo. My eye caught a line near the bottom: *The astonished man stood under the ceiling: Who can that be? Who in the world can that be?* Without warning, a sob came over me like a violent wave, a wave that had traveled across a flat and otherwise placid ocean with the express purpose of crashing down on my head. It pulled me under.

After that I got up and went to the cabinet where Lotte kept her papers and files. I didn't know what I was looking for, but imagined that sooner or later I would find whatever it was. There were old letters from her editor, birthday cards from me, drafts of stories she never published, postcards from people I knew and others I didn't. I looked for an hour but didn't find anything that referred in any way to the child. Nor did I find any letters from Daniel Varsky. After that I went downstairs, where Lotte was just waking up. We went out together for a walk, as we had done every afternoon since I had retired. We got as far as Parliament Hill, where we watched the kites tossed by the wind and then turned home for dinner.

That night after Lotte had fallen asleep I slipped out of bed, made myself a cup of chamomile tea, paged through the newspaper in a leisurely manner, and then, as if the thought had only just occurred to me, made my way up to the attic. I opened other drawers and other files, and when I had finished with these more drawers and more files sprung up in the place of those I'd already gone through, some marked and others not. Pages seemed to drift out of their own accord and migrate across the floor, like a paper autumn staged by a bored child. There seemed no end to the amount of paper that Lotte had squirreled away in that deceptively small cabinet, and I began to lose hope of ever finding what I was looking for. And all the while, as I read snatches of letters, notes, and manuscripts, I couldn't escape the feeling that I was betraying Lotte in the way she would have found most unforgivable.

It was well past three in the morning when at last I found the plastic folder holding two documents. The first was a yellowed release from the East End Maternity Hospital, dated June 15, 1948. Under Patient's Name, someone, a nurse or secretary, had typed Lotte Berg. The address given wasn't of the room near Russell Square, but another street I'd never heard of, which I looked up later and found was in Stepney, not far from the hospital. Below that it said that Lotte had given birth to a boy on June 12th, at 10:25 in the morning, and that he had weighed seven pounds and two ounces. The second was a sealed envelope. The glue was ancient and dry, and gave way easily when I tried to open it with my finger. Inside was a small lock of dark, fine hair. I picked it up and held it in the palm of my hand. For reasons I can't explain, what came to mind was a tuft of hair stuck to a low branch I had once found walking in the woods as a boy. I didn't know what kind of animal it was from, and in my mind I saw a majestic beast as large as a moose, but very graceful, making its way silently across the forest floor, a magical creature that never revealed itself to humans, but that had left a sign behind for me alone to find. I tried to shake that ancient image, which really I hadn't thought of for more than sixty years, and to concentrate instead on the fact that what I held in my palm was the hair of my wife's child. But no matter how I tried, all I could think about was that beautiful animal that strode with silent footfalls through the forest, an animal that didn't speak but knew all and looked with great sadness and pain on the ravages of human life, against its own kind and every other. At one point I even wondered whether fatigue was making me hallucinate, but then I thought to myself, No, this is what happens when you get old, time abandons you and all your memories become involuntary.

There was nothing else in the envelope. After a moment, I dropped the lock of hair back in, and sealed the envelope with tape. I tucked it back into the plastic folder, and laid it back at the bottom of the drawer I'd found it in. Then I cleared up all of the papers, put them back in order as best I could, closed the drawers of the bureau, and turned off the lights. By now it was near dawn. I crept down the stairs and went into the kitchen to put the water on to boil. In the pale light, I thought I saw something move under the azalea by the garden door. A hedgehog, I thought with delight, though I had no reason to believe as much. What has happened to the hedgehogs of England? Those friendly creatures I used to find everywhere as a boy, though even then they were often dead by the roadside. What has killed all the hedgehogs? I thought as the tea bag steeped in the steaming water, and in my mind I made a note to myself, a note I might remember or not, to tell Lotte that once upon a time you could find them everywhere in this country, those lovely nocturnal animals whose large eyes belie their terrible eyesight. The fox knows many things, but the hedgehog knows one big thing, as Archilochus said, but what was it? Time passed and then I heard her calling me from the bedroom. Yes, my love, I called, still looking out at the garden. Here I come.

LIES TOLD BY CHILDREN

I met and fell in love with Yoav Weisz in the fall of 1998. Met at a party on Abingdon Road, farther down that road than I'd ever been. Fell in love, which was still something new for me. Ten years have passed, and yet that time stands out in my life as few others do. Like me, Yoav was at Oxford, but he lived in London, in the house in Belsize Park that he shared with his sister, Leah. She was studying piano at the Royal College of Music, and often I could hear her playing from somewhere behind the walls. Sometimes the notes would stop abruptly and a long silence would pass, punctuated by the scrape of the piano bench or footsteps across the floor. I thought she might appear to say hello, but then the music would start up again from inside the woodwork. I was at the house three or four times before I finally met Leah, and when I did I was surprised by how much she looked like her brother, only more elfin, and less reliable to still be there if you happened to look away.

The house, a large and dilapidated brick Victorian, was too big for the two of them, and filled with darkly beautiful furniture that their father, a famous antiques dealer, kept there. Every few months he came through London, and then everything would be magically rearranged according to his impeccable taste. Certain tables, chairs, lamps, or settees were crated up and removed and others arrived to take their place. In this way the rooms were always changing, taking on the mysterious, dislocated moods of houses and apartments whose owners had died, gone bankrupt, or simply decided to bid farewell to the things they had lived among for years, leaving it to George Weisz to relieve them of their contents. Occasionally potential buyers came to the house to see one of the pieces in person, and then Yoav and Leah had to clear up whatever dirty socks, open books, stained magazines, and empty glasses had accumulated since the cleaner's last visit. But most of Weisz's clients had no need to see for themselves what they were buying, either because of the antiques dealer's world-class reputation, or because of their wealth, or because the pieces they were buying held a sentimental value that had nothing to do with their appearance. When he wasn't traveling to Paris, Vienna, Berlin, or New York, their father lived on Ha'Oren Street in Ein Karem, Jerusalem, in the stone house choked with flowering vines where Yoav and Leah had lived as children, whose shutters were always closed to keep out the punishing light.

The house where I lived with them from November of 1998 to May of 1999 was a twelve-minute walk from 20 Maresfield Gardens, the home of Dr. Sigmund Freud from September of 1938, after he fled the Gestapo, until the end of September 1939, when he died of three doses of morphine administered at his request. Often, heading out for a walk, I'd find myself there. When Freud fled Vienna almost all of his belongings were crated up and shipped to the new house in London, where his wife and daughter lovingly reassembled, down to the last possible detail, the study he'd been forced to abandon at 19 Berggasse. At the time I didn't know anything about Weisz's study in Jerusalem, and so the poetic symmetry of the house's nearness to Freud's was lost on me. Maybe all exiles try to re-create the place they've lost out of their fear of dying in a strange place. And yet, during the winter of 1999, when I would linger on the worn Oriental rug in the doctor's study, comforted by the hominess of the place and the sight of his many figurines and statuettes, I was often struck by the irony that Freud, who shed more light than anyone onto the crippling burden of memory, had been unable to resist its mythic spell any better than the rest of us. After he died, Anna Freud preserved the room exactly as her father left it, down to the glasses he removed from the bridge of his nose and laid on the desk for the last time. From twelve to five, Wednesday through Sunday, you can visit the room stalled forever at the moment the man who gave us some of our most enduring ideas of what it is to be a person ceased to be. In the leaflet given out by an elderly docent who sits in a chair by the front door, the visitor is encouraged not only to consider her tour as one through an actual house, but also, given the various exhibits and collections on display in its rooms, as a tour through that metaphorical house, the mind.

I say *the house where I lived with them* rather than *our house*, because though I resided there for seven months it in no way ever belonged to me, nor could I ever have been considered anything more than a privileged guest. Aside from me, the only regular visitor was a Romanian cleaner named Bogna, who fought the ever-encroaching chaos that seemed to threaten the siblings like a squall on the horizon. After what happened she left, either because she couldn't battle the mess any longer or because no one paid her. Or maybe she sensed that things were headed in a bad direction and wanted to get out while she could. She had a limp, water on the knee, I think, a cup of the Danube that sloshed around as she thumped from room to room with her mop and feather duster, sighing as if freshly reminded of a disappointment. She kept the knee thickly bandaged under her housecoat, and bleached her hair with a home brew of dangerous chemicals. If you got close enough, she smelled of onions, ammonia, and hay. She was an industrious woman, but sometimes she would pause in her work to tell me about her daughter in Constanţa, a horticultural expert poorly paid by the state whose husband had left her for another woman. Also her mother, who owned a small piece of land that she refused to sell and suffered from rheumatism. Bogna supported them both, sending money each month and clothes from Oxfam. Her own husband had died fifteen years earlier of a rare blood disease; now there was a cure for it. She called me Isabella, instead of my real name, Isabel, or Izzy, as most people call me, and I never bothered to correct her. I don't know why she talked to me. Perhaps she saw an ally in me, or at the very least someone who was an outsider, not being part of the family. Not that I saw myself that way, but back then Bogna knew more than I did.

Once Bogna was gone the house went to seed. It slumped and turned in on itself as if to protest the abandonment of its only advocate. Dirty plates piled up in every room, spilled food was left where it had scattered or congealed, the dust thickened, achieving a fine gray fur in the wilderness under the furniture. Black mold colonized the fridge, windows were left open to the rain, souring the curtains and leaving the sills to peel and rot. When a sparrow flew in and became trapped, batting its wings against the ceiling, I made a joke about the ghost of Bogna's feather duster. It was met with a sullen silence, and I understood that Bogna, who had looked after Yoav and Leah for three years, was not to be mentioned again. After Leah's trip to New York, and the beginning of the terrible silence between the siblings and their father, they stopped leaving the house altogether. Then I was the only one they had to bring them what they needed from the outside. Sometimes, scraping dried egg yolk from a pan so that I could cook some breakfast, I thought of Bogna and hoped that one day she would retire to a cottage by the Black Sea as she had longed to do. Two months later, at the end of May, my mother became sick, and I went back home to New York for almost a month. I called Yoav every few days and then, abruptly, the siblings stopped answering the phone. Some nights I would let it ring thirty or forty times while my stomach tied itself into knots. When I returned to London in early July the house was dark and the locks had been changed. At first I thought Yoav and Leah were playing a trick on me. But days passed and I heard nothing from them. In the end I had no choice but to go home to New York, since by then I'd been thrown out of Oxford. Hurt and angry as I was, I still did everything I could to find them. But I turned up nothing. The only sign that they were still alive somewhere was the box of my belongings that arrived at my parents' apartment half a year later without a return address.

Eventually I came to accept the strange logic in their departure, a logic I'd been schooled in during my brief time with them. They were prisoners of their father's, locked within the walls of their own family, and in the end it wasn't possible for them to belong to anyone else. I'd expected nothing less than their unbroken silence all these years, and never thought I'd see them again—what they did, they did without compromise, free of the complications imposed on the rest of us by indecision, wavering, regret. But though I moved on, and fell in love more than once again, I never stopped thinking about Yoav, or wondering where he was and who he had become.

Then one day in the late summer of 2005, six years after they disappeared, I received a letter from Leah. In it she wrote that in June of 1999, a week after celebrating his seventieth birthday, their father had killed himself in the house on Ha'Oren Street. The maid had found him in his study the following day. On the table next to him was a sealed letter to his children, an empty bottle of sleeping pills, and a bottle of scotch, a drink Leah had never seen him touch in his life. There was also a small booklet from the Hemlock Society. Nothing had been left to chance. Across the room on another table was the small collection of watches that had belonged to Weisz's own father, which he had kept wound since his father's arrest in Budapest in 1944. While he was alive, the watches had accompanied Weisz wherever he traveled so that he would be able to wind them on schedule. *When the maid arrived,* Leah wrote, *all of the watches had stopped.*

Her letter was written in small, neat script at

odds with its loose and haphazard composition. There was little by way of a greeting, as if only months had passed since we'd seen each other rather than six years. After the news about her father's suicide, the letter went on at some length about a painting that had hung on the wall of his study, the room in which he'd taken his life. It had been there for as long as she remembered, Leah wrote, and yet she knew there was a time when it had not been there, when her father was still searching for it, just as he had searched for and repossessed every other piece of furniture in that room, the same pieces that had sat in his own father's study in Budapest until the night in 1944 when the Gestapo had arrested his parents. Another person would have considered them lost forever. But that was what set her father apart, what led him into his field and distinguished him in it above all others: Unlike people, he used to say, the inanimate doesn't simply disappear. The Gestapo confiscated the most valuable items in the apartment, which were many, since Weisz's family on his mother's side had been wealthy. These were loaded—along with mountains of jewelry, diamonds, money, watches, paintings, rugs, silverware, china, furniture, linens, porcelains, and even cameras and stamp collections—onto the forty-two car "Gold Train" the SS used to evacuate Jewish possessions as the Soviet troops advanced toward Hungary. What was left behind the neighbors looted. In the years after the War, when Weisz returned to Budapest, the first thing he did was knock on these neighbors' doors and, as the color washed out of their faces, entered their apartments with a small gang of hired thugs who seized the stolen furniture, carrying it out on their backs. A woman who had grown up and moved away, taking his mother's vanity table with her, Weisz hunted down in the city's outskirts; entering her house in the middle of the night, he helped himself to some wine, left the dirty glass on the table, and carried out the vanity himself, all while the woman slept soundly in the other room. Later, in his business, Weisz hired others to do such work. But his own family's furniture he always appeared to claim himself. The Gold Train was seized by the Allied troops near Werfen, in May of 1945. Most of its load was sent to a military warehouse in Salzburg, and later sold through army exchange stores or at auction in New York. These pieces took Weisz longer to find, often years or even decades. He made contact with everyone from the high-ranking U.S. military officers who had overseen the dispersion of goods, to the workers employed by the warehouse to move them. Who knows what he offered them in exchange for the information he wanted.

He made it his business to know personally every serious dealer of nineteenth- and twentieth-century furniture in Europe. He scoured the catalogues of every auction, befriended every furniture restorer, knew what came through London, Paris, Amsterdam. His father's Hoffmann bookcase showed up in a shop on Herrengasse in Vienna in the autumn of 1975. He flew direct from Israel and identified the bookcase by the long scrape along its right side. (Other bookcases had turned up without this mark and been rejected by Weisz.) His father's dictionary stand he tracked to a banking family in Antwerp, and from there to a store on Rue Jacob in Paris, where it lived for some time in the window under the watch of a large white Siamese cat. Leah remembered the arrival of certain of these long-lost pieces at the house on Ha'Oren Street, tense and somber events that had terrified her so much that as a small child she would sometimes hide in the kitchen when the crates were pried open, in case what popped out were the blackened faces of her dead grandparents.

About the painting, Leah wrote the following: *It was so dark you had to stand at a certain angle to make out that it was of a man on a horse. For years, I was under the impression that it was Alexander Zaid. My father never liked the painting. Sometimes I think that had he allowed himself to live as he wanted to, he would have chosen an empty room with only a bed and a chair. Anyone else would have let the painting go the way of the rest that was lost, but not my father. He was burdened with a sense of duty that commanded his whole life, and later ours. He spent years tracking down the painting and paid quite a sum to convince its owners to sell it back to him. In the letter he left, he wrote that the painting had hung in his own father's study. I nearly choked, or screamed at the absurdity. It's possible I even laughed out loud. As if I hadn't known that everything in his study in Jerusalem was laid out exactly as my grandfather's study in Budapest had once been, down to the millimeter! Down to the velvet of the heavy drapes, the pencils in the ivory tray! For forty years my father labored to reassemble that lost room, just as it looked until that fateful day in 1944. As if by putting all the pieces back together he might collapse time and erase regret. The only thing missing in the study on Ha'Oren Street was my grandfather's desk—where it should have stood, there was a gaping hole. Without it, the study remained incomplete, a poor replica. And only I knew the secret of where it was. That I refused to hand it over to him was what tore our family apart in the year when you lived with us, a few months before he killed himself. And yet he refused to acknowledge it! I thought I'd killed him with what I'd done. But it was just the opposite. When I read his letter,* Leah wrote, *I understood that my father had won. That at last he'd found a way to make it impossible for us ever to escape him. After he died, we went home to the house in Jerusalem. And we stopped living. Or maybe you could say that we began a life of solitary confinement, only with two of us instead of one.*

The letter went on at some length about certain rooms of the house. *What falls apart we stop using. We pay someone to do the shopping, and to bring us the things we need. A woman who needs the money and has seen enough in her life that she doesn't raise an eyebrow. We used to venture out sometimes, but now hardly at all. A kind of inertia has taken hold. We have the garden, and Yoav goes outside a little, but it's been months since he last left the house.*

She came to the point of her letter: *It can't go on like this or we really will stop living. One of us will do something terrible. It's as if my father is luring us closer to him every day. It gets harder to resist. For a long time now I've been working up the courage to leave. But if I go, I can't ever come back, and I can't tell Yoav where I am. Otherwise we'll get sucked back in, and I don't think I'll be able to escape again. So he doesn't know anything about it. If you haven't figured it out already, Izzy, I'm writing to ask you to come here. To him. I don't know the first thing about your life now, but I know how much you loved him then. What you two meant to each other. You're still alive in him, and there isn't much else that is. I was always jealous of what you let him feel. That he had found someone who made him feel what I'd never been allowed to.*

At the end of the letter, she wrote that she couldn't leave unless she knew for sure that I would come to him. She didn't want to think about what would happen to him alone. She said nothing about where she planned to go. Only that she would call me for my answer in two weeks.

Her letter awakened a tidal wave of feeling—sadness, anguish, joy, and also anger that Leah would think I would drop everything for Yoav after all these years, that she would put me in such a position. It also made me afraid. I knew that to find and to feel Yoav again would be terribly painful, because of what had become of him, and because of what I knew he could ignite in me, a vitality that was excruciating because like a flare it lit up the emptiness inside me and exposed what I always secretly knew about myself: how much time I'd spent being only partly alive, and how easily I'd accepted a lesser life. I had a job like anyone, even if I disliked it, I even had a boyfriend, a gentle, kind person who loved me and evoked in me a kind of tender ambivalence. And yet the moment I finished the letter, I knew that I would go to Yoav. In light of him, everything—the inky shadows, the dirty dishes, the tarred roofs outside the window—took on a different look, became more acute, altered by a rush of feeling. He awakened a hunger in me—not just for him, but also for the magnitude of life, for the extremes of all it has been given to us to feel. A hunger and also courage. Later, looking back at how easily I'd closed the door on one life and slipped away to another, to him, it seemed that all those years I'd just been waiting for that letter, and that everything I'd built up around me had been made of cardboard, so that when it finally arrived I could fold it up and throw it away.

Waiting for Leah's call, I couldn't think of anything else. I barely slept at night, and couldn't pay attention at work, forgetting things I was supposed to do, losing papers, getting in trouble with my boss who always took his anger out on me anyway, when he wasn't staring at my legs or breasts. When the day finally arrived that Leah was supposed to phone, I called in sick to work. I didn't even take a shower, afraid that I would miss her call. Morning turned into afternoon turned into evening turned into night, and still it didn't ring. I thought she had changed her mind and vanished again. Or that she couldn't find my number, even though it was listed. But then, at quarter to nine (the very early hours of the morning in Jerusalem), the phone rang. Izzy? she said, and her voice was exactly the same as it has always been, pale, if you can describe a voice like that, and quavering a little as if she were holding her breath. It's me, I said. He's sleeping upstairs, Leah said. He doesn't fall asleep until two or three in the morning, and I had to wait to call. We both fell silent, during which, without saying a word, she reached into me and took out my answer. At last she exhaled. When you come, don't bother ringing. He won't answer. I'll leave the key for you, taped to the back of the buzzer on the gate. I nodded, too choked to speak.

Izzy, I'm sorry that we—that he never— She broke off. It was so terrible, she said. There was tremendous guilt. For years we punished ourselves. And Yoav's way of punishing himself was giving you up. Leah—I said. I have to go, she whispered. Take care of him.

*   *   *

They had lived everywhere. Their mother had died when Yoav was eight and Leah seven, and after that, without his wife to anchor him, haunted by grief, their father had wandered with them from city to city, sometimes staying months, sometimes a few years. Wherever he was, he worked. According to Yoav, his fame in the field of antiques became legendary during those years. He never had need for a store; his clients always knew where to find him. And the furniture they so coveted, the desks or bureaus or chairs they longed for, had long ago sat in and thought they would never sit in again, all that furnished the lives they lost or the lives they dreamed of living, arrived into George Weisz's possession via sources, channels, and coincidences that remained the secrets of his trade. When Yoav was twelve he used to have a reoccurring dream that his father, his sister, and he lived together on a wooded shore and every night the tide would wash furniture onto the beach, four poster beds and sofas dressed with seaweed. They dragged these under the cover of the trees and assembled them in rooms demarcated by lines their father drew on the forest floor with the toe of his shoe, rooms upon rooms that began to take over the woods, without roofs or walls. The dreams were sad and eerie. But once Yoav dreamed that Leah found a lamp with the bulb still screwed in. They ran back with it to their father, who placed it on a mahogany side table and plugged it into Yoav's mouth. Crouched on the floor, his mouth clamped shut, Yoav watched the canopy of leaves illuminate. Shadows rippled in the boughs. Years later, traveling through Norway with a backpack, Yoav stumbled across a stretch of shoreline he recognized as the one from his dreams. He took a photograph of it and when he got back to Oslo he had the film developed. Then he sent the photograph to his sister without a note, because between them there was no need for explanation.

Their father took them to Paris, Zurich, Vienna, Madrid, Munich, London, New York, Amsterdam. When they arrived at the new apartment it would already be filled with furniture. The pieces would be sold until the apartment was almost empty, and then they would leave for another city. Or it was the opposite: upon arriving, the new apartment would be bare and smell of fresh paint. As the months passed it would slowly fill up with a rolltop desk, a set of nesting tables, a daybed that arrived through the window or door, on the backs of men breathing heavily through the nose, or sometimes as if on its own, materializing while Yoav and Leah were away at school or playing at the park, making itself at home in some unnoticed corner as if it had been there all its inanimate life. Yoav told me that one of his earliest memories from those transitory years was hearing the doorbell ring, going to open the door, and finding a Louis XVI chair in the stairwell. The blue damask was ripped, and the horsehair stuffing exploded through. When the apartment became too crowded, or when the memory of his wife caught up with George Weisz, or for reasons Yoav and Leah understood but couldn't explain, they would be on their way again to another city. In the new place, they would wake in the middle of the night to use the bathroom and, believing themselves still in the old apartment, in the prior city, would crash into walls. On the inside of the medicine cabinet on the third floor of the house in Belsize Park, one or both of them had carved a list of all the addresses they'd lived at: *19 Ha'Oren, Singel 104, Florastrasse 43, 163 West 83rd Street, 66 Boulevard Saint-Michel* . . . There were fourteen of them altogether, and one afternoon when I was alone in the house I copied them into my notebook.

*   *   *

Paranoid that something might happen to his children, Weisz was strict about what they were allowed to do, where they were allowed to go, and with whom. Their lives were monitored by a series of humorless nannies with a firm grasp that accompanied them everywhere, long after they were old enough to be allowed a certain freedom of movement. After their tennis, piano, clarinet, ballet, or karate lessons they were chaperoned directly home by these muscular women in thick stockings and health clogs. Any change or amendment to their daily schedule had to be first run past their father. Once, when Yoav meekly pointed out that other children did not have to live by the same rules, Weisz snapped back that perhaps such children were not so loved as his sister and he. If there was any protest at all about life under their father's rule, it came, in a muted form, from Yoav. Weisz crushed these protests with disproportionate power. As if to ensure that Yoav would never grow confident enough to stand up to him, he found ways to constantly belittle him. As for Leah, she had always done what her father asked because she lived with the special burden of knowing that she was her father's favorite, and that to stand up to him, or God-forbid disobey him, would be a betrayal of the highest order, akin to a physical assault.

When Yoav turned sixteen and Leah fifteen, their father decided to send them to board at the International School in Geneva. By then the nannies had been replaced by a driver who shadowed them everywhere just as the women had done, only from the leather-upholstered interior of a Mercedes-Benz. But Weisz could no longer ignore how ingrown his children had become. They spoke in a pidgin of Hebrew, French, and English that only they understood, and, despite their worldliness, naturally accepted and even sought a position of isolation among others their age. He recognized that they couldn't be kept on such a tight leash for much longer. It's not impossible that he sensed, as even the most blind and misguided parents can sometimes do, that the way he had chosen to raise his children might hurt or even cripple them in the end, in ways he couldn't yet imagine.

He called the headmaster, Monsieur Boulier, and had a long conversation with him about the school, how his children would be cared for, and what he expected them to find there. Experience had taught him that people behave in your favor when they feel bound to you in some way, if only through a handshake or friendly conversation. Even better if they think there is something you can do for them in return, and so by the end of the phone call Weisz had assured Boulier that he would find him a match for his Ming vase, the other of which had fallen and shattered some years ago during a dinner party thrown by his wife. Weisz didn't believe it had broken during a dinner party, but it was enough for him to know that it had broken under circumstances that still disturbed Boulier, and only a perfect replacement of the vase would allow the memory of the incident to recede.

Weisz himself did not drive—whenever possible he walked, and otherwise he took the metro like everybody else—but he insisted on accompanying Yoav and Leah in the chauffeured car from Paris to Geneva. They stopped for lunch in Dijon, and after the meal in a dark tavern on a narrow medieval street named after a seventeenth-century theologian, Weisz left Yoav and Leah to browse in a bookshop under the driver's watch while he went to see someone about some business. There was nowhere Weisz went where he did not have business of some kind; where he had none, he invented some. There was a gesture his father always made, raking his fingers across his closed eyes as if trying to wipe something from his eyelids, that was so particular to him that it seemed to Yoav a kind of identifying mark. When Yoav was young, he used to believe that at those moments his father was listening to something outside the range of human hearing, like a dog.

When they arrived in Geneva, Weisz brought his

children directly to the house of the headmaster, Monsieur Boulier. They waited in the living room with Madame Boulier and her asthmatic French bulldog, helping themselves to a plate of butter cookies while their father spoke to the headmaster behind the closed door of his study. When the two men finally emerged from the paneled study, the headmaster accompanied them to the boys' dormitory where Yoav would live, and made a point of drawing the curtains to point out the view of the wooded park. After embracing his son, Weisz accompanied Leah across town to the house of a retired English teacher where she was to live with two older girls. One was the daughter of an American businessman and his Thai wife, and the other the daughter of the man who had once been the royal engineer to the shah. When Leah got her period for the first time, the Iranian girl gave her a pair of her tiny diamond studs. Leah displayed them in a small box on her windowsill along with other souvenirs she had acquired in her travels. That year was the first and, at least until the point when I knew them, the last that Yoav and Leah lived apart.

Without his children, Weisz grew even more restless. He sent Yoav and Leah postcards from Buenos Aires, St. Petersburg, and Kraków. The messages on the backs of the cards, written in handwriting that will die with his generation (shaky, mangled by its forced leaps from language to language, dignified in its illegibility), always ended in the same way: *Take care of each other, my loves. Papa.* During the holidays, and sometimes even on weekends, Yoav and Leah would take the train to Paris, Chamonix, Basel, or Milan to meet their father, either in an apartment or a hotel. On these journeys they were sometimes mistaken for twins. They traveled in the smoking car, Leah with her head against the window and Yoav resting his chin on his hand as the silhouette of the Alps hurtled past, the butts of their cigarettes, held between long, thin fingers, glowing brighter from time to time in the near dark.

Two years after his children began school in Geneva, nine years after he had fled from it, Weisz suddenly decided to return to the house on Ha'Oren Street. He gave his children no explanation. There were many things they simply didn't talk about: between them, silence was not so much a form of evasion as a way for solitary people to coexist in a family. Though he still traveled, the trips always came to an end with Weisz carrying his small suitcase up the overgrown path to the stone house that his wife had once loved.

As for Yoav and Leah, they enjoyed the new freedom they were allowed at school, but in other ways little changed for them. If anything, being forcefully submerged in school life and living so closely with their peers only underscored their separateness, and entrenched them more deeply in their isolation. They ate lunch alone together, and spent their free time in each other's company, wandering the city or taking boat rides on the lake during which they lost all sense of time. Sometimes they shared an ice cream at one of the cafés near the water, each staring off in the opposite direction, lost in their own thoughts. They didn't make many friends. During their second year, one of the boys who lived in the dorm with Yoav, an arrogant Moroccan, tried to cajole Leah to go out with him, and when he was coolly rebuffed, he began to spread a rumor that the siblings were having an incestuous affair. They did what they could to encourage the rumor, making a show of lying in each other's laps and stroking one another's hair. The affair became an accepted fact among the student body. Even their teachers began to look at them with a mix of fascination, horror, and envy. At a certain point things reached a boil, and Monsieur Boulier felt it was his duty to inform their father about what was going on between his children. He left a message for Weisz, who promptly returned his call from New York. Boulier cleared his throat, tried to approach from one angle, retreated, approached from another, fell into a coughing fit, asked Weisz to hold, was rescued by his wife, who rushed in with a glass of water and a stern look, a look that restored his sense of necessity, and he returned to the phone and told Weisz what everyone else knew about his own children. When he was finished Weisz was silent. Boulier raised his eyebrows and shot his wife an anxious glance. Do you know what I'm thinking? Weisz said at last. I can only imagine, said Boulier. I'm thinking of how rarely I am mistaken about people, Monsieur Boulier. Judgment of character is essential in my line of work, and I pride myself on the acuity of my own. And yet I see now that I erred with you, Monsieur Boulier. I admit that I never took you for an intelligent man. But neither did I take you for a fool. Here the headmaster began to cough again, and also to sweat. Now if you'll be so kind as to excuse me, I have someone waiting, said Weisz. Good afternoon.

Mostly it was Yoav who told me these stories, often when we were lying naked together in his bed, smoking and talking in the dark, his penis resting against my thigh, my hand tracing the protrusion of his collarbone, his hand behind my knee, my head in the crook of his shoulder, feeling the special, hair-raising excitement of being newly thrown into the fragile position of intimacy. Later, when I got to know Leah, she sometimes told me things as well. But the stories were always left incomplete, something about their atmosphere elusive and unexplained. Their father was a figure only partially sketched, as if to draw him fully would threaten to blot everything else, even themselves, from view.

* * *

It isn't exactly true that I met Yoav at a party, at least not for the first time. I first encountered him three weeks after I arrived at Oxford, at the house of a young don who had once been a student of one of my college professors in New York. But we didn't speak more than a few words to each other that night. When we met again, Yoav tried to convince me that I'd made an impression on him at the dinner, enough that he had even considered finding a way to see me again. But as I remember it, he looked alternately bored and preoccupied throughout the meal, as if, while one part of him was drinking Bordeaux and cutting his food into bite-sized morsels, the other half was engaged with shepherding a herd of goats across a bone-dry plain. He didn't talk much. All I knew about him was that he was a third-year undergraduate reading English. After dessert, he was the first to leave, explaining that he had to catch a bus back to London, though when he said goodbye to our host and his wife it was clear that, when he wanted to, he could be charming.

The doctoral program was meant to take three years and had few requirements. Aside from meeting with my supervisor every six weeks, I was left to my own devices. The trouble for me began soon after I'd arrived, when the topic I'd planned to work on—the influence of the new medium of radio on Modernist literature—reached a dead end. It had been the subject of the senior thesis I'd written in college back in New York, for which I'd won praise from my professors, and even come away with an award, the Wertheimer Prize, named after a retired professor wheeled to the ceremony from the pastoral graveyard of Westchester. But the don who'd been chosen to look after my academic work at Oxford, a bald Modernist at Christ Church named A. L. Plummer, quickly tore the thesis apart, claiming that it lacked theoretical integrity, and insisted I come up with a new topic. Cramped in a rickety chair between the towers of books in his study, I tried, weakly, to argue the worth of my work, but the truth was that I myself had lost interest in the idea, and that whatever I'd had to say about it had already been said in the hundred or so pages of my undergraduate thesis. Dust motes floated down in the ray of light that fell through a small, high window (a window through which only a dwarf or child could escape), coming to rest on A. L. Plummer's head and, presumably, my own. There was little choice but to go wading into the infinite holdings of the Bodleian Library in search of a new subject.

I spent the following weeks in a chair in the Radcliffe Camera, one of those comfortable upholstered chairs stained by human secretions that can be found in almost every library in the world. It was next to a window overlooking All Souls. Outside, water was suspended in the air like a science experiment—an experiment that had been going on for thousands of years, and constituted the weather in England. Occasionally a figure or pair of figures dressed in black robes crossed through the inner quadrangle of All Souls, giving me the impression that I was watching the rehearsal of a play from which all the words and most of the stage directions had been erased, leaving only the entrances and exits. These empty comings and goings left me feeling vague and uncertain. I read, among other things, the essays of Paul Virilio—the invention of trains also contained the invention of derailment, that is the sort of thing Virilio liked to write about—but never finished the book. I didn't wear a watch, and usually I would leave the library whenever I couldn't stand to be cooped up any longer. On four or five occasions I came out of the library door at exactly the moment that a student passed by wheeling an upright bass along the cobbled street, like someone guiding an overgrown child. Sometimes he had just passed the instant before, and other times he was about to pass. But once I exited the library doors at the exact moment he was passing them, and our eyes locked in one of those looks that sometimes happen between strangers, when both wordlessly agree that reality contains sinkholes whose depths neither can ever hope to fathom.

I was living in a room on Little Clarendon Street, where I spent most of my time when not in the library. I have always been, but was especially then, a shy and overly self-conscious person who had gotten by with having one or two close friends, even a boyfriend, with whom I spent time when not alone. I figured that eventually I'd meet such a person, or people, at Oxford. In the meantime, I stuck to my room.

Aside from a large carpet remnant lugged home on the bus from the northern end of Banbury Road, an electric kettle, and a flea market set of Victorian cups and saucers, there wasn't much in it. I've always liked the feeling of traveling light; there is something in me that wants to feel I could leave wherever I am, at any time, without effort. The idea of being weighed down made me uneasy, as if I lived on the surface of a frozen lake and each new trapping of domestic life—a pot, a chair, a lamp—threatened to be the thing that sent me through the ice. The only exception was books, which I acquired freely, because I never really felt they belonged to me. Because of this, I never felt compelled to finish those I didn't like, or even a pressure to like them at all. But a certain lack of responsibility also left me free to be affected. When at last I came across the right book the feeling was violent: it blew open a hole in me that made life more dangerous because I couldn't control what came through it.

I'd majored in English because I loved to read, not because I had any idea of what I wanted to do with my life. And yet during that fall at Oxford, my relationship to books began to change. It happened slowly, almost without my noticing. As the weeks passed, I had less and less of an idea about what I could spend three years writing a dissertation about, and became overwhelmed by the immensity of the task. Anxiety, vague and subterranean, began to encroach on me whenever I was in the library. At first I hardly realized what it was, only aware of a twinge of uneasiness in the pit of my stomach. But day after day it grew stronger, closing in around my neck, as did my sense of aimlessness and futility. I read without absorbing the meaning of the words. I would flip back and begin again at the last place I remembered reading, but after a while the sentences would dissolve again and I would go back to skidding obliviously across the blank pages, like those insects you find on the surface of stagnant water. I felt more and more unnerved and began to dread going to the library. I became anxious about becoming anxious. Entering the library, I began to panic. The fact that the panic was bound up in reading—the thing that had been at the center of my life for as long as I could remember, and which in the past had formed a bulwark against despair—made it especially difficult. I'd been sad often enough before, but I'd never felt this siege from within, as if my own being had developed an allergy to itself. At night I lay awake feeling that even as I lay still there, on some other level I was becoming further and further unbound.

Unable to work, I spent my days wandering the streets of Oxford, watching movies at the Phoenix Picturehouse, browsing the old print store on the High Street, or wasting time wandering through the skeletons, tools, and little cracked bowls of lost peoples on display at the Pitt Rivers Museum. But I barely noticed the things in front of me. I felt a deadening in my mind and a muteness in my being, as if somewhere a signal box had been shut down. As the weeks passed, I lost all sense of myself. Overnight, it seemed, someone had drained the contents from my physical shell, which was still walking around as if nothing had happened. But emptiness didn't mean apathy: anxiety, loneliness, and despair seemed to lurk around every corner, waiting to sabotage my physical progress down the street. Negotiating this obstacle course, stripped of any sense of purpose, all I longed for was to be home in my childhood bedroom, tucked under the covers with their familiar smell of laundry detergent, listening to my parents murmur down the hall. Walking back to my room one evening after hours of pointless wandering, I stopped in front of a gourmet food store on St. Giles'. As I watched people come out with their bags of marmalades, pâté, chutneys, and loaves of fresh bread, I thought of my parents sitting in their kitchen in slippered feet, their backs rounded as they bent over their dinner, the evening news broadcast from the small television in the corner, and suddenly I began to weep.

I might have packed up and left had I not so dreaded my parents' disappointment. They wouldn't have understood. It was my father who had pushed me to apply, who had gone on at the dinner table about all the doors such a scholarship would open. (My parents' bathroom was mirrored, and if you opened both of their closet doors at the same time and stood in the triangle they made, a sickening infinity of doors and selves hurtled back in every direction: it was this image I thought of whenever my father used that phrase.) He had little interest in whatever it might allow me to study. I think he imagined that after I collected enough academic accolades I would end up raking in a big salary as an investment banker at Goldman Sachs or Mackenzie. But once I'd gotten the scholarship and knew I was going to Oxford, my mother, who hadn't said much on the subject until then, came into my room and with wet eyes told me how happy she was for me. She didn't say that it would have been *her* dream at my age, had such a dream been the least bit plausible. As it was, she had known better than to receive encouragement from her hardscrabble immigrant parents for her own intellectual interests, and I couldn't help thinking that, in marrying my father, my mother had decided to suffocate them in one fell swoop, as one drowns a litter of unwanted kittens. It was terrible to think that she thought there was no other way for her—her parents were religious, and my father, twelve years older than she, was not, and I suppose it was enough for my mother at the time to escape from them. But she was only nineteen when she married in 1967, and had she waited a few years all that was changing around her might have given her more courage. Though in that case I'd have never been born.

I don't pretend to know just how much my mother crushed in herself. As the years passed she couldn't hide her weariness, but she gave little clue about the weather and traffic of her inner life. All I knew was that some intractable part of my mother's curiosity and hunger had never drowned, much as she might once have wished it would.

There was always a small pile of books by her bedside that she turned to once everyone was asleep. It was many years before I even made the connection between my own love of books and my mother's, since, though there had always been books around the house, I rarely saw my mother reading until she was older and had more time. The only exception was the newspaper, which she scoured from front page to last as if she were searching for news of someone lost to her long ago. When I was in college, I'd sometimes come across my mother reading the semester course offerings at the kitchen table, lips moving soundlessly. She never asked me what I planned to take, or in any way intruded on my independence; when I entered the room, she closed the course book and went back to whatever it was she had been doing. But the night before I left for England, my mother gave me the iridescent green Pelikan fountain pen her uncle Saul had given her as a child after she had won an essay competition in school. I'm ashamed to admit that I never wrote a word with it, not even in a letter to my mother, and that I no longer know its whereabouts.

When my parents called on Sunday afternoons I went on elaborately about the wonderful time I was having. For my father, I made up stories about the debates I'd attended at the Oxford Union and anecdotes about the others on the scholarship—future politicians, law students with sharp elbows, a former speechwriter for Boutros Boutros-Ghali. For my mother, I described Duke Humfrey's Library in the Bodleian where you could order up the original manuscripts of T. S. Eliot or Yeats, and the dinner I'd had at A. L. Plummer's invitation (before he'd rejected my thesis) at the Christ Church high table. But things were going worse and worse for me. In the state I was in, it was difficult to go out and meet people. Even to open my mouth to order a sandwich at the Tuck Shop required a desperate scavenge for a few grains of assertiveness. Alone in my room, wrapped in a blanket, I whimpered and talked aloud to myself, recalling the lost glory of my youth when I considered myself, and was considered by others, a bright and capable person. It seemed that was all gone now. I wondered whether what I was experiencing was some sort of psychotic break, the sort that ambushes a person who until then has lived an ordinary life, auguring a new existence full of torment and struggle.

During the first week of November I went to see Tarkovsky's *Mirror* at the Phoenix, which has always been one of my favorite films. I continued to sit there after the lights went up, crying or on the verge of crying. At last I gathered my things and got up, and in the lobby I ran into a bright, loudmouthed, gay political science student named Patrick Clifton who was on the same scholarship as I. Flashing his pointy little teeth, he invited me to a party that night. I don't know why I agreed, since I was hardly in any shape to go. Out of desperation, perhaps, and an instinct for self-preservation. But as soon as I arrived, I regretted it. The party in South Oxford was held in a two-story house whose rooms were bathed in different shades of light, one purple, another green, giving the place a morose feeling, exaggerated by the music which I could only think to describe as Neolithic funereal. People were getting high on the stairs, and in the room where the music was loudest there was a motley collection of swaying bodies that seemed indifferent to one another. In the back was a long galley kitchen with cracked, dirty tiles, and buckets of beer on ice. Twenty minutes after we'd arrived I lost track of Patrick and, not knowing what else to do, went in search of a bathroom. The one I found on the second floor was occupied, so I leaned against the wall to wait. Laughter erupted from inside, belonging to two or even three people. It seemed unlikely that the occupants were going to come out anytime soon, but I continued to stand there. After ten minutes Yoav Weisz materialized in the blue-lit hall. I recognized him immediately, because he looked like no one else. He had thick auburn hair that rose in high waves from his head and fell in a sweep across his forehead, a long and narrow face, very wide-set dark eyes, a steep nose that ended in arched nostrils, and full lips that naturally turned down at the corners, a face that could look beatific in one instant and devilish the next, and seemed to have come down from the Renaissance, or even the Middle Ages, without revision. You, he said, with a lopsided grin.

The bathroom door opened and a couple tumbled out, and at the same time a wave of nausea came over me and I knew I was going to throw up. I dove into the bathroom, lifted the toilet seat, and sank to my knees. When I finished I looked up and to my horror Yoav was standing above me. He offered me some cloudy water from the tap. While I drank it he watched me with concern and even tenderness. I said something about the food from the kebab van I'd eaten earlier. We sat in silence, as if, now that we had it, we were bound to stay in the bathroom for as long as the other couple had. I caught a glimpse of my reflection, dark and a little deformed in the mirror; I wanted to look more closely to see how bad things had become but was embarrassed in front of Yoav. Am I that hideous? he said at last. What? I asked, and gave a little laugh, though it came out more like a snort. If anyone's hideous—I started to say. No, he said, moving a strand of hair away from my eyes, you're beautiful. He said it just like that, with a directness that took my breath away. I'm embarrassed, I said, though I wasn't.

He reached into his pocket, took out a Swiss Army knife, and unfolded the blade. For a split second, I thought he was going to do something violent, not to me but to himself. Instead, he took the bar of soap sitting on the sink, a dirty bar caked with the grime of all the hands that had drifted in and out of that bathroom, and started to whittle. It was such an absurd thing to do that I laughed. After a while he handed me the soap. What is it? I asked. Can't you tell? I shook my head. A boat, he said. It didn't look like a boat, but that was fine with me. It had been a long time since anyone had made something in my honor.

It was then, looking at his strange face, that I knew that a door had opened, but not the kind of door my father had imagined. This one I could walk through, and right away it was clear to me that I would. Another wave of nausea came over me, nausea mixed with happiness and also relief, because I sensed that one chapter of my life had ended and another was about to begin.

Of course there were awkward moments, or moments that seemed to throw things into question. The first time we slept together something strange happened. We were lying on the carpet in Yoav's bedroom on the third floor of the house in Belsize Park. The windows were open, the sky almost black with an approaching storm, everything eerily silent. He took off my shirt and touched my breasts. He had very soft and inquisitive hands. Then he took my pants off. He didn't take off my shoes first, though, he just peeled my underwear down over the top of my pants and kept pulling until he reached my feet, at which point, of course, he got stuck. A struggle ensued, as they say in Russian novels, although thankfully it was a short one. My shoes came loose, and the pants slipped free. Then he took off his own clothes. At last we were naked. But instead of continuing in the vein we'd been going in, Yoav switched course and started to roll. An actual somersault, with me attached to him. Once we'd gone around 360 degrees, he started to roll again. I had gone along with plenty of strange or kinky things during sex, but this was the strangest because there was nothing remotely sexy about it, not for me, and, as far as I could tell, not for him. We were like two people practicing for the circus. You're hurting my neck, I whispered. That was all it took. Yoav let me go. I dropped back to the floor and lay very still for a while, catching my breath and trying to decide whether I wanted things to begin again where we'd left off, or whether I wanted to get my clothes and leave.

I was still undecided when I heard the muffled sound of crying. I sat up. What's the matter? I asked. Nothing, he said. But you're crying. I was just thinking of something, he said. What? I asked.

One day I'll tell you. Tell me now, I started to say, moving closer to him, but didn't get all of the words out, because then his mouth was on mine and I was pulled into a kiss soft and deep, as if he had reached in and performed some brisk emergency surgery with the most deft and delicate touch, causing something to surge and come alive, flooding me with vitality I had been deprived of. That night we had sex three or maybe four times. From then on, we were rarely apart.

When I was with Yoav, everything in me that had been sitting stood up. He had a way of looking at me with a kind of unabashed directness that made me shiver. It's something amazing to feel that for the first time someone is seeing you as you really are, not as they wish you, or you wish yourself, to be. I'd had boyfriends before, and I was familiar with the little mating rituals of getting to know each other, of dragging out the stories from childhood, summer camp, and high school, the famous humiliations, and the adorable things you said as a child, the familial dramas—of drawing a portrait of yourself, all the while making yourself out to be a little brighter, a little more deep than deep down you knew you actually were. And though I hadn't had more than three or four relationships, I already knew that each time the thrill of telling another the story of yourself wore off a little more, each time you threw yourself into it a little less, and grew more distrustful of an intimacy that always, in the end, failed to pass into true understanding.

But with Yoav it was different. He propped himself up on one arm and stared at me as I spoke, absently stroking my arm or leg, and interrupting me to ask questions—Who's she, you never mentioned her before, OK, go on then, what happened next? And he remembered every last detail, and wanted to hear not just the highlights, but everything, not letting me skip over any parts. He clucked his tongue and his face clouded over with anger whenever I narrated a part about some cruelty or betrayal, and grinned with pride whenever I described a triumph. Sometimes the things I told him evoked a quiet, almost tender laugh. He made me feel like the entire story of my life had been lived for his audience alone. And he treated my body with the same attentiveness and wonder. He used to touch and kiss me with such seriousness—studying my face to gauge my reaction—that it made me laugh. Once, as a joke, he took out a notebook and after each caress jotted down a little note, speaking aloud as he wrote: Sucking the earlobe . . . semicolon . . . makes her . . . gasp.Then he would kiss and stroke me again, and take the notebook back up: Licking . . . the right . . . nipple while . . . letting hand . . . rove . . . over her . . . beautiful . . . butt . . . ocks . . . semicolon . . . A faraway . . . smile . . . spreads . . . across her . . . face. Another pause. Then: Putting . . . her toes . . . in mouth . . . semicolon . . . Makes the hair . . . on her arms . . . stand on . . . end and her . . . amazing thighs . . . squeeze together . . . Addendum . . . semicolon . . . A second time . . . makes . . . her . . . squeal . . . exclamation point. And yet the joke didn't end there. One day I got to the library and found the notebook tucked in among my books, and every page had been covered with Yoav's tiny writing.

His attention made me feel so clarified, so bright

and exact, so moved, that I accepted, at least in the beginning, that while there was nothing that I wouldn't tell him, there were things about his family that he seemed unable to talk about with me. He never said so directly; somehow he just always found a way to avoid answering.

I tried to learn him. I studied the beauty marks on his body, the shiny scar like a train track above his left nipple, the misshapen nail of his right thumb, the little field of golden hairs where his spine met the top of his backside. The surprising thinness of his wrists, the smell of his neck. The silver fillings in his mouth, the tiny capillaries at the top of his ears. I loved the way he spoke out of only one side of his mouth, as if the other stiffly refused to go along with what was being said. And I felt a little flood of love for the way he held his spoon while he ate cereal and read the paper, almost crudely, in opposition to the refined way he did everything else. When he read he curled a lock of hair around his finger. He had a fast metabolism. In order to avoid headaches he had to eat often. Because of this—and because, after his mother died, there was only the food the housekeeper prepared, which wasn't the same—he had learned at an early age to cook for himself.

When he slept he threw off a heat that alarmed me until I became used to it and was even drawn to it. Once I read about children who lose their mothers and spend hours huddling near a radiator, and one night, drifting off to sleep, an image came to me of those children huddling against Yoav. It's possible I even dreamed of being such a child myself. But it was Yoav who'd lost his mother, not me. Awake, he was constantly pacing or tapping his foot. He needed to get rid of all of the energy his body produced, but there was something futile about such frenetic activity because as soon as that energy was used up his body would just manufacture more. When I was with him I had the sense that things were constantly in motion, moving toward something, a feeling that after the suffocation of the months before excited me and calmed my nerves at the same time. And if I sensed his sadness, I didn't yet know where it came from or the depth of it. Don't look at me like that, he used to say. Like what? I'd ask. Like I'm in the incurable ward. But I'm such a good nurse. How do I know? he asked. Like this, I said. Silence. Don't stop, he groaned, I only have one more day to live. You said that yesterday. Don't tell me, he said, on top of everything else I have amnesia, too?

It wasn't long before I gave up sleeping in my room on Little Clarendon Street and began to spend almost all of my time in London. You could say that I fled there, to Yoav and to his world at whose center was the house in Belsize Park. From the beginning, Yoav must have sensed in me a desperation, a willingness to match his intensity, to put aside everything in order to throw myself entirely into the only sort of relationship he knew how to have, a kind of cabal in which there was no room for anyone else, or anyone but his sister, whom he thought of as part of himself.

Right away, my mental state began to improve. Improve but not altogether return to its former self: a residual fear hung on, fear of myself above all, and of what all this time had lurked within without my knowledge. It was more as if I'd been anesthetized, not cured, of whatever had ailed me.

Things were not what they once were, and though I no longer worried that things would end for me in Bellevue, and even felt embarrassed to recall my pathetic behavior during the worst of it, I felt that something in me had been permanently altered, wizened, or even impaired. Some sovereignty over myself had been lost, or perhaps it would be better to say that the very idea of a solid self, never particularly sturdy in me to begin with, had fallen to pieces like a cheap toy. Maybe that's what made it easy for me to imagine—not right away, but as time passed—that I was, almost, one of them.

*   *   *

The beginning was different. Everything about the life that went on in the Belsize Park house seemed to me foreign and elusive. Even the most banal things—the closet of expensive dresses Leah never wore, Bogna with her limp who came to clean twice a week, the habit Yoav and Leah had of dropping their coats and bags on the floor when they came in the front door—seemed to me exotic and fascinating. I studied them and tried to understand how things worked. I was aware of a private set of rules and formalities that governed things, but couldn't say what these were. I knew enough not to ask; I was nothing if not a polite and grateful guest. My mother had drilled certain manners into me. At the heart of them was the erasure of one's own leanings wherever another held in high regard was concerned.

Just as the children of a sea captain instinctively understand the sea, Yoav and Leah had a natural sense for furniture, for its origins, age, and worth, and a sensitivity to its peculiar beauty. Not that they made much use of this gift, or were so persuaded to treat such furniture with special care. They simply took note of it, as one might remark on a nice view, and carried on doing whatever they had been doing, exactly as they pleased. I began to learn from their casual observations. Wanting to be more like them, I made a point of asking Yoav questions about the various pieces that came in and out of the house. He answered in a disinterested way, without looking up from whatever it was he was doing. Once I asked him if he ever felt there was anything sad about furniture left behind after the lives it serviced had scattered or disintegrated, all of those objects that had no power of memory themselves, just standing and gathering dust. But he only shrugged and chose not to answer. No matter how much I came to know, I could never master the grace and ease with which Yoav and Leah moved among all of those antiques, nor their strange combination of sensitivity and indifference.

Growing up in New York, I had never gone without, but my family wasn't rich either. As I child I'd always had the feeling that what we did have couldn't be relied on and might crumble from under us at any moment, as if we lived in an adobe house built in the wrong climate. I sometimes overheard my parents discussing whether or not they should sell two Moses Soyer paintings that hung in the hallway. They were moody, foreboding paintings that spooked me in the dark, but the idea of my parents being forced to part with them for money worried me. Had I known that the likes of George Weisz existed he would have haunted my sleep, as would the idea of the family furniture being carted off one piece at a time. In reality, we lived in an apartment in a white brick building on York Avenue that my grandparents had helped my parents to buy, but we always shopped for clothes at discount stores, and I was often scolded for forgetting to turn off the lights because of the price of electricity. Once I overheard my father yelling at my mother that every time she flushed the toilet it was a dollar down the drain. After that, I acquired the habit of letting waste collect in the bowl over the course of the day until it reached a critical mass. When my mother's threats prevented this, I trained myself to hold it for as long as possible. If I had an accident, I bore my humiliation and my mother's anger with thoughts of the money I'd saved my parents. All the same, I could never quite work out the incongruity between the wide, murky East River that ran endlessly outside our window and the preciousness of the water in the toilet.

What furniture we did have was generally of high quality, including some antiques bestowed on us by my grandfather. The surfaces of these were fitted with pieces of glass that rested on clear rubber circles placed at each corner. Even so, I was not to rest my glass on them or play too close. These valuable things produced in us a feeling of intimidation. We knew that no matter how far we got in life, we would never really be meant for such fineness, that the few expensive antiques we did have had fallen to us from a higher life and now condescended to live among us. We were always afraid that we would inflict some damage on them, and so I was raised to move carefully around the furniture, not so much to live with it as to live alongside it, at a respectful distance. When I first began to spend time in Belsize Park it made me queasy to see how carelessly Yoav and Leah treated the furniture that passed through their house, which constituted their father's, and their own, livelihood. They rested their bare feet and glasses of wine on Biedermeier coffee tables, left fingerprints on the vitrines, napped on the settees, ate off the Art Deco commodes, and occasionally even walked atop the long dining tables when it was the most convenient way of getting from one place to another in a room crowded with furniture. The first time Yoav undressed me and bent me over I became stiff and awkward, not because of the position, which I liked perfectly well, but because I was leaning over a writing desk inlaid with mother-of-pearl. But no matter how careless they were, they seemed never to leave behind a mark or trace. At first I took this to be the grace of those brought up to consider such furniture their natural habitat, but once I knew Yoav and Leah better I began to think of their talent, if one can call it that, as something borrowed from ghosts.

* * *

The house gave away its secrets more easily, and I got to know it well. It was four floors altogether. Leah lived at the top. She slept in the back room, in a canopy bed, and in the front one she kept an upright Steinway under a stained-glass skylight; at certain hours of the afternoon the ivory keys became streaked with color. Before I met Leah, I'd been intimidated by the idea of the place she held in Yoav's life. He referred to her often in conversation, sometimes as *my sister* and sometimes just as *she*, and frequently he spoke of the two of them collectively. When her playing stopped, I was sure that she was watching from somewhere in the house, and the hair on my arms would rise. But when Leah finally appeared for the first time I was surprised at how slight and unassuming she was, as if all her being were reserved for the life inside. She seemed held together by some great pressure exerted from within. She kept a second piano, a baby grand, in a study on the ground floor. Sheet music was stacked everywhere. These pages migrated through the house, turning up in the kitchen and bathrooms. She spent a week or two memorizing a piece, breaking it down into smaller and smaller parts, playing these mechanically with an absent look on her face. She wore an old cotton kimono and rarely got dressed. A kind of grubbiness overtook her, the piano keys became smudged and even her fingernails collected dirt. Then the day would arrive when she'd swallowed the piece whole, consumed it and made it part of herself, and she would run around clearing everything up, wash her hair, and then sit down to play the piece from memory. She would play it a hundred different ways, very fast, or very slow, and with each note she would be one step closer to a kind of uncertain clarity. Everything about her was delicate and compact, full of grace, and yet when she laid her hands on the keys something enormous seethed in her. Years later, after I got Leah's letter and went to Yoav in the house on Ha'Oren Street, in an enormous, vaulted room, hanging from the ceiling in place of a chandelier, I found her grand piano rigged up via ropes and pulleys. There was a terrible violence in it. It seemed to sway infinitesimally, though there was no breeze on that stifling day. Leah would have needed a ladder to play it. How she had hauled the piano up there was a mystery. Later, Yoav claimed he hadn't helped her; one day he had gone out and when he came back it was there. When I asked why she would have done such a thing, he replied obscurely about the pureness of a note sounded in the air that rings, for a split second, without influence. But as far as I knew, Leah had stopped playing altogether after their father killed himself. Even when I was at the other end of the house I was aware of the piano hanging eerily, at times forlorn and others menacing, and I had the feeling that when it finally fell—it was just a matter of time until the ropes gave way—it would pull the whole house down with it.

Yoav's bedroom in the Belsize Park house was directly below Leah's. In general, what minimal furniture there was on both their floors was permanent, either because it was too much of an effort for things to be constantly carried up and down, or because it was a relief for them to dwell in some place that was, at least in this one regard, outside their father's influence. There was a large mattress on the floor of Yoav's room, a wall of books, and little else.

The kitchen was down a flight of stairs on the garden level. From there you could look out on the back garden. A door at the end of a short corridor took one out into it. To open it required destroying the complicated work of the spiders that lived there; as soon as you closed it again they were back at it. Bogna, who belonged to the Orthodox Church, cared too much for the sanctity of life to kill them. The garden was wild and overgrown, full of brambles. When I saw it for the first time it was November and the whole of it was dying back. At some point the garden must have been planted and cared for, but left to its own devices, the steady tenacity and stubbornness of vegetable life unchecked, only the coarser plants had survived, grown thick and tangled. The walkway had collapsed. The rhododendrons and laurel grew up in a great, dark wall against the sunlight. There was a card table on the grass. Candle wax had collected in places on the surface, and an ashtray from the Excelsior in Rome was filled with dirty water. Later, once the weather got warm, we started to use it again, sitting out with a bottle of wine. The state of the garden suited Yoav and Leah. They had a taste and respect for the private lives of things let be; they held these things in distant, high regard. Scattered throughout the house were objects abandoned, dropped, or left where they had last been put down. Sometimes these tableaux were left to sit for weeks before Bogna finally cleared them away, returning things to their proper place if they had one or throwing them out in the trash. She seemed to understand Yoav and Leah's taste and habits even when they stood in opposition to her own. She pretended at exasperation, making much of her heavy sighing and adding extra weight to the bad leg, yet it was obvious she felt sorry for them. But in the end Bogna had her job to do. It was Weisz who paid her, and to whom she had to answer if the place wasn't clean when at last he appeared.

*   *   *

Before their father arrived, I always took the bus back to Oxford. Though his work demanded a certain charm and sociability, he was a withdrawn and private person, surrounded by a kind of moat. The sort of person who creates the illusion of intimacy by drawing you out, asking you about yourself and remembering the names of your children, if you have any, or the kind of drink you like, but who, you realize later, if you realized it at all, managed not to share much about himself. When it came to his family, he didn't like the presence of outsiders. I don't remember exactly how this was explained to me—it was never said outright—but I knew it was verboten to be there when their father was. After his visits, Yoav often seemed remote and listless, and Leah disappeared for long, punishing hours of practice. As time passed and my relationship with Yoav grew more serious, my place in the Belsize Park house more entrenched, I began to become hurt and annoyed at having to remove myself like some inappropriate or unsightly guest whenever their father arrived. The feeling was made worse by the fact the Yoav refused to explain why, or to talk about it much at all. He only insinuated that there were certain unspoken rules and expectations that simply couldn't be broken. All that remained explicit was that I couldn't be present when his father was. It aggravated an insecurity in me that always lurked below our relationship: the sense that some large share of Yoav would always be held back from me, some life he lived never mine to live beside him.

*　　*　　*

By January, I was spending almost every day at the British Library. It was dark when I set out up Haverstock Hill for the Tube, and dark when I came out of the library onto Euston Road in the afternoon. I still hadn't come up with a new topic for a dissertation. I spent the days reading aimlessly, not absorbing much, still nervous about a relapse of panic. I called A. L. Plummer, for whom I seemed to hold less and less interest, and reported on the direction I thought I was taking. Carry on then, he said, and an image came to me of him perched on one of his stacks of books, bald head tucked into his robe like a sleeping vulture's. Some days I set out intending to go to the library, but when I reached the Tube station something in me couldn't steel myself for the long descent in the elevator with the other rush-hour travelers to the cavernous depths of the Northern Line, and so I would continue on my way, buying breakfast at one of the small shops on the High Street, and passing time browsing in Waterstone's or the narrow aisles of the secondhand bookshop on Flask Walk until quarter after eleven, when I would begin to make my way down Fitzjohns Avenue. The Freud Museum opened at noon. I was often the only person there, and the docents and the woman who ran the museum shop always seemed glad to see me, and would withdraw from whatever room I was in so that I would be left alone to linger in peace.

Afternoons in Belsize Park, Yoav and I, and

often Leah, would go to the movies, sometimes seeing two back-to-back, or sitting for the same movie twice. Or we would walk on the Heath. Every once in a while we would go on some expedition—to the National Gallery, or Richmond Park, or to see a play at the Almeida. But we spent most of our time in the house, which drew us back with a force I can't quite explain except to say that it was our world, and we were happy there. At night we either watched rented movies, or read while Leah practiced, and often, once it got late enough, we would open a bottle of wine and Yoav would read aloud to me from Bialik, Amichai, Kaniuk, Alterman. I loved listening to him read in Hebrew, to hear him exist so vividly in his native language. And maybe because in those moments, I was relieved of the effort of struggling to understand him.

I, at least, was happy there. One morning as I was getting dressed in the dark, Yoav reached out from under the covers and pulled me back. You, he said. I lay down next to him and stroked his face. Let's run away, he said. To where? I asked. I don't know. Istanbul? Caracas? And what will we do? Yoav closed his eyes and thought. We'll have a juice stand. A what? Juice, he said. We'll sell fresh juice. Whatever people want. Papaya, mango, coconut. I knew he was joking, but there was a pleading look in his eyes. They have coconuts in Istanbul? I asked. We'll import them, he said. It'll be a huge craze. People will line up down the street. The whole city will go crazy for our coconut juice, I said. Yes, he said, and in the afternoon, after we've sold all the coconut juice we feel like selling, we'll go back to our place, all sticky and happy, and we'll make love for hours, and then we'll get all dressed up, you in a white dress and me in a white suit, and we'll go out, all glowing, and ride all night up and down the Bosporus in a glass-bottom boat. What can you see at the bottom of the Bosporus? I asked. Suicides, poets, houses swept away by storms, he said. I don't want to see any suicides, I said. All right, so then come with me to Brussels. Why Brussels? Orders from above, he said. What? I asked. El Jefe, he said. Your father? That's the one. Seriously? I asked. Have you ever known me not to be serious? he said, pulling down my underwear and disappearing below the covers.

From time to time their father asked Yoav or Leah to assist him with some small aspect of his work—to show a client a piece, to travel somewhere to pick up something he'd acquired, or to attend an auction on his behalf. It was the first time Yoav had asked me to accompany him, and I took it as a sign that something important had changed between us. For the first time I was being trusted to take part in some private aspect of the family's affairs. We took the car, a black 1974 Citroën DS. Turning the ignition, you had to wait a moment while the hydraulic pump kicked in and lifted the back part of the car off the wheels. The front seat was one long bench, and I sat close to Yoav as he drove. The car slid onto the motorway, and we talked about places we both wanted to go (I to Japan, he to see the Northern Lights), about Hungarian versus Finnish, genius at midnight, the relief of failure, Joseph Brodsky, cemeteries (my favorite was San Michele, his Weissensee), the house of Yehuda Amichai in Yemin Moshe. Yoav told me about how when he was a child his mother used to point out Amichai on the bus or walking down the street carrying his plastic baskets full of food from the shuk. Look at him, she used to say, a man like any other, coming home laden with groceries. And yet, in his soul all the dreams, the sadness and joy, love and regret, all the bitter loss of the people he passes on the street fight for a place in his words. And then we were there, together, in the Jerusalem of his childhood. He told me about the house on Ha'Oren Street, which smelled of musty paper, damp cisterns, and spice, and how his mother had fallen in love with it the first time she visited Ein Karem years before, and how the first thing his father did when he began to make money was pay a visit to the owner of the house to ask his price. One day he asked his wife if she wanted to go for a walk, and slowly, taking a meandering route, they arrived at the house on Ha'Oren Street as if by accident, and he took the key out of his pocket and opened the gate, and she, bewildered, hung back, the way one always hangs back, a little frightened, when a dream suddenly transforms into reality.

Looking back, I don't think that I was ever happier during my time in England than on that drive, nestled against Yoav, who talked as he drove. Though soon enough we reached Folkestone, drove the car onto the train, and left England behind. The radio didn't work in the tunnel and the car didn't have a CD player or tape deck, but we kissed in the silence under the Channel until we surfaced again in Calais. We drove past signs for the battlefields of Ypres and Passendale, but headed east toward Ghent. Outside of Brussels it became foggy, and as we sped along a canal the crows scattered and then disappeared altogether as the dilapidated outskirts of the city reared up. We got lost in a maze of one-way streets and roundabouts and avenues without signs, or confusing signs, and had to stop to ask an African taxi driver for directions. He laughed at us as we drove away, as if he knew something about where we were headed that we didn't. We drove south through the expensive streets of Uccle, and soon we were on tree-lined roads in the countryside again, those wonderful tree-lined roads planted with a ruler and a whip that you can only find in a place as anal about beauty as Europe. As we drove we talked about the future as we rarely did, though not directly since it was impossible to talk to Yoav directly about anything to do with our relationship, whereas indirectly he could talk about the most raw and intimate things, the most dangerous things, the most painful and inconsolable but also the most hopeful. As for what, exactly, was said about the future, all I can say is that, speaking as indirectly as we were, transferred between us was only a feeling, or a shift in feeling, something like the sense of solid ground underfoot after walking for days or even months on spongy bog, a shift that I would be hard pressed, both then and now, but especially now, all these years later, to put into words.

It was late in the afternoon by the time we drove up to a pair of rusted wrought-iron gates. Yoav rolled down the window and pressed the buzzer. A minute or more passed before anyone answered, and just when he was about to buzz again the gates came to life and began to swing slowly open. We drove up the drive, gravel crunching under the

Citroën's wheels. Who lives here? I asked, trying to sound unimpressed by the stone castle with slate turrets coming into view behind the huge ancient oaks, because the last thing I wanted to do was make Yoav regret having brought me. Mr. Leclercq, he said, which only added to the absurdity of the situation, since I'd never heard of any Leclercq, nor had any idea who he might be.

I assumed that anyone wealthy enough to live in such a place would be attended around the clock by butlers and maids, by a staff of uniformed people that provided a buffer between himself and any possibility of physical exertion, no matter how slight. But when we rang the bell and the enormous, brass-studded door creaked open, it was Leclercq himself who stood there, in checkered shirt and sweater vest, dwarfed by the double marble staircase behind him. An enormous leaded-glass light fixture hung from a brass chain above him, swaying slightly in a gust of wind. Otherwise, the interior was dark and still. Leclercq extended his hand to each of us, though for a second or fraction of a second I was paralyzed to respond, struggling as I was to recall who, exactly, our host reminded me of, and only once my hand was clenched tightly by his, and a chill began to spread down the back of my neck, did I realize it was Heinrich Himmler. Of course the face had aged, but the tiny pointy chin, the thin lips, the round wire-frame glasses and, beginning just above their rims, that enormous flat expanse of forehead, an unbroken plane that went on far higher than proportion should have allowed, topped with the comically small, almost shrunken mound of hair—all of it was unmistakable. When he welcomed us with an anemic smile, his teeth were small and yellow.

I tried to catch Yoav's eyes, but as far as I could tell he was oblivious to the resemblance and followed Leclercq blithely into the house. He led us down a long polished corridor, his feet, scaly, swollen, and laced with bulging veins, stuffed into a pair of red velvet slippers. We passed an enormous mirror of mottled glass in a gilded frame, and for a moment our party doubled in size, making the silence more eerie. Perhaps Leclercq felt it too, because he turned to Yoav and began to speak to him in French—about our journey, as far as I could tell, and the large and venerable oaks on the property, planted before the French Revolution. I calculated that even if Himmler's suicide in the Lüneburg prison had been a hoax, the famous photograph of the corpse laid out on the floor a theatrical trick, by then he would have been ninety-eight, and the spry man we followed couldn't have been much more than seventy. But who was to say this wasn't some relative, like those of Hitler's prospering in the leafy suburbs of Long Island, a nephew or lone surviving cousin of the overseer of the extermination camps, the Einsatzgruppen, and the execution of millions? He stopped in front of a closed door, removed from his pocket a ring of heavy keys, and finding the right one, let us into a large paneled hall with a view of the gardens stretching out in all directions. I looked out, and when I turned back again Leclercq was gazing at me with an interest that unnerved me, though perhaps it was only appreciation for a little company at last. Motioning for us to sit, he disappeared to bring some tea. Apparently, he was alone in that vast place.

When I asked if he'd noticed that our host was a dead ringer for Himmler, Yoav laughed, and when he saw that I couldn't have been more serious, he said he hadn't noticed, and when I pressed him on it he admitted that, yes, perhaps there was some minor, a very minor likeness if you squinted at the old man in a certain light. But Leclercq, he assured me, descended from one of the oldest noble families in Belgium, able to trace its ancestry back to Charlemagne; his mother's father had been a viscount, and for a short time had served Leopold II as director of a rubber plantation in the Congo. The family had lost most of its fortune during the War. What remained went to their enormous property taxes, until in the end they were forced to sell off all of their estates, keeping only Cloudenberg, the beloved family home. Leclercq was the last of his siblings alive, and, as far as Yoav knew, he'd never married.

A likely story, I almost said, but at that moment a tremendous crash came from down the hall, followed by the banging or rolling of tins or pots. We followed the noise down the corridor and eventually found the large kitchen behind the dining room where Leclercq was on his hands and knees among metal bowls of various sizes that had tumbled from the cabinet above. For a moment I thought he was crying, but it turned out that he'd lost his glasses and couldn't see. We got down on the floor to help him, the three of us crawling around together. I found the glasses under a chair. One of the lenses was cracked, and Leclercq tried pathetically to reshape the wire earpiece. On the counter was a box of vanilla wafers on a tray, and when Leclercq slipped the cracked glasses back onto his face, I had to admit that his likeness to Himmler, so striking before, faltered and grew dim, and that the association I'd made was probably born of my limited knowledge about the nature of Weisz's business.

Maybe it was because he saw the world differently now, but after Leclercq's glasses broke a kind of sadness seeped out of him, trailing behind him as we followed him down the long hallways and the winding garden paths, past sheared hedges, through the boxwood maze, and up and down (mostly up) the stairs of that great stony castle, blooming into the atmosphere the way water around a harpooned seal fills with a cloud of blood. He seemed to have forgotten why we'd come—he never mentioned the table, or maybe it was a chest of drawers, or a clock, or chair, that was the reason for our trip, and Yoav was too polite to bring it up. Instead, Leclercq got lost down the long alleys, the turns and switchbacks of his own voice as it unraveled the long history of Cloudenberg that began as far back as the twelfth century. The original castle went up in a fire that began in the kitchen and raged through the great banquet hall and up the stairs, consuming tapestries, paintings, hunting trophies, and the owner's youngest son, trapped on the third floor with his milk nurse, sparing only the Gothic chapel that sat, some distance off, on a hill. At times Leclercq's voice became almost a whisper, and I could barely make out what he was saying. I thought then that if we had crept away, retraced our steps, and disappeared back down the long drive in the Citroën, Leclercq might not have noticed, so lost was he in the long, tangled affairs, the secrets, triumphs, and disappointments of Cloudenberg, and at those moments he seemed to me, with his crazily cracked glasses, his dry and swollen feet, his steep and treacherous forehead, like a nun, if that's possible, a nun who had wed herself, body and soul, not to God but to the austere stones of Cloudenberg.

By the time the tour (if one can call it that) ended it was night. The three of us sat around the scarred wooden table in the kitchen where the cooks had once chopped shoulders and loins for the enormous banquets thrown by the viscount. Leclercq looked pale and exhausted and almost vacant, as if the Leclercq inside Leclercq had gotten up and wandered off into the fiery sunset of the twelfth, thirteenth, or fourteenth century. Forgive me, he said, you must be starving by now, and got up to look in the refrigerator, a piece of gadgetry that looked out of place amid so much history. He seemed to have acquired a limp; either that or I hadn't noticed it before, doubtful as that was considering I'd been following him around all afternoon. Possibly it was one of those limps that becomes exaggerated with fatigue or certain kinds of weather. Let me help, I said, and he gave me a look of gratitude. Isabel is a wonderful cook, Yoav said. She can make a banquet out of nothing.

Leclercq went off and came back with a bottle of wine. I prepared a quiche, and while it was in the oven I set the table. Afterwards, I realized I'd put the fork and knife on the wrong sides, and when at last it came time to eat Leclercq froze, as if he'd been presented with a conundrum, one he had no hope of being able to solve, but then, summoning all the grace of his nobility, he delicately crossed his wrists over his plate and took up the utensils in the proper hands. As soon as he ate the first forkful an audible sigh escaped his lips, the uneasiness passed, and after that, as he consumed the food and wine, he seemed a little more himself again.

After dinner, Leclercq showed us to our room. If a conversation had been had about our staying the night, I'd missed it. And yet it was past ten o'clock by the time we'd finished the meal and the subject of the item we'd come for, whatever it was, had yet to be raised. We'd packed overnight bags, having planned to stop at a cozy inn on the way home. Yoav went out to get them from the car, leaving me alone with Leclercq who busied himself with the bed linens, muttering something about the housekeeper who had her day off.

Yoav and I brushed our teeth side by side in the enormous bathroom attached to our room, with a bathtub large enough for a horse. In bed, we began to kiss. Iz, what am I going to do with you? he whispered into my hair. I fit my body into his. But instead of making love as we did almost every night, Yoav started to talk in a whisper, his face pressed to my ear. He told me more stories about his childhood in Jerusalem, things he had never told me before, as if, away from the house in Belsize Park, he could speak more freely. He told me about his mother, who had been an actress until she became pregnant with him. After he was born she never went back to work, but sometimes, looking at a photograph of her from those days, he saw in her expression intimations of the things she might have told him. Before she died, he explained, his mother was a kind of buffer between their father and them. Coming through her, his commandments were softened, and she always found ways to make the things he required of them easier.

Hours later I woke up drenched in sweat. I got up to drink from the faucet and realized that I was wide awake and, as often happens to me when I wake at night, I wouldn't be able to get back to sleep. Not wanting to disturb Yoav by turning on the light to read, I found my book—something by Thomas Bernhard, I can't remember what—and crept out of the room. I made my way down the hall under the dull gaze of six or seven mounted stag heads. At the top of the stairs was a small painting by Brueghel that Leclercq had pointed out earlier. It was one of those winter scenes of gray ice, white snow, and blackened trees all overrun with a stampede of human life, so exquisitely small and yet not one life overlooked, each measured and considered: tiny scenes of merriment and despair, equally ominous and comic when seen at such a distance through the master's telescopic eyes. I stepped closer to study it. In one corner a man was pissing on the wall of a house, while in the window above a coarse, dough-faced woman prepared to empty a pot of water on his head. Some ways off, a man with a hat had fallen through the ice while around him the oblivious skaters continued to enjoy themselves—only one small boy had noticed the accident, and was trying to offer the drowning man the end of his stick. There the scene was frozen: the young boy leaning, the stick offered but not yet taken, the whole scene suddenly tilted toward that dark hole that waited to swallow it.

In the kitchen, I fumbled for the lights. When at last I found them I almost had a heart attack because there, kneeling on a chair at the wooden table scarred with cleaver marks, was a little boy with white hair gnawing on a leg of chicken. Who are you? I asked, or shouted, though the question was largely rhetorical since in that startled instant I was sure he was none other than the elfin boy I'd just studied in the Brueghel, come in to help himself to dinner. The boy, who couldn't have been more than eight or nine, drew the back of his hand across his greasy face in a leisurely manner. He was wearing Spider-Man pajamas, and on his feet he had on a pair of ratty slippers. Gigi, he said. It seemed an unusual name for a boy. No further explanation appeared to be forthcoming, because Gigi hopped down off his chair, dropped the bone in the garbage, and disappeared into the pantry. When he came out a moment later, he had his hand in a box of cookies up to the elbow. He pulled a cookie out and offered it to me. I shook my head, and Gigi shrugged and bit into it himself, chewing thoughtfully. His hair was tangled and knotty in the back, as if someone had neglected to comb it for weeks. Tu as soif? he asked. What? I said. He pretended to gulp from an imaginary glass. Oh, I said, No. And then, absurdly: Does Mr. Leclercq know that you're here? His brow furrowed. Eh? he said. Mr. Leclercq? He knows you are here? Tonton Claude? he asked. I tried to understand. Mon oncle? he said. He's your *uncle*? It hardly seemed possible. Gigi took another bite from his cookie and pushed a strand of pale hair out of his eyes.

Gigi led the way up the stairs, still nibbling at his cookie, such a weightless, nimble child, or maybe he just seemed so against the dark, oppressive architecture of Cloudenberg. When we reached the landing, I glanced at the Brueghel to see if the boy was gone, the man with the hat drowned. But the figures were too small to make out from where I stood, and Gigi was already hurrying ahead, turning the corner. Finishing the last bite of cookie, he brushed the crumbs onto his nubby pajama pants, took a small Matchbox car out of his pocket, and ran it along the wall. Then he slipped the car back into his pocket and took my hand in his. We walked down one long corridor after another, ducked through doors and up stairs, and as we walked, Gigi sometimes leaping, ambling, and scurrying ahead, sometimes doubling back to take up my hand again, I felt myself losing my bearings, a feeling that was not at all unpleasant. The surroundings became more and more stripped of ornament, until at last we were climbing a narrow set of wooden stairs that wound higher and higher, and I realized that we were inside one of the castle's turrets. At the top was a small room with four narrow windows, one facing each direction. The glass of one was cracked and the wind came through. Gigi switched on a lamp whose shade was covered in stickers of animals and rainbows, some of which someone had, in a moment of boredom perhaps, attempted to scratch off. On the floor were blankets, a pillow with a faded floral case, and some shabby stuffed animals piled together to form a kind of disheveled nest. There was also half a loaf of stale bread and an uncapped jar of jam. I had the feeling we'd arrived at one of those animal burrows one finds in children's books, filled with homey furniture, with all of the trappings of human life on a miniature scale, only instead of descending down under the earth we had ascended into the sky, and, instead of warmth and comfort, the boy's feral hideaway reeked of isolation and loneliness. Gigi went to one of the windows, looked out, and shivered, and as he did I had a vision of our turret from the outside, a shining glass cabin containing two experiments in human life floating in a dark sea. There were three or four metal soldiers with chipped paint frozen in battle on the sill. I wanted to put my arm around the boy, to tell him that everything would be all right in the end, not perfect, not even happy perhaps, but enough. But I didn't move to touch or console him, and didn't speak for fear that I might startle him, and because I lacked the proper words in French. Taped to one wall was a photograph of a woman with wild hair and a scarf thrown around her neck. Gigi turned and saw me looking at it. He came over, took the photo down off the wall, and placed it under the pillow. Then he slipped under the pile of blankets, curled into a ball, and fell asleep.

I slept, too. When I woke for the second time during that long night Gigi was snuggled against me like a cat and the sky was turning pale. Not wanting to leave him alone, I lifted him into my arms as gently as I could. Having never had siblings, he was, as far as I can remember, the first child I ever lifted and carried, and I was surprised by his lightness. Years later, carrying my own son, mine and Yoav's, I would sometimes think of Gigi. Stirring, he muttered something incomprehensible, sighed, and resumed sleeping on my shoulder. I walked down the stairs with him, his body limp and legs dangling, back through doors and down corridors, and by some trick or accidental shortcut I emerged at last through a low door that led into a short corridor, which itself spilled into another corridor that finally deposited me in the large foyer where Leclercq had first greeted us under the enormous glass light fixture, just barely swaying above his head like the sword of Damocles, or so I thought then, unnerved as I was by the castle at night, which I only had the courage to navigate because Gigi continued to exhale his warm and gentle breath in my ear. I retraced the steps Yoav, Leclercq, and I had taken the day before. Passing the large mirror again, I half expected to find the boy exposed as a ghost, void of reflection, but, no—there, in what little light there was, I could make out the outlines of our two figures. When I came to the door, or what I thought was the door Leclercq had unlocked for us in order to show us the view of the garden, I shifted Gigi's weight into one arm and tried the handle. It gave way easily. Leclercq must have forgotten to lock it behind us, I thought, and stepped into the room, intending just to glance for a moment at the view of the garden in the gray light of dawn, a light I've always loved for the threadbare fragility it brings out in all things. But the room I now stood in was dark and had no view, or the view had been cut off by heavy drapes, and though it was possible that Leclercq had returned to draw them before going to sleep, it seemed unlikely. As the seconds passed, I began to sense that the room was far larger than the one I had previously been in, more like a hall than a room, and I became aware of some sort of mute presence in the shadows, shadows, I soon was able to make out, that were crowded with shapes of various sizes assembled in long rows, a great, melancholy mass that seemed to extend in all directions before dissolving into the far corners of the vaulted hall. Although I could see very little, I sensed what the shapes were. I was suddenly reminded of a photograph I'd come across some years earlier while researching the work of Emanuel Ringelblum for one of my college history courses, an image of a large group of Jews in Umschlagplatz, adjacent to the Warsaw Ghetto, all of them crouching or sitting on shapeless bags or on the ground, awaiting deportation to Treblinka. The photo had struck me at the time, not just because of the sea of eyes all turned toward the camera suggesting that the scene was subdued enough that the photographer could make himself heard, but because of the thoughtful composition which the photographer had clearly taken pains over, taking note of the way the pale faces topped with dark hats and scarves were mirrored by the seemingly infinite pattern of light and dark bricks of the wall behind them that trapped them in. Behind that wall was a rectangular building with rows of square windows. The whole gave the sense of a geometric order so powerful that it became inevitable, where each common material—Jews, bricks, and windows—had its proper and irrevocable place. As my eyes now adjusted and I began to see, rather than just vaguely feel with some unnameable sense, the tables, chairs, bureaus, trunks, lamps, and desks all standing at attention in the hall as if waiting for a summons, I remembered why that photograph of the Jews in Umschlagplatz had come back to me at exactly that moment, remembered, in other words, that it had been during that same period of research that I'd also come across photographs of various synagogues and Jewish warehouses that had been used as depots for the furniture and household items the Gestapo looted from the homes of deported or murdered Jews, photographs showing vast armies of upended chairs, like a dining hall closed for the night, towers of folded linens, and shelves of sorted silver spoons, knives, and forks.

I don't know how long I stood there, at the edge of that field of unemployed furniture. By then Gigi had grown heavy in my arms. I closed the door behind me, and found my way back to our room. Yoav was still asleep. I lay Gigi down next to him on the bed and watched them, two motherless boys, asleep side by side. Something creaked and strained in the low depths of my stomach. I was aware that it had been left to me to watch over them, and, while the sky slowly lightened, I did. Remembering it now, I can't help but feel that the soul of the child Yoav and I would have together, little David's soul, at that moment crossed quietly, unnoticed, through the room. My eyes became heavy, then closed altogether. When I woke the bed was empty, and the shower was on in the bathroom. Yoav emerged in a cloud of steam, freshly shaven. There was no sign of Gigi, and when Yoav made no mention of him, neither did I.

Breakfast was served in the smaller of the two dining rooms, at a table still large enough to seat sixteen or twenty. At some point in the night or early morning, Kathelijn, the maid, had returned. Leclercq sat down at the head of the table, dressed in the same sweater vest he'd worn the day before, though now he wore a gray sports jacket on top. I searched his face for some evidence of cruelty, but found only the dilapidated features of an old man. In the daylight, all I had imagined about the hall of furniture seemed absurd. The obvious conclusion was that it had been collected from the many estates the Leclercq family had owned before they went bankrupt and were forced to sell them, or simply that it had been moved to that room from the unused parts of the castle.

There was no sign of Gigi. The maid appeared at various stages of the breakfast, but always retreated quickly to the kitchen. I thought she looked at me with a touch of displeasure, but couldn't be sure. Toward the end of the meal our host turned to me. I understand you met my grandnephew, he said. Confusion clouded Yoav's face. Leclercq continued: I hope he didn't disturb you. He often gets hungry at night. Normally Kathelijn leaves a snack by his bed. I must have forgotten. Who do you mean? Yoav asked, turning from me to Leclercq and back again. My niece's son, said Leclercq, buttering a piece of toast. Is he visiting? Yoav asked. He's lived here with us since last year, Leclercq said. I'm very fond of him. It's quite a change to have a child running around the place. What about his mother? I interrupted. There was an uncomfortable pause. The muscles in Leclercq's face strained as he stirred his coffee with a small silver spoon. She doesn't exist for us, he said.

It was clear that nothing more would be said on

the subject, and after an awkward silence Leclercq apologized for having to hurry off, explaining that he planned to leave for town soon to have his glasses fixed. Then he stood abruptly and asked Yoav to follow him so at last they could discuss whatever it was we had come so far for. I was left alone. I got up and peeked into the kitchen, hoping to catch sight of Gigi. It saddened me to think I wouldn't see him again. There was a tray laid with a child's cup and bowl, but the kitchen was empty.

We loaded our bags into the trunk of the Citroën. A large cardboard box lay across the backseat. Leclercq came out to see us off. It was a cloudless winter day, everything bright and sharpened against the sky. I looked up at the turrets of the castle, hoping to see a movement, or even the boy's face, but the windows were white and blind in the sunlight. Come again, Leclercq said, though of course we never would. He opened the passenger door for me, and when he closed it again it was with unnecessary force and the windows of the old car rattled. As we drove away, I twisted around in my seat to wave at our host. He remained motionless, demented and sad in his broken glasses, the great hull of Cloudenberg rising up behind him, taller and taller by some trick of perspective, as if a sunken ship were rising back up out of the depths of the sea, until the driveway turned a corner and I lost sight of him through the trees.

On the drive home, Yoav and I were both quiet, huddled in our own thoughts. It was only as we left the depressed outskirts of Brussels behind and once again were on the open motorway that I asked what it was his father had sent him for. He glanced at the rearview mirror and let a car overtake us. A chess table, he said. We must have spoken of other things then, but what they were I no longer remember.

* * *

In the months that followed, Yoav, Leah, I, and even Bogna, who had not yet left, began to settle into a familiar routine. Leah was absorbed in learning pieces by Bolcom and Debussy for her first recital at the Purcell Room, I was doing my time at the library, Yoav began to study for his exams in earnest, and Bogna came and went, returning everything to its proper place. On the weekends, we rented a pile of movies. We ate when we felt like it, and slept when we felt like it. I was happy there. Sometimes, waking early before the others, wandering the rooms wrapped in a blanket or drinking my tea in the empty kitchen, I had that most rare of feelings, the sense that the world, so consistently overwhelming and incomprehensible, in fact has an order, oblique as it may seem, and I a place within it.

Then one rainy evening in early March the telephone rang. Sometimes it seemed that Yoav and Leah knew when it was their father even before lifting the receiver: a glance, quick and deft, flew between them. It was Weisz calling from the train station in Paris to say he would be arriving that night. Immediately a tense mood swept through the house, and Yoav and Leah became restless and agitated, coming and going in and out of rooms and up the stairs. If we leave for Marble Arch now you could be back in Oxford by half past nine, he said. I became furious. We argued. I accused him of being embarrassed of me and wanting to hide me from his father. In my own mind, I became again the daughter of those who covered the fine sofa with a plastic slipcover only removed for guests. The daughter of those who aspired to a higher life while never believing they were worthy of it, who bowed to an idea of all that hung above them, out of reach—not only materially, but spiritually, that part of the spirit that tends to satisfaction if not happiness—while diligently tending their disappointment. And if I became those things in my mind, Yoav, too, became something he wasn't: a person born into an elevated life, who, as much as he loved me, could only ever play host to me there. Looking back, I see how much I misunderstood, and it pains me to think of how blind I was to Yoav's pain.

We fought, though what we said, exactly, I can't now say, since in our arguments what began as something direct always, deflected by Yoav, became indirect. It only ever occurred to me afterwards: he had talked about something, reasoned with me about something, defended himself against something without ever really addressing or even naming the thing at all. But this time I dug my heels in and carried on. In the end, exhausted, or at a loss for further strategies, he grabbed my wrists, forced me down onto the sofa, and began to kiss me hard enough to silence me. Sometime later we heard the front door open and then Leah's footsteps on the stairs. I pulled up my jeans and buttoned my shirt. Yoav said nothing, but even then the pained look on his face filled me with guilt.

Weisz stood in the tiled entryway in polished shoes holding a walking stick with a silver handle, the shoulders of his wool overcoat shiny with rain. He was a diminutive man, smaller and older than I'd imagined, scaled back in all dimensions as if occupying space at all were a compromise he'd accepted but refused to embrace. It was hard to believe that this was the man who wielded such authority over Yoav and Leah. But when he turned his face in my direction his eyes were live, cold, and piercing. He spoke his son's name, but his gaze didn't leave me. Yoav hurried down a few steps ahead of me, as if to intercept any conclusion his father might draw, or preempt it by a few quick strokes in a private language. Weisz took Yoav's face in his hands and kissed his cheeks. The emotion in it struck me; I'd never seen my own father kiss a man, even his own brother. Weisz spoke quietly to Yoav in Hebrew, turning back to glance at me—something to the effect of having intruded on something, I assumed, because Yoav hurried to deny it, shaking his head. As if to atone for this grievous misunderstanding, he helped his father off with his coat and took him gently by the arm to guide him further into the house. During all of this, Leah stood off to the side, as if to make clear that this little unfortunate incident, this mistake standing awkwardly in untucked shirt and sneakers on the stairs, involved her not at all.

This is Isabel, a friend from Oxford, Yoav said when they'd arrived at the stairs, and for a moment I thought he might keep walking, leading his father away down the hall, as though there were a houseful of guests to introduce him to, and I, by chance, the first. But Weisz let go of Yoav's arm and stopped in front of me. Not knowing what else to do, I stepped down off the stairs like some sort of clumsy debutante.

It's so nice to meet you at last, I said. Yoav has told me a lot about you. Weisz winced and took me in with his eyes. My stomach contracted in the silence. And yet he has told me nothing at all about you, he said. Then he smiled, or rather lifted ever so slightly the corners of his mouth in an expression that could have been either kind or ironic. My children tell me so little about their friends, he said. I glanced at Yoav, but the man who only minutes before had been fucking me with such force had been transformed into something meek, subdued, almost childlike. With slumped shoulders he studied the buttons of his father's coat.

I was just leaving to catch a bus back to Oxford, I said. At this hour? Weisz raised his eyebrows. It's pouring out. I'm sure my son would be kind enough to make up a bed for you, won't you, Yoav? he said, without taking his eyes off of me. Thank you, but I really should be going, I said, because by now I'd lost all interest in sticking around to take a stand. In fact, I had to suppress the instinct to flee past Weisz and out the door, back into the world of streetlamps, cars, and London crosswalks in the rain. I have an appointment tomorrow morning, I lied. You'll take an early bus, Weisz said. I glanced at Yoav for help, or at least some guidance as to how to extricate myself without causing offense. But he avoided my eyes. Leah was also absorbed in staring at something on the cuff of her shirt. It really isn't any trouble to go tonight, I said, but weakly, perhaps, because by now I worried that to continue to protest might seem rude, and because I had begun to sense just how difficult it was to refuse their father.

We sat in the living room—Yoav and I each in a high-backed chair, and Weisz on a pale silk sofa. The walking stick with the silver handle, a ram's head with curled horns, rested on the cushion beside him. Yoav's gaze remained fixed on his father, as if being in his presence demanded all of his focus and concentration. Weisz presented Leah with a box tied in ribbon. When she opened it, a silvery dress fell out. Try it, Weisz insisted. She carried it off draped over her arm. When she returned, transformed into something lithe that shimmered and reflected light, she was carrying a tray with a glass of orange juice and bowl of soup for her father. You like it? Weisz demanded. Eh, Yoav? Doesn't she look beautiful? Leah smiled thinly and kissed her father's cheek, but I knew she would never wear it, that it would be relegated to the back of her closet with all of the other dresses her father had bought. It struck me as strange that, with everything Weisz seemed to know about his daughter's life, he hadn't yet understood that she had no interest in the extravagant clothes he always bought for her, clothes for a life she didn't lead.

While he ate, Weisz asked his children questions to which they replied diligently. He knew about Leah's upcoming recital, and that she was now working on a Liszt transcription of a Bach cantata. Also that one of her music teachers, a Russian who'd taught Evgeny Kissin, had taken a leave of absence and been replaced by another. He asked about the new teacher, where he came from, whether he was good, whether she liked him, and listened to the answers with a gravity that struck me—listened, it seemed, with the suggestion that if his daughter's answers had implied anything less than her complete contentment, those responsible would have him to answer to, as if, with a single phone call, a dangled threat, he were capable of arranging for the poor new teacher to be sent away, and for the departed Russian, recovering from a breakdown in the south of France, to be forced back into service. Leah went to lengths to assure her father that the new teacher was excellent. When he asked her whether she had plans for the weekend, she said she was going to a birthday party for her friend Amalia. But I had never heard of any Amalia, and in all my time at the house I'd never known Leah to go out to any parties.

There was little of his children in his elongated, sagging features. Or if there had once been, it had been distorted beyond recognition by all that had happened to him in life. His lips were thin, the watery eyes hooded, the veins in his temples lumpy and blue. Only the nose was the same, long, with the high, curved nostrils that were permanently flared. If Yoav and Leah's auburn hair had come from him it was impossible to say: what was left of his was thin and washed of color, combed back from the high, smooth forehead. No, the burden of his inheritance was not easily detectable in his children's faces.

Satisfied with Leah's answers, Weisz turned to Yoav and asked about the preparations for his exams. Yoav's answers were fluent and polished, as if he were reciting something he had composed in anticipation of such an interview. Like Leah, he made every effort to assure his father that things were going as well as they could, that there was no cause for alarm or worry. Listening to him, I was amazed. I knew perfectly well that Yoav thought his tutor was an arrogant fraud, and that the tutor, in turn, was threatening to put Yoav on academic probation if he didn't turn in some tangible evidence of the work he claimed to be doing. He lied with grace, without the slightest hint of guilt, and I wondered whether, if the need arose, he could lie like that to me. But worse than that, as I watched Weisz hungrily spoon the soup into his mouth holding the utensil between his long crooked fingers, I was filled with guilt about the lies I'd been telling my own parents. Not only about all of the wonderful things I was supposedly doing at Oxford, but that I was there at all. Exploiting my father's constitutional inability to pass up a money-saving deal, I made up a story about a cheap method of calling the States using a special phone card. In this way, I'd orchestrated it so that instead of their calling me every Sunday, I called them. They were creatures of habit, and I knew they wouldn't break from ritual unless something was wrong. To be sure, I called my answering machine on Little Clarendon Street every night. Thinking of them as I sat before Weisz, how they must have waited anxiously by the phone each Sunday morning, my mother at her station in the kitchen and my father in the bedroom, I felt a gnawing regret and sadness.

At last Weisz wiped his mouth and turned to me. A trickle of sweat slid down the hollow in my chest. And you, Isabel? What do you study? Literature, I said. An odd smile cracked across his bloodless lips. Literature, Weisz repeated, as if he were trying to put a face together with a name he knew from long ago.

During the next quarter of an hour Weisz interrogated me about my studies, where I came from, where my parents were from and what they did, and why I had come to England. At least those were how the questions were worded, but in truth (or so I believed) the words out of Weisz's mouth were only a code for something else he wished to uncover. I felt as if I were trying to pass a test whose requirements were hidden from me, and struggled for the right answers, feeling that with each fanciful arrangement of the truth I was further trampling the love and dedication of my parents. I had lied to my parents, and now I was lying about them. Weisz took the shape of their representative, the counsel assigned to the poor and downtrodden who can't be relied on to defend themselves. As we spoke, all the sad and noble furniture in the room fell away, the Bavarian grandfather clock and the marble table, even Yoav and Leah, and all that was left in that cold and cavernous space was Weisz and me, and somewhere, hovering on a higher plane, my wronged and injured parents. He makes shoes? Weisz asked. What kind of shoes? From the description I gave of my father's business, one could have been forgiven for thinking that Manolo Blahnik came on bended knees to my father when in need of someone to manufacture his most extravagant, complicated designs. The truth was that he produced the uniform shoes for nuns and Catholic schoolgirls in Harlem. As I went on exaggerating my father's business, imbuing it with glamour and prestige, a memory came to me of an afternoon spent in my grandfather's old factory, which my father had carried on overseeing until it was run into the ground, and his only choice was to become a middleman between Harlem and the belching factories of China. I remembered how my father had hoisted me up to sit at his giant Herman Miller desk, while on the other side of the wall the machines clattered nervously under his command.

That night I slept in a narrow cot in a small room down the hallway from Leah's bedroom. I lay awake, and now that I was alone I was overcome first by humiliation, then fury. Who was Weisz to interrogate me, to make me feel I had to prove my worth? What business was it of his who my family was and what my father did for a living? It was bad enough that he cowed his own children into such a pathetic position, rendering them unable to strike out in their own lives. Bad enough that he had succeeded in coercing them into a form of confinement of his own design, a condition they didn't resist because it was not within the realm of possibility for them to refuse their father. He ruled over them not with an iron fist or a temper, but rather with the unspoken threat, much more haunting, of the consequences of even the slightest discord. Now I had appeared to challenge Weisz's order, to unbalance the delicate triangle of the Family Weisz. And he had spared no time in making clear that I was wrong if I thought Yoav and I could go about our relationship without his knowledge or consent. What right did he have? I thought angrily, tossing in the narrow bed. He might be able to control his children, but I wouldn't allow him to bully me. Let him try: I wouldn't be frightened off so easily.

As if on cue, suddenly the door creaked open and Yoav was on me, coming at me from all sides like a pack of wolves. After we'd finished with every other orifice, he turned me over and forced himself into me. It was the first time we'd done it like that. I had to bite my pillow so as not to scream out at the first thrust. When it was over I fell back asleep against the heat of his body, a deep sleep from which I woke alone. Whatever I'd been dreaming receded, and all I could remember was finding Weisz hanging upside down in the pantry like a bat.

It was almost seven in the morning. I got dressed and washed my face in the child-sized Victorian sink decorated with pink flowers in Leah's bathroom. Tiptoeing down the hall, I paused in front of her room. The door was ajar, and through it I could see the enormous virginal white canopy bed, a bed as large and majestic as a ship, and thinking of it so I imagined her sitting aloft it in flooded waters. Standing there I suddenly knew that it, too, must have been a gift from her father, one that carried the same subtle message about the sort of life he expected her to live. She never brought home friends, though surely she must have had some at the college. Nor had I ever heard her make reference to a boyfriend, past or present. The demands her father and brother made on her loyalty and love left any outside relationship with a man almost impossible. I thought of the birthday party Leah had invented the night before. I hadn't understood the point of such a gratuitous lie, but now I wondered whether it was her only way of resisting her father.

Yoav was still asleep in his bed on the floor below. My fury from the night before had abated and with it my confidence. I wondered again how long our relationship could last. Perhaps it was only a matter of time before Weisz won. I'd forced Yoav into the first battle with his father over me and no sooner had he entered it than he had forfeited, grown pliant like a little boy, and then come at me in the dark with teeth and claws. The image of the hanging Weisz returned to me. Does one ever get free of such a father?

I wrote Yoav a note and left it on his desk, eager to get out of the house before I ran into Weisz. It was still drizzling outside, the fog low and heavy, and by the time I reached the station the damp had seeped through the coat my mother had bought for me. I took the Tube to Marble Arch, and from there I caught the bus back to Oxford. As soon as I unlocked the door of my room a crushing sadness descended on me. Away from Yoav, my life in Belsize Park took on the uncertain quality of a play whose stage could be dismantled, its players disbanded, and the heroine left alone in her street clothes in the darkened theater. I crawled under the blankets and slept for hours. Yoav didn't call that day or the next. Not knowing what else to do, I dragged myself to the Phoenix where I watched *Wings of Desire* twice. It was dark by the time I walked home along Walton Street. I fell asleep waiting for the phone to ring. I hadn't eaten all day, and at three in the morning the gnawing in my stomach woke me. All I had was a bar of chocolate, which only made me hungrier.

For three days the telephone didn't ring. I slept,

or sat immobile in my room, or dragged myself to the Phoenix where I sat for hours in front of the flickering screen. I tried not to think, and lived on a diet of popcorn and candy that I bought from the incurious punk anarchist who ran the concession stand, to whom I felt gratitude for possessing principles that approved of whiling away one's days alone in a cinema. Often he gave me free candy or a large soda when I'd only paid for a small. If I'd really believed things between Yoav and me had come to an end I would have been in far worse shape. No, what I felt was the torment of waiting, stuck between the end of one sentence and the beginning of the next which might or might not bring a hail storm, plane crash, poetic justice, or a miraculous reversal.

At some point the telephone finally did ring. One sentence ends and another always begins, though not always in the place the last one left off, not always continuous with the old conditions. Come back, Yoav said in something close to a whisper. Please come back to me. When I unlocked the door in Belsize Park, the house was dark. I saw his profile illuminated by the bluish glow of the television. He was watching a Kieślowski film we'd seen at least twenty times. It was the scene where Irène Jacob goes to Jean-Louis Trintignant's house for the first time to return the dog she'd hit with her car, and finds the old man eavesdropping on his neighbors' telephone calls. *What were you,* she asks, disgusted, *a cop*? *Worse*, he says, *a judge*. I slid onto the couch next to Yoav, and he pulled me to him without a word. He was alone in the house. Later I found out that their father had sent Leah to New York to retrieve a desk he had spent four decades searching for. In the week that she was gone, Yoav and I fucked all over the house, on every imaginable piece of furniture. He said nothing more about his father, but there was a violence in the way he wanted me, and I knew that something painful had taken place between them. One night, always a light sleeper, I woke suddenly with the feeling that a shadow had passed over us in silence, and when I crept down the stairs and turned on the hall light Leah was standing there with the strangest look on her face, a look I'd never seen before, as if she had cut the fraying ties to whatever had moored us. We had underestimated her, but no one more so than her father.

II

TRUE KINDNESS

Where are you, Dov? It's past dawn already. God knows what you do out there among the grasses and nettles. Any moment now you'll appear at the gate covered in burrs. For ten days we've lived together under the same roof as we have not for twenty-five years, and you've hardly said a thing. No, that isn't true. There was the one long monologue about the construction down the road, something about drainpipes and sinkholes. I began to suspect it was a code for something else you were trying to tell me. About your health, perhaps? Or our collective health, father and son's? I tried to follow but you lost me. I was thrown from the horse, my boy. Left behind in the sewage. I made the mistake of telling you as much, and a pained look gripped your face before you reverted back to silence. Afterwards I began to suspect that it had been a test you'd concocted for me, one for which the only possible outcome was my failure, leaving you free to curl back into yourself like a snail, to go on blaming and despising me.

Ten days together in this house, and the most we've done is stake out our territories and inaugurate a set of rituals. To give us a foothold. To give us direction, like the illuminated strips in the aisles of emergency-stricken planes. Every night I turn in before you, and every morning, no matter how early I rise, you are awake before me. I see your long gray form bent over the newspaper. I cough before entering the kitchen, so as not to surprise you. You boil the water, setting out two cups. We read, grunt, belch. I ask if you want toast. You refuse me. You are above even food now. Or is it the blackened crusts you object to? Toasting was always your mother's job. With my mouth full, I talk about the news. Silently, you wipe the sputtered crumbs and continue to read. My words, to you, are atmospheric at most: they come through vaguely, like the twitter of birds and the creak of the old trees, and, as far as I can tell, like these things they require no response from you. After breakfast, you retire to your room to sleep, exhausted from your nighttime rambling. Close to noon you appear in the garden with your book to stake out the only lawn chair whose seat has not broken. I claim the easy chair in front of the TV. Yesterday I followed the news report of an obese woman who died in Sfat. She hadn't moved from her sofa for over a decade, and when they discovered her dead they found that her skin had grafted to it. How it was possible for things to have gotten so far—this they didn't get into. The report was limited to the fact that she had to be cut loose from the sofa, and hoisted through the window with a crane. The reporter narrated the slow descent of the enormous body wrapped in black plastic because, as a final humiliation, there was no body bag in all of Israel big enough to fit her. At two sharp you reenter the house for your solitary monk's meal: a banana, a cup of yogurt, and a meek salad. Tomorrow, perhaps, you will appear in a hair shirt. At two-fifteen, I fall asleep in my chair. At four, I wake to the sound of whatever odd job you have chosen for yourself that day—clearing out the shed, raking, mending the roof gutter—as if to earn your lodging. To keep things fair and square, so that you won't owe me. At five, I summarize the late-breaking news to you over tea. I wait for an opening, a crack in the hard glaze of your silence. You wait for me to finish, wash out the cups, dry them, and return them to the cupboard. You fold the dish towel. You remind me of someone who walks backwards, sweeping away his footsteps. You go up to your room and close the door. Yesterday I stood and listened. What did I think I would hear? The scratching of a pen? But there was nothing. At seven you emerge to watch the news. At eight I eat dinner. At nine-thirty, I go to sleep. Much later, perhaps close to two or three in the morning, you leave the house to walk. In the dark, in the hills, in the woods. I no longer wake with a hunger that drives me out of bed to gorge myself before the open refrigerator. That appetite, which your mother called biblical, abandoned me long ago. Now I wake for other reasons. Weak bladder. Mysterious pains. Potential heart attacks. Clots. And always I find your bed empty and neatly made. I return to bed and when I get up in the morning, no matter how early, I find your shoes lined up by the door and your long gray form bent over the table. And I cough so that we can begin again.

Listen, Dov. Because I'm only going to say this once: We're running out of time, you and I. No matter how miserable your life may be, there is still more time left for you. You can do what you wish with it. You can waste it wandering the forest, following a trail of turds left by a burrowing animal. But not I. I'm rapidly approaching my end. I will not come back in the form of migrating birds, or pollen dust, or some ugly, debased creature befitting my sins. All that I am, all that I was, will harden over into ancient geology. And you will be left alone with it. Alone with what I was, with what we were, and alone with your pain that will no longer stand any chance of being allayed. So think carefully. Think long and hard. Because if you came here to be confirmed in what you have always believed about me, you're bound to succeed. I'll even help you, my boy. I'll be the prick you always took me to be. It's true that it comes easily to me. Who knows, perhaps it will even excuse you from regret. But make no mistake: While I'm buried in a hole void of all feeling, you will live on in an afterlife of pain.

But you know all of this, don't you? I sense that it's why you came. Before I die there are things you want to say to me. Let's have it out. Don't hold back. What's stopping you? Pity? I see it in your eyes: While I fly up in my mechanical chair I can see your shock at my diminishment. The monster of your childhood defeated by something as mundane as a flight of stairs. And yet, I only need to open my mouth in order to send your pity scurrying back under the rock it came out from. Just a few well-chosen words to remind you that despite appearances I am still the same arrogant, obtuse asshole I've always been.

Listen. I have a proposal for you. Hear me out and then you can accept or reject it as you choose. What would you say to a temporary truce, for as long as it takes for you to say your piece and me to say mine? For us to listen to each other as we have never listened, to hear one another out without becoming defensive and lashing out, to put, for a moment, a moratorium on bitterness and bile? To see what it's like to occupy the other's position? Perhaps you will say it is too late for us, that the moment for compassion is long past. And you might be right, but we have nothing more to lose. Death is waiting just around the corner for me. If we leave things like this it's not I who will pay the price. I will be nothing. I won't hear or see or think or feel. Maybe you think I'm belaboring the obvious, but I'd venture a bet that the state of nonbeing is not something you spend much time thinking about. Once you did perhaps, but that was long ago, and if there's one idea the mind can't sustain it is its own nullification. Perhaps the Buddhists can, the Tantric monks, but not the Jews. The Jews, who have made so much of life, have never known what to make of death. Ask a Catholic what happens when he dies and he will describe the circles of hell, purgatory, limbo, the heavenly gates. The Christian has populated death so fully that he has excused himself altogether from the need to wrap his mind around the end of his existence. But ask a Jew what happens when he dies and you'll see the miserable condition of a man left alone to grapple. A man lost and confused. Wandering blindly. Because though the Jew may have talked about everything, investigated, held forth, aired his opinion, argued, gone on and on to numbing lengths, sucked every last scrap of meat off the bone of every question, he has remained largely silent about what happens when he dies. He has agreed, simply, not to discuss it. He who otherwise tolerates no vagueness has agreed to leave the most important question mired in a nebulous, fuzzy grayness. Do you see the irony of it? The absurdity? What is the point of a religion that turns its back on the subject of what happens when life ends? Having been denied an answer—having been denied an answer *while at the same time* being cursed as a people who for thousands of years have aroused in others a murderous hate—the Jew has no choice but to live with death every day. To live with it, to set up his house in its shadow, and never to discuss its terms.

Where was I? I'm excited, I've lost the thread, you see how I'm frothing at the mouth? Wait, yes. A proposal. What do you say, Dov? Or don't say anything at all. I'll take your silence as a yes.

Here. Let me begin. You see, my child, a little bit every day I find myself contemplating my death. Investigating it. Dipping my toe, as it were. Not practicing so much as interrogating its conditions while I still possess powers of interrogation, and can still fathom oblivion. In one of these little excursions into the unknown I uncovered something about you that I'd almost forgotten. For the first three years of your life you knew nothing of death. You thought that it would all go on without end. On the first night you left your crib behind to sleep in a bed, I came to say good night to you. Now I'm going to sleep in a big-boy bed forever? you asked. Yes, I said, and we sat together, I imagining you on a flight through the halls of eternity clutching your blankie, you imagining whatever a child imagines when he tries to conceive of forever. A few days later you were sitting at the table playing with the food that you refused to eat. So don't eat, I said. But if you don't eat, you can't leave the table. It's as simple as that. Your lip began to tremble. Go ahead and sleep there for all I care, I said. This isn't how Mama does it, you whined. I don't care how she does it, I spat, this is how I do it, and you're not moving until you eat! You burst into tears, protesting and carrying on. I ignored you. After a while silence filled the room, punctuated only by your little whimpers. Then, out of nowhere, you announced, When Yoella dies, we'll get a dog. I was surprised. Because of the bluntness of the statement, and because I had no idea you knew anything of death. Won't you be sad when she dies? I asked, forgetting for a moment the war of the food. And you, very practically, replied, Yes, because then we won't have a cat to pet. A moment passed. What does it look like when people die? you asked. As if they're asleep, I said, only they don't breathe. You thought about this. Do children die? you asked. I felt a pain open in my chest. Sometimes, I said. Perhaps I should have chosen other words. *Never*, or simply, *No*. But I didn't lie to you. At least you can say that of me. Then, turning your little face to me, without flinching, you asked, Will I die? And as you said the words horror filled me as it had never before, tears burned my eyes, and instead of saying what I should have said, *Not for a long, long time*, or *Not you my child, you alone will live forever*, I said, simply, Yes. And because, no matter how you suffered, deep inside you were still an animal like any other who wants to live, feel the sun, and be free, you said, But I don't want to die. The terrible injustice of it filled you. And you looked at me as if I were responsible.

You'd be surprised by how often in my little peripatetic wanderings through the valley of death I meet the child you once were. At first it surprised me, too, but soon I came to look forward to these encounters. I tried to think about why it was that you would appear like that when the subject had so little to do with you. I came to realize it had to do with certain feelings I felt for the first time when you were a child. I don't know why Uri didn't arouse the same feelings before you. Maybe I was caught up in other things when he was an infant, or maybe I was still too young. There were only three years between you, but in those years I grew up, my youth officially came to an end and I entered a new stage of life as a father and a man. By the time you were born I understood, in a way that I could not have with Uri, just what the birth of a child means. How he grows, and how his innocence is slowly ruined, how his features change forever the first time he feels shame, how he comes to learn the meaning of disappointment, of disgust. How a whole world is contained inside of him, and it was mine to lose. I felt powerless against these things. And of course you were a different kind of child than Uri. From the beginning you seemed to know things and to hold them against me. As if you somehow understood that built into raising a child are inevitable acts of violence against him. Looking down into the crib at your tiny face contorted by screams of grief—there is nothing else to call it, I've never heard any baby cry like you—I was guilty before I'd even begun. I know how this sounds; after all you were only a baby. But something about you attacked the weakest part of me, and I backed away.

Yes, you as you were then, with your fair hair before it turned coarse and dark. I've heard others say that when their children were born they tasted their own mortality for the first time. But it wasn't that way for me. That isn't the reason I find you hiding there in the shallows of my death. I was too caught up in myself, in the battles of my life, to notice the little winged messenger come to take the torch from my hand and silently pass it on to Uri and you. To notice that from that moment on I would no longer be the center of all things, the crucible where life, to keep itself alive, burns most vividly. The fire began to cool in me, but I didn't notice. I carried on living as if it was life that needed me and not vice versa.

And yet you taught me something of death. Almost without my being aware of it, you smuggled the knowledge into me. Not long after you asked me whether you would die, I heard you talking aloud in the other room: When we die, you said, we'll be hungry. A simple statement, and then you went on humming off-tune and pushing your little cars across the floor. But it stayed with me. It seemed to me that no one had ever summed up death quite like that: an unending state of longing with no hope of receiving. I was almost scared by the equanimity with which you faced something so abysmal. How you looked at it, turned it over in your mind as best you could, and found a form of clarity that allowed you to accept it. Maybe I am ascribing too much meaning to the words of a three-year-old. But however accidental, there was beauty in them: In life we sit at the table and refuse to eat, and in death we are eternally hungry.

How can I explain it? The way you frightened me a little. How you seemed just the tiniest bit closer than the rest of us to the essence of things. I would walk into a room and find you staring at something in the corner. What's so fascinating? I wanted to know. But your concentration would be broken, and you would turn to me, a wrinkle in your brow, a faint look of surprise at being disturbed. After you left the room I would go to see for myself. A spiderweb? An ant? A disgusting hairball coughed up by Yoella? But there was never anything there. What's wrong with him? I asked your mother. He has no friends? By that time Uri had already befriended the whole neighborhood. There was an endless stream of kids coming in and out of the house for him. The only time Uri spent in the corner was when he was wrapping his arms around himself and wriggling as if he were French-kissing. He would run his hands up and down his back, squeeze his own ass, and give a little yelp, screwing his head back and forth in an imitation that made everyone roll on the floor. But amid the laughter you were nowhere to be found. Later, pruning the tomato plants, I came across a patch of the garden where you had mysteriously assembled little piles of dirt in rows, alternated with squares or circles etched into the ground with a stick. What the hell is this? I asked your mother. She cocked her head to study it. It's a city, she announced without a shade of doubt in her voice. Here is the gate, she pointed, and the fortifications, and this here is a cistern. Then she walked away, leaving me defeated again. Where I saw little pathetic piles of dirt she saw a whole city. From the beginning you had given her the keys to yourself. But not to me. Never to me, my son. I spotted you crouching near the hose. Come here, I shouted. You lumbered toward me on your short legs, your face crazily stained from a Popsicle. What is the meaning of this? I demanded, gesturing with the clippers. You looked down and sniffed. Then you squatted and carried out some lightning renovations—hurriedly sweeping, patting, refashioning a lump. You stood to examine it again from above, cocking your head at the same angle your mother had. So that was the secret, I thought. You have to turn your head at a special angle to make sense of it! No sooner had I absorbed this clue than you lifted your foot and, with a few quick stomps, leveled the entire thing and retreated into the house.

Which came first? Was it I who backed away, or you? A strange child with secret knowledge that I came to resent, who grew to be a young man whose world was barred to me. Do you want to know the truth, Dov? When you came to me to tell me about the book you planned to write I was taken aback. I couldn't understand what made you decide to come to me of all people—me, with whom you shared so little of yourself, whom you only spoke to as a last resort, when it was absolutely necessary. I was too slow to respond as I might have liked. I couldn't change so fast. I assumed the old position. A certain tone of voice, a roughness that had always been my defense against all I couldn't grasp in you. To reject you before you could reject me. Afterwards, I regretted it. The moment after you walked out of the room I realized that I'd lost my chance. I understood that you had offered me a reprieve, and I'd squandered it. And I knew it would not come again.

A shark that is a repository for human sadness. Who takes all that the dreamers cannot bear, who bears the violence of their accumulated feeling. How often I thought about that beast and the chance I lost with you. At times I felt I was on the verge of understanding everything the great fish stood for. One day I went into your room looking for a screwdriver you'd borrowed, and on your desk I found the opening pages. My first feeling was of relief that I had not, after all, dissuaded you. No one else was home, but I closed the door anyway and sat down to read about the terrible animal with the bared teeth suspended in a tank that glowed in an otherwise dark room. Electrodes and wires attached to its greenish body. Machines that hummed at all hours of the day and night. Somewhere also the persistent sound of a pump that kept the shark alive. The beast twitched and rolled, and expressions—is it possible for a shark to have expressions? I asked myself—passed over its face at a rapid speed, while in small, windowless rooms the patients continued to sleep and dream.

I don't need to tell you that I've never been much of a reader. It was always your mother who loved books. It takes me a long time, I have to make my way slowly. Sometimes the words are a puzzle to me and I have to read them two or three times until I can crack their meaning. In law school it always took me longer to study than the others. My mind was sharp, my tongue sharper, I could debate with the best of them, but I had to work harder with my books. When you learned to read so easily, almost on your own, I was amazed. It seemed impossible that a child like you could have come from me. It was yet another effortless understanding you shared with your mother that I stood outside of and would not be let into. And yet without your knowledge or consent, I read your book. Read it as I had never read a book before, and have never since. For the first time, I'd been given a way into you. And I was in awe, Dovik. I was frightened and overwhelmed by what I found there. When you enlisted and left for basic training, I was distraught to think that my secret reading would come to an end, that the doors onto your world would be closed to me again. And then, lo and behold, you began to send back the packages every couple of weeks, wrapped in brown tape, and decorated with the words PRIVATE!!! DO NOT OPEN!, with express instructions for your mother to place them in your desk drawer. I was happy. I convinced myself that you knew, that you had known all along, and that your extravagant charade of secrecy was simply a way to save me—to save us both—from embarrassment.

In the beginning I used to read the pages in your room. Always when your mother was out doing the shopping, volunteering at WIZO, or visiting Irit. With time I became bolder, sitting in the kitchen or making myself comfortable in a lawn chair under the acacia tree. Once she arrived home earlier than expected and caught me off guard. Not wanting to arouse her suspicions, I carried on reading, pretending it was a brief for one of my cases. A landlord who wants to evict, I muttered, glancing up at her over my glasses. But she only nodded and gave me that semi-smile she always offered up when consumed by other thoughts—of Irit, perhaps, and her pathological needs and her noisy emergencies to which your mother always arrived like an ambulance. As easy as that, I thought, but not wanting to test my luck I snuck back to your room and put the pages away in your desk.

I didn't always understand what you wrote. I admit that in the beginning I was frustrated by your refusal to state things plainly. What does it eat, this shark? Where is this place, this institution, this hospital, for lack of a better word, with the enormous tank? Why do these people sleep so much? They don't need to eat either? No one eats in this book? It was all I could do to keep myself from making a note in the margin. Many times you lost me. Just as I was finding my way around Beringer the janitor's room with only the tiny window way up high (and why was it always raining outside?) and his shoes lined up like soldiers under his little hard bed, just as I was getting the feel of the place, to smell the odor that a man gives off when he sleeps alone in a small room, suddenly you threw me out and started to drag me through the forest where Hannah used to go to hide from everyone when she was a girl. But I did my best to stifle my complaints. I gave up my questions and put aside my editorial suggestions. I put myself in your hands. And as the pages turned, my objections came less and less often. I gave in to your story and it picked me up and carried me away with it, with poor Beringer fingering the crack in the tank while in the little rooms attached by wires to the great hall that held the tank the dreamers lay dreaming, the boy Benny, and Rebecca who dreamed of her father (tell me, Dovik, was it me you modeled him after? Did you really see me like that? So heartless, and arrogant, and cruel? Or am I being as egotistical as he to think I had any place in your work?). I developed a soft spot for little, feverish Benny and his still-undying belief in magic, and I took a special interest in the dreams of Noa, the young writer, who, of all of them, reminded me the most of you. I even felt, God knows how, a strange compassion for that great, suffering shark. When the bundle of pages came to an end I was always a little saddened. What would happen next? And what about the terrifying leak that Beringer watches helplessly, and the sound of the water, *drip drip drip*, which filters into all of their dreams at night, invading them, becoming a hundred different echoes of the saddest things? Sometimes I had to wait weeks when you were especially busy in the army, even months for the next section. I would be left in the dark, not knowing what would happen next. Only that the shark was getting sicker and sicker. Knowing what Beringer knew, but which he kept from the dreamers in their windowless rooms: that the shark wouldn't live forever. And then what, Dovik? Where would they go, these people? How would they live? Or were they already dead?

I never found out. The last section you sent home was three weeks before you were sent to Sinai. Afterwards, there was no more.

* * *

On that Saturday in October, your mother and I were at home when we heard the air raid sirens. We turned on the radio but, being Yom Kippur, there was only dead air. It crackled in the corner of the room for half an hour until at last a voice came on saying that the sirens had not been a false alarm; if we heard them again we were to go down to the shelter. Then they played Beethoven's *Moonlight Sonata*—to what? to soothe us?—and at some point the broadcaster returned to say we had been attacked. The shock was terrible: we had convinced ourselves that we were finished with wars. Then more Beethoven, interrupted with coded mobilization messages for the reserves. Uri called from Tel Aviv, speaking loudly as if to the nearly deaf; even halfway across the room I could hear what he was saying to your mother. He joked with her; he might have been going to perform a magic show for the Egyptians. That was Uri. Afterwards the army called looking for you. We thought you were with your unit on Mount Hermon, but they told us you'd taken leave for the weekend. I wrote down the location you were to report to in a matter of hours.

We called everyone but no one knew where you were, not even your girlfriend at the university. Your mother worked herself into a wreck. Don't jump to conclusions, I told her. I who had known about your midnight ramblings for years, who was familiar with your way of escaping the rest of us, of finding a way to live a little in the world while it was unpolluted by people. It gave me pleasure to know something about you that your mother didn't.

Then we heard the keys in the door and you burst in, agitated and excited. We didn't ask where you'd been and you didn't tell us. It was some time since I'd last seen you, and I was surprised by how broad you'd become, almost physically imposing. The sun had tanned you and given you a new sturdiness, or maybe something else, a kind of dynamism I hadn't noticed in you before. Looking at you, I felt a pang for my own lost youth. Your mother, full of nerves, hurried around the kitchen preparing food. Eat, she urged you, you don't know when you'll get your next meal. But you didn't want to eat. You kept going to the window to look at the sky for planes.

I drove you to the meeting point. Do you remember that car ride, Dov? Afterwards, there were things you couldn't remember, so I don't know if you do. Your mother didn't come. She couldn't bring herself to do it. Or maybe she didn't want to infect you with her anxiety. Your gun sat across your knees along with a bag of food from her. We both knew you were going to throw it out or give it away, even she knew. As soon as we got on the road, you turned to look out the window, making it clear you were in no mood for conversation. So fine, we won't talk, I thought to myself, what's new? And yet I was disappointed. Somehow I thought that the circumstances, the emergency brewing around us, the fact that I was delivering you to a war—I thought the pressure of it all would force the cork and that something of you would come trickling out. But it was not to be. You made yourself clear, turning sharply away to stare out the window. And though I was disappointed I was also, I admit, a little relieved. Because I, who always had something to say, who leaped to have the first word and pressed on until I had the last—I was at a loss. I saw how your body had grown around the gun. How casually you held it, how at home you felt with it in your hands. As if you had absorbed its mechanism—all it demanded of you, its power and its contradictions—right into your flesh. The boy whose own arms and legs were once alien to him had ceased to be, and in his place, sitting next to me in dark sunglasses, his sleeves pulled up to show bronzed forearms, was a man. A soldier, Dova'leh. My boy had grown up to be a soldier, and I was delivering him to war.

Yes, there were things I wanted to say but I couldn't just then, so we drove in silence. A huge convoy of trucks was already there, the soldiers eager and restless. We said goodbye—it was as simple as that, a kind of hurried pounding on each other's backs—and I watched you disappear into the sea of uniforms. At that moment you were no longer my son. My son had gone off somewhere to hide for a while. Wherever it was you'd been before you came home—walking some trail alone in the hills—it was as if you knew what was to come, and had gone off to bury yourself in a hole. To hide there, beneath the cool earth, for as long as it took for the danger to pass. And what was left once you'd subtracted yourself from the equation was a soldier who had grown up eating Israeli fruit, with the dirt of his forefathers under his nails, who was leaving now to defend his country.

In those weeks your mother hardly slept. She wouldn't speak on the phone so as not to occupy the line. But it was the doorbell we feared the most. Across the street they arrived at the Biletskis' to say that Itzhak, little Itzy whom you and Uri played with as children, had been killed in the Golan. He had burned to death inside of a tank. After that, the Biletskis disappeared inside their house. Wild grass grew up around it, the curtains were always drawn, sometimes, very late at night, a light came on inside and someone could be heard playing two notes on the piano over and over, *pling plong pling plong pling plong*. One day when I went to deliver a piece of mail that came to our house by mistake I saw a pale spot on the doorframe where the mezuzah had been. That could have been us. There was no reason it had happened to their son and not to ours, why it was Biletski playing two notes and not me. Every day sons were being sacrificed. Another boy in the neighborhood was exploded by a shell. One night we got into bed and turned off the lights. If I lose one of them, your mother said to me in a low, trembling voice, I will not be able to go on. Either I could have said, *You will go on*, or I could have said, *We will not lose them*. We will not lose them, I said, holding her thin wrists tightly. She did not say, *I will not forgive you*, but she didn't have to say it. Uri was stationed on a mountain overlooking the Jordan Valley. He managed to call us once, so we knew he was there. Much later, years later, he told me how he could hear on the radio transmitter the desperate Israeli tank units fighting in the Golan. One after another simply vanished from the radio network, extinguished into silence, and he couldn't stop listening, knowing he was hearing those soldiers' last words. We knew from him that your brigade had been sent to Sinai. Every day we waited for the doorbell to ring, but it did not ring, and each dawn that broke without it ringing was another night you had survived. There were many things your mother and I didn't say to each other during those days. Our fears drove us deeper and deeper into a bunkered silence. I knew that if something happened to you or Uri, she would not have allowed me the right to suffer as she would suffer, and I held it against her.

That night, two weeks after the war began, the telephone rang close to eleven. That's it, I thought, and the bottom opened out in the depths of me. Your mother had fallen asleep on the sofa in the other room. Bleary-eyed, with static hair, she stood now in the doorway. As if I were moving through cement, I rose from my seat and answered. My eyes and lungs burned. There was a pause, long enough for me to imagine the worst. Then your voice came through. It's me, you said. That's all: *It's me*. But in those two syllables I could hear that your voice was slightly different, as if a tiny but vital piece had broken inside of it like the filament of a lightbulb. And yet in that moment it didn't matter. I'm all right, you said. I couldn't speak. I don't think you'd ever heard me cry. Your mother began to scream. It's him, I said. It's Dov, I choked. She rushed to me and we both put our ears to the phone. Our heads were coupled together and we listened to your voice. I wanted to listen to you talk forever. Talk about anything, it didn't matter. The way we used to listen to you babble on in your crib in the mornings before you called to us. But you didn't want to speak much. You told us you were in a hospital near Rechovot. That your tank had been hit, and that you'd been wounded from the shrapnel across your chest. It isn't bad, you said. You asked about Uri. I can't talk much now, you said. We'll come for you, your mother said. No, you said. Of course we're coming, she said. I said no, you snapped back, almost angrily. And then, softer again: They'll bring me home tomorrow or the next day.

That night your mother and I held each other in bed. In our reprieve, we clung and forgave one another everything.

When you came home at last you were neither

the soldier I had watched disappear into the crowd, nor the boy I knew. You were a kind of shell, emptied out of both of those people. You sat mute in a chair in the corner of the living room, a cup of tea untouched on the side table, and winced when I went to touch you. From your wound, but also, I sensed, because you could not bear such contact. Give him time, your mother whispered in the kitchen, preparing pills, teas, swabs. I sat in the living room with you. We watched the news and spoke little. When there was no news we watched the cartoons, cat-and-mouse chases, How many lumps do you want? and then the mallet on the head. In time it came out—not to me of course, only to her—that two others in the tank had died. The gunner who was only twenty, and the commander who was just a few years older. The gunner had died instantly, but the commander lost a leg and threw himself out of the tank. You climbed out after him. The communications system was dead, there was smoke and confusion, and the driver, who in all of this had perhaps not understood that the others had evacuated, started it up again in reverse and drove away through the sand. Perhaps he panicked, who knows; you never met him again.

You and the wounded commander were left alone in the dunes. How many times I tried to imagine it as if it had been me. Nothing but the endless dunes and the wires on the ground left from Egyptian missiles. The sound of explosions. Trying to carry the wounded man on your back, but it being impossible to make any headway in the sand. The commander, in shock, begging you not to leave him. If you stayed there, you both would die. If you left to find help, he might. You were taught never to leave another soldier wounded in the field. It was a cardinal rule the army had driven into you. How you must have struggled with yourself. Only there was no self to struggle with. The dumbstruck look on his face when he understood you were going. How with difficulty he removed his watch and held it out: This is my father's. Does it surprise you that I imagined it, that I tried, I really did, to put myself in your shoes? There was no one left in you, and so like the walking dead you abandoned the commander. Put him gently down in the sand, became the last thing he would ever see except for the endless repeat of sand, and walked away. You walked and walked. In the desert, in the heat, with the explosions in the distance, and the missiles overhead. Dizzier and dizzier, losing your senses, hoping you were headed in the right direction. Until at last, like a mirage, a rescue unit appeared and you were lifted up among the dead and the barely living. The truck was full of the wounded and dying, so they could not go for him then, they told you, they would have to return for him later. Either they returned and couldn't find him, or they never returned. He was not heard from again, and was listed among the missing. Even after the war they never found his body.

The watch sat on your desk for days. When you finally got the address of the family in Haifa, you borrowed the car and drove yourself. I don't know what happened there. When you returned that night you went into your room and closed the door without a word. Your mother bit her lip as she washed the dishes, holding back tears. All I know is that the commander was an only child, and that you returned the watch to his parents. We thought that would be the last of it. In the weeks that followed, you improved a little. Uri came to visit you every few days, and the two of you walked together. But about three weeks later a letter came to the house from the dead soldier's father. I discovered it in the pile of mail, and put it aside for you. I barely looked at the return address, I was entirely ignorant of what it contained, but it was I who delivered it to you and I, in the end, who became wrapped up in its accusations. A father writing to a son, only he was not your father, and you were not his son, and yet all the same, through associations I was powerless against, I was dragged into it.

It was not an eloquent letter, but the crudeness made it worse. He blamed you for the death of his son. *You took his watch*, he wrote in spindly handwriting, *and let my son die. How do you live with yourself?* He had survived Birkenau, and brought this into it. He summoned the courage of the Jewish inmates at the hands of the SS, and called you a coward. In the last line of the letter, scratched so hard that the pen had broken through the paper, he wrote: *It should have been you.*

The letter destroyed you. Whatever fragile wholeness you had managed to preserve was shattered when you read it. You lay in bed with your face to the wall, and you wouldn't get up and you wouldn't eat. You refused to see anyone, numbing yourself with the opiate of silence. Or perhaps you were trying to starve the little surviving portion of yourself to death. Your mother now feared for your life in a new way. (How many ways are there to fear for your child's life? Pass over it.) At the beginning your girlfriend used to come, but you turned her away and she left in tears. She had long brown hair, crooked teeth, and wore a man's shirt, and all of this somehow only strengthened her vitality and beauty. You will think I go on too much about the beauty of your young girlfriends, but I have a point, which is that in all of your suffering up until then you had not been blind to beauty, one might even say you found a certain shelter in it. But no longer; now you turned away this beautiful girl who cared for you. You wouldn't even speak to your mother. If I am honest, I have to admit that a little part of me was glad to see her receive the same treatment as I. That she should feel what all my life I felt from you. That she should have to exist a little on my side of the fence, and see what it felt like to throw oneself against that impenetrable barrier. And as if she sensed my satisfaction, whatever gentleness had come to visit us after we found out you were alive, whatever benefit of the doubt we silently agreed to give each other, dried up. Our discussions about you—in low voices in the kitchen, or at night in bed—became tense. Your mother wanted to call the father in Haifa, to shout at him, to defend you. But I wouldn't let her. I grabbed her hand and pried the phone loose. It's enough, Eve, I said. His son is dead. His parents were murdered and now he has lost his only son. And you expect him to be fair? To be *reasonable*? Her eyes turned hard. You have more sympathy for him than you have for your own son, she spat, and walked away.

We failed each other then, she and I. Failed to support each other as we should have. Instead we each retreated alone into our own anguish, the special, unique hell of watching your child suffer and being helpless to do anything for him. Maybe she was right, in a way. Not about my lack of sympathy—you were my child, for God's sake, you are still my child even now. But right, perhaps, about a lack of generosity in the way I viewed your reaction to the tragedy that had befallen you. You ceased to live. Your mother believed that something had been confiscated from you. But to me it seemed you forfeited it. As if all your life you had been waiting for life to betray you, to prove what you had always suspected of it—how little it held for you except disappointment and pain. And now you had an irreproachable reason to turn away from it, to break from it at last, just as you had broken with Shlomo, with so many friends and girlfriends, and long ago with me.

Terrible things befall people, but not all are destroyed. Why is it that the same thing that destroys one does not destroy another? There is the question of will—some inalienable right, the right of interpretation, remains. Another person might have said: I am not the enemy. Your son died at their hands, not mine. I'm a soldier who fought for my country, no more and no less. Another might have closed the door to the agonies of self-doubt. But you left it open. And I admit that I couldn't understand this. When you didn't get better after two or three months, the pain of watching you suffer turned to frustration. How can you help someone who won't help himself? After a certain point, one can't help but see it as self-pity. You resigned from all ambition. Sometimes, passing the closed door of your room, I would pause in the hall. What about the shark, my son? What about Beringer and his mop and the ceaseless drip from the leak in the tank? What about the doctor, and Noa, and little Benny? What will become of them without you? But instead, when I found you hunched over a plate of food you refused to eat, I demanded, Who are you punishing? Do you really think life will be hurt if you deny it?

Wherever you went the hurt rattled in you, the old injuries mixed up with the new. In all of this I became deeply implicated. From every angle I was given only your back. My resentment grew, for both you and your mother who had formed an exclusive camp together from which I, the brute, was excluded—to punish me for my vast misunderstanding, and many other things of which I was guilty. He feels hurt by you, she said when, in the course of a gratuitous argument, I lashed out about her complicity in your silence, the special glass silence you reserved only for me. And you think he has a good case for these feelings? I asked. You think he is right that—what? I didn't treat him fairly? That I didn't love him properly? Aaron, she said sharply, sucking in her breath in frustration. I loved him as I knew how to love him! I shouted, aware even as I shouted I was only adding to her mounting evidence, yours and hers. Perhaps I even threw a bowl—a bowl of strawberries it was—across the room, and the glass shattered. It's possible I did this. If memory serves. It's true there were times my temper got the better of me. The glass shattered, and in the wake of that crash her righteous silence seeped into the room. I would have liked to throw more.

I only had to open my mouth for you to grow angry and pained. He is a victim in everything now, I said to your mother. He toils to cultivate his right to suffer. But, as always, she took your side against me. One night, fed up, I shouted at her, So now it is I who am responsible for the commander's death? It was unfair, yes, and I regretted it immediately. A moment later I heard the front door slam and knew you had heard me. I went after you and tried to bring you back. On the street you were crying and tried wildly to throw me off. I grabbed you and held your head to my chest until you stopped struggling. I hugged you to me as you sobbed and if I could have spoken I would have said, *I'm not the enemy. I'm not the one who wrote that letter. I would rather a thousand died instead of you.*

The months passed and nothing changed. Then one day you came to see me at the office. I returned from a meeting with a client, and you were sitting there at my desk, gloomily scratching a design onto my message pad. I was surprised. For so long you had barely left the house and now you sat before me like the living dead. I couldn't remember the last time you'd come to see me at work. At a loss for words, I said, I didn't know you were coming. I came to tell you I've made a decision, you said gravely. Good, I said, still standing, wonderful, although I had no idea what the decision was. Just the idea that you had begun to be able to imagine a future for yourself was enough. You sat in silence. So? I said. I'm going to leave Israel, you said. To go where? I asked, trying to control a flare of anger. London. To do what? You hadn't met my eyes until then, but now you lifted your head and looked squarely at me. I'm going to study law, you said.

I was speechless. Not only because you had never before expressed an interest in law, but because since you were a child you had made a point of not modeling yourself on me. No, it was more than that—a point of defining yourself in opposition to me. If I spoke loudly you would be the one who always spoke quietly, if I loved tomatoes then you would hate them. I was flabbergasted by this sudden reversal, and struggled to understand what it could mean. Had you not been so earnest a person, I might have thought you meant to mock me. I admit that I couldn't picture you as a lawyer, but then to picture you as anything in those days was not at all easy.

I waited for you to say more but you didn't. Abruptly, you stood and said you had to go meet a friend. You who had refused to see anyone for months. After you were gone, I called your mother. What is the meaning of all this? I asked. All what? she asked. One day he is catatonic in his room, I said, and the next he's enrolling to study law in London? He's been talking about it for a while, she said. I thought you knew. Knew? *Knew?* How could I know? In my own house there is no one who speaks to me. Stop it, Aaron, she said. You're being ridiculous. So now I was not only a brute, but ridiculous, too. A fool that no one thought to talk to anymore, the way one puts out a moody and burdensome cat and forgets to feed it in the hopes that it will wander off and find some other family to care for it.

You went. I could not bring myself to drive you

to the airport. I drove you to war, but I could not deliver you to the plane that would take you away from your country. I had a trial. Maybe I could have canceled it, but I didn't. The night before your mother stayed up finishing a sweater she had knit for you. Did you ever wear it? Even I could see that it was unflattering, bulky with her fear that you might freeze to death. We left our goodbyes to the morning. But when the time came for me to leave for work, you were still asleep.

From the beginning your marks were tremendous. You rose easily to the top of your class. The suffering did not vanish but appeared to go into remission. You kept it buried under endless, obsessive work. When you graduated, we thought you would come home, but you didn't come. You became a barrister and were accepted in a prestigious set of chambers. You worked impossible hours, leaving no room for anything else, and quickly made a name for yourself in the criminal field. You prosecuted and defended, balanced the scales of justice, the years passed, you married, divorced, were appointed judge. And only later did I come to understand what perhaps you had meant to tell me that day so long ago: you would not come back to us.

* * *

All of this was long ago. And yet against my will I find myself returning to it. As if to touch, ritually, one last time, every enduring pocket of pain. No, the powerful emotions of youth don't mellow with time. One gets a grip on them, cracks a whip, forces them down. You build your defenses. Insist on order. The strength of feeling doesn't lessen, it is simply contained. But now the walls begin to buckle. I find myself thinking of my parents, Dovi. Of certain images of my mother in shadowy evening light, in the kitchen, and I see that her expression meant something different than I had understood it to mean as a child. She would lock herself in the bathroom and was reduced to mere sound. Muffled, through the door, my ear to it. To me my mother was first and foremost a smell. Indescribable. Pass over it. Then a feeling, her hands on my back, the soft wool of her coat against my cheek. Then the sound of her, and at the end of all that, a distant fourth, the sight of her. How she looked to me, only in parts, never the whole. So large, and I so small that at any one time I could only take in a curve, or the swelling flesh over a belt, or the slope of freckles down to the bosom, or the legs sheathed in stockings. Any more was impossible. Too much. After she died, my father lived on almost another decade. Steadying the one shaking hand with the other. I used to find him in his underwear, unshaven, with the blinds drawn. A meticulous, even a vain man, in a stained undershirt. It took him a full year before he began to dress again. Other things were never righted or repaired. Something toppled within. His conversation gave way to gaping holes. Once I found him on all fours, inspecting a scratch in the wood floor. Muttering and applying to it some Talmudic knowledge he had acquired as a boy and, having no use for it, had forgotten until now. I have no idea, no idea at all, what his thoughts were about the afterlife. We didn't speak of personal things. We saluted each other from across a great distance, from mountain peak to mountain peak. The clinking of the spoon in the teacup, or the throat cleared. A discussion of the best kind of wool, from where it came, type of animal, how manufactured, when there was discussion at all. He died peacefully in his bed, not a dirty dish in the sink. After filling a glass of water he would wipe the sink dry so that the steel would remain, true to name, stainless. For a few years I lit the yahrzeit candle for them both, but then I lost the habit. I can count on one hand the number of times I visited their graves. The dead are dead, if I want to visit them I have my memories, this is how I looked at it, if I looked at it at all. But even the memories I kept at bay. Is there not always some slight but unmistakable rebuke in the death of those closest? Is that what you will make of my death, Dov? A final installment of the long rebuke you took to be my life?

*   *   *

I was nearing the end and then you came home. You stood holding your suitcase in the hall, and I thought—it seemed—a beginning. Am I too late? Where are you? You should have been home hours ago. What's keeping you? Something isn't right, I can feel it. Your mother is no longer here to worry. Now it falls to me. For ten days I woke up and found you here, sitting at this table. So short a time, and yet already I had come to depend on it. But this morning, the morning I came down the stairs prepared to break the silence and offer a truce at last, the table was empty.

There's a pressure mounting in my chest. I can't

pass over it. For ten days we have lived under the same roof and you've hardly spoken, Dov. We move through the day like two hands of a clock: sometimes we overlap for a moment, then come apart again, carrying on alone. Every day exactly the same: the tea, the burnt toast, the crumbs, the silence. You in your chair, I in mine. Except today, when I woke and for the first time I coughed in the hallway, entered the kitchen, and no one was there. Your chair was empty. The newspaper still wrapped in a bag outside the door.

I promised myself I would wait until you were ready, that I wouldn't push. Yesterday I came across you standing in the garden, a strange stiffness in your posture as if you carried a wooden yoke like the old Dutch, only instead of water it was great reserves of feeling that you wished not to spill. I tried not to disturb you. Afraid to say the wrong thing, I've said nothing at all. But every day there's a little bit less of me. Just the tiniest bit, almost immeasurable, and yet I feel life slipping away. You don't have to tell me what you don't want to tell me about your life. I won't ask you what happened, why you resigned, why you suddenly gave up the only thing that has kept you bound to life all these years. I can live without knowing that. But what I need to know is why you've come back to me. I need to ask. Will you visit me once I'm gone? Will you come from time to time and sit with me? It's absurd, I'll be nothing, just a handful of inert material, and yet I feel it would help me to go more easily if I knew that you would come sometimes. To sweep around the headstone, and pick a stone to set there with the others. If there are others. Just to think that you would come, even once a year. I know how it sounds given the oblivion I've never doubted awaits me. When I first began my little wanderings through the valley of death and discovered within myself this desire, I, too, was surprised. I remember exactly how it happened. Uri came to take me to the eye doctor one morning. Overnight, a tiny spot of darkness had lodged in the vision of my right eye. It was just a speck, but this little void drove me crazy, everything I looked at was marred by it. I started to panic. What if another spot appeared, and then another? Like being buried alive one shovel of dirt at a time, until there was only a prick of light left, and then nothing. Having worked myself into a state, I called Uri. An hour later he phoned back that he'd made an appointment and would come for me. We went to see the doctor, none of this is important, afterwards we got in the car to go home. We were driving when out of nowhere a rock hit the windshield. The bang was tremendous. Both of us flew out of our skin, and Uri slammed on the brakes. We sat in silence, barely breathing. The road was empty, there was no one around. By some miracle it took us a moment to fully grasp, the glass had not broken. The only mark in it was a divot the size of a fingerprint almost exactly between my eyes. A moment later I saw the rock resting in the recess for the windshield wipers. Had it gone through the glass it might have killed me. I got out of the car, my legs trembling, and took hold of the stone. It filled my palm, and when I closed my fingers around it, it fit perfectly in my fist. Here is the first, I thought. The first stone to mark my grave. The first stone placed like a period at the end of my life. Soon the mourners will come bringing stone after stone to anchor the long sentence that was my life to its final, strangled syllable—

And then, my child, I thought of you. I realized that I didn't care if the others came. That the only one whose stone I wanted was yours, Dov. The stone that can mean so many things to a Jew, but in your hand could mean only one.

My child. My love and my regret, as you were when I first laid eyes on you, a tiny old man who hadn't had time to brush off his ancient expression, naked and misshapen in the nurse's arms. Dr. Bartov, my old friend who broke the rules so that I could be present, turned to me and asked if I wanted to cut the cord, bulging, whitish blue and twisted, so much thicker than I'd ever imagined, more like a rope for tying a boat, and without thinking I agreed. Just like this, he said, he who had done it a thousand times before. So I did, and suddenly it began to dance like a snake in my hands, and blood spurted around the room, splashing the walls like the scene of a heinous crime, and you opened your eyes, I swear you opened your tiny wet eyes, my child, and looked at me, as if to fix in your mind forever the face of the one who had separated you from her. At that moment I was filled with something. It was as if a pressure had blown into me, expanding everything, pushing at the walls from within, as if I were being besieged from the inside, if that's possible, and I thought I would explode from it all, from love and regret, Dov, love and regret as I never thought possible. In that instant I understood with surprise that I had become your father. The surprise lasted less than a minute because your mother began to hemorrhage, and one nurse gathered you up and hurried you away, while the other pushed me out the door and deposited me in the waiting room, where the men who had not yet seen their children looked at my bloody shoes and trembling lip and began to cough and shake.

I want you to know that I never gave up being your father, Dovik. Sometimes driving to work I found myself talking aloud to you. Pleading, reasoning with you. Or consulting with you about an especially difficult case. Or just telling you about the aphids attacking my tomatoes, or the simple omelet I made for myself one morning before your mother was awake, and ate alone in the bright silence of the kitchen. And when she fell ill, it was you I talked to while I sat in hard plastic chairs waiting for her to emerge from another procedure, another treatment, another test. I made a little scarecrow of you in my head and I talked as if you could hear me. The second time they bombed the number 18 bus I was two blocks away. Blood, so much blood, Dovi. The remains were everywhere. I watched the special Orthodox arrive to collect the splattered dead, to scrape the bits from the sidewalk with tweezers, to go up a ladder to peel a shred of ear from a high branch, to retrieve a child's thumb from a balcony. Afterwards I couldn't talk to anyone about it, not even your mother, but I talked to you. True Kindness, that's what they call themselves, the ones who arrive in their kippot and their Day-Glo yellow vests, always the first there to hold the dying as they go in shocked silence, to gather up the child without limbs. True kindness, because the dead cannot repay the favor. Yes, it was you I spoke to when I woke with nightmares. You I addressed when I looked at myself to shave in the mirror. I found you everywhere, hiding in the most unlikely places, and though at first I wondered why, soon enough I realized it was because I believed I could learn something from you, from your example. You who had always been so gifted at giving up, of letting go, of making yourself lighter and lighter, less and less, one friend at a time, one father less, one wife less, and now you have even given up being a judge, there is almost nothing anymore to tether you to the world, you're like a dandelion with only one or two hairs left, how easy it would be for you, with a little cough, a little sigh, to blow the last one away—

Suddenly I'm frightened, Dov. I feel a shiver, a coldness is seeping into my veins. For once I think I understand. What do I understand? Is it possible you've come to say goodbye again? That you intend to put an end—at last?

Wait, Dovik. Don't go. Remember how I used to put you to sleep at night, always you wanted one more question? Where does the sun go at night? What do wolves eat? Why is there only one of me?

One more question, Dovik. One more song. Five more minutes.

What would she do?

Where are you? All your life I've been asking.

I'll put on my shoes. I'll get down on my knees. I'll never mention it again.

I'll do what your mother would have done. I'll call every hospital.

ALL RISE

Your Honor, in the dark and stony coolness of my room I slept like someone rescued from a typhoon. A restless disquiet, the awareness of some misfortune, fluttered at the edge of my dreams, but I was too exhausted to investigate it. It gathered and coalesced over long hours of sleep, until at the moment I opened my eyes it burst into consciousness as an almost fanatical dread. Just beyond my reach was an insistent question that needed an answer, but what was the question? I felt a terrible thirst and fumbled in the dark for the little glass bottles of cold water. I had no sense of the time, but through the crack under the shutters I saw that it was still light out, or had become light again. The question pressed up more insistently, but when I tried to grasp it it eluded me. I groped for the key to open the door to the veranda, knocking over a bottle that shattered on the floor. The lock stuck then gave way to the violent light of Jerusalem. I looked out at the walls of the Old City, deeply moved by the view, and yet still the question was there, and my mind went to it like a tongue probing the tender spot of a missing tooth: it hurt but I wanted to know. When the sun went down and darkness slipped over the hills like a hood, everything in my head became amplified as if in a theater with perfect acoustics, a wretched clamminess seeped back in, and the urgent question rose up again, but what was it, what, until with a shock of nausea it surfaced at last:

What if I had been wrong?

* * *

Your Honor, for as long as I can remember I set myself apart. Or rather I believed that I had been set apart from others, chosen out. I won't waste your time with the injuries of my childhood, with my loneliness, or the fear and sadness of the years I spent inside the bitter capsule of my parents' marriage, under the reign of my father's rage, after all, who isn't a survivor from the wreck of childhood? I have no desire to describe mine; I only want to say that in order to survive that dark and often terrifying passage of my life I came to believe certain things about myself. I didn't grant myself magical powers or believe myself to be under the watch of some beneficent force—it was nothing so tangible as that—nor did I ever lose sight of the immutable reality of my situation. I simply came to believe that one, the factual circumstances of my life were almost accidental and didn't grow out of my own soul, and two, I possessed something unique, a special strength and a depth of feeling that would allow me to withstand the hurt and injustice without being broken by it. In the worst moments I only needed to pull myself beneath the surface, to dive down and touch the place within where this mysterious giftedness lived in me, and so long as I found it I knew that one day I would escape their world and make my life in another. There was a hatch in our apartment building that led to the roof and I used to run up four flights and scale a wall to where I could see the hard glimmer of the overpass where the trains ran, and there, where I knew no one could find me, a secret quiver of joy slid coolly through my veins and the hairs stood up on the back of my neck, because I sensed, in the raw stillness of the moment, that the world was revealing something of itself to me alone. When I couldn't get to the roof I could hide under my parents' bed, and though there was nothing to see I felt the same thrill, the same sense of privileged access to the underpinnings of things, to the currents of feeling on which all of human existence delicately rests, to the almost unendurable beauty of life, not mine or anyone else's, but the thing itself, irrespective of those who are born into and die out of it. I watched my sisters trip and tumble, one who learned to lie and steal and cheat, and the other who was destroyed by self-loathing, who tore herself up until she could no longer remember how to put the pieces together again, but I stayed the course, Your Honor, yes, I believed myself to be somehow chosen, not protected so much as made an exception of, imbued with a gift that kept me whole but was nothing more than a potential until the day came that I would make something of it, and as time passed, in the depths of me, this belief transformed itself into law, and the law came to govern my life. In so many words, Your Honor, that is the story of how I became a writer.

Understand: it isn't that I was excused from self-doubt. All my life it has shadowed me, a gnawing sense of doubt and the loathing that accompanied it, a special loathing I saved only for myself. Sometimes it lived in an uneasy opposition with my sense of chosenness, coming and going, troubling me until, in the end, my secret belief in what I was always won out. I remember all those years ago how I almost balked when the movers brought Daniel Varsky's desk through the door. It was so much larger than I remembered, as if it had grown or multiplied (had there been so many drawers?) since I'd seen it two weeks earlier in his apartment. I didn't think it would fit, and then I didn't want the movers to leave because I was afraid, Your Honor, of being left alone with the shadow it cast across the room. It was as if my apartment were suddenly plunged into silence, or as if the quality of the silence had changed, like the silence of an empty stage versus the silence of a stage on which someone has placed a single, gleaming instrument. I was overwhelmed and wanted to cry. How could I be expected to write at such a desk? The desk of a great mind, as S said the first time I brought him back to my place years later, possibly the desk of Lorca for God's sake? If it fell it might crush a person to death. If my apartment had felt small before, now it seemed tiny. But while I sat cowering beneath it I remembered, for some reason, a film I'd once seen about the Germans after the War, how they starved and were forced to chop down all the forests for firewood so that they wouldn't freeze, and when there were no trees left they turned their axes on the furniture—beds, tables and armoires, family heirlooms, nothing was saved—yes, suddenly they rose up before me wrapped in coats like dirty bandages, hacking away at the legs of tables and the arms of chairs, a little hungry fire already crackling at their feet, and I felt the tickle of a laugh in my belly: imagine what they'd have done with such a desk. They'd have swooped down on it like vultures on the carcass of a lion—what a bonfire it would have made, enough wood for days—and now I actually chortled out loud, biting my nails and practically grinning at that poor, overgrown desk that had so narrowly escaped becoming ash, had risen to the heights of Lorca, or at the very least of Daniel Varsky, and now had been abandoned to the likes of me. I ran my fingers along the nicked surface and reached up to caress the knobs of its many drawers as it stooped under the ceiling, because now I began to see it in a different light, the shadow it cast was almost inviting, Come, it seemed to say, like a clumsy giant who reaches out its paw and the little mouse jumps up into it and away they go together, over hills and plains, through forests and vales. I dragged a chair across the floor (I still remember the sound it made, a long scrape that gouged the silence), and was surprised to discover how small it appeared next to the desk, like the chair of a child or the baby bear in the story of Goldilocks, surely it would break if I tried to sit in it, but no, it was just right. I placed my hands on the desk, first one hand and then the other, while the silence seemed to strain against the windows and doors. I lifted my eyes up and I felt it, Your Honor, that secret quiver of joy, and either then, or soon enough, the immutable fact of that desk, the first thing I saw each morning when I opened my eyes, renewed my sense that a potential in me had been acknowledged, a special quality that set me apart and to which I was beholden.

Sometimes the doubt receded for months or even years, only to return and overwhelm me to the point of paralysis. One night, a year and a half after the desk arrived at my door, Paul Alpers called on the phone: What are you doing? he asked, Reading Pessoa, I said, though the truth was that I had been asleep on the sofa, and as I uttered this lie my eyes fell on a dark spot of drool. I'm coming over, he said, and fifteen minutes later he was standing at my door, looking pale and clutching a wrinkled brown bag. It must have been some time since I'd last seen him, because I was surprised at how much thinner his hair was. Varsky disappeared, he said, What? I said, though I'd heard him perfectly well, and then we both turned at the same time to stare at the towering desk, as if at any moment our tall, thin friend with the big nose might leap out, laughing, from one of the many drawers. But nothing happened except that a trickle of sadness began to leak into the room. They came to his house at dawn, Paul whispered. Can I come in? and without waiting for a reply walked past me, opened the cupboard, and returned with two glasses that he filled from the bottle of scotch in the paper bag. We raised our glasses to Daniel Varsky, and then Paul refilled the glasses and we toasted again, this time to all the kidnapped poets of Chile. When the bottle was finished and Paul sat hunched in his coat in the chair across from me, a hard but vacant look in his eyes, I was overwhelmed by two feelings: one, the regret that nothing ever stays the same, and two, the sense that the burden I labored under had now gotten immeasurably heavier.

I became haunted by Daniel Varsky and had difficulty concentrating. My mind would wander back to the night I met him, when I stood looking at the maps on the walls of all of the cities he'd lived in, and he told me about places I'd never heard of—a river outside of Barcelona the color of aquamarine where you could dive down through an underwater hole and surface in a tunnel, half-air, half-water, and walk for miles listening to the echo of your own voice, or the tunnels in the Judean Hills no wider than a man's waist where the followers of Bar Kochba lost their minds waiting out the Romans, through which Daniel had slid with nothing but a match to light his way—while I who have always suffered from a mild claustrophobia nodded meekly, and soon afterwards listened to him recite his poem which he did without blinking or looking away. *Forget Everything I Ever Said*. It really was quite good, Your Honor, the truth is that it was an astounding poem, and I never forgot it at all. There was a naturalness about it that it now seemed to me I would never possess. It was painful to acknowledge, but I'd always suspected it about myself, this little lie beneath the surface of my lines, how I piled the words on like decoration while for him it was like stripping everything away, more and more until he lay utterly exposed, writhing like a little white larva (there was something almost indecent about it which made it all the more breathtaking). Remembering it as I sat across from Paul, who by that point had fallen asleep, I felt a pain in my stomach just below my heart, like a deep stab from a tiny pocketknife, and I doubled over on his sofa, the sofa on which I had so often fallen asleep thinking about nothing, about little things, on what day of the week my birthday would fall, how I needed to buy a bar of soap, while somewhere in the desert, plains, or basements of Chile Daniel Varsky was being tortured to death. After that the sight of the desk every morning made me want to cry, not just because it embodied the violent fate of my friend, but also because now it only served to remind me that it had never really belonged to me, nor would it ever, and that I was only an accidental caretaker who had foolishly imagined that she possessed something, an almost magical quality, which, in fact, she'd never had, and that the true poet who was meant to be sitting at it was, in all likelihood, dead. One night I had a dream in which Daniel Varsky and I were sitting on a narrow bridge above the East River. For some reason he was wearing a patch over one eye like Moshe Dayan. But don't you feel, deep down, that there's something special about you? he asked me, carelessly swinging his legs while down below us swimmers, or perhaps dogs, tried to make their way against the current. No, I whispered, trying to hold back tears, No, I don't, while Daniel Varsky looked at me with a mixture of bewilderment and pity.

For a month I wrote almost nothing. At that time one of my many odd jobs was folding origami birds for a Chinese caterer owned by the uncle of one of my friends, and I outdid myself folding birds, cranes of every color, until my hands were first numb, then so stiff I couldn't curl my fingers around a cup and had to drink right from the faucet. Yet I didn't mind, there was something almost comforting about the way I began to see every object in the world as a variation on the eleven folds it took to make a crane, the flock of cranes a thousand strong that I packed into boxes that took up what little space there was not occupied by the desk. In order to get to the mattress where I slept I had to squirm between the boxes and the desk, so that for a moment my whole body was pressed against it and inhaling the smell of the wood, at once unplaceable and painfully familiar, I felt a bolt of misery so acute that I gave up the mattress and slept on the sofa until the day the man came to pick up the boxes of cranes (he let out a low whistle of surprise, then proceeded to count out the money), and my apartment was empty once again. Or rather, empty but for the desk, sofa, chest, and chairs of Daniel Varsky. After that, I did my best to ignore the desk, but the less attention I paid to it the more it seemed to grow, and soon I began to feel claustrophobic and took to sleeping with the windows open despite the cold, which lent my dreams a strange austerity. Then, passing the desk one night, I caught sight of a sentence on a page I'd written some months before. The sentence stayed in my head as I continued on to the bathroom, something about it was off, and while I was sitting on the toilet the right constellation of words suddenly leaped into my head. I went back to the desk, crossed out what I'd written, and wrote down the new sentence. Then I sat down and began to rework another sentence, and another after that, the thoughts crackled inside my skull, the words snapped together like magnets, and soon, without ceremony, I forgot myself in my work. I remembered myself again.

And so it happened time after time, the unspoken conviction always returned and won out over the anxious uncertainty. And though as the years passed one book after another fell short, each a new form of failure, I remained wedded to an unspoken belief that the day would come when

I would fulfill my promise at last, until simply, with stark lucidity, as if a knock on the head had shifted my perspective and everything clicked into place, it seized me—*What if I had been wrong?* Wrong for years, Your Honor. From the beginning. How obvious it suddenly seemed. And how unbearable. Over and over the question tore through me. Gripping my mattress like a raft, tossed into the whirlpool of the night, I turned and thrashed in my bed, consumed by feverish panic, waiting desperately for the first sign of light in the sky over Jerusalem. Come morning, exhausted, half dreaming, I wandered the streets of the Old City, and for a moment I felt on the verge of an exquisite understanding, as if I might turn a corner and discover, at last, the center of everything, the thing I had been striving to say all my life, and that from then on there would be no need to write, no need even to talk, and that like that nun walking ahead of me, disappearing through a door in the wall, wrapped in the mystery of God, I would live out the rest of my days in the fullness of silence. But a moment later the illusion was shattered and never had I been farther away, never was the extent of my failure more breathtaking. I'd set myself apart, believing myself to be in contact with the most essential things, not the mystery of God, which is a locked and foregone conclusion, but—what else can I call it, Your Honor?—the mystery of existence, and yet now, as the sun beat down and I stumbled along another narrow alley, tripping on the uneven paving stones, the growing horror unfolded that I might have been mistaken. And if I had, the repercussions of that mistake would be so vast they would leave nothing untouched, the columns would come crashing down, the roof would collapse, a void would open up and swallow everything. Do you see? I devoted my life to that belief, Your Honor. I gave up everything and everyone for it, and now it is the only thing left.

It wasn't always like this. There was a time when I imagined my life could happen in another way. It's true that early on I became used to the long hours I spent alone. I discovered that I did not need people as others did. After writing all day it took an effort to make conversation, like wading through cement, and often I simply chose not to make it, eating at a restaurant with a book or going for long walks alone instead, unwinding the solitude of the day through the city. But loneliness, true loneliness, is impossible to accustom oneself to, and while I was still young I thought of my situation as somehow temporary, and did not stop hoping and imagining that I would meet someone and fall in love, and that he and I might share our lives, each one free and independent, and yet bound together by our love. Yes, there was a time before I closed myself off to others. All those years ago when R left me I hadn't understood. What did I know of true loneliness? I had been young and full, bursting with feeling, overflowing with desire; I lived closer to the surface of myself. One night I came home and found him curled into a ball on the mattress. When I touched him his body flinched and the ball tightened, Leave me alone, he whispered or choked, his voice arriving as if from the bottom of a well. I love you, I said, stroking his hair, and the ball became tighter yet like the body of a frightened or sick porcupine. How little I understood of him then, of how the more you hide the more it becomes necessary to withdraw, how soon enough it becomes impossible to live among others. I tried to argue with him, in my arrogance I thought that my love could save him, could prove to him his own worth, his beauty and goodness, Come out, come out, wherever you are, I sang in his ear, until one day he got up and left, taking all of his furniture with him. Was it then that it began for me? True loneliness? That I, too, started not to hide but to retreat, so gradually that I hardly noticed it at first, during those stormy nights when I sat poised with the little wrench in my hand, jumping up to tighten the window bolts, sealing myself in to keep out the howling wind? Yes, it's possible that was the beginning, or nearly so, I can't really say, but it took years for the journey inward to become complete, for me to seal up all of the routes of escape, first there were other loves and other breakups, and then the decade of my marriage to S. By the time I met him I'd already published two books, my life as a writer had been established and so was the covenant I'd made with my work. The first night I brought him home we made love on the shag carpet with the desk hunched a few feet away in the darkness. It's a jealous beast, I joked, and thought I heard it groan, but no, it was only S, who at that moment perhaps foresaw something, or recognized the little grain of truth lurking inside the joke, how my work would always win over him, luring me back, opening its great black mouth and letting me slip in, sliding down and down, into the belly of the beast, how silent it was in there, how still. And yet for a long time I continued to believe it was possible to dedicate myself to my work and share my life, I didn't think that one need cancel out the other, though perhaps I already knew in my heart that if it were necessary I would not side against my work, could not any more than I could side against myself. No, if my back were pushed to the wall and I had to choose I would not have picked him, would not have picked *us*, and if S sensed that from the start soon enough he came to know it, and worse yet, for my back was never pushed to the wall, Your Honor, it was less dramatic and more cruel, how little by little I grew lazy with the effort required to hold and to keep us, the effort to share a life. Because it hardly ends with falling in love. Just the opposite. I don't need to tell you, Your Honor, I sense that you understand true loneliness. How you fall in love and it's there that the work begins: day after day, year after year, you must dig yourself up, exhume the contents of your mind and soul for the other to sift through so that you might be known to him, and you, too, must spend days and years wading through all that he excavates for you alone, the archaeology of his being, how exhausting it became, the digging up and the wading through, while my own work, my true work, lay waiting for me. Yes, I always thought there would be more time left for me, more time left for us, and for the child we might one day have, but I never felt that my work could be put aside as they could, my husband and the idea of our child, a little boy or girl that I sometimes even tried to imagine, but always only vaguely enough that he or she remained a ghostly emissary of our future, just her back while she sat playing with her blocks on the floor, or just his feet sticking out of the blanket on our bed, a tiny pair of feet. What of it, there would be time for them, for the life they stood for, the one I was not yet prepared to live because I had not yet done what I had meant to do in this one.

One day, three or four years into our marriage, S and I were invited for Passover at the house of a couple we knew. I don't even remember their names: the kind of people who enter easily into your life, then leave it just as easily. The Seder started late, after the couple had put their two young children to sleep, and we—all the guests—were talking and joking, maybe fifteen of us around the long table, in the sheepishly embarrassed and so overly jocular way of Jews who are reenacting a tradition they are far enough removed from to cause a painful self-consciousness, but not far enough to give up. Suddenly, into this raucous roomful of adults enters this child. We were all so busy with each other that we didn't notice her at first; she couldn't have been more than three, dressed in those pajamas with the feet, her bottom still saggy with a diaper, and clutching a sort of cloth or rag, the shredded remains of a blanket, I suppose, to her cheek. We had woken her from sleep. And suddenly, bewildered by this sea of strange faces and the clamor of voices, she let out a cry. A wail of pure terror that cut through the air, and silenced the room. For a moment everything froze as the scream hung above us like the question to end all the questions that particular night, of all nights, is designed to pose. A question which, because wordless, has no answer, and so must be asked forever. Perhaps it was only a second, but in my mind that scream went on, and still goes on somewhere now, but there, on that night, it ended when the mother stood, knocking over her chair, and in a single fluid motion rushed to the child, gathered her in, and held her aloft. In an instant the child quieted. For a moment she tipped her head back and looked up at her mother, and her expression was illuminated with the wonder and relief of finding, again, the only comfort, the infinite comfort, she had in the world. She buried her face in her mother's neck, in the smell of her mother's long lustrous hair, and her cries slowly grew dimmer and dimmer as the conversation around the table started up again, until at last she became silent, curled against her mother like a question mark—all that was left of the question that, for the time being, no longer needed to be asked—and fell asleep. The meal went on, and at some point the mother rose and carried the limp body of the sleeping child back down the hallway to her room. But I hardly noticed the conversation that swelled around me, so absorbed was I by the expression I'd glimpsed the moment before the girl had buried her face in her mother's hair, which filled me with awe and also grief, and I knew then, Your Honor, that I would never be that to anyone, the one who in a single motion could rescue and bring peace.

S, too, had been moved by what had happened, and that night after we arrived home he began to talk about having a child again. The conversation led, as it always did, to the old obstacles, the name and shape of which I can no longer remember exactly, beyond that they were well known to both of us, and, as we had identified them, required solutions before we could proceed with bringing our child, the one we imagined separately and together, into the world. But under the spell of that mother and little girl, that night S argued harder. There might never come a right time, he said, but despite the grief the child's expression had torn open in me, or maybe because of it, because I was afraid, I argued just as hard against it. How easy it would be to make a mess of it, I said, to crush the child as we had each been crushed by our parents. If we were going to do it we had to be ready, I insisted, and we weren't ready, far from it, and as if to prove the point—it was already dawn now, sleep was out of the question—I walked away, closed the door to my study, and sat down at the desk.

How many arguments and difficult conversations and even moments of great passion over the years ended the same way? I have to work, I'd say, untangling myself from the bedsheets, separating from his limbs, leaving the table, and as I walked away I could feel his sad eyes following me, as I closed the door behind me and returned to the desk, folding myself in, pulling my knees to my chest and crouching over my work, spilling myself out in those drawers, nineteen drawers, some big and some small, how easy it was to pour myself into them as I never could or tried to do with S, how simple to put myself into storage; sometimes I forgot whole parts of myself that I put away for the book I was going to write one day, the one that was going to be filled with everything. The hours would pass, the whole day, until suddenly it was dark out and there would be a tentative knock on the door, the little scuff of his slippers, his hands on my shoulders, which, I couldn't help it, became tense under his touch, his cheek next to my ear, Nada, he whispered, that's what he used to call me, Nada, Come out, come out, wherever you are, until at last one day he got up and left, taking all of his books, his sad smiles, the smell of his sleep, his film canisters filled with foreign change, and our imaginary child with him. And I let them go, Your Honor, as I had been letting them go for years, and I told myself I'd been chosen for something else, and comforted myself with all the work yet to be done, and lost myself in a labyrinth of my own creation without noticing that the walls were closing in, the air growing thin.

* * *

At sea in the night, losing myself in the city by day, almost a week passed lost inside a question that could no more be answered than that child's wordless question posed inside her terrified scream, though for me there was no comfort, no beneficent, loving force to gather me up and alleviate the need to ask. Those days after I arrived in Jerusalem run together in my mind into one long night and one long day, and I remember only that one afternoon I found myself sitting in the restaurant of the guesthouse, Mishkenot Sha'ananim, which looked out onto the same view as the veranda behind my room: the walls, Mount Zion, the Valley of Hinnom where the followers of Molech sacrificed their children by fire. In fact I'd eaten there every day, sometimes twice, since it was easier than trying to eat outside (the hungrier I became, the more impossible it seemed to enter a restaurant)—often enough that the heavyset waiter who worked there had taken an interest in me. While he scraped the crumbs from empty tables he glanced at me out of the corner of his eye, and soon he gave up trying to hide his curiosity and leaned on the bar watching me. When he came to clear my dishes he did so slowly, and asked whether everything had been to my liking, a question that seemed not to be so much about the food, which I often left untouched, but other, more intangible things. On that afternoon, after the dining room had emptied out, he approached me carrying a box displaying a variety of tea bags. Take, he said. I hadn't asked for tea, but I sensed there was no choice. I selected one, hardly looking at which. I'd lost my taste for everything and the sooner I chose one the sooner I thought he would leave me alone again. But he didn't leave me alone. He brought over a teapot of hot water, unwrapped the tea bag himself, and dropped it in. He lowered himself into the chair across from me. American? he asked. I nodded, pressing my lips together, hoping he would sense my desire to be left alone. They told me a writer, yes? I nodded again, though this time an involuntary squeak slipped out from between my lips. He poured the tea into my cup. Drink, he said, it's good for you. I offered him a tight little smile, more like a grimace. Over there, where you were looking, he said, pointing with a crooked finger toward the view. That valley under the walls used to be no-man's-land. I know, I said, crumpling my napkin in impatience. He blinked and continued. When I arrived here in 1950 I used to go to the border and look out. On the other side, five hundred meters away, I could see buses and cars, Jordanian soldiers. I was in the city, on the main street of Jerusalem, and I was looking at another city, at a Jerusalem I thought I would never be able to touch. I was curious, I wanted to know, what was it like there? But there was also something good about believing I would never reach that other side. Then there was the war of '67. Everything changed. At first I didn't regret it, it was exciting to finally walk those streets. But later I felt differently. I missed the days when I looked out and didn't know. He paused and glanced at my untouched cup. Drink, he urged again. A writer, eh? My daughter loves to read. A shy smile flickered across his thick lips. She's seventeen now. She studies English. I can buy one of your books here? You'll write something to her, maybe, she could read it. She's smart. Smarter than me, he said, with an irrepressible smile that revealed a wide gap between his front teeth and receding gums. His lids were heavy, like a frog's. When she was a little girl I used to tell her, Yallah, go outside, play with your friends, the books will wait for you but one day your childhood will be over forever. But she didn't listen, all day she sat with her nose in a book. It's not normal, my wife says, who will want to marry her, boys don't like girls like that, and she swats Dina over the head and tells her if she keeps going like that she's going to need glasses, and what then? I never told her that maybe if I was young again I would like a girl like that, a girl who is smarter than me, who knows things about the world, who gets a look in her eyes when she thinks about all of those stories in her head. Maybe you could write in one of your books for her, To Dina, Good luck with everything. Or maybe, Keep reading, whatever you think, you're the writer, you'll find the right words.

It became clear that he had come to the end of the long string of words wound up inside of him and now he was waiting for me to speak. But it had been days since I'd spoken to anyone and it was as if a weight were tied to my tongue. I nodded and mumbled something incomprehensible even to me. The waiter looked down at the tablecloth and wiped the sweat from his upper lip with a hairy forearm. With regret I realized that he was embarrassed, but I was helpless to extricate either of us from the awkward silence that was settling around us like cement. You don't like the tea? he asked at last. It's fine, I said, forcing down another sip. It's not a good one, he said. When you took it I was going to tell you. No one likes that one. At the end of the day all of the little compartments have only one or two packets left, but the compartment with that one is always full. I don't know why we still carry it. Next time choose the yellow one, he said. Everyone likes the yellow. Then he stood with a cough, cleared my cup, and retreated to the kitchen.

And that might have been the end of the story, Your Honor, and I wouldn't be here talking into the semi-darkness, and you wouldn't be lying in a hospital bed, if that evening, unable to forget the fallen look on the waiter's face, holding it up as proof of my chronic indifference to all but my work, I hadn't returned to the restaurant clutching a copy of one of my books, bought an hour earlier and signed to Dina. It must have been close to seven-thirty, late enough that the sun had already set but the city was still aglow like embers, and when I arrived in the restaurant I didn't see the waiter and feared his shift had ended for the day, until one of the other waiters gestured toward the terrace outside. Below the row of outdoor tables was a road, an extension of the guesthouse driveway that could only be accessed after passing through the security barricade. There, standing at the curb next to an idling motorcycle, was the heavyset waiter animated by a discussion, or perhaps an argument, with the driver.

The waiter's back was to me and I couldn't see the driver's face behind the dark visor of his helmet, only his thin frame clad in a leather jacket. But he saw me because all at once the loud discussion broke off and the driver deftly unsnapped the chinstrap, pulled off his helmet, shook out his black hair, and thrust his chin in my direction to alert the waiter to my presence. The sight of his young face, of his big nose and full lips and his long hair that I knew would smell like a dirty river, sent a shock through me no greater than if the boy I'd known for one night so long ago had at last emerged, perfectly preserved, from hiding for a quarter-century in the underground tunnels of Bar Kochba. I felt a shot of pain, and it took my breath away. The waiter swiveled to look. When he saw me he turned back to the driver and uttered a few rapid words in warning, then approached me. Hello, miss, you'd like to order something? Please take a seat here, I'll bring you the menu. No, I said, unable to tear my eyes away from the young man straddling the motorcycle, whose lips now curled into a faint, mischievous smile. I just came to bring you this, I said, holding out the book. The waiter fell back a step, brought his hand to his mouth in an exaggerated show of surprise, came forward as if to take the book from me, but then pulled his hand away and stepped back again, rubbing the bristles of his jaw. You're kidding me, he said, you really brought it? I don't believe it. Here, I said, pressing the book on him, For Dina. Now the young man's nostrils flared, as if he had caught the smell of something. You know Dina? The waiter turned and shot him a few more tense words. Ignore him, he's going now. Come sit down, how can I thank you, have some tea. But the young man made no movement to go. What is it? he asked. What is it he asks, listen to him, such a barbarian, it's a book, probably he never read one, and now he spat some more words in a different voice to the driver, who was balancing the motorcycle with one leg on the pedal and one on the street. You wrote it? the young man asked, unruffled. The evening air was fragrant, as if somewhere a nocturnal flower had opened itself. I did, I said, finding my voice at the last possible moment. Forgive me, miss, the waiter interjected, he's hassling you, come inside, it's quieter there, but now the driver flicked down the kickstand with his heel and in three quick strides was upon us. Close up, he was no less the image of Daniel Varsky, so much so that I was almost surprised that he didn't seem to recognize me, despite how many years had passed. Let me see, he said. Get out of here, the waiter growled, holding the book away from him, but the young man was quick and towered over the short, stubby waiter, and with a single swipe he plucked it away. Carefully opening the cover, he glanced from me to the waiter then back down at the book. To Dina, he read aloud, Wishing you luck. Yours, Nadia. Very nice, he said. I'll give it to her.

Now the waiter let loose a barrage of angry words, the veins pulsing in his neck as if they might burst, and the young man fell back a step, a wince of sadness flickered for a moment across his face, just the tiniest quiver, but I saw it. With delicate fingers, taking his time, he flipped through the pages. Then at last, ignoring the waiter's outstretched palm, he handed it back to me. It seems I'm not welcome here, he said. Maybe sometime you can tell me what it's about—his lips flicked into a smile—Nadia. It would be my pleasure, I whispered, and a door in the room of my life opened. Without a glance at the waiter, he pulled the helmet down over his head, mounted the motorcycle, revved the engine, and peeled away into the darkness.

A moment later I was seated at a table, and the waiter was hurrying around me laying a place with silverware. Accept my apologies, he said, that boy is a curse. A cousin on my wife's side, a troublemaker, nothing good will come of him. But his parents died, he doesn't have anyone, he comes to us. He lurks around and we can't turn him away. What's his name? I asked. The waiter looked at my glass, held it up to the light, noticed a smudge, and switched it with a glass from another table. What a gift, he went on, if only you could be there to see my Dina's face when I give it to her. I'd like to know his name, I repeated. His name? Adam, the sooner I hear the last of it the better. Why did he come here? I asked. To drive me crazy, that's why. Forget him, how about an omelet, you like an omelet, or maybe some pasta primavera? Look at the menu, anything, it's on the house. My name is Rafi. I'll bring you tea, take the yellow this time, you'll see, everyone loves the yellow.

But I did not forget him, Your Honor. I did not forget the tall, thin young man in the leather jacket whose name was Adam, but who I knew was also my friend, the disappeared poet Daniel Varsky. Twenty-seven years ago he was in that New York City apartment that looked as if a storm had swept through it, arguing about poetry and rocking back on his heels as if at any moment he might leap up like a pilot ejected from his seat, and then, in an instant he was gone, slipped through a hole, fallen into an abyss, and resurfaced here, in Jerusalem. Why? The answer seemed perfectly clear to me: to retrieve his desk. The desk he had left behind as collateral, which he had entrusted to me, of all people, to guard, which had lain for all these years on my conscience, at which I had enacted my conscience, and whose departure into other hands he had not wished for any more than I had wished to cease working at it. At least, that is how, in my addled mind, I allowed myself to imagine it, even as on another level I knew that such a story was no more than a hallucination.

That night in my room I contrived various reasons to give the waiter, Rafi, for needing to see Adam again: I wished to take a tour, by motorcycle, of the Dead Sea valley, and required a driver and guide, yes it absolutely had to be by motorcycle, and I could offer a generous fee for the service. Or: I needed someone to deliver an urgent package to my cousin Ruthie who lived in Herzliya, whom I had not seen in fifteen years and never liked, a package I could not trust to just anyone, and could he please send Adam, just a small favor to return the favor of the book for Dina, though of course I would be happy to offer a generous etcetera, etcetera for the service. I was not even above offering to "help" Rafi by bestowing on his wife's errant cousin, the family black sheep, some guidance from a benevolent outsider, the writer from America, offering to take him under my wing for a little while, to lend him some wisdom, set him on the right path. All night and all the next day I schemed about how to wrangle another encounter with Adam, but in the end it was unnecessary: the following evening, walking home along Keren Hayesod lost in thought, waiting for the light to change, a motorcycle pulled up alongside the curb. It was the roar of the engine first that pierced my daydreaming, but I didn't put it together with the young man who had flitted in and out of my thoughts all day until, still crouched on the motorcycle, he flipped up the darkened visor and gave me a long look, his eyes flashing with a joke that was either his alone or ours to share, I couldn't yet say, while the traffic grew restless, honked, and made its way around him. He said something I couldn't make out over the noise of the engine. I felt my breath quicken and stepped closer, I saw his lips move: Do you want a ride? The guesthouse was only ten minutes away by foot, but I didn't hesitate, at least, not in my mind, though once I accepted the offer it was not immediately clear to me how exactly to mount the motorcycle. I stood helplessly by, staring at the remaining portion of the seat not taken up by

Adam, unable to figure out how to vault myself up onto it. He offered his hand, and I gave him my left, but he let it drop and firmly took hold of my right, and in an elegant and practiced motion lifted me and guided me effortlessly onto the seat. He removed his helmet, revealing the same inscrutable smile I'd seen the night before, and delicately slipped it down over my head, gently sweeping aside my hair in order to fasten the strap. Then he took my hand and guided it firmly to his waist, and the tingle that had begun in the depths of my groin spread upward and ignited, jolting my body to life. He laughed, opening wide his mouth, it was nothing for him to laugh like that, and the motorcycle lurched under us and shot out into the street. He drove in the direction of the guesthouse, but as we approached the turnoff he shouted something back to me, What? I yelled from inside the muffled depths of the helmet, and he shouted something else, of which I heard only enough to know that it was a question, and when I didn't answer in time he passed the guesthouse entrance and kept going. For a moment I wondered blackly whether I'd been naïve to put myself in the hands of this troublemaker who haunted the edge of Rafi's family, but then he turned back and smiled at me, and it was Daniel Varsky turning back, and I was twenty-four again, the whole night lay ahead of us, and all that had changed was the city.

I clung to his waist, the wind caught his hair, we drove through the streets past the city's otherworldly residents I'd come to know well, the haredim in their dusty black coats and hats, the mothers leading their gaggle of children whose clothes trailed hundreds of loose threads as if the children themselves had been ripped unfinished from the loom, the pack of yeshiva boys who slammed past at a stoplight squinting as if newly let out of a cave, the old man stooped over his walker with the Filipino girl clutching the baggy elbow of his sweater, pulling a loose piece of yarn that she wrapped around her hand, unraveling him until his last words would be pulled out of him like a knot, him and her and the Arab sweeping the gutter, all of them unaware that we who sailed past them were only an apparition, ghosts more out of time than they. I would have liked to keep driving on, into the wilderness of the desert, but soon we turned off the main road and pulled into a parking lot with a wide view that looked north over the city. Adam cut the engine and reluctantly I let go of his waist and struggled to remove the helmet. Looking down at my crumpled pants and dusty sandals, my little reverie evaporated and I felt embarrassed. But Adam seemed not to notice, and motioned for me to follow him toward the promenade where little clots of tourists and walkers had gathered to watch the sunset play out its extravagant drama across Judea.

We leaned against the railing. The clouds turned brass, then purple. It's nice, no? he said, the first words of his that I'd understood that evening. I looked out at the crowded rooftops of the Old City, Mount Zion, Mount Scopus to the north, the Hill of Evil Counsel to the West, the Mount of Olives to the east, and maybe it was the bruising light, or the clarifying wind, or the relief of an unobstructed view, maybe it was the smell of pine, or of stone releasing heat before absorbing the night, or my nearness to the ghost of Daniel

Varsky, but it swept me away, Your Honor, and at that moment I joined them all, if I hadn't joined them already, the ones who have streamed toward this city for three thousand years and, upon arrival, lost their grip, went out of their minds, became the dream of a dreamer who is trying to strain the light out of the dark and gather it back up in a broken vessel. I like it here, he said. Sometimes I come with my friends, sometimes by myself. We stood in silence, looking out. You wrote that book? he asked. The one for Dina? Yes. That's what you do? It's your profession? I nodded. He thought about this, tearing off a broken nail with his teeth and spitting it out, and I winced, thinking of the nails they had torn out from the long fingers of Daniel Varsky. How did you become that? You went to school for it? No, I said. I started when I was young. Why do you ask? Do you write? He shoved his hands into the pockets and hardened his jaw. I don't know anything about those things, he said. An awkward silence followed, and now I saw that it was he who was embarrassed, perhaps for his boldness in taking me there. I'm glad you brought me, I said, it's beautiful. His face softened into a smile. You like it, eh? I thought so. Another silence. Trying to make conversation, I said, stupidly, Your cousin Rafi also likes a view. His face turned dark. That asshole? But he didn't bother to say more. Dina likes your books? he asked. I doubt she's ever read them, I said. Her father asked me to sign a book to her. Oh, he said, disappointed. My eyes fell on a small scar above his lip, and this tiny line, no longer than an inch, unleashed in me a torrent of bittersweet feeling. You're famous? he asked with a smile. Rafi said you're famous. I was surprised but I did not bother to correct him. It suited me to let him go on believing that I was something other than what I was. So what do you write? Detective stories? Love stories? Sometimes. But not only. You write about people you know? Sometimes. He cracked a grin, showing his gums. Maybe you'll write about me. Maybe, I said. He reached into his jacket pocket, pulled a cigarette out of a crumpled pack, and shielded it from the wind to light it. May I have one? You smoke?

The smoke singed my throat and chest, the wind got colder. I began to shiver and he lent me his jacket that smelled of old wood and sweat. He asked me more questions about my work, and though from someone else they would have made me groan (You ever write a murder mystery? No? So, what? You write things that happen to you? Your life? Maybe someone tells you what to write? They hire you? What do you call it, the publisher?), coming from him in the gathering dusk I didn't mind. When he, too, began to shiver and the silence between us grew thick it was time to go, and I found myself searching for another excuse to see him again. He handed me the helmet, though this time he didn't offer to help. Listen, I said, rummaging in my bag, there's somewhere I have to go tomorrow. I pulled out the wrinkled note that had migrated from my suitcase to my bedside table, from between the pages of my books to the bottom of my bag, but had not yet been lost. This is the address, I said. Could you give me a ride? I might need a translator, I don't know if they speak English. He seemed surprised but pleased, and took the piece of paper from me.

Ha'Oren Street? In Ein Karem? Our eyes met. I told him there was a desk there that I wanted to see. You need a desk to write at? he asked, interested now, even excited. Something like that, I said. You need one or you don't? he demanded. Yes, I need a desk, I said. And they have one here, he jabbed the note with his finger, at Ha'Oren Street. I nodded. He paused to think, running his hand through his hair again while I waited. He folded the note and put it in his back pocket. I'll pick you up at five, he said. OK?

That night I dreamed about him. Or rather sometimes it was him and sometimes it was Daniel Varsky, and sometimes through the generosity of dreams it was both of them at once, and we were walking through Jerusalem together, I knew it wasn't Jerusalem at all, but somehow I believed that it was Jerusalem, a Jerusalem that kept opening up into smoking gray fields which we had to cross to get back to the city, the way one tries to get back to a melody played long ago. For some reason Adam or Daniel was carrying a small case in his hand, a little case that contained some sort of instrument he planned to play for me if and when we found the place he was searching for, a kind of horn, perhaps, though it might also have been a weapon. At last the dream found its way into a room. But by then the case was gone, and while I watched Adam or Daniel slowly removed his clothes and folded them on the bed with the obsessive neatness of a man who has lived for many years under a severe authority, in a prison, perhaps, where he was schooled in a precise way to fold his clothes. The sight of his nakedness was tormenting, sad, and sweet, and I woke filled with tenderness and longing.

At four forty-five the following afternoon I was waiting in the lobby, having looked at myself too many times in the mirror, chosen a strand of red beads and dangling silver earrings. He was twenty-minutes late and I began to pace, sick at the thought of what awaited me in my room if he changed his mind and didn't come, the interminable night ahead, tearing myself to pieces. But at last I heard the bike in the distance and he appeared around the bend, and the ill feeling was drowned in a flat lake of shining pleasure, nothing could dim it, not even the spare helmet he held out this time, a sparkling red one that no one needed to tell me usually fit onto the heads of girls his own age who listened to the same bands and spoke his language, girls who could undress in daylight, with feet smooth as a baby's.

We made our way through the streets, coasting downhill, and I was happy, Your Honor, happy as I had not been for months or even years. When he leaned into a turn I felt his waist shift beneath my hands and that was enough, more than enough for someone who had so little left, and I did not think much about what I would say when we arrived at the house of Leah Weisz, the girl who had come five weeks ago to take away the desk. When we arrived in the sleepy village of Ein Karem, Adam stopped to ask for directions. We sat down in a café and he ordered for us in blunt, quick Hebrew, joking with the young waitress, cracking his knuckles, tossing his phone onto the table. A mangy dog limped across the street, but even it couldn't darken my mood or detract from the beauty of the place. Adam stirred a sugar into his coffee and sang along with the pop song drifting out of the café speakers. The light hit his face and I saw how young he was. Behind the cocky, off-tune singing, I caught the nervous shadow of uncertainty and understood that he didn't know what to say to me. Tell me about yourself, I said. He straightened up, lit a cigarette, grinned and licked his lips. So you're going to write about me after all? That depends, I said. On what? What I find out about you. He tipped back his head and exhaled a column of smoke. Go ahead, he said. You can use me in your book. I'm free. What do you want to know?

What did I want to know? What it looked like, the place he went home to at night. What hung on the walls and whether he had a stove that had to be lit with a match, whether the floors were tile or linoleum and whether he wore shoes when he walked across them, and the expression he wore when he looked in the mirror to shave. What his window looked out on, and what did his bed look like, yes, Your Honor, already I was imagining his bed, with its rumpled blankets and cheap pillows, his bed which, on the nights he spent alone, he sometimes slept across diagonally. But I didn't ask about any of it. I could wait, I could bide my time. Because he was singing, you see, and the evening would be coming on soon, and now I saw that something was different, yes, he had washed his hair.

He finished the army two years ago, he said. First he got a job with a security agency, but the boss accused him of certain things (he didn't say what) so he quit, and then he got a job painting houses with a friend of his who started a business, but the fumes got to him so he had to stop. Now he was working in a mattress store, but what he really wanted was to become an apprentice to a carpenter because he had always been good with his hands and liked to build things. And your family? I asked. He stubbed out his cigarette, glanced around distractedly, checked his phone. He didn't have any, he said. His parents died when he was sixteen. He did not say where or how. He had an older brother he had not spoken to for many years. Sometimes he thought of trying to look him up, but he never did. What about Rafi? I asked. I told you, he said, he's an asshole. The only reason I bother with him is because of Dina. If you met her you'd never be able to figure out how someone so beautiful came from that baboon. Tell me about her, I said, but he said nothing and turned away to hide the contortion that seized his face, a split second only in which all of his features collapsed and another face came through, a face he quickly wiped away with his sleeve. He stood up and threw some coins on the table, called goodbye to the waitress who smiled at him. Please, I said, reaching for my wallet, let me. But he clucked his tongue, swung his helmet up and pulled it down over his head, and at that moment, for some reason, I thought of his dead mother, of how she must have bathed him as a child, how she must have lifted him out of his crib at the bottom of the night and felt his wet lips on her face, unwrapped his little fingers from her long hair, sung to him, imagined his future, and then the needle of my mind slipped and it was Daniel Varsky's mother I was imagining, and as if in a mirror image it was the son who was dead and the mother who went on living. For the first time in the twenty-seven years I had been writing at his desk the magnitude of his mother's loss dawned on me, a window swung open and I saw out to the unutterable nightmare of her grief. I stood next to the motorcycle. The wind was still. There was the smell of jasmine. What is it, I thought, to go on living after your child is dead? I climbed onto the bike and gently clasped his waist in my hands, and each of my hands were those mothers' hands, the one who couldn't touch her child because she was dead, and the one who couldn't touch her child because she went on living, and then we arrived at Ha'Oren Street.

We did not immediately find the house because the number was hidden behind a riot of vines that grew up along the wall that surrounded it. There was an iron gate locked by a chain, but through it, half obscured by the trees, we could see a large stone house with green shutters, almost all of which were closed. To imagine the girl, Leah, living there was to give her an entirely new dimension, a profundity I hadn't sensed. Peering into the dusty garden, I was myself filled with a sadness that came from the uncanny feeling of being in a place that had been touched, however obliquely, by Daniel Varsky: inside that shuttered house lived a woman, or so I believed, who had once known and most likely loved him. What had Leah's mother thought about her daughter's search, and how had she felt when the desk of the man, the father of her child, who had been so brutally ripped from the world, had arrived home to her like a giant wooden corpse? As if that weren't enough, now I was here to deliver his ghost. I considered making up an excuse, telling Adam I'd made a mistake, this wasn't the place, but before I could he found the bell under the leaves and rang it. A tinny electric rasp sounded. Somewhere a dog barked. When there was no answer he pressed it again. You have a telephone number maybe? he asked, but I did not so he held it down for a third time and the lack of even the faintest stirring, the paralysis of the stones and the shutters and even the leaves came back as sheer stubbornness. They know you're coming? Yes, I lied, and Adam shook the bars of the gate to see if the chain would give. I guess I'll have to come back, I began to say, but at that moment an old man appeared, or rather lengthened like a shadow from behind the wall, holding an elegant walking stick. Ken? Ma atem rotsim? Adam answered him, gesturing to me. I asked if he spoke English. Yes, he said, gripping the silver handle of his cane which I saw now was the shape of a ram's head. Does Leah Weisz live here? Weisz? he said, Yes, I said, Leah Weisz, she came to see me last month in New York to pick up a desk. A desk? the old man echoed, uncomprehending, and now Adam fidgeted impatiently and said some more words to the man in Hebrew. Lo, the old man said, shaking his head, lo, ani lo yodea klum al shum shulchan, He doesn't know anything about a desk, Adam said, and the old man balanced on his cane and made no movement to unlock the gate. Maybe they gave you the wrong address, Adam said. He pulled Leah's crumpled note out of his jeans and offered it through the bars. Unhurriedly the old man reached into his breast pocket, unfolded a pair of glasses and slipped them onto his face. It seemed to take him a long time to understand what was written there. When he finished reading, he turned it over to look at the other side. Finding it blank, he turned it back again. Ze ze o lo? Adam demanded. The old man neatly folded the note and passed it back through the bars. This is 19 Ha'Oren Street, but there is no one by that name here, he said, and I was surprised by his accent, which was fluent and refined.

Now it occurred to me that there was something cunning I had missed in Leah Weisz. That she might have deliberately given me the wrong address in case I changed my mind and tried to get back the desk. But then why give any address at all? I hadn't asked, and the fact that she had left one had almost struck me, I realized now, as a kind of invitation. The old man stood in meticulously ironed shirtsleeves while behind him the house held its breath beneath the leaves. What was it like inside, I wondered. What did the kettle look like, was it old and dented, the cup for the tea, were there books, what hung there in the gloomy hallway, something biblical, a little etching of the binding of Isaac perhaps? The old man studied me with sharp blue eyes, the eyes of a tamed eagle, and I sensed that he, too, was curious about me, as if there were a question he wished to ask. Even Adam seemed to notice it, and looked from the old man to me, then back to the old man, and the three of us hung in the balance of the silence that surrounded the house until at last Adam shrugged, ripped off another sliver of nail with his teeth, spat it out, and turned back to the bike. Good luck, the old man said, his hand tightening around the curled silver horns of the ram, I hope you find what you're looking for. I don't know what possessed me, Your Honor, I blurted out, I didn't want it back, the desk, I only wanted—but I stopped because I couldn't say what it was that I had wanted, and a look of pain flickered across the old man's face. Adam started up the engine behind me. Let's go, he said. I didn't want to leave yet, but there seemed to be no choice. I got onto the motorcycle. The old man lifted his stick in farewell and we drove away.

Adam was hungry. I didn't care where we went, so long as he didn't bring me back to the guesthouse. I tried to understand what had happened. Who was Leah Weisz? Why had I so blithely accepted everything she'd told me without the least bit of proof? So willing had I been to give up that desk around which I had bent my life that one might have thought I had been eager, keen to be relieved of it at last. It's true that I'd always thought of myself as its guardian, sooner or later, I told myself, someone would come for it, but the truth was that it was merely a convenient story I told myself, a story like so many others that excused me from the responsibility of my decisions, that lent them an air of the inevitable, and beneath it all I had been convinced that I would die at that desk, my inheritance and my marriage bed, so why not also my bier?

Adam took me to a restaurant on Salomon Street where he was friends with some of the waiters. They clapped him on the back and looked at me appraisingly. He grinned and what he said made them laugh loudly. We sat down by the window. Outside, on a balcony that hung above the narrow street, a man sat on an old mattress hugging his young son and talking to him. I asked

Adam what he had said to his friends. With lips half curled in a smile he looked around at the other diners to gauge their reaction, as if he had walked in with a celebrity, as absurd as that may seem. With a pang I realized that I was deceiving him, but it was too late. What could I say: No one reads my books, perhaps soon they will stop publishing me? I told them you're writing about me, he said and flashed another grin. Then he snapped his fingers and his friends laughed and brought us plates stuffed with food, then more plates after that. They looked me over and I saw the amusement in their eyes, as if they sensed my desperation and knew something about their friend that I did not. From the back of the restaurant they watched us, enjoying their friend's luck at having netted this older woman, a rich and famous American, or so they believed, until Adam snapped again and they came forward again with a bottle of wine. He ate ravenously, as if he had not eaten for many days, and it was a pleasure to watch him, Your Honor, to sit back with my glass of wine and enjoy his beauty and his hunger. When the meal was finished (he devoured almost all of it), his friends put the check in front of me, and I saw that they had chosen for us the most expensive bottle of wine. While I fumbled with my money, trying to count out the right bills, Adam rose and joined them, joking and chewing on a toothpick. When I stood I felt the wine in my head. I followed him out of the restaurant, and I knew he could feel my eyes on him, knew that he knew I wanted him, though I would like to say, Your Honor, in my defense, that it was not only lust I felt for him, it was also a kind of tenderness, as if I might be able to lessen the pain I had seen in the face he had wiped away with his sleeve. He winked at me when he tossed me the helmet, but it was the awkward and unsure young man behind the posturing that made me want to ask him home with me. We arrived at the entrance of the guesthouse and I groped for the right words, but before I could say them he announced that a friend of one of the waiters had a desk, and if I wanted he could bring me to see it tomorrow. Then he kissed me chastely on the cheek and drove away without saying what time he would come for me.

That night I found a number for Paul Alpers in my address book. I had not spoken to him for many years and when he picked up after two short rings I almost hung up. It's Nadia, I said, and because that did not seem like enough, I added, I'm calling from Jerusalem. For a moment he was silent, as if he were trying to get back to the place where that name—mine or the city's—meant something to him. Abruptly, he laughed. I told him that I had gotten divorced. He told me that he had lived for some years with a woman in Copenhagen but it was over now. We did not go on for long, hurried by the long distance of the call. After we cleared the particularities of our lives aside I asked him if he sometimes thought about Daniel Varsky. Yes, he said. I was going to call you a few years back. They found out that he was kept on a boat for a while. A boat? I echoed. In the hold, Paul said, with other prisoners. One of them survived, and some years later he met someone who knew Daniel's parents. He said they kept him alive for some months, though only barely. Paul, I said at last, Yes, he said, and I heard a lighter click, then the drag of his cigarette. Did he have a child? A child? Paul said. No. A daughter, I asked, with an Israeli woman he was with not long before he disappeared? I never heard of a daughter, Paul said. I doubt it, really. He had a girlfriend in Santiago, and that's why he kept coming back when he shouldn't have. Her name was Inés, I think. She was Chilean, that much I know. It's strange, Paul said, I never met her but suddenly I remember now that a while back I had a dream about her.

As Paul spoke it occurred to me with something like surprise that if it weren't for the peculiar logic of Paul's dreams I would never have met Daniel Varsky, and all these years it would have been someone else writing at his desk. After I hung up I couldn't sleep, or perhaps I didn't want to sleep, afraid to turn off the lights and meet whatever the dark would bring. In order to distract myself from thinking about Daniel Varsky, or worse yet about my life and the question that tormented me as soon as I let my thoughts slip, I concentrated on Adam. In extravagant detail I imagined his body and the things I would do to it and those he would do to mine, although in these fantasies I allowed myself another body, the one I had before mine began to blur and lose shape and go off in a different direction from me, the one who existed inside of it. I showered at dawn, and at seven sharp I was there when the guesthouse restaurant opened. Rafi's face clouded over when he saw me and he retreated to the bar and occupied himself with drying the glasses, leaving the other waiter to attend to me. I lingered over my coffee, and, discovering that my appetite had returned, went back twice to the buffet. But he continued to avoid my eyes. Only as I left did he run after me in the hall. Miss! he called. I turned. He kneaded one broad hand with the other, and glanced over his shoulder to make sure we were alone. Please, he groaned, I'm asking you. Don't get involved with him. I don't know what he says to you, but he's a liar. A liar and a thief. He's using you to make a fool of me. I felt a flash of anger, and he must have seen it on my face because he hurried to explain. He wants to turn my own daughter against me. I forbid her to see him and he wants—he began to say, but at that moment the director of the guesthouse approached from the other end of the hall and the waiter bowed his head and hurried away.

From then on I dedicated myself to seducing Adam. He was, that waiter, no more than a fly buzzing around a desire I no longer had any control over, which I did not wish to control, Your Honor, because it was the only live thing left in me, and because so long as I was consumed by it I did not have to face the view of my life that had come so sickeningly into focus. I even took a certain amused pleasure in the fact that it had taken a man less than half my age with whom I had nothing in common to awaken such a passion in me. I went back to my room and waited; I could wait all day and all night, it didn't matter. Close to dusk the phone rang and I picked it up on the first ring. He would come for me in an hour. Perhaps he knew I'd been waiting, but I hardly cared. I waited some more. An hour and a half later he arrived and took me to a house down an alley somewhere off Bezalel. A necklace of colored lights was strung up in the fig tree and people were eating around the table beneath it. Introductions were made, folding chairs brought from inside, space created around the already tightly packed table. A girl in a thin red dress and high boots turned to me. You're writing about him? she asked, incredulous. I looked across the table at Adam drinking a bottle of beer and felt a yearning and also the special warmth of knowing I had come with him, and it was me he would leave with. I smiled at the girl and helped myself to olives and salted cheese. They seemed nice, those kids, people who would not have tolerated a liar and a thief among them; Rafi had been unfair to him. Dessert was brought out, then tea, and eventually Adam motioned to me that it was time to leave. We said goodbye to the others and walked out with a boy who had long blond dreadlocks and delicate glasses. He ducked into an old silver Mazda, rolled down the window and waved for us to follow. But when we arrived at his apartment the desk in question was not there either, and I waited while Adam and the dreadlocked boy passed a joint back and forth in the tiny, stained kitchen under last year's calendar showing views of Mount Fuji. They discussed something in rapid Hebrew, then the boy went away and came back jingling a set of keys on a Mogen David key chain which he tossed to Adam. Then he showed us out, waving a cloud of hashish out into the hall, and we drove to a third place, a group of tall apartment buildings overlooking Sacher Park, hewn of the same sallow stone as everything else in the city. We rode up to the fifteenth floor, thrown together in the tiny mirrored elevator. The hallway was dark and as he groped for the switch I felt a throb of longing and almost reached out and pulled him to me. But the fluorescent lights buzzed and flickered awake in the nick of time, and with the keys dangling from the little metal Mogen David Adam unlocked the door to 15B.

Inside it was dark as well, but I'd lost my nerve and so waited with arms wrapped around my waist until the lights came on again and we found ourselves in an apartment stuffed with heavy, dark furniture incongruous with the blinding desert light: mahogany vitrines with leaded-glass cabinets, Gothic high-backed chairs with carved finials, their seats upholstered with tapestry. The metal blinds were drawn over the windows as if whoever lived there had gone away for an uncertain amount of time. There was hardly a foot of exposed space left on the walls, so cluttered were they with thickly impastoed fruit and flowers, pastoral scenes so dark that they seemed to have survived the smoke of a fire, and etchings of little humped beggars or children. Improbably mixed in with the rest were cheap Plexiglas frames with blown-up panoramic shots of Jerusalem, as if the inhabitants were unaware that the real Jerusalem lay just on the other side of the blinds, or as if they had made a pact to refuse the reality outside the windows and chosen instead to go on yearning for Eretz Yisrael just as they had when they dwelled in whatever part of Jewish Siberia they'd come here from, because they had arrived too late in life and did not know how to adapt themselves to this new latitude of existence. While I studied the faded colored photographs of children that colonized the sideboard—smiling, rosy-cheeked toddlers and gawky bar-mitzvahs who by now probably had children of their own—Adam disappeared down a carpeted hall. After a few minutes he called to me. I followed his voice to a small room whose shelves were lined with paperbacks on whose cumulative surface a thick layer of dust had settled, visible even in the lamplight.

This is it, Adam said with a sweep of his hand. It was a desk of blond wood whose rolltop had been drawn back to reveal an intricate inlaid pattern whose gleam, protected all this time from the democratizing blanket of dust, was unnerving, as if the person who had been sitting at it had only moments ago gotten up and walked away. Eh, he said, you like it? I ran my finger along the pattern of wood which felt as smooth as if it were one piece, not the many hundreds from how many different varieties of trees it must have taken to produce the revelatory geometry of cubes and spheres, collapsing and expanding spirals, of space folding in on itself before suddenly expanding to reveal a glimpse of infinity, that hid some meaning the maker had obscured by an overlay of birds, lions, and snakes. Go ahead, he urged, sit at it. I was embarrassed and wanted to protest that I could no more work at such a desk than I could write out my grocery list with a pen that had belonged to Kafka, but I didn't want to disappoint him and sank into the chair he had pulled out. Who does it belong to? I asked. Nobody, he said. But surely the people who live here— They don't live here anymore. Where are they? Dead. But then why is everything still here? This is Yerushalayim, Adam smirked, maybe they'll come back. I was seized by a feeling of claustrophobia and wanted to get out of there, but when I rose and stepped back from the desk Adam's face fell. What, you don't like it? I do, I said, I like it very much, So what? he said, It must cost a fortune, I said, For you he'll make a good price, he replied with a grin and something rusted but sharp flashed in his eyes. Who will? Gad. Who is Gad? The one you met just now, But who is he to them? The grandson, he said. Why would he want to sell only the desk? Adam shrugged, and nimbly closed the rolltop. How should I know? he shrugged. He probably hasn't had time for the rest.

Adam took a thorough tour of the place, opening the drawers of the sideboard and turning the delicate key in a glass cabinet to inspect the little collection of Judaica. He made use of the bathroom, relieving himself in a long stream that I heard through the door left ajar. Then we left the apartment, returning it to the dark. But in the elevator down we went on discussing the desk, and, as the conversation continued in a dim bar, moving to other subjects, but always returning to the desk, I began to feel the thrill of the unspoken thing I believed we were actually negotiating, for which the desk, with its hidden meanings, was only a stand-in.

* * *

Of the days and nights that followed, I want to spare you, Your Honor, without sparing myself:

Here we are in an expensive Italian restaurant and Adam, in the same shirt and jeans that he has worn for four days straight, clinks my glass of wine with his beer and asks with a conspiratorial smile whether I have come up yet with the story of which he will be the hero. When we share a tiramisu with two spoons, of which I let him eat most, he returns, like an organ-grinder with a limited repertoire, to the question of the desk. Having felt out the situation, he thinks he can get Gad to come down a little, though it should not be forgotten that it is a one-of-a-kind antique, the work of a master that on the open market would fetch many times more. I play along, pretending to be swayed by his salesmanship while searching for his foot under the table. So long as I almost let myself believe what I am saying it's fine, at least until I suddenly remember with a bolt of nausea that I don't know if I will ever write anything again.

Here we are having lunch in the café of the Ticho House, which Adam has heard from one of his friends is the sort of place that writers like to go. I am wearing a billowy floral dress and a purple suede drawstring purse with gold brocade that I bought the day before after seeing them in the window of a boutique. It has been a long time since I bought myself anything new, and it is exciting and strange to be wearing these things, as if changing my life could begin so simply. The shoulder straps keep falling off and I let them. Adam plays with his phone, gets up to make a call, comes back and pours the rest of the sparkling water into my glass. Someone, somewhere, has taught him the rudiments of chivalry, and he has taken these and refashioned them into his own erratic code. When we walk he hurries ahead of me. But when we arrive at a door he opens it and waits for as long it takes for me to catch up and go through. Often we go without talking. It is not talking that interests me.

Here we are in a bar on Heleni Ha'Malka. Some of Adam's friends arrive, the same ones I'd met around the table under the fig tree, the girl with the thin red dress (now it's yellow) and her friend with dark bangs across her forehead. They greet me with kisses on the cheek as if I were one of them. The band swaggers onto the stage, the drums begin to thump, and at the first few notes of the guitar the straggly crowd claps, someone whistles from behind the bar, and though I know I am not one of them, that I am in every way a stranger in their midst, I am filled with gratitude to be so simply accepted. I feel an urge to take the girl in the yellow dress by the hand and whisper to her, but I can't think of the right words. The music gets louder and more discordant, the lead singer screams in a raw voice, and though I don't want to distinguish myself from the others I can't help but think he's taking it a bit far, exaggerating things a little, so I find my way to the bar to buy myself a drink. When I turn, the girl with dark bangs is standing next to me. She shouts something to me, but the music overpowers her tiny voice. What? I shout back, trying to read her lips, and she repeats it, bursting into a giggle, something about Adam, but I still can't understand, so the third time she leans right up to my ear and yells, He's in love with his cousin, then leans back, covering her smile, to see if I've heard. I scan the crowd and when my eyes find Adam making a show of holding up his lighter while the singer croons I turn back and return the girl's smile, and with a look I tell her that if she thinks she knows the whole story she's wrong. I walk away. I have that drink and then I have another. The singer goes back to screaming in excess, but now the music grows rounder, brighter, and suddenly Adam grabs my hand from behind and tugs me outside, and I know I won't have to wait much longer now. We get onto his bike—it's nothing now for me to climb on behind and fit myself to him—and I don't need to ask where we're going because I'll go anywhere.

Here we are back in the grimly lit concrete entryway of Gad's apartment. We're going up the stairs and Adam is singing off-key, he's taking the steps by twos. I'm breathless. Inside everything is the same, only Gad isn't home. Adam searches the drawers and shelves for something while I switch on the stereo and press play, so sure am I of what he is searching for and what is about to happen. The CD skips to life, the music floats out of the speakers; it's possible I begin to sway or to dance. Turn it off, he says, coming up behind me, and before I can feel him I can smell him like an animal. Why? I ask, turning with a flirtatious smile, Because, he says, and I think, All the better in silence. I reach up and take his face in my hands. With a moan I press my body into his, searching with my groin for something hard, I part my lips and bring them to his, my tongue slips in and tastes the heat of his mouth; I was starving, Your Honor, I wanted everything at once.

It lasts only a moment. Then he shoves me away. Get off of me, he growls. Not understanding, I reach for him again. With his palm he pushes my face and throws me down with such force that I fall back onto the sofa. He wipes his mouth with the back of his hand, his hand which I see now holds the keys to the apartment filled with the dead people's furniture. From far off, the understanding arrives that they are not dead after all. Are you out of your mind? he hisses, his eyes shining with hostility and also something familiar I cannot place at first. You could be my mother, he spits, and then I realize that it is disgust.

I lie sprawled on the sofa, astonished and humiliated. He turns to leave, but stops at the door. The purple suede purse sits in the entry where I'd left it when we came in. He picks it up. In his hands it becomes what it must have always been on me: absurd and pathetic. With his eyes pinned on me, he digs his hand in up to the forearm and rifles through it. When he does not find what he is looking for he overturns it and the contents scatter. Quickly he leans over and plucks up my wallet. Then he throws the purse down, kicks it out of his way with his boot, and, with a final look of repugnance in my direction, walks out, slamming the door behind him. My lipstick continues to roll across the floor until it hits the wall.

The rest hardly matters, Your Honor. I only want to say that the devastation tore through me, pulling the roof down at last. What was he, after all? Nothing more than an illusion I had conjured to deliver the answer that I could not give myself, though I had known it all along. When at last I roused myself and with shaking hands filled a glass from the kitchen faucet, my eyes fell on a little dish with some loose change and Gad's car keys. I did not hesitate. I picked them up, walked past the scattered contents of my purse, and out of the apartment. The car was parked across the street. I unlocked it and slid into the driver's seat. In the rearview mirror I saw that my face was swollen from crying, my hair matted, the gray showing through. I am an old woman now, I thought to myself. Today I have become an old woman, and I almost laughed, a cold laugh to match the coldness inside of me.

I steered the car into the road, bumping over the curb. I followed one road and then another. When I came to a familiar intersection I turned in the direction of Ein Karem. I thought of the old man who lived on Ha'Oren Street. I did not think of going to him, but I drove toward him. Soon I lost my way. The headlights slipped over the trunks of trees, the road led into the Jerusalem Forest and fell away to one side, sloping down into a ravine. All it would have taken was a jerk of the wheel to throw the car down into the dark below. Tightening my knuckles, I imagined the headlights bouncing in the darkness, the upturned wheels spinning in silence. But I do not have whatever it is that makes a person capable of extinguishing herself. I drove on. I thought, for some reason, of my grandmother whom I used to visit on West End Avenue before she died. I thought of my childhood, of my mother and father who are both dead now, but whose child I cannot escape being any more than I can escape the nauseatingly familiar dimensions of my mind. Now I am fifty, Your Honor. I know that nothing will change for me. That soon, maybe not tomorrow or next week, but soon enough the walls around me and the roof above me will rise again, exactly as they were before, and the answer to the question that brought them down will be stuffed into a drawer and locked away. That I will go on again as I always have, with or without the desk. Do you understand, Your Honor? Can you see that it is too late for me? What else would I become? Who would I be?

A moment ago you opened your eyes. Dark gray eyes, completely alert, that caught and gripped me for a moment in their gaze. Then you closed them again and drifted away. Maybe you sense that I am coming to the end, that the story that has been hurtling toward you from the start is about to turn the bend in the road and collide with you at last. Yes, I wanted to weep and gnash my teeth, Your Honor, to beg your forgiveness, but what came out was a story. I wanted to be judged on what I did with my life, but now I will be judged by how I described it. But perhaps that is right, after all. If you could speak, perhaps you would say that is how it always is. Only before God do we stand without stories. But I am not a believer, Your Honor.

The nurse will come soon to administer another dose of morphine, touching your cheek with the gentle ease of one who has made a life of caring for others. She said they will wake you tomorrow, and now tomorrow has almost come. She washed the blood from my hands. She took a brush out of her purse and ran it through my hair, just as my mother used to do. I reached up and stilled her hand. I'm the one who—I began to say, but stopped there.

You stood pinned in the headlights, so still that I thought, in the fraction of a second left for me to think, that you were waiting for me. Then the screech of brakes, the body blow. The car skidded and was still. My head hit the wheel. What have I done? The road was empty. How long until I heard the abysmal moan of pain, and understood that you were alive? Until I found you crumpled in the grass and took your head in my hands? Until the wail of the siren, the red splash of lights, gray dawn through the window in which I saw, for the first time, your face? What have I done, what have I done?

They swarmed around you. They hung you back up on life, like a coat that has fallen from its hook.

Talk to him, she said, fixing the electrode that had come loose from your chest. It's good for him to hear you. Good? She said, It's good for you to talk. About what? Just talk. For how long? I asked, though I knew I would sit by your side for as long as they let me, until your true wife or lover arrived. His father is on the way, she said, and drew the curtains around us. For a thousand and one nights, I thought. More.

SWIMMING HOLES

Lotte remembered me until the very last. It was I who often felt I could no longer remember the person she had once been. Her sentences began easily enough, but quickly faltered and became submerged in oblivion. Nor did she understand me. At times she gave the impression of understanding, but even if some combination of words I struck on had ignited a glimmer of sense in her mind, by the next moment she'd lost it. She died quickly, without pain. On the 25th of November we celebrated her birthday. I bought a cake from the bakery she liked in Golders Green, and the two of us blew out the candles together. For the first time in weeks I saw a flush of happiness in her cheeks. The following night she came down with a very high fever and had trouble breathing. Her health wasn't good, and she was frail by then; in the last years of her life she had aged a great deal. I called our doctor, who came to see her at the house. Her condition worsened, and some hours later we brought her to the hospital. The pneumonia came over her rapidly and overwhelmed her. In her last hours she begged to be let to die. The doctors did everything they could to save her, but when there was nothing more to do they left us in peace. I climbed onto the narrow bed with her and stroked her hair. I thanked her for the life she'd shared with me. I told her that no one could have been happier together than we had been. I told her again the story of the first time I saw her. Soon after that she lost consciousness and slipped away.

About forty people came to Highgate Cemetery on the afternoon I buried her. Long ago, we had decided to be buried together there, where we had walked so many times among the overgrown lanes, reading the names on the toppled gravestones. That morning I was flustered and nervous. Only as the rabbi began to say Kaddish did I realize that some part of me believed her son might attend. Why else had I published the small announcement in the newspaper? Lotte would certainly have disapproved. To her, private life was exactly that. Through eyes blurred by tears, I scanned the trees for a figure in the landscape. Hatless. Coatless, perhaps. Quickly drawn, as the masters sometimes drew a portrait of themselves hidden in a dark corner of the canvas or concealed in a crowd.

Three or four months after Lotte died I began to travel again, as I had been unable to do while she had been unwell. Mostly in England or Wales, and always by train. I liked to go where I could walk from village to village, staying in a different place each evening. Making my way like that, with only a small rucksack, I felt a sense of freedom I hadn't known for many years. Freedom and peace. The first trip I took was to the Lake District. A month later I went to Devon. From the village of Tavistock, I set out across Dartmoor, losing my way until at last I saw the chimneys of the prison rise up in the distance. About two months after that I took a train to Salisbury to visit Stonehenge. I stood with the other tourists under the monstrous gray sky, imagining the Neolithic men and women whose lives so frequently came to an end with blunt-force trauma to the cranium. There was some litter on the ground, shiny metallic wrappers and so on. I went around picking these things up, and when I stood up again the stones were even larger and more frightening than before. I also began to paint, a hobby I'd had when I was young, but had abandoned when I realized that I lacked talent. But talent, worshipped for all that it promises when one is young, seemed at last utterly irrelevant: nothing could be promised to me now, nor did I wish for it to be. I bought a small collapsible easel and took it with me on my trips, unfolding it whenever a particular view struck me. Sometimes someone would stop to watch and we would find our way into a conversation, and it occurred to me that there was no need to tell such people the truth about myself. I would say I was a country doctor from outside Hull, or an airman who'd flown a Spitfire in the Battle of Britain, and as I said it I could actually see the pattern of fields below, opening out in all directions like a code. There was nothing sinister in it, nothing I wished to hide, only a certain pleasure in leaving myself and becoming someone else momentarily, and then a different sort of pleasure, watching the stranger's back recede into the distance, of slipping back into myself again. I felt something similar on nights when I would wake up in some bed-and-breakfast and forget for an instant where I was. Until my eyes adjusted enough to make out the lines of the furniture, or some detail of the previous day came back to me, I hung suspended in the unknown, the unknown which, still loosely tethered to consciousness, slips so easily into the unknowable. A fraction of a second only, a fraction of pure, monstrous existence free of all landmarks, of the most exhilarating terror, stamped out almost immediately by a grasp of reality which I came to think of at such times as blinding, a hat pulled over one's eyes, since though I knew that without it life would be almost uninhabitable, I resented it nevertheless for all it spared me.

On one such night, waking before I was able to remember where I was, an alarm rang out. Or rather it was the alarm that woke me, though there must have been a delay between the break from my sleep and an awareness of the earsplitting noise. I jumped out of bed and my arm swept the bedside lamp onto the floor. I heard the bulb shatter, and remembered that I was staying in the Brecon Beacons National Park in Wales. There was a smell of acrid smoke as I fumbled for the light switch and pulled on my clothes. The stench of burning in the hallway was overpowering, and I heard shouts coming from the bowels of the building. Somehow I found the stairs. On the way down I met others in various stages of dress. There was a woman holding a barefoot child, a child who was utterly still and silent, like the eye of a storm. Outside, there was a small group assembled on the green in front of the building, some with rapt faces turned upward and illuminated by the fire, others doubled over coughing. Only once I'd made it to their circle did I turn back to look. Flames were already consuming the roof and leaping out of the windows of the top floor. The building must have been more than a hundred years old, a mock Tudor with great wooden ceiling beams made from the masts of old merchant ships, according to the hotel's brochure. It went up like dry timber. The impassive child watched it quietly, resting her head on her mother's shoulder. The night porter appeared with a list of guests and began a roll call. The child's mother answered to the name of Auerbach. I wondered if she was German, perhaps even Jewish. She was alone, there was no husband or father, and for a moment, as the fire raged and the firefighters pulled up in their trucks and my belongings, the easel and my paints and what clothes I'd brought, went up in smoke, I imagined placing a hand on the woman's shoulder and guiding her and the child away from the burning building. I pictured the grateful look on her face as she turned to me, and the placid, accepting expression of the child, both of them aware that my pockets were full of crumbs and from then on, from forest to forest, I would guide them, protect them, and care for them as my own. But this heroic fantasy was interrupted by a murmur of excitement that shot through the group: One guest was missing. The porter went down through the roll again, calling each name in a loud voice, and this time everyone became hushed, touched by the seriousness of the task at hand and the luck of their salvage. When the porter arrived at the name Rush no one answered. Ms. Emma Rush, he called again, but it was met with silence.

It was another hour before the fire was put out entirely and her body was discovered, brought out to the driveway covered in a black tarp. She'd jumped from the top floor and broken her neck. Only one other guest remembered her, and described her as middle-aged, always in possession of a pair of binoculars that she'd used, presumably, for bird-watching in the valleys, gorges, and woods of the Brecon Beacons. One ambulance left for the morgue and the other, carrying those suffering from smoke inhalation, to the hospital. The rest of us were divided up for various inns in nearby towns on the edge of the park. The Auerbach woman and her child were assigned to Brecon, and I to Abergavenny in the opposite direction. The last I saw of them was the child's matted hair as she disappeared into the van. The following day there was a piece about the fire in the local paper, in which it said that the fire had been electrical, and the deceased a primary school teacher from Slough.

A few weeks after Lotte died, my old friend Richard Gottlieb had come round to see how I was getting on. He was a lawyer, and years before he had persuaded Lotte and me to draw up our wills—neither of us had ever been practical in that regard. He'd lost his own wife some years earlier, and since then he had met someone else, a widow eight years younger than he who took care of her appearance and hadn't let herself go. A force of life, he said of her, stirring the milk into his tea, by which I knew he meant that it's terrible to die alone, to grow old and fumble with one's pills, to slip in the bath and crack one's skull, that I should think about my future, to which I replied that I thought I might travel a bit when the weather got warmer. Either way, he let the subject, so briefly raised, drop. Before he left he laid a hand on my shoulder. Might you want to think about revising your will now, Arthur? he asked. Right, I said, of course, but at the time I had no intention of doing as much. Twenty years ago when we'd drawn up the wills, Lotte and I had each left everything to the other. In the case that both of us died in a single stroke, we'd divided things up among various charities, nieces, and nephews (mine, of course; Lotte had no family). The rights to Lotte's books, which earned a pittance, we left to our dear friend Joseph Kern, an old student of mine who had promised to act as her executor.

But on the train ride back from Wales, my clothes still reeking of smoke and ash, the photo of the dead teacher from Slough gazing up at me from the paper folded in my lap, it was as if death's iron door had swung open and through it, for an instant, I glimpsed Lotte. *Deep within herself*, as the poem goes, *Filled with her vast death, which was so new, / she could not understand that it had happened*. And seeing her like that, something broke in me, a little valve that could no longer hold back such pressure, and I began to weep. I thought about what Gottlieb had said. Perhaps it was time to revise after all.

That night, back at home, I made myself a supper of fried eggs and ate them listening to the news. Earlier in the day, General Pinochet had been arrested at London Bridge Hospital where he had been convalescing after back surgery. A number of Chilean exiles, victims of his torture, were interviewed; celebration could be heard in the background. The boy, Daniel Varsky, came back to me briefly, vividly, as he had stood that night at our door. I switched on the television to follow the story, and also, I suppose, to see if there would be any report of the fire, or the woman from Slough, but of course there wasn't. Images of Pinochet in military uniform, saluting his army, waving from the balcony of La Moneda, were interspersed with blurry footage of an old man dressed in a canary yellow shirt semi-reclining in the back of a car driven by Scotland Yard.

There was an old feral tomcat who sometimes stalked our garden and knew to come to me for food. At night he screamed like a newborn. I left a bowl of milk out to let him know I was back again. But he didn't come that night, and in the morning a dead fly was floating belly-up in the bowl. As soon as it turned nine, I took out our old address book filled with Lotte's handwriting and found Gottlieb's number. He answered, full of cheer. I told him about my trip to the Brecon Beacons, but not about the fire; I didn't want to disturb the silence around it, I suppose, or betray it by turning it into a story. I asked if I could come by to speak to him in person, he expressed his enthusiasm, called to his wife, and after a muffled pause he invited me over that afternoon for tea.

I spent the morning reading Ovid. I read differently now, more painstakingly, knowing I am probably revisiting the books I love for the last time. At a little after three I set off across the Heath to Well Walk where Gottlieb lived. The windows were decorated with his grandchildren's paper cutouts. When he opened the door his cheeks were ruddy and the house exhaled a smell of allspice, like those sachets women put in their lingerie drawers. So good of you to come, Arthur, he said, patting me on the back, and led me to a sunny room off the kitchen where the table was already set for tea. Lucie came in to say hello, and we talked about a play she had seen at the Barbican the night before. Then she excused herself, saying she had a friend to visit, and left us alone. When the door closed behind her, Gottlieb took his glasses out of a small leather case and put them on, glasses that magnified his eyes many times their normal size, like the eyes of a tarsier monkey. The better to see me with, I couldn't help but think, or to see through me.

What I'm about to tell you might surprise you, I began. It surprised me when I discovered it myself, some months before Lotte died. Since then I haven't grown any more used to the idea that the woman I lived with for nearly fifty years was capable of hiding from me something of this scale, a secret that I have no doubt remained a vivid and haunting part of her inner life for all those years. It's true, I said to Gottlieb, that Lotte rarely spoke about her parents murdered in the camps, or about the childhood she was exiled from in Nuremberg. That she displayed a capacity, even a talent, for silence perhaps should have alerted me to the possibility of other chapters of her life she might have chosen to withhold from me, to sink deeply into herself like a wrecked ship. But, you see, the subject of her parents' fate and the loss of her former world were known to me. She had managed to communicate these nightmarish parts of her past at some point early on in our relationship in the form of a shadow play, without ever dwelling on them or giving them away too fully, and had managed at the same time to make clear to me that they were not subjects I should expect ever to be raised by her, nor should I attempt to raise them myself. That her sanity, her ability to carry on with life, both her own and the one we had forged together, depended on her ability and my solemn agreement to cordon off those nightmarish memories, to let them sleep like wolves in a lair, and to do nothing that might threaten their sleep.

That she visited these wolves in her dreams, that she lay down with them and even wrote about them, however many times metamorphosed into other forms, I knew well enough. I was a complicit if not equal partner in her silences. And as such, they were not what one might call secrets. I should also say that despite my acceptance of these terms and my desire to protect her, despite the tender understanding and sympathy I aspired always to show her, and my guilt for having lived a life sheltered from such torment and suffering, I was not always above suspicion. I admit that there were times I am not proud of when I sank to imagining that she had kept something hidden from me in order to willfully betray me. But my suspicions were small and petty, the suspicions of a man who fears that his powers (I trust I can speak frankly to you about these things, I said to Gottlieb, that you are no stranger to what I'm trying to say), his sexual powers which are expected to last decade after decade, have diminished in his wife's esteem, that she, whom he still considers beautiful, who still evokes in him a feeling of lust, is no longer excited by his sagging and dilapidated state revealed beneath the covers, a man who, to further compound the matter, has taken the example of his own lust for total strangers, certain of his students, or the wives of his friends, as incontrovertible proof of the lust his wife must feel for men other than him. You see, when I doubted her it was her loyalty that I doubted, though I would like to say in my own defense that it was not often, and also that to respect one's wife's right to silence as I tried to do, to muffle your own need for reassurance, to suffocate your questions before they rise up and escape through your mouth, is not always easy. A man would have to be better than human not to wonder, at times, whether she hadn't smuggled into those greater forms of silence, the ones to which you both long ago agreed, other, cheaper, forms—call them omissions or even lies—to mask what amounts to a betrayal.

Here Gottlieb blinked, and in the peace of that sunny afternoon I heard his lashes, magnified many times, brush against the lenses of his glasses. Otherwise, the room, the house, the day itself seemed to have emptied of all sounds but my voice.

I suppose there was something else that laid the groundwork for my uneasiness, I continued, something from Lotte's life before I knew her. Being part of her past, I felt I didn't have the right to interrogate her about it, though at times I was frustrated by her reticence, and resented her unspoken demand for privacy on the matter, since as far as I knew it had nothing to do with her loss. Of course I knew that she had other lovers before me. After all, she was twenty-eight by the time I met her, and for many years she had been alone without any family in the world. She was an awkward woman in many ways, a woman unlike the sort many men her age would have encountered, but if my own feelings can be used as any example, I have to guess that this drew those men to her all the more. I don't know how many lovers she had, but I assume there were enough of them. I suppose she kept silent about them not only out of a desire to contain her past, but also so as not to arouse my jealousy.

And yet, I was jealous all the same. Vaguely

jealous of them all—of how and where they had touched her, and what she might have told them about herself, of her laughter given up for something they'd said—and agonizingly jealous of one in particular. I knew nothing about him except that he must have been the most serious of all, most serious to her, because he alone had been allowed to leave behind a trace. You have to understand that in Lotte's life, a life reduced to fit the smallest possible space, there was almost no trace of her past at all. No photographs, no keepsakes, no heirlooms. Not even any letters, or none that I ever saw. The few things she lived among were entirely practical, and held no sentimental value to her. She made sure of this; it was a rule by which she lived in those days. The only exception to it was her desk.

To call it a desk is to say too little. The word conjures some homely, unassuming article of work or domesticity, a selfless and practical object that is always poised to offer up its back for its owner to make use of, and which, when not in use, occupies its allotted space with humility. Well, I told Gottlieb, you can cancel that image immediately. This desk was something else entirely: an enormous, foreboding thing that bore down on the occupants of the room it inhabited, pretending to be inanimate but, like a Venus flytrap, ready to pounce on them and digest them via one of its many little terrible drawers. Perhaps you think I'm making a caricature of it. I don't blame you. You'd have to have seen the desk with your own eyes to understand that what I'm telling you is perfectly accurate. It took up almost half of her rented room. The first time she allowed me to stay the night with her in that tiny pathetic bed that cowered in the shadow of the desk, I woke up in a cold sweat. It loomed above us, a dark and shapeless form. Once I dreamed that I opened one of the drawers to find that it held a festering mummy.

All she would say was that it had been a gift; there was no need, or perhaps it would be better to say she saw no need, or resisted the need, to say from whom. I had no idea what had become of him. Whether he had broken her heart, or she his, whether he was gone for good or whether he might still come back, whether he was alive or dead. I was convinced she had loved him more than she could ever love me, and that some impossible obstacle had come between them. It tore me apart. I used to fantasize about encountering him in the street. Sometimes I gave him a limp or dirty collar, just so he would leave me alone and let me get some sleep. It struck me, the gift of that desk, as an act of cruel genius—a way to stake his claim, to insinuate himself into the unreachable world of her imagination, so that he might possess her, so that every time she sat down to write it would be in the presence of his bestowal. Sometimes I would roll over in the dark to face a sleeping Lotte: Either he goes or I do, I imagined saying. During those long, cold nights in her room there was no distinction in my mind between him and the desk. But I never had the courage to say it. Instead I would slip a hand under her nightdress and begin to stroke her warm thighs.

In the end it all came to nothing, I told Gottlieb, or almost nothing. With each passing month, I became more confident of Lotte's feelings for me.

I asked her to marry me, and she agreed. He, whoever he was, was part of her past, and like the rest it had sunk away into the dark, irretrievable depths of her. We learned to trust each other. And for the better part of fifty years the suspicions I sometimes harbored, the ridiculous idea that she might betray me with another man, proved unfounded. I don't believe that Lotte was capable of doing anything that would have in any way threatened the home we two had so carefully built together. I think she knew that she couldn't have survived in another life, one of unknown specifications. Nor do I think she had the stomach to hurt me. In the end, my doubts always fizzled out on their own, without the need for confrontation, and in my mind things again returned to the way they'd always been.

It was only in the final months of Lotte's life, I told Gottlieb, that I discovered there was something enormous she had kept from me all those years. It happened quite by accident, and many times since then I've been struck by how close she came to keeping her secret until the end. And yet she didn't, and though her mind was failing her, I can't help but believe that in the end she made a choice not to. She chose a form of confession that suited her, that made, in her obscure state of mind, a kind of sense. The more I've thought about it, the less it has seemed to me an act of desperation, and the more it has seemed the culmination of an oblique logic. Alone, she found her way to the magistrate. God knows how. There were times when she could hardly find her way to the lavatory. And yet, there were still moments of lucidity when her mind suddenly reassembled itself, and then I was like a sailor at sea who suddenly sees the lights of his hometown illuminate on the horizon, and begins to make wildly for shore, only to see them go out again a moment later and find himself alone again in the infinite dark. It must have been in such a moment, I told Gottlieb, who sat unmoving in his chair, that Lotte rose from the sofa where she had been watching TV, and, while the nurse was busy talking on the phone in another room, quietly left the house. Some ancient reflex would have reminded her to pick up her bag from the hook in the front hall. Almost certainly she took the bus. She would have had to change once, something too complex for her to have worked out on her own, and so I have to imagine that she put herself in the driver's hands, asking him to show her the way, just as we did as children. I still remember my mother putting me on the bus in Finchley at the age of four, and asking the conductor to see me off on Tottenham Court Road where my aunt would be waiting for me. I remember the sense of wonder I had as we drove through the wet streets, the view I had of the back of the driver's muscular neck, the shiver of joy I felt at the privilege of traveling alone, combined with a shiver of fear brought on by disbelief that at the end of all of those seemingly random turns of the driver's enormous black wheel my aunt, with her ruddy cheeks and funny red-brimmed hat, would actually materialize. Perhaps Lotte felt the same. Or perhaps, determined as she must have been, she felt no fear at all, and, as the driver signaled to her the right stop, and which bus to take next, she gave him one of those broad smiles she reserved for strangers, as if she were aware of being able to pass, in their eyes, for an ordinary woman.

As I told Gottlieb what had taken place between Lotte and the magistrate, then described the hospital certificate and lock of hair I found among her papers, I felt a sense of relief, of a tremendous unburdening, knowing that I would no longer be the only one responsible for her secret. I told him that I wished to find her son. Gottlieb straightened up in his chair and let out a long sigh. Now it was I who waited to hear what would come next, knowing I had put myself in his hands and would proceed only as he decided. He took off his glasses and his eyes shrank and became reduced again to the sharpened eyes of a lawyer. He rose from the table, left the room, and returned a moment later with a pad of paper, then took out the fountain pen he kept at all times in his pocket. He asked me to repeat to him the information on the hospital certificate. He also asked exactly when Lotte had arrived in London on the kindertransport, and the addresses of the places she had lived before she met me. I told him what I knew, and he made a note of everything.

When he finished writing, he put down the pad. And the desk? he asked. What happened to the desk? One night in the winter of 1970, I said, a young man, a poet from Chile, rang our bell. He was a fan of Lotte's books and wanted to meet her. For a few weeks he became part of her life. At the time I didn't understand what it was about him that moved her—normally so private and introverted a person—to give so much of herself. I became jealous. One day I came back from a trip and discovered that she'd given him the desk. At the time I was baffled. The desk she had clung to and refused to give up, had dragged with her ever since I'd met her. Only much later did I come to understand that the young man, Daniel Varsky, was the same age as the son she gave away. How he must have reminded her of her own child, and what it would have been like with him. How moving those days with Daniel must have been for her, in ways he himself could never have grasped. He, too, must have wondered what she saw in him, and why she gave him so much of herself. All those years she had submitted to that monstrous piece of furniture that her lover had given her, with which he had bound her to him—to him and later to the dark secret of their child she gave up. All those years she had borne it as she had borne her guilt. How right it must have seemed to her, in the mysterious poetry of the mind's associations, to give it away at last to this boy who reminded her of her own son.

I turned to look out the window, tired after saying so much. Gottlieb shifted in his chair. They're cut from a different cloth from us, he said quietly, by which I took him to mean women, or our wives, and I nodded, though what I wished to say is that Lotte was made of something else entirely. Give me a few weeks, he said. I'll see what I can find.

*   *   *

That autumn the frost came late. A week after I planted the spring bulbs, I packed my bag, locked up the house, and took a train to Liverpool. It had taken Gottlieb less than a month to track down the name of the couple who had adopted Lotte's child and to find an address. One evening he dropped round to hand me a piece of paper with the information. I didn't ask him how he'd come by it. He had his ways—his work led him to know people in every walk of life, and as he was someone who went out of his way for others there were plenty who owed him favors he was not above returning one day to collect. Perhaps I, too, am one of those people. Are you sure you want to do this, Arthur? he asked, brushing a thatch of silver hair from his forehead. We stood in the hallway, the collection of unworn straw hats assembled on the wall like the costumes of another, more theatrical life. The motor of his car was still idling outside. Yes, I said.

But for some weeks I did nothing. A part of me had remained convinced that all traces of the child had vanished, and so I hadn't adequately prepared myself to receive the names of his parents, the ones he'd gone through life with. Elsie and John Fiske. John who perhaps went by Jack, I thought on my knees as I divided the hostas a few days later, and I imagined a burly man hunched at the bar in the pub, a chronic cougher, extinguishing his cigarette. Separating the tangled roots with my fingers, I imagined Elsie, too, scraping food off a dirty plate into the bin, dressed in a robe with her hair still in curlers, lit by the grim light of a Liverpool dawn. It was only the child that I couldn't fathom, a boy with Lotte's eyes or her expressions. Her own child! I thought, placing my rucksack on the rack above my seat, but as the train pulled out of Euston Station I imagined in the windows of a passing train the flickering faces of those Lotte had said goodbye to in her life—her mother and father, brothers and sisters, school friends, eighty-six homeless children bound for the unknown. Could she really be blamed for encountering in her own depths a refusal—the refusal to teach a child to walk, only to watch him walk away from her? In a way I'd never thought of before, her loss of memory, the loss of her mind at the end, made grotesque sense: a way for her to leave me effortlessly, slipping away an immeasurable amount each hour of each day, all to avoid a final, crushing goodbye.

That was the beginning for me, the beginning of a long and complicated journey I didn't know I was taking. Although maybe some part of me sensed it after all, because when I locked the door of the house a melancholy feeling came over me that I've only ever had when leaving for a long trip, a hollow feeling of uncertainty and regret, and when I looked back over my shoulder and saw the dark windows of our house I thought that it was not impossible, given my age and all the things that can befall one, that I would never see it again. I imagined the garden overgrown, turned wild again as it had been when we first saw it. It was a melodramatic thought and I rejected it as such, but many times along the way I was reminded of having had it. In my bag among the usual items of clothes and books I had the lock of hair, the hospital certificate, and a copy of *Broken Windows* to give to Lotte's son. On the back cover was a photograph of her, and it was because of that photograph that I chose that book of hers and not another. In it she looked as much like a mother as she ever would, so young, her face so soft and full, the skull not yet showing through as it begins to do by forty, and I thought that was the Lotte her son might like to see, if he wished to see her at all. But whenever I reached into my bag I would encounter her bruised eyes staring up at me, and sometimes it seemed she was admonishing me, and sometimes asking me a question, and sometimes attempting to bring me some news of death, until at last I couldn't bear it anymore and tried to lose her at the bottom, and when I couldn't (she kept rising up), I pushed the book down and buried it under the weight of other things.

The train pulled into Liverpool close to three in the afternoon. I was watching a flock of geese wing across the iron gray sky and then we plunged into a tunnel and came up under the glass dome of Lime Street station. The address Gottlieb had given me for the Fiskes was in Anfield. I'd planned to walk past the house before finding a bed-and-breakfast nearby to spend the night, then to call the following morning. But making my way down the platform I felt a heavy ache in my legs, as if I had arrived from London on foot rather than sat idle for two and a half hours on the train. I stopped to switch my bag to the other shoulder, and without looking up I sensed the gray sky pressing down on the glass roof from above, and when the letters on the flip board above the platform began to whir and click, times and destinations disintegrating, leaving us, the newly arrived, in limbo, a sickening wave of claustrophobia came over me and I had to struggle to resist the urge to walk straight to the ticket office and purchase a ticket for the next train back to London. The letters began to clatter again, and for a moment I was seized by the thought that the whirring letters were spelling the names of people. Though what people, I couldn't say. I must have stood for some time, because a man from the railway company wearing a gold-buttoned uniform approached to ask me if I was all right. There are times when the kindness of strangers only makes matters worse because one realizes how badly one is in need of kindness and that the only source is a stranger. But I managed to resist self-pity, thanking him and continuing on my way, heartened by my luck at not being forced to wear a hat like his, a perky box with a shiny visor that would make the daily battle for self-dignity before the mirror immeasurably more difficult. My satisfaction only lasted as far as the information desk, though, where I joined the line of travelers trying the patience of the girl who looked as if she had closed her eyes in one place and opened them to find herself there, in that little circular booth, dispensing information about Liverpool she never knew she had.

It was almost dark by the time I arrived at the hotel. The walls of the tiny, overheated foyer were papered with a flowery design, bunches of silk flowers were set out on the small tables clustered at the back, and hanging on the wall, though it was still some weeks before Christmas, was a large plastic wreath, the whole thing giving one the feeling of having stepped into a museum dedicated to the memory of long-extinct floral life. A wave of the claustrophobia I'd felt at the station came back to me, and when the receptionist asked me to fill out a registration form I was tempted to make something up, as if going under a false name and occupation might bring the relief of another, untapped dimension. My room looked out on a brick wall, and it, too, continued and elaborated the floral theme, so that for the first minutes during which I stood in the doorway, I did not believe that it would be possible for me to stay there. If it weren't for the heavy ache in my legs and my feet that felt like a pair of anvils, I almost certainly would have turned around and left; it was only exhaustion that made me enter and collapse on the chair with its dense print of exuberant roses, though for more than an hour I was unable to close the door behind me for fear of being shut in alone with so much choked, artificial life. As the walls seemed to lean in toward me, I couldn't help but ask myself, not in so many words, but in the fragmentary shorthand of thoughts one thinks alone to oneself, What right do I have to turn over a stone she wished to leave unturned? It was then that the sense rose up in me like bile, a sense I tried but failed to keep down, that what I was really doing was trying to expose her guilt. To expose it against her wishes, in order to punish her. For what, you might ask, punish the poor woman for what? And the answer that comes to me, which is only part of the answer, is that I wished to punish her for her intolerable stoicism, which made it impossible for me to ever be truly needed by her in the most profound ways a person can need another, a need that often goes by the name of love. Of course she needed me—to keep order, to remember the shopping, to pay the bills, to keep her company, to give her pleasure, and, in the end, to bathe, and wipe, and dress her, to bring her to the hospital, and finally to bury her. But that she needed it to be *me* who performed these duties and not some other man, equally in love with her, equally at the ready, was never entirely clear to me. I suppose it could be said that I never demanded she make the case for her love, but then I never really felt I had the right. Or maybe I feared that, honest as she was, unable to tolerate the smallest insincerity, she would fail to make the case, that she would stutter and grow silent, and then what choice would I have but to get up and leave forever, or continue with things as they had always been, only now with the full knowledge that I was simply one example where there could have been many? It isn't that I thought she loved me less than she might have loved another man (though there were times I feared as much). No, what I'm speaking of now, or trying to speak of, is something else, the sense that her self-sufficiency—the proof she carried within her that she could withstand unthinkable tragedy on her own, that in fact the extreme solitude she had constructed around herself, reducing herself, folding in on herself, turning a silent scream into the weight of private work, was precisely what enabled her to withstand it—made it impossible for her to ever need me as I needed her. No matter how bleak or tragic her stories were, their effort, their creation, could only ever be a form of hope, a denial of death or a howl of life in the face of it. And I had no place in that. Whether I existed downstairs or not, she would continue to do what she had always done alone at her desk, and it was that work that allowed her to survive, not my care or company. All our lives I'd insisted that it was she who was dependent on me. She who needed to be protected, who was delicate and required constant care. But in truth it was I who needed to feel needed.

With great difficulty I managed to drag myself down to the hotel bar for a gin and tonic to calm myself. The only other drinkers were two old women, sisters, I think, perhaps even twins, perilously frail, their hands deformed around their glasses. Ten minutes after I'd arrived, one got up, departing so slowly she might have been performing a pantomime, leaving the other alone, until at last the second one vacated her spot just as slowly, like some demented version of the Von Trapps exiting to the tune of "So Long, Farewell," and as she passed me she swiveled her head and gave me a terrifying grin. I smiled back, the importance of manners, my mother always said, is inversely related to how inclined one is to use them, or, in other words, sometimes politeness is all that stands between oneself and madness.

When I returned to Room 29 an hour later the air itself seemed to have taken on a sickening floral odor. I dug out the number Gottlieb had given me from my bag. I dialed and a woman answered. May I speak to Mrs. Elsie Fiske? I asked. Speaking. Really? I almost said, because no small part of me still held out for the possibility that Gottlieb's detective work would lead to a dead end, and that I would return home to London, to my garden and books and the grudging company of the tomcat, having tried and failed to find Lotte's child. Hello? she said. I'm sorry, I said, this is bound to be awkward. I don't mean to throw you off guard, but I was hoping to discuss with you a rather personal matter. Who is this? My name is Arthur Bender. My wife—this really is very awkward, forgive me, I assure you I don't wish to make you uncomfortable in any way, but some time ago my wife died and I learned that she had a child I never knew about. A boy she gave up for adoption in July 1948. There was a heavy silence on the other end of the line. I cleared my throat. Her name was Lotte Berg—I began to say, but she cut in. What is it you want, exactly, Mr. Bender? I don't know what possessed me to speak so frankly, perhaps something in the tone of her voice, the clarity or intelligence I thought I heard in it, but what I said was, If I were to answer that question honestly, Mrs. Fiske, I might have you on the phone all night. To be as straightforward as possible, I've come to Liverpool and I wondered if it would not be too much of an imposition to ask to meet you, and perhaps, if you come to think it would be all right, to meet your son. There was another pause, a pause that seemed to go on a long time as the vegetation unfurled and advanced along the walls. He's dead, she said simply. He's been dead twenty-seven years.

The night was long. The heat in the room was unbearable, and from time to time I would get up to open the window, only to remember that it was sealed shut. I threw all of the covers onto the floor and lay spread-eagle on the mattress, inhaling the heat rising off the radiator, a heat that infected my dreams like a tropical fever. They were dreams beyond language, grotesque images of raw, wet, bloated flesh strung up in black nets, and white bags that secreted a slow colorless drip echoing off the floor, images from the nightmares of my childhood at last come back to me, even more horrifying now than they were then since I grasped, in that semi-hallucinatory state, that they could only belong to my death. We have to draw some distinctions, I repeated over and over in my head, or not I but a disembodied voice that I took to be my own. But there was one dream that stood apart from that monstrous parade, a simple dream of Lotte on a beach, drawing long lines with her bony toe in the sand while I watched, lying back on my elbows in the body of a much younger man which I sensed, like a nimbus at the edge of that bright day, didn't belong to me. When I woke, the blow of her absence made me gag. I stood gulping from the bathroom tap, and when I tried to urinate there was only a drip and a burning sensation, as if I were trying to pass sand, and suddenly, out of nowhere, the way news of oneself so often arrives, it dawned on me what a ridiculous thing it was to have dedicated one's life to being a scholar of the so-called Romantic poets. I proceeded to flush the toilet. I took a shower, dressed, and checked out of the hotel. When the receptionist asked if everything had been to my satisfaction I smiled and said that it had been.

A long walk in the hours after dawn, of which I remember little. Only that I arrived at the house before nine, though Elsie Fiske had asked me for ten. All my life I have arrived early only to find myself standing self-consciously on a corner, outside a door, in an empty room, but the closer I get to death the earlier I arrive, the longer I am content to wait, perhaps to give myself the false sensation that there is too much time rather than not enough. It was a two-story terraced house, indistinguishable from the others on the road apart from the number next to its front door—the same dull lace curtains, the same iron rail. It was drizzling, and I walked up and down the opposite side of the street to stay warm. Something about the sight of the lace curtains filled me with a sickening guilt. The boy was dead, the story I'd asked Mrs. Fiske to tell would end badly. All those years Lotte had kept from me the story of her child. However he had haunted her, he had not been allowed to intrude on our lives. On our happiness, I should say, since that was always ours. Like a strongman under an enormous weight, she'd borne her silence alone. It was a work of art, her silence. And now I was going to destroy it.

At ten o'clock sharp I rang the bell. The dead take their secrets with them, or so they say. But it isn't really true, is it? The secrets of the dead have a viral quality, and find a way to keep themselves alive in another host. No, I was guilty of nothing more than advancing the inevitable.

I thought I saw the curtains move but it was some time before anyone came to the door. At last I heard footsteps and the lock turned. The woman who stood there had very long gray hair, hair that must have gone all the way down her back when it was loose, but which she had plaited and coiled on top of her head in the style of one who had just stepped off a stage where she'd been performing Chekhov. She had a very erect carriage and little gray eyes.

She showed me into the living room. Right away, I knew that her husband had died and that she lived alone there. Perhaps a person who lives on his own has a special sense for the shades, tones, and peculiar echoes of that life. She gestured to the tasseled sofa decorated with an abundance of crocheted pillows, all of which, as far as I could tell, pictured various species of dogs and cats. I took a seat among them; one or two slipped onto my lap and nestled there. I proceeded to stroke a little black stuffed dog on the head. On the table, Mrs. Fiske had laid out a pot of tea and a plate of digestives, though for a long time she didn't move to pour it, and by the time she did the tea was too strong. I don't remember how we began to talk. I only remember that I made the acquaintance of that stuffed little dog, a spaniel of some kind, and then Mrs. Fiske and I were deep into conversation, a conversation that both of us had been waiting a long time to have, though neither had known it. There was very little (or so it seemed, sitting in that room that I soon realized was filled with canine and feline likenesses of every kind, not just the pillows but the figurines that crowded the shelves and the paintings on the wall) that we couldn't say to each other, even if we did not choose to say it all, and yet it wasn't intimacy that existed between us, certainly not warmth, but something more desperate. At no time did we ever address each other as anything but Mr. Bender and Mrs. Fiske.

We spoke of husbands and wives, of the death of her husband eleven years earlier, who had gone by a heart attack while singing "You'll Never Walk Alone" in the football stadium, of the hats and scarves and shoes of the dead that keep turning up, diminishing powers of concentration, letters returned in the mail, of train travel, of standing over graves, of all the ways that life can be squeezed out of the human body, at least I have the impression now that we spoke of these things though I admit it is possible we spoke of the difficulty of growing lavender in a wet climate, and that those other things were only the subtext, so clearly understood between Mrs. Fiske and me. But I don't think so, I don't think we discussed lavender or gardens at all. The bitter tea grew cold, despite the tea cozy. A few strands of Mrs. Fiske's gray hair came loose from arrangements made earlier.

You have to understand, she said at last. I was thirty by the time I met John, and some weeks earlier I had caught sight of myself in the reflection of a shop window before I had a chance to compose my face, and afterwards, on the bus ride home, I came to accept certain things. It was not a revelation, she said, it was more a question of things having reached a certain point, and the image I saw reflected back at me was the last straw. Not long after that, I was at my sister's and her husband brought a friend back from the office. John and I found ourselves trying to pass one another in the narrow hall that led to the kitchen, pass without touching, and he asked, rather awkwardly, whether he could see me again. The first night he took me out I was taken aback by how, when he laughed, you could see his fillings, and also the darkness gathered at the back of the throat. He had a way of throwing his head back and opening his mouth to laugh that took me some time to get used to. I was what you might call the solemn type, Mrs. Fiske said, looking past me out of the window, solemn and shy, and despite the music of his laughter I was frightened by what I thought I saw there at the back of his throat. But we found our way with one another, and were married five months later in front of a small group of family and friends, many of whom were surprised to find themselves there, having come to believe that I would become an old maid, if I wasn't one in their eyes already. I made it clear to John that I didn't want to waste any time before trying to have a child. We tried, but it didn't come easily. When at last I became pregnant—this is strange to say—the sensation I had was of a tide washing in and out of me, and when the tide came in the child was safe within me, and when it washed out it was the child being pulled away from me, as if he had seen something bright and shining elsewhere, and no matter how I tried to hold him back I couldn't. The pull of that other thing, that other, shining life, was too hard to resist. And then one night asleep in bed I felt the tide wash out of me for good, and when I woke I was bleeding. We tried again after that, but deep down I no longer believed I was capable of bearing a child. Those were painful times for me, and if normally I laughed little now I laughed hardly at all, but I remember thinking that John's laughter remained constant. It isn't that he wasn't saddened, but he had a merry disposition, he could turn a corner and see things from another angle, or hear a joke on the radio and that was enough for him. And when he laughed, throwing his head back, the darkness at the back of his throat seemed to me even more foreboding than before, and a little shiver ran through me. I don't mean to give the wrong impression. He was very supportive, and did his best to cheer me up. In a way I can't explain, said Mrs. Fiske, the darkness I saw there had nothing, or very little, to do with John himself and everything to do with me; the back of his throat just happened to be the place where it dwelled. I began to turn away when he laughed so as not to see it, and then one day I heard his laughter switch off like a light, and when I turned back his mouth was clamped shut and there was a look of shame on his face. I felt awful then, cruel, really, absurd and self-absorbed, and soon afterwards I made sure that things began to change between us. By and by a kind of tenderness was allowed in that had not been before. I learned something about controlling certain kinds of feelings, about not giving in to the first emotion that presents itself, and I remember thinking at the time that such discipline was the key to sanity. About six months later we decided to adopt a child.

Mrs. Fiske leaned forward and stirred what was left of her tea as if she might drink it, or as if the words for the rest of her story were resting among the bits of tea leaves at the bottom of the china cup. But then she seemed to think better of it, returned the cup to its saucer, and leaned back again in her chair.

It didn't happen right away, she said. We had to fill out endless forms, there was a process. One day a lady in a yellow suit came to our house. I remember staring at her suit and thinking that it was like a small piece of sunshine, and she an envoy from a different climate where children thrived and were happy, and that she had arrived at our house to shine herself and see how it looked, how so much light and happiness might reflect back off of our colorless walls. I spent the days before her arrival on my knees scrubbing the floors. I even baked a cake on the morning of her arrival so that there would be the smell of something sweet in the air. I wore a blue silk dress and made John wear a houndstooth jacket that he'd never have chosen for himself, because I thought it had an optimistic flair. But as we sat waiting uneasily for her in the kitchen I saw how the sleeves were too short and how the jacket, the way John sat hunched in that ridiculous jacket, instead gave away our desperation. But it was too late to change, the doorbell rang, and there she was with her patent-leather bag containing our file tucked under her arm, this bright yellow guardian from the land of tiny fingernails and milk teeth. She sat down at the table and I put a slice of cake in front of her, which she didn't touch. She took out some papers for us to sign, and proceeded to conduct her interview. John, who was easily intimidated by authority, began to stutter. Embarrassed and insecure, cowed by the power she had over us, I lost my way in the answers I tried to give, became flustered, and made a fool of myself. As she looked around, an artificial little smile pulled tightly at her lips, I saw her shiver, and I realized that the house was cold. I knew then that she would not give us a child.

After that I entered into what I suppose is called a depression, though I didn't know it then. When I emerged many months later, I'd accustomed myself to the idea of a life without children. Then one day, visiting my sister who had moved to London, I was reading the paper and my eye happened to catch a small ad near the bottom of the page. I could have easily missed it, it was just a few words in small print. But I saw it: *Baby boy of three weeks available for immediate adoption*. Below it was an address. Without hesitating, I took out a piece of paper and wrote a letter. Something took hold of me. My pen hurried across the page, trying to keep up with the words pouring out of me. I wrote all I'd been unable to express to the lady in yellow who had come from the adoption agency, and as the letters flew off the point of my pen I knew that ad had been meant for me alone. The boy for me alone. I posted the letter, and said nothing about it to John. I didn't want to put him through more than I had already; having seen me through the worst of my depression only to watch me fall prey to blind hope, again, would be more than he could bear. But I knew it wasn't blind hope. Sure enough, as soon as I returned home to Liverpool a few days later, a letter was waiting for me. It was signed with only her initials: L.B. Until you called last night, I never knew her name. She asked me to meet her five days later, at four o'clock on the 20th of July, in the ticket hall at West Finchley Station. I waited until John left for work at eight and then I hurried out on my way. I was going to meet my child, Mr. Bender. The one I had waited so long for. Can you imagine what I felt, stepping aboard that train? I could barely sit still. I knew I was going to call him Edward, after the grandfather I'd loved. Of course he must have had a name already, but I didn't think to ask, and she didn't tell me. We said so little. I could barely speak and neither could she. Or perhaps she could have spoken, but chose not to. Yes, I think it was that. There was a strange calmness about her—it was my hands that shook. Only later, during those first days, with the house filled with the smells of a new baby, did I think about that other name hiding behind the name we had given him, like a shadow. But in time I forgot about it, or if I didn't entirely forget it I rarely thought of it, except at odd moments when I would hear a name being called on the street, in a shop, or on the bus, and I would stop and wonder if that was it.

When I got to London I took the Tube to West Finchley. It was a warm, sunny day and she was the only one indoors in the ticket hall. She fixed me in her gaze, but didn't step forward. I felt she was looking inside me, under my skin. A strange calmness, that's what struck me. For a moment I thought it was possible that she wasn't the mother, but rather a surrogate sent in her place to carry out the bitter task. But when she moved the blanket away and I stepped forward and saw the baby's face, I knew he could only be hers. When she spoke at last her accent was heavy. I didn't know where she was from, Germany or Austria, maybe, but I understood that she was a refugee. The baby was asleep, his little knotted fists balled on either side of his face. We stood there in the empty ticket hall. He doesn't like it when the hat falls too low on his forehead, she said. Those were her first words to me. A few moments later, very long moments, she said, If you put him on your shoulder after he eats, he cries less. And then, His hands get cold easily. As if she were giving me instructions on how to run a finicky car instead of giving away her own baby. And yet later, once I had him a few weeks, I began to see it differently. I understood that those few things were the precious discoveries of someone who had studied and tried to understand the mystery of her child.

We sat side by side on the hard bench, Mrs. Fiske said. She patted the bundle in her arms one more time then handed it to me. I felt the warmth of his body through the blanket. He squirmed a little, but continued to sleep. I thought she would say something else, but she didn't. There was a bag on the floor and she nudged it toward me with her foot. Then she looked out of the window and something she noticed on the platform seemed to jar her because she stood abruptly. I continued to sit because my legs were weak and I worried that I might drop the baby. Just like that, she began to walk away. Only when she reached the door did she stop and look back. I pulled the baby to my chest and held him tightly. I felt him snuffling there, and then I began to rock him a little and he relaxed and even cooed a little. You see! I wanted to shout to her. But when I looked up she was gone.

I sat without moving. I rocked the baby and sang to him quietly. I bent my head over his to block the light from his eyes, and when I pressed my lips to his head a cloud of warmth seemed to come off him, and I smelled the sweetness of his skin and also a fetid odor from behind his ears. He jerked his face toward me and opened his mouth. His eyes were wide with shock and his arms sprang up, as if he were trying to catch himself from falling. He began to cry. A sudden heat rose to my face and I began to sweat. I jiggled him, but he began to cry louder. I looked up, and there, peering through the window, was a young man in a strange, almost pitiful coat with a matted fur collar. He had very black shining eyes. A shiver went up my spine as he looked at us, the baby and me. He looked at us with the hunger of a wolf, and I knew he could only be the baby's father. The moment seemed elongated, pulled thin, while some starved longing or awful regret churned inside him. Then a train pulled into the station and he boarded it alone and that was the last I saw of him. When you called last night, Mr. Bender, I was sure that you were he. Only when you rang the bell did I realize that you couldn't be.

* * *

At that point I stood and asked Mrs. Fiske the way to the lavatory. The black spaniel dropped to the floor and bounced in a sickening way. A dizzy spell had come over me and I felt faint. I closed the door and sank down on the toilet seat. There was a wooden rack set up in the bath where two or three pairs of tights were drying, the shriveled brown feet still dripping, and above the tub was a window fogged from the humidity. I imagined escaping through it and running down the street. I put my head between my knees to stop the dizziness. For forty-eight years I had shared my life with a woman who was capable of coolly giving her child away to a stranger. A woman who had put an advertisement in the paper for her own baby—*her own baby*—as one advertises an item of furniture for sale. I waited for this new knowledge to throw its stark light, waited to understand, for the door to swing open, waited to come into a lifetime of hoarded truth. But no revelation came.

Are you all right? Mrs. Fiske asked, her voice coming from far away. I don't know how I responded, only that some minutes later she led me up the stairs to a small room with a twin bed where I proceeded to lie down without protest. She brought me a glass of water, and when she leaned over to put it down on the night table the view of her throat reminded me of my own mother. May I ask a question? I said. She said nothing. How did he die? She sighed and squeezed her hands together. It was a terrible accident, she said. Then she left me alone, closing the door softly behind her, and only as I listened to her footsteps recede down the stairs, fainter and fainter, and the room began slowly, almost leisurely, to spin, did it occur to me that I was lying in the room that had belonged to him, to Lotte's child.

I closed my eyes. As soon as this passes, I thought, I'll thank Mrs. Fiske, say goodbye, and return home on the next train to London. But even as I thought it I didn't really believe it. Once more I had the feeling that it would be a long time before I would see the house in Highgate, if I saw it again at all. It was getting cold, the tomcat would have to find his dinner elsewhere. The swimming holes would freeze over. What was it that slept there on the soft, slimy bottom that drew Lotte back down day after day? Every morning she would go, as Persephone went down, to touch again that dark thing, vanishing into the black depths. In front of my eyes! And I could never follow. Can you understand what it was like? As if a small rip had been made in the day and she alone slipped through it. A splash, and then a stillness that seemed to last forever. A kind of panic crept over me. And just when I was convinced that she had hit her head on a rock or broken her neck, the surface would break and she would appear again, blinking water out of her eyes, her lips blue. Something had been renewed. On the walk home we spoke little. There was only the sound of the leaves and twigs crunching under our feet like broken glass. I haven't gone back since she died.

It must have been some hours later when I woke again. It was dusk outside. I lay still looking up at the mute rectangle of sky. I turned my face to the wall. And as I did, an image came to me of Lotte in the garden. I have no sense of the provenance of the memory, and in fact I can't say for certain whether it happened at all. In it, she stands near the back wall, unaware that I am watching from a second-story window. A small fire smolders at her feet that she tends with a stick or perhaps the fire poker, bending over her work, heavy with concentration, her shoulders covered in a yellow shawl. From time to time she adds a few more pieces of paper to the blaze, or perhaps shakes a book whose pages float down into the fire. The smoke rises in a twisting violet plume. What she was burning, and why I watched in silence from the window, I couldn't say, and the more I tried to remember, the less vivid the image became, and the more agitated I felt.

My shoes were lined up under a chair, though I didn't remember removing them. I put them on, smoothed the lace bedcover, and went down the stairs. When I came to the kitchen Mrs. Fiske was standing with her back to me over the stove. It was that hour before dark when one hasn't yet thought to turn on the lights. Steam rose from the pot she was stirring. I pulled a chair out from the kitchen table and she turned, face flushed from the heat. Mr. Bender, she said. Please, I said, call me Arthur, though immediately I regretted it because I knew that it was my strangeness to her that allowed her to speak so openly. She said nothing, only took down a bowl from a shelf, ladled some soup into it, and wiped her hands on her apron. She set the bowl down in front of me, and took a seat opposite, just as my own mother used to do. I wasn't hungry, but there was no choice but to eat.

After a long silence, Mrs. Fiske began to speak again. I always thought that she would contact me. Of course she knew where we lived. In the beginning I was terrified that I would receive a phone call or letter, or that she would simply appear at the door to say that a mistake had been made, that she wanted Teddy back. Rocking him to sleep at night, or standing still in the dark so as not to creak the floorboards and wake him, I used to silently plead my case. She gave him away! And I took him in. I loved him like my own! And yet a feeling of guilt weighed on me. He used to cry so much, his face knotted, his mouth agape. He was inconsolable, you see. The doctor said it was colic, but I didn't believe it. I thought he was crying for her. At times, in my frustration, I would shake him and shout for him to stop. For a moment he would look at me, surprised or maybe frightened into silence. In his dark eyes I saw the hard glimmer of willfulness. Then he would begin to shriek louder than before. Sometimes I slammed the door and let him cry. I would sit here, where I'm sitting now, with my hands over my ears, until I became nervous that the neighbors might hear and suspect me of neglect.

But neither the call nor the letter ever came, said Mrs. Fiske. And after three or four months Teddy began to cry less. Together he and I discovered things, little rituals and songs that calmed him. A kind of understanding, however tentative, began to unfold between us. He learned to smile at me, a crooked, gaping smile, but it filled me with joy. I began to gain confidence. For the first time since I brought him home, I began to take him out in the pram. We would walk to the park and he would sleep in the shade while I sat on the bench, almost the same as any other mother. Almost, but not quite, because in a little, hidden cell of each day—arriving often at the hour of dusk, or after I'd put the baby to sleep and was running myself a bath, but sometimes without warning at the exact moment my lips brushed his cheek—a feeling of fraudulence took hold of me. It would slip around my neck like a pair of tiny, cold hands, and in an instant it would obliterate the rest. At first it filled me with despair, said Mrs. Fiske. I hated myself for carrying on as if I really were his mother, something that, in that chilling, lucid moment, I felt I could never be. While I was feeding or bathing or reading to him, there would always be a part of me that was somewhere else, riding a tram in a foreign city in the rain, walking along a foggy promenade on the edge of an alpine lake so large that a scream would falter and become lost before it ever reached the other shore. My sister had no children, and I didn't know many other young mothers. Those I did know I would never have dared to ask if they ever felt the same. I took it to be my own failure, a failure that had something to do with having not conceived Teddy myself, but which ultimately came down to an inadequacy at the core of me. And yet, what could I do but continue to try despite myself? No one came for him. He only had me. I made an enormous effort, lavishing no end of attention on him in order to make up for it. Teddy grew into a contented child, though there were times that I saw in his eyes, or thought I saw, a fleeting look of some long-unrelieved desperation, though afterwards I could never be sure that it wasn't just thoughtfulness, which for some reason always carries the faint impression of sadness when passing across the face of a child.

By then I no longer worried that she was going to come back to claim him, Mrs. Fiske said. I thought of him as my own, no matter my faults, no matter the failing of attention from which he would call me back with increasing determination, my impatience with certain little games he wished to repeat over and over again, no matter the sense of paralyzing boredom that sometimes took hold after I'd dressed him and the day stretched out again before us like an endless car park. I knew that he loved me despite all of this, and when he crawled into my lap and found the place where he fitted most naturally, I felt that no two people could understand each other better than he and I, and that it must be that, after all, which was what was meant by being a mother and child. Mrs. Fiske stood to clear my bowl, put it in the sink, and looked out the window at the small garden behind the house. She seemed to be in something close to a trance, and I didn't speak for fear of breaking it. She filled the kettle, put it on the stove, and returned to the table. I saw then how tired she seemed. She fixed her eyes on mine. What is it that you came here to find out, Mr. Bender?

Taken aback, I didn't speak right away.

Because if you came to understand something about your wife, I can't help you, she said.

A long silence passed. And then Mrs. Fiske said:

I never heard from her again. She never wrote. Sometimes I thought of her. I watched the baby sleeping and I wondered how she could have done what she did. Only later did I come to understand that to be a mother is to be an illusion. No matter how vigilant, in the end a mother can't protect her child—not from pain, or horror, or the nightmare of violence, from sealed trains moving rapidly in the wrong direction, the depravity of strangers, trapdoors, abysses, fires, cars in the rain, from chance.

With time I thought of her less and less. But when he died she returned to me. He was twenty-three when it happened. I thought that in the whole world, only she could fathom the depth of my grief. But then I realized that I was wrong, said Mrs. Fiske. She couldn't know. She didn't know the first thing about my son.

* * *

Somehow I made it back to the railway station. It was difficult to think clearly. I took the train back to London. Every station we passed through I saw Lotte on the platform. What she had done, the cold-bloodedness of it, filled me with horror, a horror amplified by the fact that I had lived with her for so long without having the faintest idea of what she was capable. Everything she had ever said to me I now had to consider in this new light.

That evening I returned to Highgate to find that the front window of the house had been smashed. From the large hole a magnificent, delicate web of cracks radiated outwards. It was something to behold, and a feeling of awe came over me. On the floor inside, lying among the broken glass, I found a rock the size of a fist. Cold air filled the living room. It was the special stillness of the scene that shook me, the kind that comes only in the wake of violence. At last I saw a spider crawling very slowly across the wall and the spell was broken. I went to get the broom. When I had finished cleaning up, I taped a sheet of plastic over the hole. The rock I saved and put on the living room table. The next day, when the glazier arrived, he shook his head and said something about rowdy kids, hoodlums, the third window they'd broken that week, and I felt a sudden pang and realized I had wanted that rock to be meant for me, the work of someone who wished to throw a rock through *my* window, and mine alone, not just any window. And when the little feeling of pain passed, I began to resent the glazier with his loud and gleeful voice. Only after he left did I understand how lonely I was. The rooms of the house sucked me in and seemed to scold me for having left them. You see? they seemed to say. You see what happens? But I did not see. I had the feeling of understanding less and less. It was becoming difficult to remember—or not to remember, but to *believe* what I remembered of what Lotte and I used to do in those rooms, how we passed our time, where and how we used to sit. I sat in my old chair, and tried to summon Lotte as she used to sit across from me. But it all became touched with absurdity. The plastic rippled over the gaping hole, and the spectacular cracked glass hung suspended. One heavy step or gust of wind, it seemed, and the whole thing would fall into thousands of pieces. The following day when the glazier returned I excused myself, and went out to the garden. When I came back the window was whole again, the glazier smiling at his handiwork.

I understood, then, what deep within myself I had always understood: that I could never punish her as much as she had already punished herself. That it was I, after all, who had never admitted to myself just how much I knew. The act of love is always a confession, Camus wrote. But so is the quiet closing of a door. A cry in the night. A fall down the stairs. A cough in the hall. All my life I had been trying to imagine myself into her skin. Imagine myself into her loss. Trying and failing. Only perhaps—how can I say this—perhaps I *wanted* to fail. Because it kept me going. My love for her was a failure of the imagination.

* * *

One evening the doorbell rang. I was not expecting anyone. There is no longer anyone or anything to expect. I put down my book, carefully marking the page with a bookmark. Lotte had always put her books down open-faced and when we first met I used to tell her that I could hear the little high-pitched cry as its spine was broken. It was a joke, but later when she left the room or went to sleep I would pick up her book and slip a bookmark in, until one day she lifted her book, ripped the bookmark out, and dropped it on the floor. Don't ever do that again, she said. And I understood that there was one more place that belonged to her that I would be now and forever barred from. From then on I no longer asked about her reading. I waited until she volunteered something—a sentence that moved her, a bright passage, a character vividly drawn. Sometimes it came and sometimes it didn't. But it was not for me to ask.

I walked the few paces down the hallway to the door. Hoodlums, I thought, the word of the glazier coming back to me. But through the eyehole I saw it was a man close to my own age dressed in a suit. I asked who was there. He cleared his throat on the other side of the door. Mr. Bender? he asked.

He was a small man, dressed with simple elegance. The only flourish was a walking stick with a silver handle. It seemed unlikely that he was there to bludgeon or rob me. Yes? I said, standing in the open doorway. My name is Weisz, he said. Forgive me for not calling in advance. But he did not offer any excuse. There's something I'd like to discuss with you, Mr. Bender. If it isn't too much of an imposition—he looked past me, into the house—may I come in? I asked what it was about. A desk, he said.

A weakness came into my knees. I was paralyzed, certain that it could only be he: the one she had loved, in whose shadow I had eked out a life with her.

As if in a dream, I showed him into the living room. He moved without hesitation, as if he knew his way. A coldness slid through me. Why had it never occurred to me that he might have been here before? He walked directly to Lotte's chair and stood waiting. I gestured for him to sit as my legs began to crumple under me. We sat face to face. I in my chair, he in hers. As it had always been, I thought now.

I've intruded on you, he said, I'm sorry. And yet he spoke with a composure that belied his words, with a confidence that was almost intimidating. His accent was Israeli, though tempered, I thought, by the vowels and accents of elsewhere. He looked as if he were in his late sixties, perhaps seventy, which would have made him a few years younger than Lotte. Then it dawned on me. How could I not have guessed before? One of her charges on the Kindertransport! A boy of fourteen, perhaps fifteen. Sixteen at most. In the beginning those few years might have seemed like a lot. But as time passed, less and less. When he was eighteen she would have been twenty-one or twenty-two. They would have shared an unbreakable bond, a private language, a lost world condensed into blunt syllables that each had only to utter for the other to understand completely. Or no language at all—a silence that stood for all that could not be spoken aloud.

His appearance was impeccable: not a hair out of place or a speck of lint on his dark suit. Even the soles of his shoes looked unscuffed, as if he hardly touched the ground. Just a few minutes of your time, he said. Then I promise to leave you in peace.

In peace! I almost cried out. You who tormented me all these years! My enemy, the one who occupied a corner of the woman I loved, a corner of her like a black hole that, through some sorcery I never understood, contained the deepest volumes of her.

I find it difficult to describe my work to others, he began. I'm not in the habit of talking about myself. My business has always been to listen. People come to me. At first they don't say much, but slowly it comes out. They look out the window, at their feet, at some point behind me in the room. They don't meet my eyes. Because if they were to remember that I was there, they might not be able to say the words. They begin to talk and I go with them back to their childhoods, before the War. Between their words I see the way the light fell across the wooden floor. The way he lined his soldiers up under the hem of the curtain. How she laid out the little toy teacups. I am there with him under the table, Weisz continued. I see his mother's legs move about the kitchen, and the crumbs the housekeeper's broom missed. Their childhoods, Mr. Bender, because it is only the ones who were children who come to me now. The others have died. When I first started my business, he said, it was mostly lovers. Or husbands who had lost their wives, wives who had lost their husbands. Even parents. Though very few—most would have found my services unbearable. The ones who came hardly spoke at all, only enough to describe a little child's bed or the chest where he kept his toys. Like a doctor, I listen without saying a word. But there's one difference: when all of the talking is through, I produce a solution. It's true, I can't bring the dead back to life. But I can bring back the chair they once sat in, the bed where they slept.

I studied his features. No, I thought now. I had been mistaken. He could not have been the one. I don't know how I knew, but looking at his face, I knew. And to my surprise I felt the bitter taste of disappointment. There is so much we might have said to one another.

There is an amazement that comes over each one, Weisz continued, when at last I produce the object they have been dreaming of for half a lifetime, that they have invested with the weight of their longing. It's like a shock to their system. They've bent their memories around a void, and now the missing thing has appeared. They can hardly believe it, as if I'd produced the gold and silver sacked when the Romans destroyed the Temple two thousand years ago. The holy objects looted by Titus that mysteriously disappeared so that the cataclysmic loss would be total, so that there would be no evidence left to keep the Jew from turning a place into a longing he could carry with him wherever he wandered, forever.

We sat in silence. That window, he said at last, gazing behind me. How did it break? I was surprised. How did you know? I asked. For a moment I wondered whether there was not something sinister I'd missed in him. The glass is new, he said, and the putty is fresh. Someone threw a stone through it, I told him. His sharp features became softened by a thoughtful expression, as if my words had awakened a memory in him. The moment passed, and he began to speak again:

But the desk, you see—it isn't like the other pieces of furniture. I admit that there were times when it was impossible to find the exact table, chest, or chair that my clients were seeking. The trail reached a dead end. Or never began at all. Things don't last forever. The bed that one man remembers as the place where his soul was overwhelmed is, to another man, just a bed. And when it breaks, or goes out of style, or is no longer of use to him, he throws it away. But before he dies, the man whose soul was overwhelmed needs to lie down in that bed one more time. He comes to me. He has a look in his eyes, and I understand him. So even if it no longer exists, I find it. Do you understand what I'm saying? I produce it. Out of thin air, if need be. And if the wood is not exactly as he remembers, or the legs are too thick or too thin, he'll only notice for a moment, a moment of shock and disbelief, and then his memory will be invaded by the reality of the bed standing before him. Because he needs it to be that bed where she once lay with him more than he needs to know the truth. You understand? And if you ask me, Mr. Bender, whether I feel guilty, whether I feel I am cheating him, the answer is no. Because at the moment that man reaches out and runs his hand across the rail, for him there are no other beds in the world.

Weisz reached up, rubbed his hand across his forehead, and kneaded his temple. I saw now how tired he looked, despite the keen sharpness of his eyes.

But the one searching for this desk isn't like the others, he said. He doesn't have the capacity to forget just a little. His memory cannot be invaded. The more time passes, the sharper his memory becomes. He can study the strands of wool on a rug he sat on as a child. He can open a drawer of a desk he hasn't seen since 1944 and go through its contents, one by one. His memory is more real to him, more precise, than the life he lives, which becomes more and more vague to him.

You can't imagine how he hounds me, Mr. Bender. How he calls and calls. How he torments me. For him, I traveled from city to city, I made inquiries, I called, I knocked on doors, I scoured every conceivable source. But I turned up nothing. The desk—enormous, unlike any other—had simply vanished like so much else. He wouldn't hear it. Every few months he would call me. Then once a year, always on the same day. And always the same question: Nu? Anything? And always I had to give him the same answer: Nothing. Then a year came when he didn't call. And I thought, not without relief, that maybe he had died. But a letter from him arrived in the mail, written on the date he always called. An anniversary, of sorts. And I understood then that he could not die until I found the desk. That he wanted to die, but he could not. I became afraid. I wanted to be through with him. What right did he have to burden me with this? With the responsibility of his life if I didn't find it, and his death if I did?

And yet I couldn't forget about him, Weisz said, lowering his voice. So I began to search again. And then one day, not long ago, I received a tip. Like a tiny bubble of air rising from the depths of an ocean where leagues below something is breathing. I followed it, and it led me to another. And another. Suddenly the trail was alive again. For months I've been following it. And at last it led me here, to you.

Weisz looked at me, waiting. I shifted under the burden of the news I would have to give him: that the desk that had haunted us both was long gone. Mr. Bender—he began to say. It belonged to my wife, I said, only my voice came out as a whisper. But it isn't here. It hasn't been here for twenty-eight years.

His mouth twisted and a tremor seemed to clench his face for a moment, then dropped away, leaving his expression painfully blank. We sat in silence. Far off, the church bells chimed.

She lived alone with it when I first met her, I said quietly. It hovered above her, and took up half the room. He nodded, his dark eyes glassy and bright, as if he, too, was seeing it rise up before him. Slowly, as if with a black pen and simple lines, I began to draw for him a picture of the desk and the room that was its dominion. And as I spoke, something happened. I sensed something hovering on the far edge of my understanding that Weisz's presence brought near, something I could feel but not quite grasp. It sucked up all the air, I whispered, groping for an understanding just out of my reach. We lived in its shadow. As if she had been lent to me from out of its darkness, I said, to which she would always belong. As if—and then something flared hotly within and when it faded to black again I felt the sudden coolness of clarity. As if death itself were living in that tiny room with us, threatening to crush us, I whispered. Death that invaded every corner, and left so little room.

It took me a long time to tell him the story. The live, pained look in his eyes and the way he listened, as if memorizing every word, drove me onward, until at last I arrived at the story of Daniel Varsky who rang our bell one evening, who tormented my imagination, and then receded as quickly as he had come, taking with him the terrible, overbearing desk. When I was finished we sat in silence. Then I remembered something. Just a minute, I said, and went to the other room where I opened the drawer of my own desk and took out the small black diary that I'd kept for almost thirty years, filled with the tiny handwriting of the young Chilean poet. When I returned to the living room, Weisz was staring absently at the window the glazier had replaced. After a moment he turned to me. Mr. Bender, are you familiar with the first-century rabbi Yochanan ben Zakkai? Only the name, I said. Why? My father was a scholar of Jewish history, Weisz said. He wrote many books, all of which I read years later, after he was dead. In them I recognized the stories he used to tell me. One of his favorites was about ben Zakkai, who was already an old man when the Romans besieged Jerusalem. Fed up with the warring parties within the city, he staged his own death, Weisz said. The corpse bearers carried him through the gates for the last time, and delivered him to the tent of the Roman general. In return for his prophecy of Roman victory, he was permitted to go to Yavne to open a school. Later, in that small town, he received the news that Jerusalem had burned. The Temple was destroyed. Those that survived were sent into exile. In his agony, he thought: What is a Jew without Jerusalem? How can you be a Jew without a nation? How can you make a sacrifice to God if you don't know where to find him? In the torn clothes of the mourner, ben Zakkai returned to his school. He announced that the court of law that had burned in Jerusalem would be resurrected there, in the sleepy town of Yavne. That instead of making sacrifices to God, from then on Jews would pray to Him. He instructed his students to begin assembling more than a thousand years of oral law.

Day and night the scholars argued about the laws, and their arguments became the Talmud, Weisz continued. They became so absorbed in their work that sometimes they forgot the question their teacher had asked: What is a Jew without Jerusalem? Only later, after ben Zakkai died, did his answer slowly reveal itself, the way an enormous mural only begins to make sense as you walk backwards away: Turn Jerusalem into an idea. Turn the Temple into a book, a book as vast and holy and intricate as the city itself. Bend a people around the shape of what they lost, and let everything mirror its absent form. Later his school became known as the Great House, after the phrase in Books of Kings: *He burned the house of God, the king's house, and all the houses of Jerusalem; even every great house he burned with fire.*

Two thousand years have passed, my father used to tell me, and now every Jewish soul is built around the house that burned in that fire, so vast that we can, each one of us, only recall the tiniest fragment: a pattern on the wall, a knot in the wood of a door, a memory of how light fell across the floor. But if every Jewish memory were put together, every last holy fragment joined up again as one, the House would be built again, said Weisz, or rather a memory of the House so perfect that it would be, in essence, the original itself. Perhaps that is what they mean when they speak of the Messiah: a perfect assemblage of the infinite parts of the Jewish memory. In the next world, we will all dwell together in the memory of our memories. But that will not be for us, my father used to say. Not for you or me. We live, each of us, to preserve our fragment, in a state of perpetual regret and longing for a place we only know existed because we remember a keyhole, a tile, the way the threshold was worn under an open door.

I handed Weisz the diary. Perhaps this will help you, I said. He held it for a moment in his palm, as if measuring its weight. Then he slipped it into his pocket. I walked him to the door. If I can ever do anything for you in return, he said. But he did not offer me his card or any way to contact him. We shook hands and he turned to go. Something seized me then, and unable to control myself I called out: Was it him that sent you? Who? he asked. The one who gave the desk to Lotte. Is that how you found me? Yes, he said. I began to cough. My voice came out as a wretched croak. And is he still—? but I couldn't bring myself to say the words.

Weisz studied my face. He tucked the stick under his arm, reached into his breast pocket and took out a pen and a small leather case holding a pad of paper. He wrote something down, folded it in half, and handed it to me. Then he turned toward the street, but after a step he stopped and turned back to look up at the windows of the attic study. He was easy enough to find, he said quietly, once I knew where to look.

The headlights of a dark car parked in front of the neighbor's house came to life, illuminating the fog. Goodbye, Mr. Bender, he said. I watched him walk down the front path and slide into the backseat of the car. Between my fingers I held the folded paper with the name and address of the man Lotte had once loved. I looked up at the wet, black boughs of the trees, the tops of which she had looked out at from her desk. What would she have read in them? What would she have seen in the crosshatch of black marks against the sky, what echoes and memories and colors that I could never see? Or refused to see.

I slipped the paper in my pocket, went inside, and gently closed the door behind me. There was a chill, so I lifted my sweater off the hook. I laid some logs in the fireplace, crumpled a sheet of news-paper, and crouched to blow on the fire until it took. I put the kettle on to boil, poured some milk into the tomcat's bowl, and left it in the pool of light the kitchen cast on the garden. Carefully, I placed the folded paper on the table in front of me.

And somewhere the other one turned on his lamp. Put the kettle to boil. Turned the page of a book. Or the radio dial.

How much we might have said to one another, he and I. We who collaborated in her silence. He who never dared to break it, and I who bowed to the borders drawn, the walls erected, the areas restricted, who turned away and never asked. Who each morning stood by and watched her disappear into the cold, black depths, and pretended not to know how to swim. Who made a pact of ignorance and smothered what churned within so that things might carry on as they always had. So that the house would not flood, nor the walls come crashing down. So that we would not be invaded, crushed, or overcome by what dwelled in the silences around which we had so delicately, so ingeniously built a life.

I sat there for many long hours into the night. The fire died down. The price we paid for the volumes of ourselves that we suffocated in the dark. At last, near midnight I picked up the folded paper from the table. Without hesitating, I dropped it into the fire. It singed and burst into flames, for a moment the fire roared with new life, and in an instant was consumed.

WEISZ

A riddle: A stone is thrown in Budapest on a winter night in 1944. It sails through the air toward the illuminated window of a house where a father is writing a letter at his desk, a mother is reading, and a boy is daydreaming about an ice-skating race on the frozen Danube. The glass shatters, the boy covers his head, the mother screams. At that moment the life they know ceases to exist. *Where does the stone land?*

*   *   *

When I left Hungary in 1949 I was twenty-one. I was thin, a person partially erased, afraid to stand still. On the black market I turned a gold ring I found on a dead soldier into two crates of sausages, and the two crates into twenty vials of medicine, and the twenty vials into a hundred and fifty packages of silk stockings. I sent these in a shipping container with other luxuries that were to be my livelihood in my second life, the one waiting for me in Haifa port the way a shadow waits under a rock at noon. In the container, folded among the other items, were five silk shirts cut to fit me like a second skin, my initials monogrammed on the breast pocket. I arrived, but the container never did. The Turk in customs who stood under the Carmel claimed to have no record of it. Behind me the boats rocked on the waves of the sea. A sliver of shadow slipped out from a rock near the Turk's enormous right foot. A woman in a thin dress was bent over kissing the scorched ground, crying. Perhaps she had found her own shadow under a different stone. I saw something glint in the sand and picked up a half lira. A half can become a whole can become two can become four. Six months later I rang the doorbell of a man's house. The man had invited his cousin, and his cousin, my friend, had brought me along. When the man opened the door he was wearing a silk shirt and sewn above the breast pocket were my initials. His young wife brought out a tray of coffee and halva. When the man reached over to light my cigarette the silk of his sleeve brushed my arm, and we were like two people pressing on either side of a window.

* * *

My father was a scholar of history. He wrote at an enormous desk with many drawers, and when I was very young I believed that two thousand years were stored in those drawers the way Magda the housekeeper stored flour and sugar in the pantry. Only one drawer had a lock, and for my fourth birthday my father gave me the little brass key. I couldn't sleep at night, trying to think of what to put in the drawer. The responsibility was crushing. In my mind I went over my most prized possessions again and again, but all of them suddenly seemed flimsy and grossly insignificant. In the end I locked the empty drawer and never told my father.

* * *

Before my wife fell in love with me, she fell in love

with this house. One day she brought me to the garden of the Sisters of Zion convent. We had tea under the loggia, she tied a red scarf around her hair, her profile against the cypress trees dated from ancient times. She was the only woman I'd ever met who didn't want to bring the dead back to life. I pulled my white handkerchief from my pocket and laid it down on the table. I surrender, I whispered. But my accent was still heavy. You remember what? she asked. Afterwards we walked back to the village and on the way she stopped in front of a large stone house with green shutters. There, she pointed, under that mulberry tree, our children will play one day. She was only flirting, but when I turned to look where her finger was pointing I saw a streak of light flash in the shadows under the boughs of the old tree, and I felt pain.

My business grew, the one I started with a carved walnut commode I bought cheaply from the Turk in customs. Later he sold me a drop-leaf table, a porcelain mantel clock, a Flemish tapestry. I discovered I had certain talents; I developed an expertise. Out of the ruins of history I produced a chair, a table, a chest of drawers. I made a name for myself, but I didn't forget the streak of light under the mulberry tree. One day I went back to the house, knocked on the door, and offered the man who lived there a sum he couldn't refuse. He invited me in. We shook hands in his kitchen. When I came here, he said, the floor was still littered with pistachio shells the Arab had eaten before he fled with his wife and children. Upstairs, I found the little girl's doll, he said, with real hair that she had lovingly braided. For some time I kept it but one day the glass eyes began to look at me in a strange way.

Afterwards the man let me walk through the house that would be our house, hers and mine. I walked through room after room, searching for the one. None were right. And then, opening a door, I found it.

*   *   *

When I returned to the house in Budapest where I grew up, the War was over. The place was filthy. The mirrors were smashed, there were wine stains on the carpets, on the wall someone had drawn with charcoal a man sodomizing a donkey. And yet never had it been more my home than in its desecration. On the floor of her ransacked closet, I found three strands of my mother's hair.

I brought my wife to the house she had loved before she loved me. It's ours, I said. We walked through the halls. A house built so that people could become lost in it. Neither of us mentioned the cold. There's one thing I ask, I said. What? she said, distracted, breathless. Let me have one room, I said. What? she said again, more faintly. One room that is mine alone, that you will never enter. She looked out the window. The silence unspooled between us.

*   *   *

When I was a boy, I wanted to be in two places at the same time. It became an obsession of mine, I spoke of it endlessly. My mother laughed, but my father, who carried two thousand years with him wherever he went the way other men carry a pocket watch, saw it differently. In my childish desire he saw the symptom of a hereditary disease. Sitting by my bed, wracked by a cough he couldn't shake, he read me the poems of Judah Halevi. With time, what began as a fantasy transformed into a deeply held belief: while I lay in bed, I sensed my other self walking down an empty street in a foreign city, taking a boat at dawn, driving in the back of a black car.

*   *   *

My wife died and I left Israel. A man can be many more places than two. I took my children from city to city. They learned to close their eyes in cars and trains, to fall asleep in one place and wake in another. I taught them that no matter the view from the window, the style of the architecture, the color of the evening sky, the distance between oneself and oneself remains immutable. I always put them to sleep together in the same room, I taught them not to be afraid when they woke in the middle of the night not knowing where they were. So long as Yoav called out and Leah answered, or Leah called out and Yoav answered, they could put themselves back to sleep without needing to know. A special bond developed between them, my only daughter and my only son. While they slept I rearranged the furniture. I taught them to trust no one but themselves. I taught them not to be afraid when they went to sleep with the chair in one place, and woke up with it in another. I taught them that it doesn't matter where you put the table, against which wall you push the bed, so long as you always store the suitcases on top of the closet. I taught them to say, We're leaving tomorrow, just as my father, a scholar of history, taught me that the absence of things is more useful than their presence. Though many years later, half a century after he died, I stood on top of a sea wall watching the undertow and thought, Useful for what?

* * *

Years ago, when I first began my business, I received a phone call from an old man. He wanted my services, and mentioned the name of a mutual acquaintance who had recommended me. He told me he no longer traveled; indeed, he rarely left the room where he lived on the edge of the desert. It happened that I was going to be passing not far from the town where he lived, so I told him I would come to see him in person. We sat drinking coffee. In the room was a window, and on the floor beneath was a dark half-moon from years of forgetting to close the window in the rain. The man saw me looking at the stain. I didn't always live this life, he said. I used to live a different life, in other countries. I met many people, and discovered that each had his own way to cope with reality. One man needs to reconcile a floor stained by rain in a room of a house on the edge of the desert, he said. But for another, the contradiction itself is the form the reconciliation takes. I nodded and drank my coffee. But all I understood was that his regret was a stain on the floor from the rain falling in a city he hadn't been to in years.

* * *

My father died fifty years ago on a death march to the Reich. Now I sit in his room in Jerusalem, a city he only imagined. His desk sits locked in a storage room in New York City, and my daughter holds the key. I admit that I did not foresee this. I underestimated her courage and will. Her cunning. She thought she was denying me. In her eyes I saw a hardness I had never seen before. She was terrified, but her mind was made up. It took me some time, but soon the sense in it dawned on me. I could not have invented a more fitting end myself. She had found a solution for me, though it was not the one either of us had intended.

The rest was simple. I flew to New York. From the airport I took a taxi to the address where I'd sent my daughter to retrieve the desk. I spoke to the superintendent. He was a Romanian, I knew how to make myself understood to him. I offered him fifty dollars to remember the name of the moving company that had taken away the desk. He drew a blank. I offered him a hundred, and still he couldn't remember. For two hundred dollars his memory came back to him with dazzling clarity; he even looked up the phone number. From his small dingy office in the basement where his street clothes hung on a pipe, I made the call. I was put through to the manager. Sure I remember, he said. The lady said a desk, I sent two men, it nearly broke their backs. I told him I wanted to know where to send the tip they deserved. The manager gave me his name and address. Then he gave me the address of the storage warehouse where his men had delivered the desk. The Romanian hailed me another taxi. The tenant who owned that desk, he said, she went on a trip. I know, I said. How do you know? She came to see me, I said, and then the driver pulled away, leaving the surprised Romanian standing in the street.

The warehouse stood near the river. I could smell the silt and in the dingy grey sky gulls were carried aloft by the wind. In the office at the back I found a young woman painting her nails. She screwed the top on the polish when she saw me. I sat down in the chair on the other side of her desk. She straightened up and turned down the radio. One of the units in this facility is registered under the name of Leah Weisz, I said. The only thing it contains is a desk. I'll give you a thousand dollars if you let me sit at it for one hour.

She will never have children of her own, my daughter. I've known that for a long time. The only thing she ever let escape from herself were notes. She began when she was a child: *pling plong pling plong.* Nothing else can come of her. But Yoav—there is something unanswered in Yoav, and I know there will be a woman for him, perhaps many women, in whom he will spill himself in order to seek the answer. One day a child will be born. A child whose provenance is the union of a woman and a riddle. One night as the infant sleeps in the bedroom, his mother will sense a presence outside the window. At first she will think it is just her own reflection, haggard in her milk-stained robe. But a moment later she will sense it again, and suddenly afraid, she will switch off the lights and hurry to the baby's room. The glass door of the bedroom will be open. On top of the pile of the child's tiny white clothes his mother will find an envelope with his name, written in small, neat handwriting. Inside the envelope will be a key and the address of a storage room in New York City. And outside, in the dark garden, the wet grass will slowly straighten up again, erasing my daughter's footsteps.

*   *   *

I opened the door. The room was cold, and had no window. For an instant I almost believed I would find my father stooped over the desk, his pen moving across the page. But the tremendous desk stood alone, mute and uncomprehending. Three or four drawers hung open, all of them empty. But the one I locked as a child, sixty-six years later was locked still. I reached out my hand and ran my fingers across the dark surface of the desk. There were a few scratches, but otherwise those who had sat at it had left no mark. I knew the moment well. How often I had witnessed it in others, and yet now it almost surprised me: the disappointment, then the relief of something at last sinking away.